'Dreda Say Mitchell confi... ...
in crime writing with this taut novel *Eric, Read...*

'As good as it gets . . . Mitchell is English fiction's brightest
new voice' Lee Child

'An interesting, original novel, worth reading, even if you don't
get half the references and in real life would block your ears
to the noise' *Literary Review*

'KILLER TUNE is a sharply observed, incisive and moving
story of radical politics, conflicting loyalties and unfinished
business.' *Guardian*

'Brilliant – a gripping roller-coaster for the reader'
*Independent*

'Mitchells' plot is elaborate but tightly played, with a
backbeat of racial abuse. KILLER TUNE lays the breezy muscial
name-checking of Hornby's *High Fidelity* over a well-crafted
murder mystery.' *Financial Times*

'Publishing folklore has it that second novels are generally
weaker than their predecessors – not KILLER TUNE . . . It makes
it encouragingly clear that Dreda Say Mitchell will be a figure
in the crime-writing world for the forseeable future.'
*Times Literary Supplement*

'Dreda Say Mitchell is an exciting new talent and her
second novel, KILLER TUNE, shows her distinctive take on
current urban noir . . . The narrative throbs with energy and
has a refreshing directness' *Sunday Telegraph*

*Also by Dreda Say Mitchell*

Running Hot

# Dreda Say Mitchell

# KILLER TUNE

**HODDER**

First published in Great Britain in 2007 by Hodder & Stoughton
An Hachette Livre UK company

First published in paperback in 2008

4

Copyright © Dreda Say Mitchell 2007

The right of Dreda Say Mitchell to be identified as the Author of the
Work has been asserted by her in accordance with the Copyright, Designs
and Patents Act 1988.

A CIP catalogue record for this title is available from the British Library

ISBN 978 0 340 93709 9

Typeset in RotisSerif by Palimpsest Book Production Limited,
Grangemouth, Stirlingshire

Printed and bound by Clays Ltd, St Ives plc

Hodder & Stoughton policy is to use papers that are natural, renewable
and recyclable products and made from wood grown in sustainable forests.
The logging and manufacturing processes are expected to conform to the
environmental regulations of the country of origin.

Hodder & Stoughton Ltd
338 Euston Road
London NW1 3BH

www.hodder.co.uk

For Maggie Hamand
Thanks for your friendship, support and inspiration

# ACKNOWLEDGEMENTS

So many people to thank . . .

A big debt of gratitude to the Arts Council for their much-appreciated writing bursary.

For helping me fine-tune the writing, my editor Carolyn Mays, Emma Dunford and my amazing agent Jane Gregory.

Anastasia and Tony for their continued support and encouragement.

To my music experts, Sam Wright, Ros Wynne-Jones, Samantha Spence, Exley, Lydia, Jacob and Joanne.

For sharing their memories – Professor Harry Goldbourne, Finsbury Park's finest The New beacon bookshop, Professor Victoria Paisley, Danny and Russ, Poet Abe Gibson, Tim Spafford, David Davies, Marc Thompson, Graham Smith, Eddie, Uncle Moses, Irma, Auntie Gracelyn, Lydia, Lorraine and Gloria and her posse.

To Stav Sherez for his brilliant tour of Notting Hill.

I couldn't have written this book without inspiration from the works of Linton Kwesi Johnson, Lloyd Bradley, Imani Perry and Chris Morrow and the 'Back to Black' exhibition at the Whitechapel Art Gallery and the 'Black British Style' exhibition at the V&A Museum.

DISC 1

# 'BLOOD AND FIRE'

**PLAYLIST**

Intro – SEVEN DEVILS IN HELL

1. GASOLINE GHETTO (FEATURING CURTIS)
2. KILL THE VOLUME
3. SLAMMIN' WITH THE B-LINE
4. LOOTIN' AND SHOOTIN'
5. TRANS-HOXTON EXPRESS
6. REWIND
7. 'WHAT'S GOING ON'
8. 'PRESSURE DROP'
9. 'AN EVERLASTING LOVE'
10. KBW (FEATURING THE KING)
11. 'A TRAIN A-COMING'
12. WHO KILLED EMMETT TILL?
13. FACE DOWN
14. THE BONEYARD
15. REVIVAL SELECTION: 1976, VOLUME 1 (LP)
16. COVER VERSION
17. 'THE HANDSWORTH REVOLUTION'
18. THE CROWD PULLER
19. PUNK BEAT

His voice dipped low as he said his final words.

'Son, let me tell you a secret. It is whispered that on August bank holiday, the Devil and his six disciples, wearing smiles flashing like molten lightning, travel across the world. Underground. From west to east. From Trinidad to England. Balancing drums on their left hips and bamboo sticks in their right claws. When they reach Notting Hill they beat their drums throughout the multicoloured memories of the day and the black-and-white fusion of the night, making the streets of West London ripple and roll to their badass, hellfire groove.

'Watch the ground beneath your feet, son, because the human experience comes back to one thing – rhythm.

'The sun goes up, the sun goes down.

'The days get longer, the days get shorter.

'People live, people die.

'Simple.'

# TRACK 1: GASOLINE GHETTO
## (Featuring Curtis)

On Wednesday, 16 August, Curtis stood, MP3 player in one hand,
large bottle of rum in the other, in one of East London's most
desirable squares. Rhodes Square was a cut-through for the kids
who went to the local school – the one that residents took care
their Sophie and Sebastian did not go to. He faced a large Victorian
house. Number 12. It stood one door down from the house with
the Mercedes parked outside and two doors up from the house
with a black fist as its knocker.

He moved his lanky body one step closer. The afternoon breeze
brushed over his golden, teenage face. Brushed over his du-rag.
The du-rag fitted the crown of his head like a silk stocking and
blew loose at the back and side of his neck with the flare of a
Foreign Legion cap. He gazed down at his MP3 player. Pulled it
up, just below his chin. His thumb shifted to the side. Pressed
the power button. The black screen lit up with blood-red touch-
sensitive controls. His thumb glided over the screen. Found 'menu'.
Hit it. The selection bar came up.

All
Favourites
Top 20

His thumb hit 'favourites'. The title of a single song ignited the
screen.

'Gasoline Ghetto'.

His thumb caressed the horizontal volume strip. Bottom to top, just like when Betty Dean had taught him to French-kiss from tonsil to tip. Guaranteed max-i-mum, ear-thumping, boom-bass madness. His thumb hit 'play'. He waited. Waited in his low-riding black-and-white-striped tracksuit for the high-rising music. He counted. One. Two. Three. Then it came. The violins from Vivaldi's Winter Concerto, stabbing behind a red-hot, pepper-sauce R 'n' B beat. He waited for the singing to start. One. Two. Three. It came. A gruff, male voice with its tell-it-as-it-is street lyrics.

He shoved his MP3 player into his tracksuit pocket. Looked back up at the house. Now was the right time to do it because he couldn't see anyone inside the house. He used the fingers of one hand to untie his du-rag. Tugged it from his head. Tucked it under his arm. He looked at the rum bottle. Read the label.

White. Overproof. Full-strength rum.

He unscrewed the lid. Grabbed the du-rag. Held it out. Tipped some rum on to it until it turned from bone-dry black to juice-soaked jet. He screwed the lid back on to the bottle. Then he tied the alcohol-soaked du-rag around its neck.

'Could I ask about 1976?' she asked behind him.

King Stir It Up, aka Isaiah Augustus Cleveland Scantleberry on his medical records, tensed at her question as he clutched his box of bones.

Shit.

'76.

The one year he never talked about.

He stared at the panoramic view of the Victorian square across the road from his hospital window, desperately trying to think of a way to hitch a ride away from her question. His gaze settled on a young man, who stood with a bottle in his hand in front of one of the houses. The youth pulled something from his head. It looked like one of them du-rags some of the young kids wore these days.

'Could I ask about 1976?' she repeated.

Shit.

She wouldn't leave '76 alone.

His guest moved to stand with him in the warmth of the window. He quickly buried his box of bones in his dressing-gown pocket. Turned his head to face her. Her blonde hair was chopped and clipped back. Nothing, including hair, was getting in this woman's way. He caught the hope in her blue bright eyes as she stared at him. He flicked his head back towards the window. Back towards the square. Back towards the youth.

'OK, 1976. That summer . . .' he began, the same time as the youth in the square tied the cloth in his hand around the neck of the bottle.

Curtis finished tying the du-rag. He wedged the bottle under his left arm as the music from his MP3 soaked into his body. His right hand moved to the back pocket of his trousers. He pulled out the magazine that was sticking out of it. It unfolded in his hand. It was already on the correct page. The only page he was interested in. He looked at the advertisement in the top right corner.

THE CONCERT OF THE YEAR
Wednesday 16th August
FEATURING
M.C. Insanity
And Lord Tribulation – He's the DADDY!

The R 'n' B backing track of the song playing on his MP3 fell silent. Just violins. Then the violins were joined by a woman's voice. Soft. Quiet. The vulnerability of her vibrato made his thoughts stop; made him taste her melody; see the face of his mother. The magazine fell from his fingers. Fluttered on to the ground. He searched in his pocket. Pulled out a lighter. He placed the bottle in his right hand. Turned his body sideways. Shifted his feet wide, but steady. Twisted his waist, so his upper body faced the house. His eyes snapped over it, searching for a target. He found it. A second-floor window. He flicked the lighter on.

Held up the bottle. Lit the dripping du-rag around the bottle's neck. His hips and shoulders rotated forward. With a flourish the petrol bomb left his hand. His eyes squinted in the sun as he followed its path. Upwards. Towards the target. He stumbled back. Startled. Startled by the two unexpected young faces peering from the second-floor window.

'That summer.' King Stir It Up picked up the words he'd left floating in the air, as he continued to stare out of the window. 'Do you know what the killer tune was?'

'Killer tune?' She took a step, pushing her curiosity closer to him.

'The killer tune is the song everyone's playing. Dancing to. That year's memorable rhythm-and-bass ride. In '76, for us black youth, it was Junior Murvin's "Police And Thieves".'

'But did anything stand out that year? Was there anything different?'

He said nothing. Just half cocked his head and watched the youth in the square pull something from his pocket.

'It was a turbulent year, wasn't it?' Her voice was soft. Low.

'Tings got out of control,' he finally whispered, as something bright flickered in the youth's hand.

'What things?'

He saw the youth touch the bright object to the cloth around the neck of the bottle. There was an instant gush of light. He moved his head forward to get a better look. Fire.

'What things?' she coaxed.

The youth pulled the bottle back. Threw it at one of the houses.

'Oh my God,' King Stir It Up yelled as his face pressed against the window.

'What?'

He swung his head to face her.

'Call the police.'

Curtis took a shocked step forward as he watched the bottle sail towards the faces at the window. His arm lunged up. He knew it was too late. No way was he going to pull the bottle back. The children at the window scurried back when they saw the bottle arching towards them. The petrol bomb smashed into the glass. Dived into the room. Glass splintered and fell to the ground outside. Fell on to Curtis. Shredded into his arm and face. He closed his eyes. Heard a bang. Looked up at the same time as the fire started licking from the window. He heard two screams. Together. Blistering the scene like bewildered alto and soprano saxophones. That's when he started running.

King Stir It Up watched the youth run. The tumour tightened in his gut. He shut his eyes. Tried to cut the pain out. Cut the fire out. Cut the memories of 1976 out. But he couldn't because '76 had been just the same. The sounds. The fire. A youth running away. A youth that had been him. Running from a burning, dead body.

Thirty-year-old rap artist Lord Tribulation – LT to his friends – stood outside the Hugh Gaskell hospital ward contemplating the best way to make an entrance. Life was all about making entrances. Well, that was his philosophy. It did not matter what type of door you went through – car door, lover's door, record company door – you had to make an entrance. Make people remember you. Years of treading the stage had also taught him that an entrance is only as good as the walk you take with you. He chose his walk. Strut 'n' sway. Head held high, shoulders and hips loose, moving to the rhythm of a carefree summer reggae track. He moved his lean, six-one frame in easy steps. Always take it easy. Never rush it.

People stopped to look at him, in his knee-length leather jacket, vintage Levi jeans, black beret and smoke-tinted aviator sunglasses, as he made his way down the corridor.

He took it easy.

As the suppressed hush bounced against the white walls and tiled floor.

He took it easy.

As the trio of nurses at the desk ran their eyes over him.

He took it easy.

As he moved through the acrid sting of disinfected air.

He took it easy.

As a porter, with a mop, admired his L and T lettered earrings in his left ear.

He took it easy.

As he reached his father's private room.

His steps faltered. Stopped. He sucked a sharp breath into his body. He might be trying to take it easy, but it never got any easier however many times he came knocking at his dying father's door. He pushed down the handle. Entered the room. He did not know where the King got the readies to afford a private room. He never asked. Every man was entitled to his privacy, especially if they were told their time was up. For his money his father got a blanched tight one-person sofa, a recently upholstered armchair, a portable TV, which was on, and soothing paintings of bowls of fruit and seascapes on the green pastel walls. And, of course, a bed. Nothing special, but slightly wider than the ones in the public wards. In the bed sat his father, King Stir It Up, or the King as everyone affectionately called him.

The King was propped up on his pillows, hunched over, talking into a Dictaphone. Where the King went so did his Dictaphone. The King had taught him from an early age that a Dictaphone was an essential tool of any songwriter's trade. You never knew when the lyrics would come to you. The barbershop. The bathroom. That final groan at the end of making love.

The King stopped talking. Mid-sentence. He punched the stop button on the Dictaphone. Put it down next to the scattered dominoes on the mobile table over the bed. He straightened his head and shoulders. Father and son looked at each other with faces that were once a mirror image of each other. The same alert brown eyes, long bone structure and a mouth they were both proud of, with its bottom lip slightly puffed forward as if a constant bank of lyrics bubbled behind it. But in the last six months the King's terminal illness had distorted their shared reflection. While LT retained a skin tone that was a deep saturated brown with a fiery glaze of old oak rum, his father's had become a tired grey, as if the gravediggers were already throwing earth on top of him. The sharpness of his cheekbones stretched his skin. But he defiantly had his hair and now a beard, just so they knew he didn't want anything to do with that chemo shit. The only medication he was willing to take was a new drug that helped to relieve the suffering of people with stomach tumours.

The King pinned LT with those black eyes of disapproval. LT hated that look because it reminded him that since he had injected what he called his cash raps (or craps, as the King like to sneer) – songs about money, women, women, money – into his act, his father's pride in his achievements had started to be eroded by disappointment.

'Well, if it isn't Huey Newton,' the King rasped in a voice that had once been serene and smooth; now his illness made sure he could no longer control the chord changes.

Baffled, LT followed the path of his father's eyes as they glided over his leather jacket and black beret. He'd borrowed the image from one of his stylist's books – but who the hell was Huey Newton?

'. . . and take those darkers off, boy – life's moving into the night.'

LT pulled off his shades. Folded them. Tucked them into the flap pocket of his jacket. He sat down on the armchair by the King's bed, near the vase of assorted flowers he knew the King's girlfriend, May, bought every day. He pulled off his beret, revealing a small Afro. One that was plaited in the night and finger-combed in the morning. He ran his long fingers through it. His father looked at him with a spark of merriment in his eyes. He knew the King was getting ready for their light-hearted call-and-response routine.

'What you call that masquerading on your head?' the King started.

'This is an Afro, also known as a 'fro . . .'

'Also known as a natural . . .'

'Which you should know all about as it dates back to your heyday . . .'

'When people knew what good music sounded like . . .'

'Music's as good as the number of punters you pull in . . .'

'You call that boom-boom, bang-bang business you sing music?'

The King's voice ended in a ragged rush. His eyes screwed closed.

'You all right, Dad?' LT asked as he leaned over the dominoes. His hands rested on his father's shoulders.

Now the King was sick LT realised that maybe their little routine was too quick for a man dying to keep up. For years they had played call-and-response – the King would say something mildly contentious and he would respond. It was always quickfire. As soon as the last word left one mouth, the other grabbed the space. Sometimes it got so quick it was hard to know where one voice started and the other ended.

'It ain't easy thinking back sometimes, you check me?' the King answered wearily.

'So what's the latest?' LT asked, easing back in his chair, trying to lighten the mood.

'The latest?' The King's eyes sprang open with the kind of life LT wished the rest of his father's body showed.

'Yeah, you know. On the news.' LT nodded his head towards the portable television.

'It's the usual – the rich are bombing the poor. And the rich are winning again . . .' The King shook his head as a jet fighter arced across the TV screen before a splash of orange burst where a missile had exploded. 'The damn rich are always winning. The last time we won anything was when Che and Fidel rode into Havana in 1959, you check me?'

'Who were they?' LT asked.

'Who was who?'

'Che and Fidel . . .' LT had heard the names in the house as a youth but he couldn't place them.

'Well, kiss my sweet black rah-rah, you mean to tell me, Jeremiah, you don't know who Che Guevara and Fidel Castro are?' His father was incredulous.

The King was one of the only people who ever used his birth name, Jeremiah.

'No. Unless they're giving me a helping hand up the musical ladder, why should I?'

LT shook his head. Che Guevara? Fidel Castro? Huey Newton? Since the tumour had been diagnosed it was like the King lived in a completely different world. The King's chest rumbled in a small chuckle. Then he lifted his eyebrow mischievously and explained, 'They were musicians . . .'

'Musicians . . . ?' LT was interested now.

The King rearranged himself so he was full on with his son. A half-crooked smile crinkled his lips and tilted the right corner of his beard.

'That's right. They played maracas in a rumba band in Cuba. They were big for a while; they cut a few records and had a few hits. Then of course those damn communists took over and Che, Fidel and the boys had to move to the States. They finished their days playing bossa nova for gamblers in Las Vegas . . .'

LT had met a few Latin Americans around town. Sharp, snappy dressers. Maybe this Che and Fidel knew how to make the clothes talk as they walked.

'So what kind of rig did they go around town in?'

'Rig?' The King's smile spread full across his lips. 'Well, let's see – they use to dress in olive-green battle fatigues – and sombreros. Man, when they shook those maracas, all them American gals were on the dance floor shaking their ting – you check me?'

LT had a think about that. He couldn't use the sombrero but the battle fatigues sounded cool. Very outlaw – very rebel. He decided to ask his stylist what olive green would look like against dark, brown skin. LT looked at his watch. Five minutes to six.

'What are you looking at your watch for, boy? You got some place you need to be?'

'I've got a really important gig tonight and . . .'

'Gig?' the King scoffed. 'Gig? You call that song-and-dance routine you do a "gig"? You call that gyrating around you do trying to catch the avaricious eye of those record companies a "gig". Some "gig", boy . . .'

That pissed LT off. His body tightened in the chair as his mouth let loose.

'Yeah, that's right, a "gig" – and you might like to know that Paradise Records will be there and we're talking about a deal at the moment. You know what a deal is, don't you? Only of course you don't because all you ever did was make a few loser records for your friends and family to buy. You know what I think? I think you're jealous because I'm making a living out of my music while all you did was earn some beer money playing for your mates in community centres . . .'

The King interrupted with a whisper, 'Music's not "a living", boy. Music is living . . .'

'Music is money,' LT asserted. Hard.

The King shook his head as they both fell silent, chewing their own thoughts.

LT shook his head, feeling annoyed with himself for his angry outburst at a man who almost gave up his life so that he could have his. His mother had left to live in Canada when he was a baby, leaving the King to bring him up on his own. Until her death five years earlier she'd never visited him, which suited him fine. The tension eased its hand from his shoulder. He relaxed into the softness of the chair.

'Dad, I came up because I want to share something with you.'

'Never been in no threesome before.'

They both chuckled, looking more alike than they had in a long time.

'My first TV interview is coming on in about . . .' He looked at his watch. ' . . . two minutes.'

'Well, I can't watch my boy on the box with a dry throat.'

LT knew exactly what the King wanted. He got up and bent down to search under the bed for his father's black holdall bag. He found it near the King's slippers. He unzipped the side pocket, searched inside and pulled out a joint. Doing drugs and alcohol had never been his rush. He had seen one too many people, including the King, lose their focus on life. Even so, he passed the joint to his father. The King lit up. Sucked the smoke in. Let it find its resting ground inside his body. Blew the residue out and snuggled back into the pillows.

'That makes me almost feel alive, Jerry.'

LT couldn't understand why the King wouldn't have the

chemotherapy. Didn't he understand it meant they would have more time together? The King caught the anguished look on his face.

'Son, I'm going anyway so I'd rather be laid out in the box with my own hair. You should keep your pity for the two young ones downstairs.'

'What young ones?' LT asked as he used the remote to switch the television to Shake Up TV, a satellite channel specialising in mainly British rap.

'This afternoon two kids got burned badly in an arson attack in the square over the road. Before I forget, son, I want to be buried with my best jacket . . .'

LT did not hear his father because his eyes were fixed to the television screen. The final part of a report about Sean Sparkle, a legendary musician and producer receiving a lifetime achievement award at the Brits musical event, was on.

'Jerry, did you hear me? This is important, son.'

LT nodded his head, but kept staring at the television as he said, 'Yeah, sure. Let's chat about it after the interview.'

He settled himself in his seat as the presenter, Courtney Cross, or Cee Cee as she liked to be known, came on to the screen. She was street sexy and street cool, wearing a cropped white sequin top over blue hipster jeans. Her port-liquored hair brushed her shoulders and cupped her healthy white face. She sat with LT in a minimalist pale studio on an even paler leather couch. LT smiled as he watched the programme. Yeah, he had got the pose just right. Part insolent, part cheeky grin, like the studio lighting was the best sunshine he'd tasted in his life. The lighting shone against his white du-rag, which had his trademark 'He's The Daddy' logo on it.

Cee Cee introduced him with a carefully crafted smile. Then breathed her first question at him.

'Your music has got this unique, melting, stand-out style. Everyone calls it the Ice Shack sound. There are so many myths about how your music got its defining sound and name.' Her eyelids fluttered down, then curled up to flirt with him.

'Tell us what the real story is.' She spoke like she was asking him if he liked to do it on top, underneath or over the dressing-room table in front of the mirror.

He did that half-turn into the camera his stylist had taught him and grinned back at the presenter just before he answered her question.

'My father, King Stir It Up, as you know, is a musician. So I grew up with loads of music around me. His band, like other sound systems, were always experimenting with different sounds – echo chambers, vibrations, raw bass lines. One night when I was a kid I heard him playing one of his sound systems tunes. It had this really funky sound. A bit like heavy breathing. Kind of a half-beat in, a half-beat out . . .'

Suddenly the hospital room filled with a wheezing sound. High pitched, soaked in agony. LT quickly turned away from the television to stare at his father. The King was holding his chest and gulping air like his time had come. LT shoved out of the chair. Leaned over his father.

'Dad, you all right?' His hands fluttered over the King's chest.

The King's hands reached out. Clawed into LT's leather jacket. He yanked LT close. Whispered, 'Box of bones.'

LT's hand shot into the mix of dominoes on the table to steady himself. The King tugged him closer. Drank in some air. Whispered, 'Bury . . . best jacket.'

The King's hands loosened. Then he collapsed on to the bed. Silent. LT shook his father's shoulders.

'Dad? Dad?' he repeated as each shake became harder. The King did not move. LT rushed out of the room, yelling, 'Help. My dad.'

The ward sister at the desk looked up. Heard his high-pitched call. She ran over to him. Past him into the room. LT did not follow her. He leaned against the wall. Took shallow breaths. The tears stuck in his throat. He didn't want to be here. He did not want to see his old man like this. He closed his eyes. Kept them closed for three minutes.

'Mr Scantleberry?'

He let his mind and vision come back into the world. Sister stood next to him.

'He'll be fine, but he needs to rest. I've given him something so he gets a good night's sleep.'

She raised her hand and held the smoking spliff in front of his face. 'What were you thinking, giving this to him? It's no wonder he collapsed.'

'But . . .'

'Your father has over-exerted himself today. I've explained to you in the past that the drug your father has been prescribed means he can't afford to be under any more stress. I think it's best if you go.'

She walked away from him, carrying the pungent joint. He turned to the King's closed door. Lay his palm flat against it. Felt the warmth of the King one more time. He removed his hand. Let it drop. He looked over at the retreating figure of Sister, and he was sure he could see a freshly exhaled billow of smoke hanging over her body. Her back tightened. She stopped. Relaxed. Another cloud of smoke rose above her. He shook his head. Checked his watch. He still had more than enough time to dress to impress Paradise Records at his concert at the Minus One club tonight.

The illegal aroma of marijuana hit the woman as soon as she entered her house. She twisted her lip with annoyance, knowing that her daughter was home. She closed the door. Hard. So her daughter heard, to give her enough time to get rid of the evidence. She moved into the hall and laid her briefcase on the table under the huge mirror. She looked at her steel-grey suit. Straightened it and moved towards the lounge. She opened the door. Her daughter and two friends sat huddled on the sofa as they watched the television.

'Hi, Mummy. You're back early.' Her daughter kept her voice easy. Innocent. She didn't get up to greet her. No kiss. They had stopped doing that when she'd sent her to boarding school.

She delicately sniffed the air.

'You girls are wearing an interesting perfume these days.'

She peered over her daughter's head to watch the television with indifferent eyes. She wasn't surprised to see her daughter's musical idol, Lord Tribulation, being interviewed. His posters dominated her daughter's bedroom. Her daughter often listened to his tracks, which she had downloaded on to her MP3 player while eating breakfast. She hated that. Such bad manners.

When the interviewer asked Lord Tribulation how he got his distinctive musical sound her daughter swung back to the television. She started to turn her head away from the screen. Then she heard the rapper answer the question. She became still. Motionless. The brightness left her eyes and dark patches of blood spotted over her face. The stench of the marijuana choked her senses. Marijuana that had nothing to do with her daughter and everything to do with her memories. She swayed. Her hand gripped the edge of the sofa. 'Mummy, are you OK?'

She heard her daughter. But didn't answer. Couldn't answer.

'Mummy?'

The distress in her daughter's tone made her finally pull herself straight. Her hand left the sofa. Heaved through her hair. She smiled at her anxious daughter and said, 'I'm fine, darling. You know I hate the television on this loud, so can you please turn down the volume.'

She left the room as her daughter picked up the remote and killed the volume. She closed the door. Her hand tightened on the door handle. Every expletive she knew crammed her mind, overloading her head. She slammed her briefcase down on the table near the mirror. Opened it. Pulled out her mobile phone. Went straight to the address book. Scrolled down until she got his number. In her line of work she was given many numbers. When his had come her way she had stored it just in case. She punched the buttons as she marched into the chilled openness of the kitchen. She put the phone to her ear as she gazed out of the French window.

'It's Anne . . . yes, I know it's been thirty fucking years, and believe me, if I never had to speak to you again I wouldn't do it. We're in trouble.'

She swung away from the window. Listened. Then her words exploded.

'How do I know?' Her voice was clipped, the saliva drying in her mouth. 'That doesn't matter. What matters is he's still got it.'

She stopped. Took a single breath that stretched her lungs. The rise and fall of her chest softened. She was back in control.

'We need to meet to decide how to play this one out. In the meantime do anything you can to get it. Have you got people who can get on to this straight away?

'Good.' She smiled at his answer. 'But your people are going to need to know what they're looking for. Where do you think the King would have kept it?'

She listened to his answer. Sighed. Smiled a bit more widely.

'Of course,' she said softly. 'It was one of the only things he ever talked to me about. His best jacket.'

# TRACK 3: SLAMMIN' WITH THE B-LINE

'Who's the rebel?' Lord Tribulation blasted out on the stage at the Minus One club.

The jubilant two-hundred-strong crowd shouted, hollered and screamed.

'What's my name?'

'Tribulation.'

'What's my name?'

'Tribulation!'

'People – I said, what's my name?'

'Trib-u-la-tion!'

LT stood in front of his fan base with his mic hiked high. Arm outstretched. Legs wide apart. Silver lights flashed and arced behind him. They illuminated his white leather military-style Napoleonic jacket and white leather trousers. The sweat on his forehead deepened the trademark logo on his white silk du-rag – 'He's The Daddy'. His head moved rapidly to the drum-and-bass beat that his sometime collaborator M.C. Insanity pumped out at her decks on the right side of the stage.

He began to prowl, his steps moody. Intimidating. The crowd joined in his motion, elevating themselves on to the final jive of their musical journey. As he moved he let his gaze swing to the A&R crew that Paradise Records had sent down to check him out. There were two of them. A man and a woman. She was white, he was black. They stood at the left side of the stage, in the front row, arms folded, observing his performance and how the crowd responded to it. For too many years he'd been one of many rap acts scrapping a living on London's nocturnal music scene. Then three months ago – bingo – an art house film used two of his tunes on its soundtrack. When the film got a standing ovation at Cannes it springboarded his music from the underground to potential prime time over night. Now everyone wanted a slice of his lyrical whack. Paradise Records were not the first to come banging on his door, but they were the biggest players yet.

Now it was time to turn up the heat. To show Paradise Records' A&R people that he had the ability to revolutionise lives and wallets. He knew that as far as the record companies were concerned they were the same thing. As one record executive had explained to him once, 'Black rebels are always good box office.' He pulled his head up, eyes dancing across the crowd, looking for a novice, a newcomer who remained on the margins of the music. He searched – up, down, right side, left side, middle. He stopped when he found the face he was looking for. Young, white, male, lilting in a motion that said he was almost frightened to cut it with the music. LT's stare zoomed in so that they stood eye to eye, roaring brown meeting reticent blue. The best way to make a new devotee move on was to start with what they knew. LT started moving to the young man's tune.

One beat.

Two.

Three.

On the fourth he changed the gear. Revved it up. The groove of his body became faster, looser, chanting, It's just you and me, me and you. The young man's rhythm changed.

That's right, son, let it go.

Their motion went backwards, forwards, forwards, backwards, until an electric swing moved between them that no one could break.

That's it, baby, let it flow.

The young man closed his eyes and tipped his head back, and

LT knew that he had done his job. Like the King always said, no jam is a success until the crowd closes its eyes and feels the things it cannot see.

When each head in the crowd began to flop back, arms spread wide, LT knew they were ready for the final revelation. He turned his head and nodded to M.C. Insanity. With a flick of her wrist, she shut the music down. The crowd eased down. Waited. He bowed his head and raised his right hand in a black fist salute. It was a parody of a poster the King had that showed three black men standing on rostrums with their fists in the air. They looked like they had won something, like at the Olympics. It was a great image. Although he never asked what the story was behind the picture he borrowed it for his stage act. LT brushed his gaze towards the A&R pair and smiled as he saw them lean forward like everyone else. They did not know what was coming but the crowd did. He raised his head, ready to deliver his killer tune.

Curtis groaned as he slammed his back against one of the metal doors at the rear entrance to the Minus One club. He slid down and gulped in a single breath. He checked his watch. Seven minutes, that was all the time left before the concert finished. He closed his eyes. His chest pinched in pain as his nails cut into his balled palms. He unwrapped his hands. Opened his eyes. Six hours, that was how long he'd been running. Running from the two boys' faces at the window. Running from the smoke suffocating the air. Running from the blood he'd washed off himself in the public toilet. He'd run until the pulse of the daylight had swerved into the anonymous heartbeat of the night.

He checked the time again. Five minutes. He shoved up. Took three steps forward. He twisted around to face the club. His eyes swung between the three doors evenly spaced on the back wall. Shit, he didn't know which one to choose. Always start with what you know, Mr James, his violin teacher, had said. His violin. Pain squeezed his chest. The one thing he couldn't think about was his beloved violin. His hand shot out and grabbed the handle of the door he'd been leaning against. He pushed down. The door didn't move. He skipped to the second door. No joy there either. Moved to the last door. He pushed the handle down with the force of desperation he was feeling. The door did not budge. He kicked his trainer against the metal. Once, twice, three times. He had to get in. He felt the tears tear into his face. He pressed down on the handle and viciously kicked the door one more time. The door sprang open.

LT watched as M.C. Insanity spun the sampled disc with the power of the last move she might ever make. Vivaldi's violins mixed with an R 'n' B beat spun on. Laced behind both was LT's trademark sound of erratic human breathing. A half-breath in, a half-breath out. The Ice Shack sound, his musical MO. The words to his rap began to swell behind his front teeth. His mouth burst open, allowing his rap to come in his own unique bragging, nasal, vocal style that was a remix of Caribbean dance hall and cockney chat.

>*'Fire it up in the morning*
>*Send that match way high*
>*Gasoline Ghetto make over*
>*Burn down the system*
>*Die baby die.'*

He kept his eye on the A&R pair. The woman started moving. Yes, she was buying into his shit. LT strolled to the edge of the stage. Rocked his body into a wide-leg stance until his rhythm was balanced. Then he recited with the guile of a master storyteller:

>*'Gasoline Ghetto make over*
>*Die baby die.'*

He bellowed it a second time. Third time. Fourth time. He raised a finger, pointing it to the crowd, conducting them to join in. They did not disappoint him with their fanatical response. Over and over their mantra kicked against the walls. The couple from Paradise Records shook their bodies, in a more modest beat set by the crowd, but that did not matter because he knew that they finally felt it. M.C. Insanity cut the violins. Cut the R 'n' B track. Only the sound of heavy breathing filled the venue. LT added his voice to the breathing. The crowd added theirs. A half-beat in, a half-beat out. Higher and higher, their voices rose in a wordless refrain.

LT and the mic twisted, whirling dervish-style, in a hectic dance. Halfway through a whirl, he caught sight of someone standing in the wings. His movements slowed as his eyes ruffled over the newcomer. Teenage kid, stained clothing – plain untidy or an upcoming style, he could not tell. What he did know was that the kid was in the wrong place. Only performers and security were allowed backstage. He could see that the kid was a bad moon rising on his perfect performance. He noticed that most of the boy's tension seemed to be locked into one of his arms. His eyes skidded down the kid's right arm, which was clenched into a fist at his side.

The kid moved forward and flexed his right arm sideways at the same time. LT dropped his gaze to the youth's hand. He didn't see anything in the hand but he wasn't taking any chances. He held up his own hands, face up, loose, peacemaker style, as he said, 'Take it easy. Everything's cool.'

The boy moved into the light. Took a step closer to him. Now LT could see the boy's face, which was long, supported by a graceful neck. A face LT remembered as belonging to one of the fans the night before who'd waited for him to sign autographs after the gig at the Jamdown club in Notting Hill. He remembered that just as he got to the boy he'd decided to stop signing autographs. Thoughts of last night disappeared as LT saw the boy's arm push up. LT stepped back.

'Security,' he yelled.

Two huge men dressed in black with microphones clipped to their ears and ID badges hanging from their lapels rushed on to the stage.

'I think he's got a piece, he's got a piece,' one of them growled.

As the two security men dived on the youth, dragging him down, the crowd reacted, slamming the room with a bass line brimming with panic. People started shoving and screaming in a desperate attempt to get to the neon-lit exits. The smaller ones tumbled over as the survival instinct drove the bigger ones on. One woman crouched, left alone at the front, her hands over her head, sobbing. LT scanned the crowd, searching for the A&R pair, but the crush of people made it impossible for him to find them. The youth being wrestled to the ground screamed. The woman crouching below the stage finally dashed, still clutching her head, towards the nearest exit. The security men had immobilised the youth, so he lay locked flat down on to the stage.

LT swore. Furiously. When you're doing ghetto music the last thing you need appearing is the ghetto. His fingers ground into the mic in his hand. The mic. Shit, he had a job to do. He turned away from the youth and the security men. Rushed to the front of the stage. Brought the mic to his lips and announced, 'Chill, everybody, just chill. This party is still freebasing.'

Most of the revellers ignored him and continued pressing towards the doors, but a few people stopped, turned and faced him. Damn. None of the faces belonged to the A&R people.

'Watch out, he's still got the gun,' one of the security men said as he pushed his weight harder against the kid.

LT twisted back around at the same time as the youth pushed up, making one of the security men tumble half off his back. The youth raised his arm up. Towards LT. There was a loud crack and a flash. People screamed. LT felt his legs giving way at the same time as he noticed the drops of blood falling on to his white jacket.

# TRACK 4: LOOTIN' AND SHOOTIN'

At seven minutes after eleven the mobile phone next to the King's hospital bed started to ring. The second ring lifted the King from his painkiller-induced sleep. The third made him open both eyes and sit up. By the sixth ring his arm was slowly reaching out to grab the phone. He didn't know what the time was but he felt the lateness pressing against the air. He placed the phone against his face. His mouth was dry, his voice drowsy as he said, 'Yeah?'

'Thirty years is a long time,' came the reply.

The voice, not the words, slammed the King's upper body in shock against the pillow. The male voice was gentle, but insistent, just the way it had been back in '76. The King's vocal cords froze for maybe one of the first times in his life. His fingers gripped the phone as the caller carried on speaking.

'I hear you're dying, but before you depart this life to join that great sound system in the sky I think we need to meet. Tomorrow. Joe's Café. I'm sure you remember which end of town it's in. I know you musicians find the morning light unhealthy, but let's say ten.'

He let the caller's instruction hang in the air with his disbelief. He steadied his breathing. Got some control back. Then he abruptly ended the call. He hadn't said yes, he hadn't said no, but he knew he would have to go. It had been thirty years but they had finally found out that he had kept it and not destroyed it as they agreed he would. Just like he had dreaded they would as he lay choking in his son's arms hours earlier.

And now he thought he was going to start choking again. But he didn't. Instead he punched a new number into his mobile. The call was diverted straight to voicemail. Awkwardly he left a message.

'It's the King. Yeah, meet me here at one . . . I'm ready to tell you all about 1976 . . .'

'What did Paradise Records say, boss?' LT grunted at his manager, as blood and anger seeped into the white du-rag he held against his nose.

He was sitting in a plastic chair in the square dressing room on the top floor of the club. The blood pressure ebbed and flowed in his face. Sweat ran from his forehead with the texture of tears and the sureness of blood. Half an hour had passed since the police had arrested the youth. An hour since everyone had dived for cover when the bang and the flash had changed the tempo of the room and he had crumpled to the stage. Hackney being Hackney, everyone had assumed the same thing – he'd been shot. But of course he had not been. The loud explosion and the flash were the result of an electrical light blowing, and it turned out that the kid hadn't been packing any heat – well, not of the lethal gun-toting variety. But his manager, Window, had vaulted on to the stage, yelling for an ambulance. When Window reached him LT whispered that he didn't need an ambulance. Window's eyes had searched him, taking in his hand rubbing against his calf muscle, his hand clutching his nose. Window had eased back, knowing LT was hurt, but not from the impact of a firearm.

Stupid. Stupid. Stupid. Why couldn't he just be like other people and get migraines or rashes or the runs? Since he was eight years old the doctors the King had dragged him to, hoping to find a cure for his son, had explained that nosebleeds and leg cramps were his body's reaction to stress. And he was stressed. The chaos caused by the youth's appearance had induced cramps and a nose-bleed right on stage. It had never happened to him in public before. The look in his eye had pleaded with Window to get everyone out. The thought that fans would see his weakness was something he couldn't deal with. Didn't want to have to deal with. Besides, it was better PR for his public to leave thinking he had taken a bullet for his art rather than that a childhood ailment had laid him low.

He dumped his thoughts as another pain coiled through his left calf, dragging him back to the dressing room. The boom-box acoustics of the room caught his cry. Rotated it against the walls. He was glad he had his shades on because the only thing more embarrassing than people hearing his pain was seeing it duplicated in his eyes.

'I left a message on their voicemail,' Window, who was also the sole owner of the Minus One club, answered as he closed the door.

LT pulled the du-rag from his face. Ran a finger like a violin bow under his nose. His finger came away clean. He flicked his head up as he watched his manager stride towards him with slow deliberate steps. Window was six foot three of the most imposing smooth-plated copper muscle most people would see this side of the river. He wore his head shaved clean so that the tattoo that stretched across his neck could be easily seen. The letters of the tattoo were of a non-Roman script. Only a few people knew what it said. LT was not one of them and he didn't ask.

Window reached him. Stopped. Looked down at him. The light from the shaded bulb in the centre of the ceiling spread Window's shadow over him.

Window shook his head and said, 'Don't worry about Paradise Records.'

His large hand clasped LT's shoulder and LT knew that he was angry. Really angry. Whoever the youth on the stage had been, he couldn't have been local. If he had been he would never have done it. No one treated Window that way. People respected Window. People feared Window. He had started his adult life as the main eyes for some of East London's major players. That's how he had got his nickname. About five years ago Window had turned legit. But legit is a relative term in the East End. He had the connections that LT needed. And LT trusted him. The King had told him too many stories of musicians in the seventies, too distracted by snorting and shagging the high life to notice their accountants and managers ripping them off.

'Paradise Records will be back,' Window continued. 'Know why? Because you're units. They don't give a toss about what you're singing, just how many times it's being downloaded. How many MP3s it's hooking up with. They only need to read this interview to know they're getting success with a capital S when you go through their door.'

Window was holding a copy of *The Lick* lad mag. They had done a one-page profile of LT. LT took the magazine. Looked it over. In the top right corner was an ad for tonight's concert. The rest of the page was a homage to him and his music.

**Tag Name:** Lord Tribulation (LT to all his mates)
**Birth Name:** Jeremiah Scantleberry
**Age:** 25
**Birthplace:** Hackney, East London
**Music:** Rap singer & pioneer of the Ice Shack sound
**Collaborators:** Renowned deck magician M.C. Insanity
**Heat Rating:** Volcano hot. Has won the Notting Hill Carnival's Writer in Residence of Ladbroke Grove rap contest two years on the trot. Will he be the first rapper to ding number three this year?
**Kiss-&-Tell Rating:** Footloose and fancy free. Whenever you're ready, ladies . . .
**Hobbies:** Music, music, music!
**Clothing:** Du-rag heaven. Trademark du-rag logo 'He's The Daddy'. Also keeps a selection of du-rags on which to write headlines he gets from the newspapers. All clothes are custom-made by his own designer
**Fan Mail:** 12 Rhodes Square, London E8
**Word On The Street:** That Paradise Records are currently negotiating a sizzling record deal
**Deep Dark Secrets:** Never gigs in Hoxton

'They got the address wrong for the fan mail,' he said, handing the magazine back to Window.

Window scrutinised the article, then said, 'I told them 12 Rhodes Street, where my office is, not Rhodes Square.'

His words were cut off as his mobile began to ring. LT's breathing quickened, hoping it was the record company. Window took the call. He nodded his head once towards LT as he listened. LT's heart pumped harder. He rubbed the tip of a finger anxiously over the dryness of his bottom lip.

'Thanks for getting back to us. My boy is as eager as you are,' Window said. Then he stopped as he listened. 'No, of course it wasn't part of the show,' Window added tightly. One minute later he clicked off.

'What did they say?' LT asked.

'They need to have an in-house chat. Then they'll contact me in a couple of days. When they do it's going to be good news. Come on, I'll run you home in your ride just in case those cramps come back.'

Since Window had become his manager everything in his career had gone according to plan, so he couldn't see why that should now change. He eased up. Picked up his walk. Took it easy. Didn't rush it, as he moved towards his jacket.

Window gave it some stick as he drove LT's beloved Pacific blue four-by-four through the brooding night streets and side roads of Hackney. The low-level throttle of the car almost sighed, like a man quenching his thirst after a hard day and looking for that woman to end the day right. LT's head lolled back against his engraved initials in the leather headrest as he relaxed in the passenger seat. Eyes half closed, he listened to the DJ chatting on Window's favourite radio outlet, Station Debt-E-Nation FM.

'This is Lady Hectic blessing all you people of the metropolis. It's that crazy groove time of the year again. Europe's biggest street jam, the one and only Notting Hill carnival, is almost jacking at our door. Just twelve days to go. On the last day of the carnival, bank holiday Monday, don't miss Ladbroke Grove's Writer in

Residence slamdown. This year's clash will be held in the open on the All Saints Road. I will be the people's MC, introducing contestants Elliott Ness, Lady Tick, Rumplestiltskin and reigning boy wonder, Lord Tribulation. This year's judges will include the legendary LA producer Sean Sparkle and community activist Beresford Clarke. It's gonna be a roadblock, so make sure you're there well before the clock strikes three.'

A quick smile shuffled across LT's mouth. The Writer in Residence of Ladbroke Grove was one of the most lucrative musical events in British rap. As the DJ so nicely put it, he was the reigning boy wonder. He liked that. The event had begun life as a response by the community to the explosion of tension between the police and the youth at Notting Hill's carnival in 1976. On the last night of the carnival the body of a well-known activist, street name Houdini, had been found. Everyone was convinced that the police had killed him. The following year, on the last night of the two-day carnival, the Jamdown club in Ladbroke Grove had held a small musical event in memory of Houdini's militant life. The main highlight had been a musical battle between calypso singers. In 1978, when Super Cool, the winner, had been asked how he had defeated his opponents, he had replied, 'It was all about the slamming power of my lyrics. All about the words, man.' From that point on, whoever won was crowned the Writer in Residence of Ladbroke Grove. As sponsorship grew the event became huge. It moved from a showcase for calypsonians to one for rappers. LT had won it for the last two years. Everyone was holding their breath this year because no artist had won it three years in a row. Some said if he pulled off the treble he should be crowned Shakespeare of Ladbroke Grove.

The DJ's voice on the radio softened as she said, 'Now chill back and enjoy our seventies reggae revival selection. Here's one for those who remember that classic movie *The Harder They Come.*'

The haunting vocals of the Slickers' 'Johnny Too Bad' wailed against the leather seats of the car's interior.

'That's the trouble with this life,' Window said as the lyrics and car took a smooth right, 'too many people just lootin' and shootin'.'

LT knew Window was referring to the abrupt ending of the concert.

'We don't need these record company people,' his manager carried on as he slow-rolled the car at a set of traffic lights.

LT didn't answer. He did not want to have this conversation. They had had it too many times. He knew Window was talking about music@yourfingertips.net, an Internet network run by a friend of his for musicians to sell their music straight to the public. It cut out the middleman, the record companies, and had minimal overheads. LT thought it sounded like a poor man's music show stuck inside a computer. He wanted the limelight, the limousines, the glamour. And the only people who knew how to do glamour with a triple G were the record companies. But his manager obviously didn't agree as he continued to coax him with his words.

'Everyone knows the industry is going that way. Musicians are taking control, setting up their own networks. You don't want to be the only one not linking arms.'

A vehicle sounded its horn behind them in a furious wake-me-up beat. LT realised that the lights had changed to green. Instead of moving the car forward, Window used the rearview mirror to check out the vehicle behind him. A large white van, the type that was used for removals. He glared for a few seconds. Then hit the accelerator.

'Like I said, too much lootin' and shootin',' Window mumbled as he bent the car into the main road, leaving the white van behind.

Ten minutes later, the white van shuddered to a halt outside a block of flats in central Hackney. One half of the block pulsed with the sound of music, while the other half slept in silence.

'We're here,' the man in the driver's seat whispered into his mobile phone.

He nodded his head a few times, listening to the person on the other end of the line. Forty-five seconds later he cut the call. Tucked the mobile into his trouser pocket. Tipped his baseball cap low over his eyes. Checked his watch. Smiled. They had made good time. He shifted his head towards the younger man next to him. The job had come through mid-evening, which had cheered him up. Late jobs meant he could charge a premium price.

'OK, if we're in and out within the hour, there's a monkey in it for you,' he told his companion gruffly.

They jumped out of the van. Took the stairs to the second floor. They walked along the balcony until they reached the address they'd been given. The older man took out a screwdriver. Usually he would have a set of keys. There was always an enterprising council worker willing to sell duplicates of keys for cash to compensate for having to work those extra years to get a full pension. But this time there had not been time. He jammed the screwdriver between the door and frame. Just under where the lock was set in the door. He applied pressure. As the door started to give he said, 'OK, we've got one hour to clean this place out.'

The following morning a bead of sweat bounced into the mug of coffee King Stir It Up stared into. He sat at a table in Joe's Café. A café in Hoxton, on the south-western tip of Hackney. The one part of Hackney he hated.

He waited in his battered suit, which was neatly buttoned over his hospital pyjamas. Fluorescent lighting bounced off the high spring-green floor and on to laminated sheets of white paper on the wall advertising the standard dishes in bubble-blue writing. A small television was mounted on a stand above the counter, where a daytime chat show debated the pressing issue 'Is your husband wearing your clothes? And does it matter?' Behind the counter stood a woman. Mid-twenties, with quick working hands that suggested this job was just a stopgap on the way to somewhere else.

He knew that they had deliberately chosen Hoxton to meet to make him feel uncomfortable. To make him remember where the bad times started. To make him remember a time that he'd rather forget. To pressurise him into giving them what they wanted. Something that for thirty years they had never realised he still had. He grimaced as he looked at the clock on the wall. Shit, it was already nineteen minutes past the time they said they would meet him. He didn't have a problem with lateness – what musician did? No, he had a problem with standing still when there were no more years left to live.

The hiss and humidity pouring from the urn behind the counter made his palms retreat from the heat of the mug. His hand grabbed the edge of the table as he looked downwards. Shit, he still had his slippers on. Satin black with Cuddle Monster machine-embroidered in white thread. A present from his lady, May. He just hoped that May and his other boy, a boy his son knew nothing about, had remembered to give Jerry what he had left with them. Maybe he should call Jerry now? His hand felt in his jacket pocket. Found his mobile. Half dragged it up. His hand stopped. Hesitated. Pushed back down. He'd talk to Jerry later. Face to face.

He checked the clock again.

'Come on,' he chanted with impatience. He dragged the mug of coffee back into his hand.

'More tea, love?' a waitress asked him.

He didn't hear her. She moved out of his shadow and left him to himself. He made his decision. He had given them enough time. As he got ready to leave, the ten thirty local news bulletin flashed up on the TV screen.

'Violence has reared its head again at a rap concert in the capital. Last night a young man was arrested at the concert of London rapper Lord Tribulation . . .'

His head shot up at the same time as a puff of steam came from the urn.

'Unconfirmed reports also suggest that the man in police custody may have also been involved in an arson attack that seriously injured two children. The police are investigating whether there are any possible connections between the two incidents. Earlier we interviewed the Minister of Culture, Clarissa Hathaway, about the incident at last night's concert.'

The screen changed to show the interview with the minister. The blood drained from his cheeks as he stared.

'Well, kiss my sweet black . . .' He didn't finish.

Instead he thrust up. The tumour in his stomach woke up, coiling pain around his body. The vomit climbed to his throat. He gulped it back. The acid made his eyes water. Stupid fool, he told himself, why hadn't he seen it? He rushed forward, skidding

on a slice of tomato on the floor. His hand crunched acciden-
tally against the mobile in his pocket. Pushed a button. One of
the music tracks his son had downloaded on to it started to play.
The one track he did not need to hear – 1976's killer tune 'Police
And Thieves'.

'You all right, mate?' one of the workmen at a nearby table
asked him.

He didn't answer. Instead, he pushed himself up. Rushed to the
door. Opened it. Stumbled into the street. Pain heaved inside his
stomach. He looked around, breathing in the unhygienic air,
deciding which was the quickest way to get to his son. Quickest
way would be the bus from the end of Gazoo Lane. The song in
his pocket still played. He didn't have time to turn it off. He
lengthened his strides. Passed a trio of drunks lazing on a blue
bench like a family unit waiting for cream tea. Passed a public
phone box. Passed a cab office. Sweat glazed his skin as he swung
into the sun-drenched Lane. The sound of the bars of a song beat
in the background coming from a car. The hum of a car began
to increase as he moved. He ignored it and hurried on. The song
got louder as the engine of a car roared behind him. He stopped,
feeling the warmth of the car breathing. He stilled, turned around
and moved to the side to let the car pass. The car stopped at the
same time as the driver jacked up the volume on the tune spinning from the car's deck. He stumbled, held the wall when he
realised that it was the same track that was playing in his pocket
– 'Police And Thieves'. The music accelerated from his phone
inside his pocket.

A slice of sunlight stroked his eyes, blinding him.

The music from the car stopped dead.

The pressure inside him dropped.

The car's engine ignited, blasting the air.

The sun slid behind a cloud.

He shook his eyes, adjusting back to the daylight.

He saw the face of the driver. Shocked, he stopped, hesitated.
The pain twisted in his stomach. Catapulted up to his chest.

The car went into full throttle towards him, with the brooding bass line of 'Police And Thieves' still kicking high in the air from his mobile phone in his pocket.

Jane Blake stood at the cab office window on the damp-ridden top floor and pulled out a pack of twenty B&H. She drew out a fag. Fag, yes, that was right. Not cigarette. That was what the English people called them. And above all she was learning the art or craft of becoming English, just like her new chosen name. She stared out through the dirt-speckled glass and saw a man hurrying down the Lane. Then she saw a car. It slowed down as it saw the man. The man skipped to the side. She pulled her lighter. Lit up. The man stopped. Turned around. The car revved its engine. Jane lowered the lighter from her fag. Her face strained at the window at the same time as the car accelerated forward. The fag fell from her fingers. Her hands gripped the curtains. Snapped them together. As most people learned back home, the best way to deal with life was to see nothing. Then she heard the screech of tyres. Her fingertips pinched into the curtains. Eased them partially open, so she could peep outside again.

The ring of his landline on the bedside table and the touch of Mel's tongue skimming inside his belly button made LT wake up. The humid air seeped into the room from the discreetly opened window, sucking the scent of Mel's counterfeit perfume on to his lips. The telephone rang a second time. He knew he should answer it in case it was Window with news from the record company. But he didn't. Mel's warm platinum-ringed hand moved lower. He groaned, but not with pleasure. One of the many snippets of advice the King had given him on relationships was 'the day your lady's touch don't make your piece get high, it's time to whisper bye-bye'. He'd been seeing Mel for three months. He knew it was finally time to whisper those words next to her gold-looped earring.

'What's wrong, babycakes?' she asked, her voice muffled as she gripped the edge of the maroon duvet with her purple acrylic nails.

She slid her body full length against his, clipping the silver ring in his left nipple. She gazed at him with her saddle-brown face and coin-round eyes. Her blonde – or champagne, as she called it – corkscrew extensions cupped her face. She fixed her mouth into a pout that always reminded him of exaggerated chat, with exaggerated lip movements, like a teenager who wanted anyone passing by to believe that the words leaving her mouth were important. He didn't answer her. Instead he slid his gaze over her and realised that she was not the type of woman he wanted hanging on his arm now he was beating at the door of success.

Getting a sniff of success hadn't been easy. No way. It had taken him twelve long years of solid graft to get where he was going. He remembered the exact date when he had decided that he was going to become the Don Dada of the British rap scene.

A Saturday in October.

A night that had hit zero degrees.

A year and a half ago.

He'd been gigging at a club in Tottenham. He'd been one of three acts. Three forgettable acts. After his performance he'd stood in front of the mirror in the dressing room and been startled to notice a single grey hair in the middle of his hairline among his short, springboard locks. The hair had shaken him up. He couldn't have grey hair – that just wasn't natural, for God's sake, because he was only . . . He'd counted and realised that he was nine months off the big three zero. And there it was, a spindle of grey hair, just like his dad's had gone at the same age. And that was very bad news – genetics could play havoc with a boy's career. It hit him then that since the age of eighteen he'd been just like the rest of the underground rap crowd doing the usual who could spit the words on the mic the fastest, who could twist the words the hardest. The realisation that he was a cut-and-paste rapper hit him with a swinger straight in his ambitions.

He knew he had to stand out from all the other snappers on the scene, so he set about remoulding his look, redefining his musical hook. The first thing he'd done was shave off his locks and five years of his life. Yeah, twenty-four felt like a good age to be. Then he'd tested his new heavy-breathing backbeat, at the One Love Festival in East London's sprawling Victoria Park. When he first hit the crowd with his new sound the audience and pigeons had stopped moving, gone silent. Then a couple had jumped up, flashing their psychedelic colours and marijuana fumes into the air, like the second coming had arrived. The park erupted. A few months on, his new style was being given its own name – the Ice Shack sound. There were many stories doing the rounds about how it got its tag. His favourite was that two ice crystal addicts were joyriding on their chosen drug and his music. One had said to the other that the music felt like she was high inside an ice house. As she started to yell, 'Ice house, baby,' her companion had pointed out that they couldn't even afford to buy a house in London – just a shack maybe. So the name Ice Shack had been born.

He moved his face a quarter of an inch closer to Mel's. He opened his mouth and yawned in her face. She sucked her teeth, jumped out of the bed, took the four minutes she needed to throw on her hipsters, tube top and four-inch cork wedge heels and then grooved her hips out of the room.

The alarm radio buzzed on: 11.45 a.m. The radio came on. Karen Carpenter's fragile, compelling voice tightened across the bedroom as she sang about 'Rainy Days And Mondays'. His nostrils flared as he breathed in her voice. A voice that he admired. He loved what other people said they hated about it – the sugar, the lullaby quality, the simple purity. He used to be upfront about his love of her voice, but not any more. Window insisted his fan base just wouldn't roll with it. Uncool. He reached over and banged the radio off.

He leaned back on the bed. Gazed up at the ceiling. The ceiling was covered in a patchwork of album covers with a few twelve-inches sown in between. They ran across the spectrum of popular music and the era of time. From the lonely night-time London depicted on The Streets' *A Grand Don't Come Free* to the clean-cut image of four men looking into the distance on Kraftwerk's hugely influential *Trans-Europe Express*. From Nas's golden Last

Supper image proclaiming himself as da man on *The Street Disciple* to the sumptuous tan belly, complete with riveting belly button, on Trojan Records' reggae compilation *Tighten Up Volume 2*. His best album cover and the King's were side by side. In the centre. His was Public Enemy's *It Takes A Nation Of A Million To Hold Us Back*. The King's was Junior Murvin's *Police And Thieves*. He eyed the King's favourite album cover. The King had given it to him last week. Since the King had learned he was dying he kept giving him stuff, little bits of his life. Before the album he'd given him a pork-pie hat. Before the hat his pineapple ice bucket.

Shit. He didn't want to think about the King. Didn't want to think about how he'd seen him yesterday, suffering in downtown Hackney. He sighed. At least his old man was being well looked after and was no doubt tucked up safe and sound in his bed right now.

He eased out of the bed. Naked. Stretched, making the muscles in his stomach and arms punch like rocks under his skin. His fingers did a frisky journey through his 'fro – front, back, centre. He put on a green-and-white-panelled polo shirt and made his way to the main room.

He lived on the south side of Hackney in a one-bedroom flat on the fourth and top floor of Ernest Bevin House. Although it was a standard T-shaped flat, everyone agreed it was unusual. What made it unusual was that his home was a living homage to music. His music collection – vinyl, CDs, singles, tapes – ran from the bedroom to the bathroom, from the kitchen to the main room. Each room was devoted to a different style of music. Rap that ran from Old Skool to Dirty South in the bedroom then spilled over into London Grime in the kitchen. The main room was his Caribbean sunrise and orgy of soul. On one side of the room was his reggae collection – dub, dance-hall, ragga and roots revival. On the other side was his celebration of soul – Stax, funk, Motown, Rare Grooves, Northern Soul and R 'n' B.

He sauntered into the main room, passed his Rare Grooves collection and went over to the answering machine.

Four messages. Hopefully one from Window about Paradise Records.

He heard Mel come into the room, bringing the scent of coffee that she held in the cup in her hand.

As he pressed the play button he said, 'Mel, when you go leave my keys on the table.'

'You what?'

He didn't answer her as he padded to the window, shaking his head, pushing the sleep out of his mind, shifting into the beginning rhythm of the day. He watched the lethargic sway of the Regent's Canal as the answer machine clicked, buzzed. The first message began to play.

'Won't believe this one. You're news headlines. Give me a bell asap.'

It was M.C. Insanity's voice. Anxious, a touch angry.

'What you say to me?' Mel asked.

Mel's question dragged him back to her. He didn't look around as he said, 'I told you from the start not to get too cosy. That all we were strictly playing were tribute band tunes.'

The second message played.

'A couple of word rats have been shaking their tails around at the club. You need to be tuned into Channel Three on your box for the lunchtime news.'

He spun around, hearing Window's voice. Word rats meant tabloid press. Why would they be looking for him? Sure, there had been the incident at the club last night, but no big thing. His face screwed up in confusion at the same time as Mel's full-flow aria took over the room.

'What, so now you're gonna be all famous with your big head on the TV, you don't want me near you?'

LT put up his hand, palm flat against the air, for her to be quiet. The third message came up.

'Hey, Lord Tribulation, this is Tad Williams from the *London News*. We'd like to give you the opportunity to put your side of the story. I left a card with your manager. Call me.'

That made him move. From the window to the machine. But Mel started to shuffle her heels against the wooden floor, mini-stamps that told the world it had better listen to her.

'Don't think I don't know all you want is one of them white chicks tweeting on your arm . . .'

'Mel, give it a rest.'

'What, my home-girl pussy getting in the way of your OK ya ting?'

Before the fourth message came on he hit 'rewind'. Pressed 'play'. Listened to the messages from the start. But Mel's voice started hurting him again. He cringed at the verbal static she was throwing in his face. Just like with a pair of cheap earphones, the sound quality wasn't going to get any better, no matter how good the music. He knew he wasn't going to be able to listen to the messages while her mouth got riper.

He pressed 'pause' on the machine. Turned to Mel and smiled at her like she was a fan.

'It was great while it lasted, Goldilocks.'

'Don't give me none of that "it's better to have loved and lost" shit.'

That threw him. He thought her reading age went as far as the instructions on the tub of Dark 'n' Lovely hair-straightening kit. He had never figured her for a Tennyson girl or the inhaler of any other type of high-grade literature.

'All right, I'm off, but let me tell you that the sparkles' – she pushed her chest out as she showed him the trio of gold necklaces he'd given her as gifts – 'are still gonna be kissing my skin when I leave here. Just you remember that a man can't be too careful in the choice of his enemies.'

She rushed out of the door and, he hoped, out of his life. He listened to the messages. He shut his eyes the same way he did when he was trying to find the lyrics that worked when he was composing a new track. He let the words float to him. *News headlines . . . word rat . . . lunchtime news . . . Your side of the story.* He looked at his watch: 11.58. He rushed over to the TV at the same time as the last message on the answering machine bombed into the room.

'Mr Scantleberry, this is Sister Begum from St Luke's hospital. We thought we should inform you that your father has gone.'

'My mum says that stuff makes you nuts if you keep smoking it,' the fifteen-year-old St Ignatius schoolgirl said to her friend as they strolled down Gazoo Lane.

Her friend defiantly took a stronger lug from the joint in her mouth. She sucked in, breathed the smoke out and said, 'Wish I'd been nuts in that maths lesson this morning instead of having to die from boredom.'

They both laughed as they moved farther down the lane. Their lemon-coloured du-rags with 'Who's The Daddy?' written across the front accentuated the haze of the lunchtime sun.

'Did you hear about Casey's brother?' the girl without the joint asked.

Her friend shook her head as the final smoke hissed from her mouth. She flicked the butt into the sunlight.

'He's in the hospital. Intensive care. Some dead-head petrol-bombed some house her brother shouldn't have been playing in. One of them houses on Rhodes Square that just got sold to some rich people.'

'How do you . . .' Suddenly the schoolgirl pulled her words back as they approached the bins with a pile of black bags around the bottom.

She pushed her head to the side so that her right ear faced the two bins.

'Can you hear that?'

'What?'

She turned back to her friend and said, 'Music coming from those black bags.'

'Don't be stupid. See, I told you that stuff makes you nuts . . .'

'No, listen.'

They both strained forward, catching the whispering bass line pulsing in the air like the distant wheels of a train.

'Someone might have dropped their MP3.'

They turned to look at each other. Smiled.

'Finders keepers,' they both yelled as they rushed towards the bags. They bent down and eagerly pushed them out of the way.

'What's that?' one girl asked as she reared back.

Her friend looked closer.

'Looks like a pair of slippers. Someone must have dumped them. Come on, help me find that MP3.'

Her friend rejoined her as they pulled back another bag.

'Oh my God,' one girl screamed.

She jostled back as she stared at a pair of legs attached to the slippers.

'Call Five-O,' she yelled at her friend. 'Call the fucking police!'

'What do you mean, he's not dead? You said he was gone,' LT said to Sister Begum in her office.

His voice was both relieved and indignant as he stood in a room that was a subtle homage to tropical green – the thin lawn carpet, the deep-sea cushioned chair Sister sat on, the charity-shop vase that stood proudly on top of the four-drawer steel cabinet and the tangy, sweet scent, like someone had dripped lime cordial over the warm radiator.

After hearing the message from the hospital, he'd bolted to the front door and shouted over the balcony for Mel to wait. He needed her to drive him to the hospital. He decided against taking his own wheels. If the King was really finally gone he knew that the cramps would eventually come. No way could he drive his ride in that condition. Seeing her opening back into his life, Mel had been more than happy to jump into the driver's seat. When they had reached the hospital Mel had made a fuss, wanting to come upstairs with him, but he'd made her wait downstairs in the reception.

'Mr Scantleberry, please take a seat.'

Sister Begum spoke to him in a carefully modulated voice that cuddled each syllable.

LT pushed his long body down in the chair, sitting across from her at the simple white desk. He wore faded large-pocket jeans, with a white V-neck undershirt propped behind a black thigh-length wet-look jacket. No du-rag. Most fans didn't recognise him without one. Besides, he suspected that until he found out what had happened to the King and why he was a headline on the box it was a day he needed to keep his life low.

She gazed at him, with a sympathetic look, waiting for him to start, so he did.

'Your message said that he was gone,' he said, staring at her name badge on her uniform. Poppy Begum.

'Which he has done,' she replied.

The way her hand curved back, with her thumb lying on the inside of her forefinger, he knew she spent most nights in bed with a book. Most probably second-hand, never brand-new, from the space left between forefinger and thumb.

'But I thought you meant he was dead.'

Her eyebrows rose as she said, 'We are not in the habit of informing relatives that their loved ones have died over the telephone.'

'So what exactly happened?' he asked as he rubbed the tiredness from his left eye.

'At about nine this morning he just started packing his belongings . . .'

'But where's he gone?'

'That I can't tell you. Hasn't he got a mobile you could try?'

'Yeah, but he hates the thing. Doesn't like being tracked. Thinks a man should be free to walk the streets without the world on his back. Why didn't you stop him?'

Her eyebrows jumped higher.

'Despite what the community might say this is not a prison camp, so I didn't have the right to stop him.'

A shaft of sunlight came through the window above Sister's head and went into his eyes. He closed them and kept them shut for a while, happy for the time to collect his thoughts. Sister started speaking again. He reopened his eyes.

'I tried to stop him but he wouldn't listen. I see this all the time. When people know that they're dying they suddenly remember all kinds of things they should have done. Maybe there was something urgent that he knew he just had to do. They are always back by the evening, so I wouldn't worry if you don't hear from him.'

He nodded his head, still feeling irritated.

'From what I've seen on the telly this morning, I know you've got your own problems today . . .' Sister began to say.

The door burst open.

'Sister, we need you urgently,' a young male nurse said, and then rushed away.

Sister rushed after the nurse, leaving LT sitting in the cold breeze from the wide-open door as his face flushed, realising he still hadn't a chance to watch the television to discover whether all the fuss was going to interfere with his chances with the record company.

As Poppy Begum rushed after her colleague she swore quietly, remembering the bag Isaiah Scantleberry had told her to give his son.

LT pressed the up button for the hospital lift and decided that if the King weren't already dying he would be tempted to drop the fatal blow himself. The King of all people knew that August was one of the most important times of the year. The Notting Hill carnival and the Ladbroke Grove's Writer in Residence competition were the ultimate time for rappers to strut their adrenalin-fused stuff. He reorganised his priorities – first find a telly and find out what all the fuss was about and then locate the King.

Best place to find out what was going on was to get to Window at the Minus One club. He debated whether to call a cab or ask Mel, who was still waiting for him downstairs in reception. He decided the easiest option would be Mel. He twisted his lips. But then being the wrong kind of easy was always Mel's problem.

His finger pressed anxiously against the lift button. He watched the red light flick from one to two, from two to three. The lift wheezed, sort of chuckled and then opened. Inside was a woman holding her head down as she hiked the padded straps of her rucksack securely to her shoulders. He moved forward at the same time as her short cropped blonde head came up. He froze, shocked, as he saw her face. A face he had not seen in fifteen years.

'Hi, Jeremiah,' she said, moving out of the lift. 'Sorry about the cliché but it's certainly been a long time.'

LT's feet tripped an unsteady two steps back, shocked, shoving his back against the corridor wall. He gaped at the woman standing in front of him.

The lift doors wheezed. Shuddered. Closed. The final sound took him out of his shock. He pulled his back off the wall. Pushed his chin out and straight. His tongue tipped on to his dry bottom lip. Glided from left to right. Then he spoke in the rhythm of a slow handclap.

'Well, well, well.'

He stopped. Did a dramatic three-second pause. Continued.

'Bernie.' His gaze stroked up over her as he said her first name.

'Ray.' His gaze stroked down over her as he said her surname.

Bernie Ray. The love of his life from the age of thirteen until he was almost sixteen. And if he was honest, the only love of his life there had ever been.

Of course, she had changed since she was a girl of fifteen, the last time he'd seen her, but not where it mattered. She still stood exactly level with his chin. Still had the type of body people remembered long after she'd left a room. Long elegant neck that showed off above a classic waistline more fitting to the 1950s than today's trim and thin look. Still held her chin, left side slanted down, like the amazing violin player she'd once been. Maybe still was. A baby black butterfly clip pinned the side of her cropped white-gold hair back behind her ear. The stark colour of her hair was heightened by the blackness of her T-shirt, bootleg jeans and trainers. Tiny lines, like the violin strings that had dominated her young life, plucked around her pale, misty-blue eyes. The only difference he saw was in her back. It was a little too strong, a little too straight, almost like if she relaxed too much she would fall apart.

'It's good to see you, Jerry,' she said, looking up at him.

Shit. He almost squeezed his eyes shut when he heard her voice. Yeah, she hadn't changed where it mattered. Still had that upmarket accent with that sandy quality that reminded him of Al Green hitting those seductive low notes on 'Let's Stay Together'.

She took a half-step towards him. Then stopped just before she touched his heat.

'I hear LT are the initials on everyone's lips these days,' she said, her tone strong and even.

He watched her, hard, trying to find out whether she was giving him a compliment or a two-way slap across his achievements. Her features were set, her eyes hooded so he couldn't see which way she flowed. But he knew how he was feeling, so he took her to where, he suspected, she didn't want to go.

'Yeah, life's moved up, babe, since you went all a cappella and doo-wopped out of my door.'

She didn't respond to his insult. Didn't respond to the way he made 'babe' sound like it came just before bastard in the 'fuck you' dictionary. But then that's what he'd loved about her – her toughness. Despite coming from a family that had money to burn she had been as streetwise as anyone else at St Ignatius school.

'So how was your father?'

Her enquiry surprised him. He took a step closer to her. The way her head moved back told him she now felt his heat.

'How did you know my dad's in here?'

'You know what Hackney's like. Everyone is always willing to tell a story except their own.'

He almost asked whether she was ready to tell her own story about why she had left fifteen years ago. But he didn't.

'Wish I could tell you how my old man is, but I can't.'

'Why not?' She hitched her head up to gaze anxiously and directly into his face.

He just smiled. Let her dangle the way she had left him hanging fifteen years ago. He moved past her to the lift and pressed the button again. It opened. He picked up his strut 'n' sway walk. Took it real easy as he moved inside the lift. He pressed the G button. Kept his gaze steady above her head as he said, 'Nice seeing you again, Bernie. Maybe I'll see you in another fifteen years' time with your Zimmer frame.'

He pushed his gaze down. Watched her baby finger rub in the groove in the middle of her collarbone, in the same place she'd once kept the key to her violin case on a chain around her neck. She turned swiftly, her rucksack slapping her back as she rushed down the corridor. Whatever she was doing here was none of his business. But he kept watching. As the lift doors sighed, getting ready to close, he saw Bernie reach the King's room. She bolted inside the room.

'What the . . .' he called out.

Both his hands dug into the coolness of the lift's steel doors. He pushed forward, trying to stop them closing. The doors stopped. Then their force fought back against him. He gritted his teeth. Groaned. The gap began to widen. He took a deep breath. Pushed again. The doors creaked in protest as they moved back. He jumped through the gap. Pelted down the corridor. He reached the King's room. Swung inside. Bernie stood by the foot of the King's empty bed. She turned. Faced him.

'What's going on?' he asked roughly, breathing hard.

'Marvin Gaye, '71. Hot-pick selection for inclusion in anyone's top ten albums of all time,' she replied.

A confident grin spread leisurely across her whole face. So she still remembered how to take it easy.

He moved towards her. Growled, 'Unlike the amazing Marvin, I'm exercising my right to use a question mark, so I repeat, what's going on?'

'Oh, didn't I mention that your father's helping me with an article I'm writing?'

His facial muscles started jerking. No way was he allowing her back into his life. No fucking way. That's when he felt that familiar feeling. Blood slicing down his nasal cavity. Thick, tiny drops tumbling out. Dyeing the sweat on his top lip a murky red.

LT was crammed into the armchair by the King's bed. He reluctantly took the tissue that Bernie offered him. He pressed it against his 'let-me-down' nose. Two bloody nosebleeds in two days. He wasn't meant to be serenading with this type of stress when mass-market stardom was stomping its foot, fist raised, ready to beat a magic treble riff on to his door. As Bernie eased up, her natural fragrance – fresh, unique – and memories dusted over him. Drew him back to the first time he had clicked with her at school.

1990.

The school canteen.

Soft summer day.

A time when PE had nothing to do with physical education and everything to do with Public Enemy.

St Ignatius school believed in music. It kept alive the Inner London Education Authority's motto that every child should have a musical instrument. LT had first seen her around in the fourth year. Knew that she was the new girl in the playground. Everywhere she went, so did the violin in its case, strapped to her body like a suckling baby, and the key to the case which she wore around her neck. With a name like Berlina he knew that she was not Hackney born and bred. The word was that she got her name from when her parents were hippies in West Berlin, waiting for the revolution to spread from East to West. She was a loner like him, preferring the company of her violin, like he did his portable microphone. So there he'd been, waiting in the queue of the canteen, his earphones on, shut off from the world, rocking to Public Enemy's 'Fight The Power'. Something had made him turn around. He was never sure what it was. The turn-your-life-around truth of the lyrics? The twist of the soothing spring breeze? That invisible tap on the shoulder?

Whatever it had been, he'd shifted around and there she was. Headphones on, nodding to the same furious beat that he was. No way, he'd thought. No way would some prissy middle-class white violinist be drawing blood with music that stuck a finger up to the world. What did she know about the song's radical A-line rhythm of aggro, anger, agitation? The only pupils at St Iggy's who got deep in that were those from the Estates. And she was no Estate girl. No, she was a big-house girl – no less than three storeys and an attic, he guessed. So he'd stared at her with the look in his eyes that asked 'What you hooked up to?' She had stared with bold, blue eyes and lobbed the question straight back at him. They had smiled at each other. When the chorus hit for a second time, in unison they had yelled it out together.

After that the four of them, including her violin and his mic, were inseparable. The intensity and energy of the way she played the violin often reminded him of the King's wailing chants as he toasted onstage. They made music together. When they hit fifteen, they made love together. Spent their adolescence never rushing it, taking it easy together. Then one day short of his sixteenth birthday, she was gone.

Now she was back and it had something to do with his father.

He didn't want her in the King's life. Or his. Not after what he'd discovered had made her run out on him fifteen years ago.

He pulled back from the memories. Ran a finger under his nose. No blood. He flicked his chin up to look at Bernie. Saw the look in her ballsy-blue shaded eyes. Knew she wasn't going to give up on her quest to find out about the King that easy. And he was equally determined to tell her nothing. She tilted her chin to the left. He kept his head dead straight. Neither one of them was willing to back down. Instinct told him that the next part of their conversation was only going to be played one way – they were going to fall straight back into what they used to call their Double D minor Rap. She'd loved playing Bach's Double Violin Concerto in D minor with another violinist. When they were young, in their haste to speak sometimes, they would behave just like the two violins and belt out what they had to say at the same time. Like they were both on the stage. Side by side. Neither willing to let the other take the lead in the performance. Their eyes caught. Firm brown meeting entrenched blue.

They started speaking. At the same time. Her voice just ahead of his.

'Where's your father?'

'Where's your violin?'

'I need to find him.'

'Do you still play?'

'He left a message on my voicemail, asking me to meet him . . .'

'Remember the first time you played it for me?'

'At twelve thirty in his room.'

'At two thirty in your bedroom.'

'Will you shut up because I'm worried about him.'

Her shout made him stop and look at her.

'What do you mean, you're worried about him?' he asked as he leaned forward in the chair. 'Since when did you know my old man well enough to be losing sleep over him?'

'After I saw him yesterday . . .'

'Bernie, stop fucking around and open that big mouth of yours wide enough to tell me what's going on.'

She looked at him as she rubbed the spot between her collarbone.

'OK, this is the story,' she started. 'I'm a freelance journalist. The Notting Hill carnival committee has organised an exhibition called "Exodus: The Story of Black London 1948 – the New Millennium". It's going to be one of the London-wide events that kick off this year's carnival. The committee has commissioned me to write a piece for the exhibition about music and 1970s radical movements. Your father seemed an obvious person for me to contact because he was a well-known face around town back then. So I arranged to meet him here yesterday to do our interview. He was fine, cracking jokes – that is until I asked him about 1976 . . .'

"76?'

'He kept trying to avoid answering questions. Got nervous. Uptight. Then the arson attack happened across the road and he didn't want to talk any more. But late last night he left a message on my voicemail and told me to get here for one to finish the interview. Said he was ready to talk about 1976.'

LT sank deeper into the chair, remembering how he'd left the King yesterday – collapsed, motionless. His mic hand moved up. Found his ear. Finger and thumb rubbed against his L-lettered earring.

'You look worried,' Bernie said as she took a step towards him. 'Did something else happen yesterday?'

He looked up at her. Opened his mouth. Almost answered her. Then he remembered who she was. What she'd been to him. That he was the one who should be flinging questions in her face about what she'd done all those years ago. He snapped his mouth shut. No, Bernie Ray wasn't waltzing that easily back into his life.

'I'm outta here.'

He thrust out of the chair. Turned towards the door. Her hand grabbed the back of his jacket. Held it tight. He turned so swiftly that her arm curled around his waist. They faced each other, closer than they had been in fifteen years.

'You can't go . . .'

'Don't tell me what I can and can't do. If you were so interested in me you would never have gone solo and pissed out of my life. The King couldn't have known who you were or he would never have agreed to help you.'

The force of his words moved him deeper into her arm. That was when he should have shaken off her arm. But he didn't.

'No.' Her tone dipped low. 'He didn't know about our past relationship. Remember, I never met him when we were young. You always came back to mine because my mother thought your estate was a bit rough.'

He felt the muscles in her arm clinging to his waist. He should step back. Move the hell away.

'Jerry, I . . .' Her words were as soft as the look she ran over his face.

The door was flung open with such force it bounced against the wall. LT twisted around to find Mel standing in the doorway. Shit, he'd forgotten all about her. Mel's eyes burned into him. Into Bernie. Sizzled on Bernie's arm. He shook the link with Bernie from his body.

'Mel . . .' he coaxed with his most charming smile hooked to his face.

'You know what they say,' Mel began, champagne curls swinging angrily against her face. 'Morality, like art, means drawing a line someplace, and I draw the line at having to queue up to share you with one of your Hampstead honeyz.'

'Come on, Mel, baby . . .'

She kissed her teeth at him. Stared Bernie down and said, 'From what they're saying on the telly you're up shit street anyway. Just you remember this, a poet can survive everything but a misprint.' Then she was gone. He swore as he stared at the empty doorway.

Bernie's mocking voice crept over to him as she said, 'A girl-friend who quotes Oscar Wilde, it must be true what they say about the quality of London's education going up in the world these days.'

He turned furiously on her.

'Now thanks to you I haven't got a ride.'

'Well, your luck's in because my faithful Mini is just outside. We can find your father together.'

His eyes savaged the cocky gleam on her face.

'You know what, Bernie, the day I take your help is the day I find myself singing cover versions in a boy band.'

He moved out of the room, rushing it, his movements anything but easy. Bernie followed him, her trainers biting into the floor and her words chewing the air.

'I need to find him. You've got to listen to the message he left me.'

But he didn't listen. He kept moving. Past the lift. Towards the emergency exit. Bernie's pace quickened behind him. He stopped abruptly. Swung around to face her. She skidded to a halt. He said the one thing that he knew would hold her back.

'I know why you left fifteen years ago.'

This time when he started moving she didn't follow him.

# 'PRESSURE DROP'

The Minus One club stood in the heart of Hackney's Stoke Newington Church Street, or what the local tourist guide raved was one of London's 'newest, thriving, artistic, multicultural, vibrant, too-cool-to-be-true communities'. Those who lived on the other side of the one-way system, which divided Church Street from the rest of Stoke Newington, said that the guide needed only to use four words – the middle-class ghetto. Some whispered that the club had sold out, gone upmarket, grooving with the high-speed tempo of the neighbouring renovated houses and open-front food holes. Others stuck by the club, saying that it might have steam-cleaned its brickwork, started advertising itself as a concert venue, but it hadn't sold out the one thing that mattered – the music.

LT pulled off his shades as he strolled into the same room that he'd performed in last night. The video to Kanye West's 'Touch The Sky' blazed from the large video screen on the wall. The tension in LT's shoulders dropped as they were massaged by the song's cruising, solar-powered backbeat, supplied by Curtis Mayfield's 'Move On Up'. He tipped his face to the side as if the sun were on his face. A small smile broke over his tense face. It was the first one he had allowed himself since he had learned the King was missing and run into Bernie. His eyes swung quickly over the room's ivory-glossed walls and the funky coloured backdrop of the stage as he looked for his manager, Window.

'What took you so long?' a voice breathed deeply behind him. He turned around and found Window.

'You don't want to know. I need a drink. A large one. I haven't watched the box yet so fill me in on what the hell has been going on with the media.'

Window laughed, deep, as he moved towards the perspex bar. LT still got freaked out when Window smiled, chuckled, gut-giggled or used any other style of showing he was high on happiness. Since he had got married midway through last year and become a father, he was a changed man. LT ran his eyes over his manager's powerful body and reminded himself that Window might now smell of baby powder and bliss, but his neck tattoo and hands told people of what he used to be and some claimed still was.

As LT followed Windows towards the bar he beat out the story about the King's bunk from the hospital. He eased himself on to a stool as Window moved behind the bar. Window knew he never touched alcohol, so he poured him the perfect summer drink – pineapple juice, with coconut water and a slice of lime. Window slid the glass across the bar and said two words:

'They called.'

The only 'they' he and Window had in common were Paradise Records. His hand shook around the glass as he hacked some air into his lungs.

'They want to meet us. Be at their house tomorrow, midday.'

The air blew out of LT's body. He felt champagne-fizz dizzy. Whether this was from the air conditioning or the glory of fame that had been deep-throating him for the last few months he didn't know. What he did know was that the temperature of life was back to max-i-mum hot. He took a long swig. Then he jumped off the stool and started singing a wild rendition of 'Move On Up'. He slid his feet in a Muhammad Ali-style shuffle to the swing of the horn section in the song. His shoulders pumped high and low, somersaulting the joy of life from one to the other. He took over the floor for a full thirty seconds then punched his arms into the air.

'Can't believe it, Window. I can't wait to tell the King when I find him.'

He swaggered back on the stool, laughing.

'Don't throw your seeds of joy and groove dust in the air just yet because it looks to me like you ain't caught the news?'

The cautious tone of Window's words pulled the laughter from his body.

'What's the story?' he asked.

Window leaned his head into his hand.

'Nothing to worry about. Just the customary puffing of steam and chests, or breasts in this case.'

Window pressed a couple of buttons under the bar so that the video screen went blank. He pressed another button and a recording of the midday news flashed up. A newsreader, male, with salt-and-pepper hair and a serious face, began to speak.

'Rap concerts could find themselves banned from national venues following a violent disturbance at a concert of London rapper Lord Tribulation last night. In the words of one witness there was "pandemonium and panic". A young man, believed to be a teenager, was arrested. Further developments today suggest that the suspect may also be implicated in an arson attack in East London, which injured two children. Clarissa Hathaway, the Minister of Culture, launched a strong attack on what she described as "senseless and provocative" rap music lyrics. We interviewed the minister earlier today.'

The screen changed to show the minister standing outside the House of Commons. Her bobbed chestnut hair settled over her sunlamp-blasted angular face with the sheen of legitimacy. She wore a formal deep green suit with an autumnal scarf loosely wrapped around her throat. She gazed at the camera with the determination of the lawyer she had once been. She started speaking with a voice that was softened, volume lowered.

'I'm a parent and like most parents I'm extremely concerned about the rising tide of street violence we see around us today. So when we hear musicians like Lord Tribulation recording inflammatory and violent lyrics that has to be a matter of concern. If the reports that the youth at the concert was the same youth who seriously injured two children in an arson attack earlier yesterday are true then we do need to ask artists who sing such reckless lyrics to be accountable for what they put on the airwaves. Councils throughout the country do have a responsibility to protect the safety of the population. If this means that they need to carefully consider the types of music licences they give to venues, then so be it.'

The screen cut back to the newsreader in the studio.

'But not everyone agrees. Community activist Beresford Clarke spoke to us earlier today.'

The screen changed to show a compact black man of about fifty, sitting comfortably and composed in a brown suit. He looked at the camera as if he'd done this many times before.

'Which came first – the violence or the music? Artists like Lord Tribulation are merely observing and recording what goes on around them. They see violence, oppression and racism – so that's what they sing about. You might as well blame a journalist who sends reports from a war zone for starting the war.'

'Are the rumours true about the knighthood the Queen will bestow on you this year?' the reporter asked.

The screen went blank.

'Are the kids hurt in this fire all right?'

'They're both in St Luke's. Sounds like one might be quite bad. From what the streets are saying they shouldn't have been in that house. No one lives there at the moment because it's being done up by a couple with cash in their pocket. But this hasn't got anything to do with you, OK.'

'On the one-to-ten worry scale, where is this?' LT asked his manager.

Window smiled softly and said, 'With Beresford Clarke on your side, you're tipping zero and below.'

'Who actually is he?'

'The best. He's one of the new judges at this years' Writer in Residence of Ladbroke Grove competition.'

LT had never seen Window stretch his neck up to admire anyone, so whoever Beresford Clarke was he must be some type of geezer.

'What about the record company?'

'They must have seen the minister doing her pulpit routine on the box today but they still want to meet us. In fact, I'm sure that having a notorious rapper on their books won't hurt their sales too much. The only badass clouds I can see blocking out your limelight is if the youth at the concert turns out to be the one who injured those kids. If that happens the minister is going to be thumping the Good Book as well, and who knows what that kind of noise will create.'

As he finished his words, LT noticed the shadows of Window's eyes become darker as they looked over his head. He decided not to pay any attention and instead strove to take the angst out of the mood.

'I can just see the headlines now – outlaw rapper sells a million in one week . . .'

'How about outlaw rapper loses father in one day,' a taut, female voice piped behind him.

Bernie.

LT looked to the heavens for guidance. He mouthed 'sorry' to Window, who cocked the side of his mouth in amusement. He flipped around to find Bernie standing with her hands on her hips, her rucksack on her back. He got up and took the floor quickly. He reached her. His hand moved towards her. Hesitated just before he touched her. What the fuck, he thought. He knew she wasn't going to like it, but he did it anyway. He grabbed her arm. He ignored the protesting sounds she shot into the room as he marched her towards the far corner, to a low-level table with four chairs. He stopped. Bent his head so she could smell the anger of his whispered words.

'Bernie, you can't just walk in here.'

'Why not? I have a pair of functioning legs.' Her words were glib but her blue eyes were bottled up with fury.

'You lived in Hackney, so you know how it works. You can't

walk into the yard of a man like Window without paying your dues first.'

'What is this, some kind of gangster flick? Oh, forgot, you love playing the gangsta.'

He ignored the mock-drama she puffed into her words. Instead he hooked his foot around a chair leg. Pulled it out.

'Wait for me.'

He turned without seeing if she had followed his instruction. As he lifted his walk into its fifth stride he heard the chair creak. Sixth stride, heard her mutter. He let out a long breath and realised that he had been shallow-breathing. As he reached his manager he opened his mouth to apologise, but Window started speaking first.

'Berlina Ray, but everyone name-checks her as Bernie. Thirty. One of St Ignatius School's highest achievers until she left at the age of fifteen. Ten days before her sixteenth birthday. Dad lives in Sussex, mum in uptown, Holland Park. She's never worn that gold ring on her finger or a fiancé on her arm. But the speculation is that she had two great passions – her violin and a music man called Jeremiah Scantleberry.'

The last words made LT blush. He knew there was no point asking Window how he knew the low-down on Bernie. He wouldn't be called Window if he didn't keep an eye on what passed up and down Hackney's byways.

Window continued in that soft voice he used when he talked about his family. 'You don't need to worry about Paradise Records because they're playing our tune and the dust from the media and Madam Minister will have blown away come tomorrow. So why don't you hang with your lady friend and try to find your old man. I'll check you tomorrow at twelve at Paradise Records.'

He nodded and smiled, reassured by his manager's words. As he turned towards Bernie, the smile evaporated from his face. He began to walk towards her and his calf muscles started hurting.

'Are you going to ride my back cheeks the whole day?' LT asked Bernie as they stood just inside the club's entrance.

'Oooh, where do you get all those sexy lines from?' she threw back at him.

'Sexy' hung in the air. They stared at each other. Their eyes caught. Uncertain brown touching anxious blue. He remembered the feel of her arm clutching his waist back in the King's hospital room. He took a step back and said, 'You've been gone fifteen years and all of a sudden you can't get enough of me.'

She ignored his remark and said, 'Have you heard from your father?'

'When I need a conscience I'll go and find one in the half-price summer sale.'

She pushed an eyebrow up. Tipped her chin to the left, defiantly waiting for him to answer her question. He kissed his teeth lightly. Pulled his mobile from his back trouser pocket. Scrolled through his message box. He flicked his head up and answered her.

'No.'

She pulled out a packet of Silk Cut. Mild. Started to light up.

'You can't do that in here. Club policy is that the only high you get is strictly generated by the dance floor.'

A telephone rang inside the club as they stepped outside. The narrow side road was cobbled with debris from the previous night's concert. The sky was turbulent, blue tousling with grey. The beat of traffic from the neighbouring main road snarled in the air. Bernie lit up. Sucked in a funnel of smoke and London air. Exhaled. Then she took the first step and they began to walk. He didn't know where they were going, but every step they took he could feel his anger stoking up. After fifteen years did she really think she could ride into town and pretend that nothing had happened? Finally the anger burst out of his mouth.

'Instead of me and you skipping along the yellow brick road looking for the King somewhere over the soddin' rainbow, why don't we have a little sit-down and clear the nasty air about fifteen years ago.'

She stopped. Looked sideways at him. He couldn't define the emotion tightening the features on her face.

'I haven't come here for a put-your-hand-in-my-hand walk down memory lane. I just need to find your father.'

'You could have called me. Could have said goodbye.'

She shuffled her head back as if an offensive odour were coating the wind.

'Instead of quoting lyrics from some fucking love song' – *fucking* bounced high and direct, like spit into his face – 'why don't you for once in your life stop struttin' your Mr Big Gold Chain stuff and think about what's happened to your father.'

He wiped an open palm over his face, annoyed. He never wore gold chains. Too obvious.

He opened his mouth, having found the words he needed to try to put her in her place, but another voice got there first.

'Jeremiah Scantleberry?'

It came from behind Bernie. They turned to find two policemen solemnly staring at them. One in plain clothes, the other sporting the Blue's finest threads. LT let out an exasperated sigh, waved his hands in the air and said, 'Look, I had nothing to do with that boy onstage last night . . .'

The plainclothes officer moved closer to him.

'Sir, this isn't concerning the events at your concert last night . . .'

LT took a step back, never comfortable about being that close to the law.

'If it's about this arson stuff, I ain't . . .'

'Please come with us so that we can tell you . . .'

'LT,' Window's voice struck out from the opposite end of the street.

LT and Bernie swung around to find his manager standing in the club's doorway.

Window pushed up the street until he stood next to LT. He shook his head. Dipped his head towards LT. Whispered, 'You need to listen to them because word just came through.'

He paused. Then his words dropped like the shadows in his eyes.

'They've found the King.'

# 'AN EVERLASTING LOVE'

LT stood in the almost-silence of the mortuary in St Luke's hospital. A furious three-chord punk beat bitched about in his head – distorted guitar clashing with the driving bottom notes of a bass – as he waited for them to show him what they claimed was the King's dead body. His arm clung on to May, the King's lady friend, who wept quietly. He wasn't sure whether she was clinging on to him or he was clinging on to her. He stood in front of two black soft chairs and a small table with red flowers in a vase on it. He couldn't smell the flowers. All of his senses were shut down as he faced the drawn green curtains covering a window. Behind the window, they said, was the body of the King. Sister Begum stood on LT's right side. When he'd arrived at the hospital she'd been waiting for him with May. She'd quietly asked whether she could be present. Behind them stood a uniformed policeman. The mortuary attendant grasped the cords of the curtain. He began to pull. As the curtain moved LT remembered the story he had been told about the one other occasion when rumours had got around that the King was dead.

1976. During the heat and upheaval at the Notting Hill carnival. An eyewitness had sworn with cross-my-heart clarity that he had seen a police truncheon strike the King on the head and split his skull. Another eye at the scene had confirmed the tale. The King had turned up at the Mangrove restaurant, a few hours later, a bit battered, but totally alive. The King always laughed at the story. You couldn't be classed a legend unless you were pronounced dead at least once in your lifetime.

May's hard sobs filled the room as the curtains were opened completely. As LT gazed at the face on the trolley he knew there was only going to be one more announcement of the King's death. A green sheet covered his body, except his head. His face was the colour of grey marble. His eyes and his memorable mouth were closed. Sombre, like he was in the deepest sleep. The top of the King's clenched fist peeped out of the sheet. Same as it did when he held his mic. The attendant saw LT's eyes watching the hand. He moved forward and whispered, 'Sorry.'

'No,' LT's voice stopped him. 'Let him have his final song.'

LT hoped the King was singing Natalie Cole's 'This Will Be (An Everlasting Love)'. The King always played the track as the final song when he did house parties in the old days. That always surprised him as the King was a hardened sound system man. When he'd asked him to explain why that tune of all the memorable classics, his father would reply, 'People have to leave the dance with a feeling of everlasting love because you want them to come back.'

LT could not understand why he wasn't crying. Why his nose was not bleeding. This was one of the greatest stresses he knew he would ever face and his body couldn't even give up any liquid in respect for the most important person in his life.

He turned to the policeman.

'Yeah, that's my dad. Isaiah Augustus Cleveland Scantleberry.'

Sister Begum whispered, 'I'm so sorry.'

He wished everyone would stop whispering.

'I've got to get back to the ward, but your father left this with me earlier today.'

He turned to her to find her holding a bag. He recognised the King's bag. He took it. He felt it for a while, connecting to its warmth. As Sister Begum turned to walk away he called out to her.

'Please, I've got something to give you.'

She faced him with a puzzled look ruffling across her face. He walked over to her, blocking the view of the policeman. He opened up the side pocket, looking for the King's secret stash of weed. He felt inside, smiled as his hand grasped weed already rolled up, ready to go.

'Sister, I know he'd want to thank you.' He placed the joints discreetly into her hand.

Her eyes flicked to the policeman as her face heated up, with discovery that her secret was out or gratitude, he didn't know. What he did know was that her fingers folded over them like they were the most precious gifts. She nodded and said, 'I'll see what I can do to make sure you find out as quickly as possible the result of your father's post-mortem.'

Then she was gone.

LT walked towards the policeman and asked, 'What happened?'

The policeman took out his notebook. Flicked through the pages. Then he coughed and replied, 'As you'll understand, Mr Scantleberry, we can't confirm anything at this stage as a post-mortem is pending, but we will be actively pursuing every line of enquiry. There will also be an inquest if the coroner's office conclude that he didn't die of natural causes.'

'So where was he found?'

The policeman checked his notes again.

'Early this afternoon his body was discovered in Gazoo Lane . . .'

'Gazoo Lane?' LT cried incredulously.

The policeman nodded.

'No, you must have got that wrong,' he shouted, as he shook his head.

The door swung open. Bernie stood in the doorway, her foot keeping the door open.

'Jerry, what's going on?'

He turned swiftly to her, his arms waving, and said, 'They're saying that they found the King in Hoxton.'

He turned back to the cop, 'You don't get it. My father would have walked down the street singing "Mammy" before he'd have

gone to Hoxton. He hated the place. There's something wrong.
There's something badly wrong here . . .'

'You OK?'

Bernie's question soothed and caressed LT as she drove through
Hackney's streets towards May's home. May sat behind them. The
erratic riff of her hiccups and soft sobs bounced in the back. The
King's bag nestled between LT's legs.

The car swerved into an east turn off Queensbridge Road, shooting
into a road that ran adjacent to the Regent's Canal. LT sank deeper
into the passenger seat of Bernie's wheels of choice. Rover Mini
Cabriolet. 1994. Caribbean blue. The windows were half down, so
he sucked in the uneasy smell of the canal travelling with the
bright rays of sun following the car. He didn't answer her. Couldn't
answer her because there was only one question bursting the bound-
aries of his mind: *What had the King been doing in Hoxton?*

Two of his fingers drummed the high swing beat to 'This Will
Be (An Everlasting Love)' against the ridge of his knee. He caught
his troubled reflection in the wing mirror. The skin on his forehead was wrinkled, his eyebrows were low. Confusion was an
uneasy companion to the grief marked on his face.

Bernie's voice drew him back to the inside of the car.

'Why are you so convinced that your father would never go
to Hoxton? I thought Hoxton was one of those "in" places where
everyone and their new leather jacket just have to be seen.'

Since the mid-1990s, Hoxton had transformed itself into one
of the trendy and artistic groove islands of the London scene.
People flocked to be seen sucking in the breeze and the latest
must-have cocktails in its numerous pubs, clubs, restaurants and
galleries. Even the designer who made LT's du-rags and T-shirts
rented a space here. Only two people he knew hadn't bought into
Hoxton's good-time vibe – him and the King. People close to him
told him that it was artistic suicide for him not to perform in
one of its many nightspots. But he wouldn't go there because
Hoxton had been a very different place before the loft apartment
mother ship had landed.

His fingers stopped strumming. The wind slicing into the car took refuge under his shirt, running through his nipple ring. He pulled some more of London's air into his body. Then he answered her.

'You know how the Angel Gabriel never goes knocking on hell's door, that's how it was with us and Hoxton.'

'What do you mean by "us"?'

He jerked his profile towards her.

'Me and the King. We took a vow that we'd never go there.'

'A vow? That's a bit dramatic.'

'No one does drama better than East London and back in '84 the worst kind of drama for any black person was to be caught in Hoxton.'

'Tell me about 1984.'

A cramp took him by surprise. Took his left calf. Twisted the muscle right. The pain jetted from his mouth as his left arm slid down his leg, found his calf muscle. His fingertips did a frantic massage.

'I can't talk about this,' he rasped, each word bumpy, serrated against the dryness of his tongue. 'And don't ask me if I'm OK because it's a fucking fool's question.'

'You should learn some respect with that mouth, boy,' May punched from the back of the car, her voice back to that of the solid, hard-working woman LT knew.

The older woman shuffled forward as she carried on speaking in her high-low-high Trinidadian accent. 'You have to tell her what you know. If this is going to help us find out what happened to my beloved King, then you keep talking.'

Although LT had never had a mother in his life he knew that when a black woman of May's generation told you to keep talking that's exactly what you did. So he kept talking.

'It was August bank holiday. '84. I was eight years old . . .'

His fingertips again caught the swing of Natalie Cole against his knee as he told the story.

# KBW
## (Featuring The King)

That summer was the first year the King took him to the adults'
day at the Notting Hill carnival on bank holiday Monday. The
King always took him to the carnival, but only on a Sunday, children's day. Now, the King said, he was ready for that next step
on his musical journey, jumping up in the streets with big people.
The time at the carnival was one that LT would never forget. Just
like he would never forget what happened to them when they
left.

After the carnival, the King took him to a gig in a basement
club in Soho. The King knew the owner, who said it was fine for
LT to be there as long as he stayed in the background. His young
eyes had been in awe of the uptempo music, the forget-me-not
clothing and the high-energy chat.

At about one in the morning they had left, walking hand in
hand towards Trafalgar Square to get the night bus home. They
entered the square with the rest of London's dislocated nightlife,
walking past the huge steps of the National Gallery. His eyes
skipped with excitement when he saw the fountains and four
lions in the centre, Nelson's Column and St Martin-in-the-Fields
church with its soaring steeple and open friendliness held up by
vast pillars that reminded him of Greek ruins he had seen in
books at school. His gaze stopped when he noticed a small group
of men and women holding candles and banners outside a huge,
imposing building. When he asked the King what they were doing,
his dad replied, 'That, my son, is freedom.' Years later he found

out that it was the twenty-four-hour anti-apartheid vigil outside South Africa House.

There was already a sizeable group of people milling near by waiting for the bus to arrive when they reached the bus stop. His palm dug deeper into the chill of the King's hand as the people pressed forward when the bus pulled up. The King yanked him forward until they were in the middle of the crush. As a laughing couple stepped up to the bus in front of them the King let go of his hand. The King's fingers dived inside the front pocket of his jacket, searching for the money for the fare. He pulled his hand out empty. He searched his left pocket. Empty. Then the King's fingers did a mad dance around his inside pocket. Empty. The King kissed and sucked his teeth violently.

'What's the matter?' LT peered up at him.

Before the King could answer a male voice slurred behind them, 'You getting on the bus or what, mate?'

The man's Bacardi breath broke over them. The King pulled LT out of the line towards the side. He hunched down, smiled and flicked the hood of LT's coat on to his head.

'Tings is cool and irie,' the King reassured him. 'Got your travelling shoes on?'

LT smiled and nodded, realising they would be walking home.

'Dad, how long will it take?' he asked as they left the square.

'Don't worry, son, the rhythm fairies will be tucking you in, in no time.'

At first the journey had been exciting, especially seeing the sleeping River Thames glide with them as they strolled along the Embankment. But as half an hour turned into one hour his feet started to drag. When they reached Tower Hill, that was when it happened. In the glare of the artificial light shrouding the Tower of London a cramp seized his leg. He cried out. Stumbled. The King caught him before he fell.

The King swung him up as tenderly as he would a newborn. When they reached the corner of Aldgate East underground station and Commercial Street the muscles in the King's arm sagged.

'Son, I've got to put you down.'

As soon as his shoes touched the ground the cramps ripped like feedback along his legs. The King bent down. Briskly rubbed his hands against first the left and then the right leg.

'Better?'

His nod said one thing but his tears told another. He did not like the look he saw in his dad's face – proud but helpless. He did not know what it meant but he didn't want to add to his troubles.

'Good boy.'

He took the King's hand and put his foot out for what became a journey of agony. Every step felt like the skin on his legs was going one way while the muscles inside went another. The tears fell but he didn't cry out. The King kept up the pace until they passed the huge, white Hawksmoor church that dominated the area of Spitalfields. It stood large and all-embracing before the public Ladies and Gents that stood almost genuflecting in front of it. Abruptly the King's pace slowed as two figures emerged from the next corner and moved towards them. LT cocooned himself into the King's side. The figures got closer. The King got tenser. Then the King's body relaxed. The figures were women. Women walking 'The Perimeter', as the locals called the nightly move of prostitutes looking for customers on Commercial Street. Both the women were white, their height elevated by their platform shoes, their eyes downcast by their chosen life. The King nodded to them. They nodded back. As the women clanked past, one of them turned back and whispered, 'Make sure you keep your eyes about you.'

The tenseness in the King's body sprang back like an elastic band. His hand became firmer, just like when he held his mic. They picked up their pace. Every third or fourth step the King's head would click sideways and start looking around. He kept this up until they reached the intersection where Shoreditch High Street becomes Kingsland Road. Suddenly the pressure of the King's hand pulled LT back. Made him stop. As if the King were saving them both from crossing into a minefield. LT looked up at his dad and saw that his face was stretched into a predatory profile, chin inched out, forehead inched back, like something was dying on the wind. It was some years later that LT realised that crossing the street meant they were going to be entering what locals called 'The Hate Estate'. The south-west of Hackney that ran from Hoxton to Haggerston and threaded through to Brick Lane and Bethnal Green was the homeland of the National Front. Saying two simple words – Hate Estate – evoked different responses in different people. Some said the words with fear crippling their eyes, while others said them and then spat on the ground.

The King spat on the ground.

A cramp slashed LT's leg, making him cry out. The King's movement was so swift that he never saw it until his hand was clamped over his mouth. The King hunkered down. Grabbed him in an embrace. Shifted back. Looked at him. They stood eye to eye.

'Sh. I know it hurts, son, but there are times in life when you just have to groove with the pain.'

LT did not know what the King was talking about. But he did know from the hard shine in his father's eyes than he meant it. The King stood up.

'Stick to my side and keep your travelling shoes moving.'

He grasped the King's chilled hand. They stepped forward.

They crossed the line.

Moved under the huge girders of the railway bridge that covered Kingsland Road. They moved quickly, walking swiftly past a 'GEORGE DAVIS IS INNOCENT' slogan painted in white on the wall. They kept moving. For one minute. Three minutes. Five minutes later they left the darkness of the bridge behind and reached the open road again. They hit the bend where Falkirk Street touches the main road on its left. That was when they heard the voices. Male, boisterous, singing, with the crude aroma of alcohol their main melody. He could not make out the words of their song, but the acoustics of the Hate Estate told them they were coming from Haggerston across the road.

'Shit,' the King growled.

The sensation in Jerry's left leg finally became numb as he stepped forward, throwing him on to the pavement.

'Jerry, you have to get up.'

As the King bent towards him, the lyrics the voices were singing tore up the air.

'There're ain't no black, there ain't no black . . .'

He couldn't hear the rest of the song. It sounded like the rhythm of the crowd that accompanied *Match of the Day* on Saturday nights.

'There ain't no black, there ain't no black . . .'

His father promptly picked him up and threw him over his shoulder in a fireman's lift, twisted into Falkirk Street and began to pick up speed.

'There ain't no black, there ain't no black . . .'

The King's head ripped to the left. Ripped to the right. Which way to go?

'. . . there ain't no black, in the Union Jack!'

The King swept them around a corner, deviating from the main road. The vibrations he felt from the King chucking air into his body told him this was bad. If he'd realised that the side street his father had turned down led into Hoxton Square he'd have known how bad it was. Even at his age he knew Hoxton wasn't a place to go, although he didn't know why. All he knew was that the older people said 'Hoxton' the way his Auntie Glad would say 'Satan'.

The voices followed their path.

'If it's white, it's all right!'

They ran past a school. A wall with the words KBW – Keep Britain White – painted in huge white strokes. A café. Past Gazoo Lane. When they reached an abandoned Georgian house, the King abruptly stopped, looked up at the house and moaned, 'I don't want to be here.'

But the King didn't stop for long as the voices came again.

'If it's black, send it back!'

The King swivelled right, into the shadow of a pub, until they reached the corner of Hoxton Square. The King's foot hit a beer can. The can ricocheted against the hard ground. The King carried him into the wet, muddied and littered grass that passed for a 'green' in the middle of the square. He turned, chest heaving, examining the empty blocks and tenements and the church that looked over them.

'If it's red, shoot it dead!'

He turned his head around and could see, through the mist created by the rain and damaged street lighting, a mixture of shadows falling in the road they had just run down to get to the square. Only a few moments and the NF would be in the square too.

'If there's a coon anywhere, we can smell him in the air.'

The King ran out of the green, his breathing heavy and hard against the night air. The smell of rotten drains tried to hold them back, but the King pressed on, knowing they had to deal with anything the street threw at them this night. As LT's weight began to droop in his father's arms they passed a skip. The skip stood outside a garment factory that was a few storeys high. Gasping and shaking, the King looked inside. The top of the skip was covered with an ageing carpet. The King pushed back the carpet. Hoisted him like a trophy. The King pointed his finger in his face. 'Stay here and don't make a sound.'

'I'm dreaming of a "white" Christmas, just like the ones we used to know . . .'

The chanting was nearly in the square.

He was lowered inside the skip. The carpet swept over him. Claustrophobic. Dark. Reeking of leather offcuts and a word the King never let him use. The rain dropped on to the carpet with the beat of an introduction to a sad song. Silent gulps tipped from his mouth. The pain began to twist in his leg again. It was savage but he knew that he couldn't cry. Mustn't cry.

The chanting had stopped. Instead there were voices and the hectic stamp of heavy boots.

'Barry, you stay here. Me and Johnny-boy will check out the rest of the square.'

Boots ran into the distance. Then silence. He felt the movement of someone by the skip. His body cringed. He was frightened. He felt something thick begin to run from his nose. His fingertips touched it and he knew it was blood. A wave of panic engulfed him. His body moved into a ball. He wanted to go home. He heard the shuffle of the one they had called Barry by the skip. Suddenly the unseen Barry started to sing Bob Marley's 'Redemption Song'.

The voice was incredible. Beautiful. Unrestrained, with the purity of youth guiding it. LT suspected Barry was just a few years older than him. Who would have thought that one of the most compelling voices he ever heard would be gifted to an enemy. He knew he should not do it. But the King had taught him that the highest thing in life was the appreciation of life-giving music. The King had trained him too well. As Barry sang the words to 'Redemption Song' LT joined in.

The voice stopped.

LT stopped.

He dipped his head. Held his breath. Quiet. So still LT was sure he could hear the moon sighing. Then the voice started again. Sang the words 'redemption song'. Quiet. 'Redemption song'. Quiet. The third time LT made it a duet. He felt the body lean into the skip as they sang together. Tranquil, hushed and in tune.

Stamping feet blistered the air. One pair. LT and Barry stopped singing at the same time. The feet stopped by the skip.

'Barry, see any foreign scum?'

LT cringed inside. The blood flowed harder from his nose. *Please don't tell. Please don't tell.*

'Nah, nothing here.'

LT heard a scuff of feet and the grating noise of a zipper being pulled.

'What you doing?' Barry asked, a layer of panic in his voice.

'I'm having a piss, what's it look like . . . ?'

There was the drumming of urine on the side of LT's skip.

' . . . I mean, what's your problem? This place is probably owned by the Yids anyway.'

When the pissing had stopped, the footsteps started and the chanting began again.

'England! England!'

The words disappeared into the distance. There was no noise but the steady beat of the rain. LT sat in silence with his hands clasped over his head, his feet contorted by cramps and cold numb patches. His nose had stopped bleeding. While he waited for something to happen or for more people to come along and start urinating against his skip, he tried wrapping bits of cloth and leather around his hands and feet in the dark to keep the cold and damp out. His eyelids drooped as the cold took him towards sleep. That was when he heard the footsteps. His heart jumped high in his chest. They ground to a halt beside the skip. Before he could think, the carpet was thrust back. Fresh rain fell on him. He squeezed his eyes tight. Opened his mouth to gulp or scream, he was never sure. He felt the heat of human flesh lean down to him. The tips of fingers grasped his waist. His body shook as he cried. The hands clasped around his whole waist. Hoisted him up and high. Fear finally made him open his eyes. He confronted his tormentor. Cried harder when he realised it was the King. The King picked him up. Cradled him and said, 'Don't worry, son, neither one of us is ever coming here again.'

They had rushed into London's shadows until they reached home. After the King had cleaned him up, he tucked him into bed and said, 'I've got your name, son.'

For months the King had been looking for a stage name for him.

'When you walk the stage your name will be Lord Tribulation. That's what you have to sing about, son, the trials and tribulations of everyday life. The ups and downs of what people go through as they walk this earth. Sometimes beneath our feet walk seven devils . . .'

'Seven devils?'

'When you're older I'll tell you all about those seven devils.'

Then the King had kissed him, pulled the covers up to his

chin and left. He tried to sleep but he couldn't. He didn't know how long he'd been lying in bed, eyes wide open, when he heard the music, coming from the sitting room. He crept into the passage and stood quietly by the half-open sitting-room door. The King was listening to one of his sound system tracks. The beat was heavy, like a human voice, a half-beat in, a half-beat out. Then he heard the other sound – the King crying. That was when he decided that music might be living but he was going to use it to make sure that he never jeopardised the life of his child just because the crunch of crisp notes was not in his pocket.

LT stopped talking. He finished the story at the part about the seven devils. Bernie and May didn't need to know the rest. His stomach rolled with the sickness of having told the tale of Hoxton for the first time.

'So now you know why I get nosebleeds and cramps and why I know the King wouldn't have been seen dead in Hoxton,' LT said quietly inside the car.

His teeth caught his bottom lip when he realised what words he'd spoken. That the King had indeed been seen dead in a place he loathed.

The car slowed outside a blue Georgian house.

'So how are we going to find out what he was doing in Hoxton?' Bernie asked, her voice insistent as she cut the engine.

Her hands fell off the steering wheel as she turned her upper body towards him. He dipped his head. Moved his mic hand to his ear. Ran a finger and thumb in a tight circle around his T-lettered earring. His hand skipped to his L-lettered earring. Did the same motion. Shit, the King was really dead. The unwelcome punk beat licked back inside his head. Bounced his finger and thumb from his ear. Suddenly he wanted Bernie gone. May gone. Just needed to be on his own. He yanked his head straight. Finger combed his 'fro. Then he said what he needed to say.

'I'm going to get ready for my meeting with the record company tomorrow and then make arrangements to bury my dad.'

Bernie pushed herself forward like she was going to jump in his seat.

'You can't bury him because there's likely to be an inquest. And what about him being in Hoxton? You know there's something strange going on.'

Anger heated his face as he belted out, 'Do you think, for once in your privileged life, you could stop thinking about what you want and consider me? Don't you get it – the King's gone and he ain't coming back.'

The silence wound like barbed wire between them. Their eyes caught. Tearful brown meeting hostile blue.

May started crying in the back.

LT grabbed the handle of the King's bag and spat out, 'You know what, Bernie, now the old man's gone, he can't help you with your little article or whatever the bollocks you were doing. So why don't you click your heels three times and disappear the same way you did fifteen years ago.'

He jumped out. Opened the back passenger seat. He stepped back, allowing May to climb out. He held the bag with one hand and May with the other and marched towards the house. Bernie's voice rang out behind him.

'If you can't be bothered to find out how and why your father died, then I will.'

He ignored her. Instead he tightened his grip on the bag containing the few possessions that the King had packed for his death. That was when the hurt started. Really started.

The wailing from number 44 Ernest Bevin House began just after the sun went down at 8.30. Some on the fourth floor shook their heads. Others shuddered. A few kicked up the volume on their wide screens. But no one called the police or the council's out-of-hours noise patrol because they recognised the natural sound of a son grieving for his father.

LT sat in his living room, hunched over the King's bag. He couldn't straighten up because memories – both good and bad – were beating against his back. Jesus, no one had warned him about this heat. This burning agony that grief brings. This suffocating sadness that grief brings. The scalding sweat that grief brings.

LT wiped back the tears as the good memories drowned out the bad and he remembered how the King had turned his life into a sprawling human album of musical discovery.

'Try everything, son, because music has no frontiers,' the King would tell him.

A letter would drop through their front door from school about their new choir – the King made him do it.

A letter about learning tap – the King made him do it.

A letter about learning about Chopin, Beethoven, Mozart – the King made him do it. When he hit eight years old, once a month the King started to take him to gigs.

'Watch and learn, boy,' was all the King said as they put on their 'good' clothes.

So that was what he did. LT learned that the excitement for musicians didn't start when the crowd arrived. No, it started long before then. With the loading of the equipment – records, turn-tables, speakers, amps, mics – checking out the acoustics of the venue, finding the spot on the stage where shadows leave their least tread to best dazzle the crowd. The house parties were the best. The kind of parties where the host said it started at eight, but everyone knew that meant 10.30. The kind of parties where the music fast-jammed from midnight and slow-jammed from 3.30. The kind of parties where a bottle was the only currency needed to join the low curve of lighting inside. The kind of parties where the revellers forgave the police if they came banging at the door because they all suspected the boys in blue were trying to swap the beat of the street for some other type of melody. The kind of parties where the children and coats were asleep on top of each other in a back room.

Of course, LT's intention had never been to sleep but to learn. He'd always peep at a pitch by the door, staring, wide eyed, real-ising that the only time dancing was mesmerising was between the yawning of the night and the sprinkling of the morning dawn. He'd realised it didn't matter how you defined yourself – whether you were soul, calypso or a ragga-roots freak; whether you liked to parade your funky dread dance moves in the centre of the room or entertain yourself in a corner; whether you liked to sip Pink Lady or down Red Stripe, everyone was united in one pastime – getting rhythmically wasted.

Wasted. He saw the King, peaceful, dead on a slab. He shook the image from his mind and looked down at the King's bag. He slipped the zip back. He pushed his hand inside. Hesitated. Stopped. He pulled his hand back. He just wasn't ready to sort through his father's things. He picked himself up and back-kicked the bag so that it skidded under the sofa he'd been sitting on. He moved out of the main room. Went into his bedroom. Stared up at the patch-work of record covers on the ceiling. The mattress on the bed dipped as he eased on to it. He steadied himself as he stood on the bed, ready to pull down the King's favourite tune – 'Police

And Thieves' by Junior Murvin. He stretched up on tiptoe. Reached up. But the grief was too heavy. Pulled him back to the soles of his feet. Just as well, he thought. Putting on this timeless classic would only make the pain stronger.

He took himself back into the main room. Slow-walked to his record collection. His hand shook as he riffled through his 1960s soul section. He got midway. '65. He pulled out the album he was looking for. Eased out the vinyl. Let his fingers touch the smooth surface, the way you were advised not to. He moved to his music system. Slipped the record on the turntable. He maximised the volume, hoping to minimise the pain. Pressed 'play'. Watched the arm move. The needle drop. The static from the record crackled in the room. 'People Get Ready' by the Impressions. He sat down. Closed his eyes. Waited for the voice to come. Curtis Mayfield's gentle falsetto began its tender, lonely journey around the room. LT tried to sing along but his vocal cords froze up. He tried once. Twice. Three times. On the fourth attempt his voice finally made it. In a quiet and shattered vibrato his voice climbed on board with the lyrics and took a devastated journey around the room.

Now he started he could not stop. Could not stop because all he could see was the King lying, mic hand ready, dead in the mortuary. Could not stop because he sensed the King's last day had been played out like the throwaway track on an album. *What was the King doing in Hoxton?* The question still tore up his mind.

A knock at the front door made him lift his head. He got up. Reached the door. Opened it. Bernie stood on the balcony, a living silhouette against the shady London night. Her fingers touched her lips like she didn't know what to say. He didn't know what to say either. Their eyes caught. Exhausted brown touching guarded blue. She tugged her lips into a weak smile as she stepped inside. He did the only thing he could when presented with a situation where he desperately needed to share his pain. He moved forward. Kissed her. He tasted the warmth from the receding evening wind on her lips. Tasted all the stories she had locked away in the fifteen years since he'd last seen her. Her mouth opened. His tongue dived inside. He banged the door closed. Pressed her against the wall. Her palm flattened against his chest, pushing his nipple ring into his flesh. Then their hands moved at the same time. Rushing it, anything but easy. Pulling. Twisting. Ripping. Her bare legs hooked around him. Two beats, that was how long it took for him to find a haven in her. Two beats, that was how long it took for him to release the pain he felt inside. Two beats, that was how long it took for him to think what the fuck was he doing letting Bernie Ray back into his life?

'You killed him, didn't you?'

The woman's voice was urgent as she walked beside the man in the peace and contentment of the darkness of London's South Bank.

He twisted his lips together at her question. He hated melodrama. And he hated the fact that despite her successful lifestyle she was still the melodramatic idiot she had been all those years ago in 1976.

'All you need to know is he isn't going to be talking any more.' She stopped swiftly. Faced him.

'I would never have consented to any of this if I knew what . . .'

'Don't kid yourself. You were the one that called me. You know why? Because you had no alternative. Instead of thanking me . . .'

She took three steps back from him, retreating into the flood-light beaming from the National Theatre.

'What are you doing?' he asked.

'Moving away from the shit you keep shovelling into my face.'

He twisted his lips some more.

'So what do think we should have done instead? Presented ourselves at Scotland Yard and confessed our sins?'

'We could tell them . . .'

His harsh laugh cut her off.

'Now who's tossing crap into the wind? You might not care about who you are now, but I do. There's no way my reputation is standing in the dock just because of what happened when I was a stupid, idealistic revolutionary in short pants. And I don't think your people would forgive you either. Remember, if you go down, your mess is going to land on their pretty, polished faces. So my advice is to dump any fucking thoughts of police stations.'

She began walking again. He followed her.

'What if the son starts asking questions about the King's death?'

'The only answers he's going to get are through an inquest. And there won't be one.'

Surprise made her twist her profile towards him.

'How can you be so sure?'

'Just believe me when I say it won't happen.'

She began walking again as she talked.

'Did your people find it in the King's best jacket?'

'My people cleaned his place out, searched his things, but it wasn't there. His best jacket wasn't there.'

'After all these years he might have a new best jacket.'

'No, he was the type of man who, when he made a commitment, stuck by it. He never did understand that everyone needs to move on.'

She swore into the wind.

'Don't worry,' he reassured her. 'We'll try the son's place next. Like we already decided, you do your bit and I'll do mine and it will just fall into our laps.'

'And if life isn't so giving?'

They passed a busker playing a flat violin rendition of a popular soap opera theme.

'Then unfortunately it's the King's son who will have to pay the price.'

LT shifted awake with a smile on his face. He rolled over on to his front. Leaned into the imprint of warmth left by another human being on the other side of the bed. Bernie. The smile died as he remembered the events of the previous day. Remembered that the King wasn't going to be hitting any high notes any more. He rolled over on to his back. Sighed and stared at the record covers above the bed. His gaze deliberately avoided the King's

*Police And Thieves* record cover. He knew he would have to think of funeral arrangements. But not now. Instead he focused on the meeting with Paradise Records at midday. He heard a faint tapping sound coming from another room. The kitchen? Bathroom? Living room? He couldn't tell, but he knew she was still here. That surprised him. He thought she would be long gone. Moved on to another story. Another fifteen years.

He pulled himself up. Eased out of the bed. Into the summer heat pushing its way through the room. Finger-combed his 'fro with his mic hand. He checked the radio clock: 10.23. He walked, body bare, except for the silver ring in his nipple and the L and T lettered earrings in his ear, towards the tapping sound. He realised that it was coming from the kitchen. Sounded like she was making him breakfast. That got the smile back. Well, half of it at least. He stopped at the threshold of the half-opened door. What the fuck was he meant to say to her after last night? After they had taken the plunge three times? Hooked into each other's bodies three fantastic ways?

He pushed the door. Eased inside. The sun pierced the room, flushing a giddy glare across the cream cupboards, the laminated floor, his Grime music collection and Bernie. She stood with her back to him, fully dressed, hunched over a work surface. One of her hands chopped downwards with the same fervour she had learnt to create violin stabs.

'What's the difference between a fiddle and violin?' he asked huskily as he lounged in the doorway.

Nothing like a bit of humour to try to deal with the aftermath of the night before, he decided. Her hand stopped moving, mid-chop. Her shoulders shot halfway to her ears. Hesitated. Stopped. Stayed where they were. She remained silent, so he nervously delivered the punchline.

'Who cares – neither one's a guitar.'

She slowly turned around. Looked up at him, her face half set in shock. He smiled. Looked down at what she'd been slicing. The smile let go of the corners of his eyes as he saw that this morning's fry-up was two lines of cocaine.

'Everyone has his or her own way of greeting the day,' she told him. She looked him straight in the eye. No apology.

He was shocked, not at the cocaine, but that the rush from the music obviously wasn't enough for her any more. He just hoped he wasn't around the day her pupils got permanently bigger than her brain cells. He moved towards her, the lines on his face cut into serious grooves. He noticed that a sprinkle of powder had fallen on to the crest of her top lip.

'If you're going to do this stuff at least make sure it ends up in the right place,' he said. Her tongue moved out to lick it. He shook his head, stopping her.

'Let me do the honours.'

He'd never tasted coke in his life and knew that after this morning he wasn't going to renew the acquaintance. But he couldn't miss an opportunity to get inside her again. He dipped his head. Flicked out his tongue. Slowly licked the powder from her dry morning mouth. His tongue continued its journey between her parted lips. Inside her mouth. He felt her tongue retreat. He pulled his tongue out and looked down at her. He smiled, twisting the right corner of his mouth.

'So, last night was your idea of grief therapy?'

She shoved her hand through her hair. The side without the butterfly clip.

'There's only one thing at the top of my priority list and that's finishing the job I've started.'

'Does that mean I can let you know when I'm grieving again?'

She upped the length of her neck, making her five-nine instead of the five-eight she was.

She went back to the work surface. Leaned down. Took in the first line. Breathed. Leaned down again. Sniffed the second. Sighed. She kept her back to him. Then she turned around and said, 'Your father went to meet someone yesterday.'

'How do you know that?'

She twisted away from him towards her open bag on the work surface. She dipped her hand inside and pulled out her mobile. She turned back and held the phone out to him.

'This is the message he left me.'

LT took the phone from her. Held it to his face and listened to the voicemail. The King's voice was awkward. Nervous.

*It's the King. Yeah, meet me here at one . . . I'm ready to tell you all about 1976. I got to meet someone else first so if I'm not here just wait for me.'*

LT lowered the phone as the blood beat in his face.

'Do you know who he might have been meeting?' she asked.

'If I did, don't you think I'd have been banging on their door last night instead of banging you?'

He regretted the words as soon as they tipped into the room. Angry, ripe, red blood pooled across Bernie's face. She grabbed her mobile from him and glared.

'Look, Bernie, I . . .'

His words were interrupted by a loud thump coming from outside the front door. He turned quickly. Left the kitchen. Hit the hallway. Needing to get away from her. Away from the terrible images of the King she kept flinging into his face. Away from the compulsion he had to keep hurting her about fifteen years ago. He opened the main door. Strewn on the ground was a pile of newspapers. He ordered three copies – one broadsheet, two tabloids – to be delivered to him every day. As well as having an extensive collection of du-rags with the 'He's The Daddy' logo on he also kept blank du-rags so that he could write headlines he got from the newspapers on them. He picked up the papers. Shut the door. Took them to the bedroom. Bernie followed him. The restless scent their lovemaking had created last night still clung to the air.

'Can I open the window?' she asked already moving to the other side of the room.

She didn't wait for his reply. She opened the window. The bubble and bustle of the noise from other people's lives dived inside. He threw the newspapers on a corner of the bed. His toes faded into the carpet as he moved to the wardrobe. He opened it. Looked at his reflection in the full-length mirror on the inside of the wardrobe door. His reflection was rumpled. Tired. There were stress lines radiating from his eyes and tightly held mouth. He flicked his eyes away from his reflection and said, 'I've got to be at the record company by midday so can we talk about this later?'

'Oh yes, I forgot, you're too busy becoming a superstar.'

'Becoming one? I'm already there, darlin',' he bit out, the corners of his mouth fluttering with fury.

His hands began shifting clothes, looking for the outfit he would wear to meet Paradise Records.

'Just listen to me,' she started. 'So far we know that your father went to meet someone. As you so eloquently pointed out in the kitchen, you don't know who this someone is. But it's likely he met this person in Hoxton. So whoever it was had the power to make him go somewhere he loathed. We also know that he was desperate to tell me something about 1976. He already told me that things got out of control in 1976, which suggests it involves other people. Maybe his death wasn't an accident and particular people didn't want him to talk.'

'What people?' He creased his face up at her as he took the items of clothing out one by one and laid them on the bed.

Bernie moved to stand by him.

'I don't know. I don't have faces, I don't have names, but my gut can feel them all around us.'

'Bernie, I don't have time to listen to you talk in tongues. I got business to get ready.'

He sat down on the bed. Picked up a newspaper. The broadsheet. Began flicking through, looking for a headline to write on his du-rag. One that would be both hard hitting and memorable to impress the people at Paradise Records. He stopped when he saw a report about his concert two days earlier. A few lines were devoted to the youth's possible involvement in the arson attack. The article was small, which meant that he was already becoming yesterday's news.

'Are you going to your father's flat today?'

'Yeah. Why?' Now he looked up at her.

'Can I tag along for the ride?'

'If it means you're going to let me bury the King in peace.'

She shifted her gaze to his clothes on the bed. A pair of three-quarter khaki trousers and a polo shirt in a lighter shade of green, spread out ready for a body to jump in.

'Is that what you're wearing to see the record company?'

'Yeah. It's a new look.' His face shone with pride. 'My stylist got it ready for me. I call it revolutionary rumba . . .'

'Revolutionary rumba?' She stared at him like he was a species that had yet to be discovered by man.

'The King told me about these Cubans called Che something or other and Fidel Castro who were members of a rumba band . . .'

Bernie let out a high-spirited laugh that finally propelled the chill out of the room.

'What's so funny?'

She shook her head as her laughter trickled away.

'Nothing. That's what I loved about your father, he knew how to make the world giggle.'

He still didn't get it. But it was the first time he had seen her laugh in fifteen years so he let it go.

'See you at the King's castle at about three,' she said.

She picked up her rucksack and laughter as she left. He turned back to the newspaper. Kept flicking until he found the headline he needed. It was a story he had not come across before. Lots of old photographs of a young black boy and others of white men. He liked the headline. Hard hitting. Memorable.

'Who killed Emmett Till?'

# TRACK 12: WHO KILLED EMMETT TILL?

LT knew that he was being seduced. Seduced by the recording contract that lay provocatively on the egg-shaped table by his leg, in the third-floor office at Paradise Records. LT was glad that the gushing light from the three massive windows and the striking white walls and floor made it an office that was easy to breathe in. He sat on a five-seater leather corner suite, with Window on his left and the two representatives of Paradise Records, Carlton and Helena, on his right.

Helena's style was all flimsy and fly – petal-sleeve summer-cut blouse; Farrah Fawcett flicked bleached hair, tinted pink at the ends like strawberry syrup on summer vanilla ice cream; an angular face whose focal point was the leopard-print glasses over her grey eyes. She had done a good job with her foundation and pressed powder, but LT could still tell she was well pass thirty-five. Carlton had done his best to look 'street' – a baseball cap turned backwards, mustard-flavoured baggy T-shirt, overlaid with a long gold chain that kissed his stomach with a lopsided silver cross and ultra-low-down jeans. The dead give-away was his nails. Probably carefully manicured every second week. But LT acknowledged that Carlton was 'street' where it mattered – he had the power to make or break LT's musical career.

'So what are the benefits of my client signing with Paradise Records?' Window directed his question to Helena.

She shook her hair behind her shoulder line. Smiled her recently whitened teeth at Window and said, 'We've already confirmed that there's absolutely no problem about what happened at the concert. As for this arson attack, that appears to be a tenuous link to Lord Tribulation. It won't be the first time that one of our people has been in the newspaper.' Her hand waved at a photograph on the wall, in the middle of a chequerboard of other pictures of past and previous celebrities joyous at award ceremonies and posing for official portraits. 'Our former client Sean Sparkle can attest to that.'

The photo showed Sean Sparkle, former musician and now legendary LA-based producer, post-punk era, greeting the Queen after a Royal Variety Performance. Rumour had it that he was so rat-faced on some South American jungle concoction that an attendant had to prise his hand from the Queen's. He had made his name as the frontman and drummer of one of Britain's first punk rock bands and moved into the New Romantic era with his own outfit. That was when he had become a legend. The parties, the three wives, the drugs had taken him to folklore hero. Then he dropped out for a few years and re-emerged on the Balearic beat scene. His wizardry with electronics had soon made him a much-sought-after producer. Now he was based in the States, with his own record label called 50p Trick, producing some of the most memorable acts in rap and rock.

Helena laughed. Window did not. He arched his eyebrow, leaned his powerful body back in the leather and said directly to her, 'Just tell me one more time how exactly your company will harness my client's rare talents.'

'I know what's needed,' she started. 'Let me get us all something to gear up our brains.'

She unfolded her legs. Got up. Her large charm bracelet created its own jingle as she crossed the room. She reached a desk. Bent. Pulled out a drawer. She pushed herself back up holding a large black padded wallet that resembled the type of wallet airlines put first-class tickets in. She moved towards Window. Looked down at him as her tongue ruffled her bottom lip. Her hand travelled along his arm as she eased down beside him. Real slow. She moved her coral-painted lips to his cleanly shaven face. Blew in his ear. 'Like I said, no one is going to offer your client a better deal than us.'

She held the wallet out for Window. He took it. Her hand remained on his arm. He unfolded the Velcro flap. LT peered over as the wallet folded out like a man's toiletry set. Inside was a small pile of Daddy C and a rolled hundred-dollar bill. Window passed it over to LT. He gazed at the cocaine, annoyed. Annoyed that he might end up working for people who didn't get the fact that the only rush he needed was music. He refolded the wallet. Passed it back to Window to let him deal with this one.

Window twisted towards Helena, making her hand fall from his arm. He leaned into her space. Let his shadowed eyes trip all over her and said, 'LT will provide his own backing singers.'

Tension gripped the room. Helena stood up nervously as she took the wallet and glanced over at Carlton. This was obviously his cue. He deliberately slouched back into the sofa, top body flat, legs apart, looking like a crack-dealing ruffian sitting in the sultry sun. LT and Window looked at each other and knew that Carlton was preparing to go ghetto-style. LT simmered with irritation.

'This is the coup, my brother,' Carlton started.

LT brushed his hand over his shirt. He hadn't dressed in uptown threads for someone to splatter him with downtown lingo. But Carlton got on with the job he had to do.

'Your rawness thang is storming. Your edginess is the bomb. From our direction your potential is heaving. But we think the edginess needs another injection. Needs to go under the knife. Punters need to understand what they're getting when they reach out to touch your soul. So first we're thinking image redefinition. We just love, love, love the du-rag gimmick, but let's reshape it. Visualise, visualise this – you replace the du-rag with white writing straight on to your forehead so we have a type of living graffiti board. Then let's throw into the mix some hardcore urban wear, like a drawing of a hand grenade or a semi, so you become a rapper laced with a topical explosion.'

LT's hands tightened. Sank into the softness of the sofa. Now nerves joined irritation in a pogo dance throughout his system. He knew that he'd have to make some image changes, but he thought they would at least be happy about the bulk of his product. He couldn't speak. His mouth felt full of words that were best left unspoken because he wanted this bad and didn't want to mess it up.

'So what do you think?' Carlton coaxed, leaning forward, his eyes flitting between Window and LT, not sure which one to speak to. Window answered.

'As you say, that has potential. But it sounds like you have a full body reshape in mind so run us through some of the other changes.'

Carlton's hands, palms up, fell on his knees, in full haggling fashion.

'Visualise, visualise this. We're thinking, radicalise your lyrics machine to make the package complete. Chatting about education, starvation, unemployment is cool. Give yourself a full round of applause. But check this, when people are driving to work they want something happy to ease their everyday stress. Your lyrics would benefit from that type of angle shift. So our people have been working on a song that we know will get you the attention you deserve.'

He bounced up. Moved to the desk that Helena had previously been to. He opened the top left drawer and pulled out two pieces of paper. He passed one each to LT and the other to Window. LT silently read the chorus:

*Honey girl you're so fine.*
*Your sugar blows my mind.*
*I'll do serious time,*
*To receive a life sentence with your booty.*

LT knew he was caught in what the underground rap scene called a zipadeedooda moment – when record companies were happy to sign you as long as you said everything was wonderful and dandy when they suggested any artistic changes. His eyes flicked to Window for help. His manger's eyes were expressionless.

'This song is . . .' He tried to think of the word he needed. Shit? Fucked up? An insult to humanity? He found it. '. . . unique. I'll tell you what I'll do, I'll take this song and the contract away and Window will call back with my decision in a few days.'

Helena smiled at that and transformed her face into something LT hadn't seen about her before. Helena was a woman who liked to get what she wanted and lick her fingers after.

LT picked up the teasing contract from the table. Folded it and put it in his top pocket. He smiled, knowing he was one step closer to the b-i-g time. Knowing that the King would have been so proud of his son.

'You better be prepared to have a blood transfusion in the future because that lot are going to suck you dry,' Window said as he bent to open the door to his ride – a silver-blue convertible Benz.

The West End traffic was brisk, busy and impersonal as it passed by.

'Maybe. But what alternative do I have?'

'It don't have to be like that. Barry is just waiting for your call. Barry's not just interested in making a quick buck, he genuinely loves music.'

He didn't answer. Why couldn't his manager get it that he didn't want to be part of any musicians' Internet network. Especially run by someone who couldn't even be bothered to find a decent tag name. Barry sounded like a tosser's name. He wanted the real deal. And if the real deal meant throwing up occasionally on too much humble pie and allowing his creativity to be taken over, then so be it.

Window shook his head. Eased down into the soft, vanilla leather of the driver's seat.

LT was glad he'd brought his wheels. He could do without Window doing the whole father routine on the way home. He already had enough troubles trying to figure out what happened to one father without having another one breathing down his throat.

LT checked his watch. Two thirty. He'd promised to meet Bernie in half an hour. He left his manager and found his motor. He jumped in. Put on his cherry tinted shades. Spun a DVD on the flip screen. Checked his appearance in the rear-view mirror. Yeah, the Emmett Till du-rag headline still looked good. He juiced the engine and made his way to the King's castle.

LT parked his wheels in front of the King's castle, which was in Clement Attlee House, or the Big C, as most residents called it. It was a typical sixties block. Four up, ten doors across with a lift shaft dividing it in two. It was also one of the most notorious blocks this side of the river. What made it notorious was that on the weekends it became an upfront, red-brick madhouse of music. The corner flat, on each floor, on the left side of the block, stacked together to become an unofficial four-tier club. Each flat was devoted to a different style of music. The first flat was strictly for B-boys and girls wanting to do their thang to rap and hip-hop. The second was for those who wanted to tear it up to dance-hall, dub and any other imported melodrama shipped in from Jamaica. The third was reserved for those wishing to sizzle to R 'n' B and classic soul. The last flat, owing to popular demand, was a fusion of all the musical sounds played on the other floors. Lately the rumble of Congolese soukous could be heard coming from the opposite corner of the second floor. Rumour had it that the council waiting list was solid for the next ten years, jammed with young people waiting for their chance to be booked into the Big C.

LT made his way up through the block. To the second floor. Right-hand side. He took the final step up. Stopped. He leaned his palm on the chipped, green-tiled wall as he bent his head. He wasn't sure he was ready for this. Ready to go through the King's belongings. He flipped his head up, knowing he didn't have a choice. He shook his shoulders at the same time as a conventional reggae riff – hard first beat, whispering snare on the third

- boomed from a flat somewhere underneath. He pushed on towards his father's place. The glare from the afternoon sun dropped on his 'Who Killed Emmett Till?' du-rag. The bass line from downstairs punched against the balcony. He reached number 27. Felt inside his pocket for the keys. Took them out. As he leaned in to push the key into the lock he noticed a slice of light slithering between door frame and door. The door was already open.

He stood there for a moment, confused. Then he realised that someone might be inside. Shit. He jumped back into the side shadow on the wall by the door. The hard first beat of the track from downstairs fisted against the wall. What should he do? Yell for help? Call the cops? No. A black man calling the police was like . . . he couldn't even think of a comparison, it was that rare. Instead he counted the classic four-on-the-floor dance beat in his head.

One.

Two.

Three.

Four.

Then he eased himself back in front of the door. He pushed his palm against it, widening the opening. He thrust his ear forward. Listening. The music from downstairs stopped. No sounds. He shifted his body into the opening. Slid into the passage. That was when he felt the heat of someone inside. Heard movement. The shuffling of feet coming from what he suspected was the sitting room. The sitting room was tucked in the right-hand corner from the passage. LT's heart reared up in his chest. A new wave of sweat dampened the du-rag to his forehead. He knew he had no choice but to go on. As he made that decisive step forward, the sitting-room door began to open. He hustled backwards. Pressed his body against the passage wall. His breathing was loud. Erratic. It wasn't easy, but he slowed his breathing down. Eased it back. Waiting. The sitting-room door was pushed wide, flushing light into the passage. The person moved into view. But not in LT's space. His first glimpse was a flash of fair hair and a body

size he knew he could tackle. The intruder's head was down,
looking at something they held in their hands. Double shit. He
knew that all over town there was a new wave of burglaries
involving gunplay. LT balled his palm into a fist. The intruder
got into his space. Flicked their head up. LT twisted. Leaped
forward. Swung his fist.

# TRACK 13 : FACE DOWN

The left side of LT's face was slammed against the floral wall-paper he'd hated since his dad had put it up in the passage back in '93. The imprint of the raised flowers on the wall dug into his flesh as fingers shoved and braced the back of his neck. The other hand of his assailant cranked his arm, wishbone-style, against his back. He tried to wriggle, but the determination of his attacker held him in place. His arm was pushed higher. He groaned. Then the pressure of the hands against his neck and arm changed, soft-ened with an almost brutal tenderness. Breath brushed his neck. The heat of lips balanced above the crest of his ear. Then a voice rasped, 'Fight tip number one: if you relax, your opponent will too, and that's when you strike.'

LT breathed more easily when he heard the familiar voice.

'Bernie, let me up, you're mashing up my mic arm.'

She relaxed her hold on him. Let him go. He leaned on the wall to catch his breath. Then he thrust around. Looked at her as he rubbed his arm.

'You nearly broke my arm. You must've realised it was me.'

'Maybe I did.'

She had freshened up since he'd seen her that morning. Her hair was tousled with no butterfly clip to hold it in place. She still wore black trousers and jacket but with a white tie-top blouse. He wondered whether the blouse was twisted or scooped behind to show off her back.

'How did you get in here anyway?'

'The same way you did. I came up as we arranged, but when I got here I could tell that the door had been forced. Whoever did it was professional because they made sure the door looked like it was still closed.'

'That's the problem with dying around here. As soon as word hits that you ain't coming back, breaking and entering is in.'

'I've never been here before but I'm not sure that's what happened here.'

'What do you mean?'

She didn't say any more but turned around, going back towards the sitting room. He followed her, flexing his arm. When he crossed the threshold, he forgot to breathe. The room was empty. Cleared of furniture, ornaments, free-standing lamp, the King's huge vinyl and dub plate record collection and even the King's classic table-top three-tier green plastic fountain. The carpet had been dragged up and rolled to the far side of the room beneath the large window. But the place was neat, like someone had run the Hoover over it and given it a thorough spring clean. The white of the walls had a forlorn feeling, reminding him of the mortuary.

He twisted around, striding towards the door. Bernie called out to him because she knew where he was going.

'I've already checked all the other rooms. Except for the fridge and cooker, they're empty as well.'

She held the double L sound at the end of the sentence. He stopped. She let the sound go.

He wandered to the middle of the room and in a dazed voice said, 'I don't get it. Maybe the council came and removed his gear?'

'Not without checking with you first. Maybe some of the neighbours saw what happened?'

'Waste of time. The only neighbours around here are too busy looking at their feet, developing their dance moves, to look up and notice anyone else's life.'

'Now do you believe me when I say there's something going on?' Bernie's tone was low, as if they were in a crowded room and she didn't want other people to hear.

He looked around the room, remembering the times on a Friday night when the King would have his mates over to splash on some hardcore tunes and thump out some dominoes. The mad noise would push up the walls, making the room and the lives of the men within it seem much bigger than they were.

Suddenly, LT could feel himself rocking. As if the pulse of the ground underneath his feet were shifting. As if he were being toppled by the overwhelming starkness of watching his father's life disappear before his eyes. He crouched, head bent, to save himself from falling or to escape staring at the four empty walls of the King's home, he didn't know. What he did know was that no one had the right to take the King's stuff before he had that last chance, that last moment, to run his mic hand over the warmth of his dad's record collection. His fingertips balanced his weight and seesawing rage against the floor.

'Are you all right?' Bernie asked.

He lifted his chin and looked at her. She took a step towards him, a funny lift of her feet as if she wasn't sure whether she should be going forward or back. Then she stopped. Reversed her movements until she was leaning on the wall next to the radiator. He quickly tipped his head back to the floor so she couldn't see how much he needed the touch of her hand to share the chill of the King's death.

The ground began to move again. This time with the energy of a tune that had been last year's one crowd puller favourite on the dance-hall circuit coming from the flat directly below. The beat pounded through LT's body. Pushed his head up. Made him straighten to his feet. He walked over to Bernie. Leaned near her against the wall and said, 'Tell me what you think is going on here.'

'This is what we've got so far. When I interviewed your father he told me that in 1976 there were things that got out of control. Then he leaves a message on my voicemail. He sounds troubled, even scared. Tells me he wants to talk about 1976, like he's got something he needs to get off his chest. Next, he disappears and is found dead hours later. We know that he was going to meet someone. We still don't know who that person was. Now his home has been robbed and emptied of all his belongings. Do you remember anything that he might have said about 1976?'

'The usual. It was hot. He was at the height of his toasting career. The gals were yummy and sweet. That was the year my mum dumped me on him and skipped town. I was eight months old when she left me with him on carnival Sunday.'

She pushed off the wall.

'Did he say anything else the last time you were with him?'

He rubbed a hand over the 'Who Killed Emmett Till?' headline on the front of his du-rag.

'Look, I don't know if this has got anything to do with anything.' Bernie moved herself in front of him, her gaze expectant, urging him to carry on. 'The last time I saw him at the hospital he got really sick. He was chewing on a bit of weed as we watched an interview I did on the box when all of a sudden he starts choking. Do you know how long I'd been telling him to knock that gear on the head? Anyway, he grabs me really tight and starts babbling about something called his box of bones and wanting to be buried in his best jacket. Then he collapsed.'

She cocked her chin to the side, as if her violin were back in its rightful place, and asked, 'What is his box of bones?'

'Do I look like an encyclopedia?'

'From the man who doesn't even know who Che Guevara and Fidel Castro are? No, I'd never mistake you for a font of knowledge,' she scoffed.

He opened his mouth to hit back but she kept on talking.

'So you don't know what this box of bones is?'

He shook his head. Bernie pushed her hand inside her pocket. Pulled out a digital Dictaphone with the initials B.R. engraved on it. Pressed 'record' and said, 'Box of bones.' She clicked 'pause'. Tilted her head back towards him.

'What did he mean, he wanted to be buried in his best jacket? Did he have a jacket that he really liked?'

'He had loads of jackets. You know all those old men, they loved their jackets. Going to a party, put on a jacket. Going to the bookie's, put on a jacket. Going to make love, put on a jacket.'

'But did he have a particular one? One that he really liked?'

'Sure, he had a few. But look at this place, baby.' His hands swept over the space in the room. 'It's been cleaned out. Along with his clothes.'

The word baby whimpered in the room. He saw her face flush. He used to call her that when they were at school. He closed his eyes. Fool, fool, fool. When he reopened his eyes her back was to him. He heard the click of her Dictaphone. 'Best jacket,' she said.

She turned back to him.

'When we went to identify his body, I'm sure I saw the sister from his ward give you a bag? Am I right?'

He nodded.

'Was that the King's?'

Again he nodded. Her eagerness pushed her towards him.

'Where is it?'

'Back at mine.'

'Why didn't you tell me this morning?'

His anger flared.

'You know what, Bernie, my dad's dead, so forgive me if keeping you sweet hasn't been at the top of my "do three things that make other people happy today" list.'

He strode over to the window. Watched the afternoon sun tease people on the ground below.

'I don't need this,' he groaned. 'I've got a record contract in my pocket. I've got one chance to be crowned Writer in Residence of Ladbroke Grove at the carnival for the third time in ten days' time. I'm going places and this is just pulling me back.'

Bernie folded her arms over her chest. Looked him up and down he as if he were in a pawnshop window.

'If this had happened to you and it was your father standing here now in your empty pad, what do you think he would do? Do you think he'd just ignore the contents of that bag?'

LT did not want to say the truth but he knew he had no alternative.

'He'd go back to Ernest Bevin House and be in that bag like a rat in a food cupboard.'

Jackie Jarvis had a sixth sense about when trouble was brewing in Ernest Bevin House. She stood outside number 16, on the first floor, her home for the last ten years. Stretched her five-two frame and peered over the balcony. Her pixie-style coral-red hair gleamed in the afternoon light as she looked hard at the white van parked in the residents-only bay. White, big, a removal van with a logo of zigzagged dirt sprayed along its side. The other residents gossiped that, as the self-appointed matriarch of the block, she had the savviest green eyes you ever saw. They were right. Jackie knew everything that happened in the block. She knew when Brenda at number 5 had found her Ted in bed with a bloke. She knew when Jamilla at number 11 had got the news that her daughter had won a scholarship to some posh school across the river. She knew when the Barratts at number 13, sleeping three to a room, had struck the match to burn down their one bedroom in an attempt to be rehoused. Yes, Jackie Jarvis knew everything that happened. But she didn't know anything about a white van.

She rushed downstairs in her backless slippers. Pushed the new entrance door. Walked into the main yard. Hustled backwards until she had a good view of the whole block. Her eyes skidded up the centre. They creased at the corners when she couldn't detect anything unusual. But her sixth sense kept prodding her just above her belly button. She took another step back and started again. Her gaze skated along the first floor. Up.

Along the second floor. Up.

Along the third floor. Up.

Along the top floor. Her gaze screamed to a halt outside number 44.

LT's place.

Two figures stood near his front door. Male or female, she could not tell, but she was going to find out. She compressed her lips into a tight line as if she were trying to keep her top teeth inside her jaw. She marched back into the block. Took the steps quickly to the top floor. Stepped on to the balcony. Strode into the stream of summer light mixing with shadows and the silky sound of Mary J. Blige's 'No More Drama' floating from the open window of one of the flats on the right. The vocals brimmed with the husky tone of world-weariness and determination. She swung to the left side of the balcony. Saw two men shuffling and pressing against LT's door.

'Oi, what you doing?' she called out.

The men swung around, their startled white faces looking at her. Jackie knew the type immediately. Geezers. Heavies who talked in dramatic baritones when they got together with the lads for a jar down the old rub-a-dub and slipped to a menacing bass when they dolled out a kicking. She'd been handling geezers as long as she could remember. She power-walked, her slippers banging against the concrete like a hand-held drum over the tinkling piano backbeat of the song. Never one to back down from a fight, she got up close. One was young, the other a good decade older. They both wore baseball caps and clothes that played at being bad boys. The younger one kept his head down with his hands fidgeting behind his back. His companion pushed out his chest, ready to take control of the situation. The young man's arms dropped by his side. The older one took a step back and smiled, showing teeth that were mainly crowns.

'We're here to do an interview with Lord Tribulation.'

Jackie strip-searched him with her eyes. No bag.

'Well, I'm his manager and I don't remember booking any appointments.'

The man's smile shortened as he stuck out his chest some more. 'You're his manager?'

'What, you don't think us women can cut it?'

'We don't want any fuss.'

'Then book an appointment like everyone else.'

The younger man finally raised his head. Thin face, grey eyes, with a freshness to his skin like he'd finally decided to take a chance on being somebody in this life. She guessed he was a few years older than she'd been when she'd done a bunk from local authority care when she was fifteen.

'You ain't his manager,' the other man said.

'Don't matter what I am and ain't, you ain't going in there, all right.'

She muscled through the middle of them, rubbing against the smells of nicotine and cats.

She put her back against LT's door, presenting to the world the Rottweiler everyone in the block appreciated she had become. The older man let out a little laugh. He took a full stride towards her. The pressure of her back against the door increased.

'How are you,' his eyes swept up her small frame, 'gonna stop us?'

'I got the best lungs this side of Watford. Besides, if you knew who my old man was you wouldn't be asking no tomfool questions.'

He stood his ground. So did she. Mary J. Blige's voice swept along the balcony in a raw, raucous pitch of elation. Jackie's heartbeat rose high in her chest as she saw the man's eyes. Eyes that reminded her of a time she would rather forget. He shifted closer. His hands balled at his side. He leaned forward. Face bearing down. Jackie cringed deeper into the door.

'Come on.' The younger man's voice broke over the balcony. 'We've got another story to do.'

His partner lifted the left side of his mouth in a soundless snarl. Held it. Then he pivoted on his heels and started to walk away. Jackie let out the air from her body. Slowly. Her head fell back against the door. She closed her eyes. She wasn't sure whether it was the hammering of her heart or the sharp, piano-driven finale of the song she heard. She looked at the back of the retreating men and noticed the red plastic-handled screwdriver poking out of the young one's trouser pocket.

LT rolled and massaged the muscles in the top of his back against the car seat as he killed the engine in the courtyard of Ernest Bevin House. Bernie sat quietly in the passenger seat beside him.

The squeals from a small group of children playing catch by the rubbish chute in the sunlight wove a daisy chain of happiness around the car.

On the drive back he had contacted the police about the burglary at the King's. He wasn't hopeful. The running joke on the street was that the last time the police had solved a burglary on an estate in Hackney was in 1066. But he felt better about doing the right thing. He'd also contacted a locksmith to repair the King's door. Not that there was anything left to take, but he didn't like the idea of anyone walking into the King's home like he didn't matter any more.

As he leaned over and touched the door to get out, Bernie said, 'I need a minute.'

He shuffled his upper body around to stare at her. She stretched that sleek neck of hers. Let it drop. She fiddled in the side pocket of her rucksack. Pulled out a nick of cocaine. He should have known that she was only interested in conducting a one-to-one with her white boyfriend.

He folded his arms across his chest and said, 'You know what, I'm not comfortable with you doing the "beam me up, Scottie" routine in my ride. In fact, I'm not comfortable with you doing it full stop.'

She played dumb. Held the powder under her nose ready to sniff.

'So did you sell your violin or give it away?' he asked, moving on to another topic that he knew would piss her straight off.

She inhaled in a ragged breath. Shut her eyes. Tipped her head back.

'All you need to know is it doesn't belong to me any more.' Her tone was confident, but her pitch was off.

A hand banged against the window on the driver's side. LT swivelled around. Jackie Jarvis's face gleamed at him, her freckles almost twitching on the glass.

'Not another Oscar Wilde-quoting girlfriend?' Bernie asked.

'Take these.' She looked startled as he threw the car keys at her. She missed the catch.

He got out of the car. Moved towards Jackie and said, 'What's happening?'

'Who's Snow White?' Jackie jerked her head towards the car. She sniffed dramatically, indicating she was not referring to a fairy tale.

'And how's Prince Charming?'

Her cheeks blushed with the bloom of suspended joy. Her Prince Charming was Schoolboy, a former small-time dealer who gave up the bad times of London's underworld for a life of cooking in Devon. Schoolboy also happened to be the brother-in-law of his manager. London was big, yet small.

'He's coming down next week and I'm hoping he'll say the M word.'

'Marriage?'

'No, maybe.' She ran her hand through her hair, rubbing in the sunshine. 'That's all I want. Maybe.'

Stark vulnerability covered her face. He turned away slightly, to give her time to recover. She hated being caught naked.

'Anyway, I found a couple of geezers at your place today,' she told him as he turned back to her.

'Inside?'

'What, with me around?' she said, puffing up her chest. 'I don't think so.'

'What did they want?'

'Said they were reporters. Funny thing was one of them had a screwdriver.'

'A screwdriver?' Bernie said behind them. She moved as quickly as the question she shot out at Jackie. 'Were they trying to break in?'

'Don't think they were trying to fit a new lock, were they, love.' Bernie compressed her lips.

'Check you later,' Jackie said, looking at the group of children by the rubbish chute. 'I got to fix the kids their tea. Ryan.' She belted out the name of her son in a rising six-note call.

'She should have been a singer,' Bernie commented, watching Jackie retreat into the block.

'Perhaps she was. Many people around here have got their own stories to tell.'

'Someone's definitely looking for something. Let's just hope that the box of bones and best jacket are in the King's bag.'

He snapped his body towards her and said in an anxious voice, 'Shit. What if Jackie was wrong and they got in and took the bag?'

They both ran towards the stairwell at the same time.

'They must have got in and taken it,' LT said as he prowled across the bare boards of the main room floor, moving from his rare grooves music collection in one corner to Northern Soul in the other.

For ten minutes they had searched the flat, looking for the bag. He'd taken the bedroom. She'd done the kitchen. He'd taken the bathroom. She'd done the main room. Now they both stood in the main room minus the bag. She leaned up against the door frame while he dug his agitated strides into the floor, moving from Northern Soul to Rare Grooves. Her voice interrupted his movements.

'But the front door lock wasn't broken and you said nothing looks liked it's been touched.'

He turned to her and watched her finger play circles in her collarbone.

'But I've searched high and low and still can't find it.'

'Just think. When was the last time you had it?'

He dropped on to the single sofa, midway between Rare Grooves and Northern Soul.

'Yesterday.' He looked up at her. 'It was when you came around and we made . . .' The words trailed off but didn't go away.

Her hand dropped from beneath her throat.

'Just cast your mind back.'

He shoved out of the sofa. Began prowling again. But softer. Looser.

'OK. I decided to put on some music. So I got up. Then I sort of kicked it with my foot and it . . .'

He stopped. Jerked his head towards the floor. Dropped to his knees beside the front of the sofa. He stretched his arm out. Pushed it under the sofa and shouted, 'Bingo, baby.' His arm pulled back, revealing the black canvas bag.

She rushed over to him. Dropped to her knees beside him. His hands shook as he unzipped the bag. Then one by one he took out each item and placed it on the sun-sanded floor.

Toothbrush.

Box of Cuban cigars.

Dictaphone.

A book – *Songs of Experience* by William Blake.

A domino set.

Underwear.

A box of mints.

An old jeans jacket.

A tub of cocoa butter.

A box as slim and as long as both of the King's hands.

An old 50p coin.

They both stared at the remaining pieces of the King's life.

'So how we going to do this?' he asked.

'A process of elimination. Whatever isn't a box or a jacket, we put to the side.'

They dumped the items they didn't need near the Rare Grooves collection – tub of cocoa butter, Dictaphone, underwear, William Blake book, 50p coin and toothbrush. They stared at what was left. Four boxes – cigars, dominoes, mints and the slim box – and a denim jacket.

'Let's start with the jacket,' Bernie said.

LT picked it up. Vintage. Wrangler. Cowboy cut. Tight fitting. Four-button front. He shoved his hand into the flap top pocket. Nothing. He turned the jacket inside out. Nothing. He shook it. Nothing. He let it drop on to the floor.

'Nothing,' he threw at Bernie, his tone full of frustration.

'You look at the mints, I'll do the cigars.'

One minute on they both realised there was nothing in either box. He kissed his teeth, hard, blowing his irritation into the room. He rubbed his hand over the 'Who Killed Emmett Till?' headline on his du-rag. He looked at the disappointment creasing Bernie's face.

'What's in this one?' Bernie asked, pointing to the slim box.

'The King's mic.'

'Don't some people give their musical instruments nicknames? Maybe he called his mic his bone?'

As his arm moved towards the box he said, 'I never once heard the King call any mic bone. I would have remembered if . . .'

His words trailed off in a tight breath that shoved harshly inside his chest. His hand changed direction and lunged for the domino set.

'What is it?' she asked, rearing up on her knees.

His hand reached the box of dominoes. Hesitated. Stopped. Hovered above the box as he said, 'Of course. His box of bones. His domino set. All the old geezers call them bones. The King and his mates use to sit up half the night playing dominoes.'

She shuffled closer to him, excitement lacing her voice as she said, 'I should have guessed. The last time I saw your father in the hospital he was holding a box of dominoes in his hand, but when he saw me looking he slipped them into his pocket. He didn't think I saw him but I did.'

LT remained transfixed by the box.

'I should have known these were bones. Do you know why they're called bones?' she carried on. 'When they were first made in China they use to make them with animal bones.'

She gently picked up the box. Held it out to him.

'You should do this.'

He took them and said, 'I still don't get it.'

'Just open it.'

He slid the lid across, revealing the top layer of dominoes stacked in a formation of seven rows. White tiles, black dots. He tipped the dominoes out. They hit the wooden floor with the ripple of musical notes. Some piled on top of each other. He peered at them. Couldn't see anything unusual.

'There's nothing in the boneyard.'

'Boneyard?' Bernie tipped her chin to the left to look at him curiously.

'Yeah. When all the dominoes are laid out together they call them the boneyard.'

'Well, I think you should check the boneyard, don't you?'

He bent his back. Leaned over the dominoes. Spread his fingers into them, the way a domino player does when he shuffles, to separate them. The double blank sat on top of another domino. He moved the double blank to reveal the domino underneath. But it wasn't a domino.

'What the . . .'

He picked it up. Examined it. Held it out to her and said, 'You know more about these things than me.'

They sat on his bed. Bernie held the King's Dictaphone. LT held what they had found with the dominoes – a Dictaphone tape. The same size as the dominoes, almost the same thickness. On the front was a tiny label with black writing that read: 'Revival Selection: 1976, Volume 1'.

'What does that mean?' Bernie asked him.

'A revival selection is when you start spinning old-time music. Reviving it. Bringing it back. Sometimes they would release reggae compilations and call them volumes. Like that one.' He pointed to one of the album covers on the ceiling. 'That's Trojan Records' *Tighten Up Reggae Compilation, Volume 2*.'

Bernie pressed 'eject' on the old-style Dictaphone. He handed her the tape. She pushed it into the slot. They both let out a breath. It fitted.

'Don't get your hopes up,' he told her. 'This could just be a bank of lyrics and music from 1976.'

She pressed 'play'. Placed the machine on the bed between them. The King's singing filled the room, a favourite that he sang with his sound system back in the seventies.

'I told you . . .' LT started, then stopped when the singing was suddenly cut off to be replaced by the King speaking.

'If this is you, son, make sure you find Berlina Ray and give her this tape. Well, if you're listening, Berlina, I suppose you want me to go straight to 1976. The year I became a soldier in the revolution. The year I stood on the street corner with my black fist in the air, Afro clenched tight, denouncing imperialism, Babylon and pigs. The year you had to decide whether you wanted to listen to Kiki Dee and Elton John's "Don't Go Breaking My Heart" or skanking to the warrior heartbeat of Junior Murvin's "Police And Thieves". We started out with a cause, but somewhere along that murky, tough road stuff started to happen. Stuff we couldn't control. I suppose there's only one place to start. It was a night in mid-February. A Friday. Man, that night was bitter. It was a night that started with a war . . .'

# TRACK 15: REVIVAL SELECTION: 1976, VOLUME 1 (LP)

'Babylon is a bitch!'

The words flew out of my mouth with the power of the Lion of Judah as I chewed up the mic on the stage at the Blue Jam nightclub. I was decked out in my butt-hugging angel pants, two-and-a-half-inch platforms, Farrar shirt and, of course, my PSA (perfectly shaped Afro). The crowd bounced with approval at my words. Any curse against Babylon was appreciated. Babylon was anything that held you back in life – third-rate education, tumble-down housing, a skin just too black to cut it and, of course, the biggest Babylon of all, the police. Just like the scriptures in the Good Book say, if you were suffering you must be living in Babylon. And that's what the mother country, England, felt like in 1976.

'Babylon is a bitch!' I roared out one more time, taking a step forward towards the edge of the stage.

The crowd bounced higher. Man, they were ready. Ready to take part in the war. A war that had, for the last two hours, been marching into a full-frontal, take-no-prisoners battle. They were there to witness the ultimate musical skirmish – a sound system clash.

That night the dance-floor turf was fought over by us, the Uprising Sound System, and one of our many rivals, Mount Zion, who hailed from South London. I lived for those clashes. There was nothing sweeter in life than competing against other sound systems to see who had the baddest tunes; who had the most militant sound; who could mash up the status quo with their lyrics and rhythms. The crowd's job was to honour the sound system that played the freshest cuts laced with the freshest lyrics with the loudest roar.

There were four of us in Uprising – me, Desmond 'Sound Man' Jay, Maximus and Sean. I was the frontman. The toaster or DJ. Being a toaster wasn't hard to define, but people being people, everyone had to fling their words into the pot. Some claimed that my job was to chat over the instrumental break or dub version of a record, others said that it was to chant. Well, if you asked me, I provided verbal vibrations because over the roots-rocking rhythms of our music I belted out our hardcore, rebel, outlaw stories. You couldn't tune into our stories on the telly, on the radio or in the newspaper. The dance hall was our BBC – Badass Broadcasting Corporation. And man, did we have stories to tell. We were tired. Tired of behaving like our parents, listening to Jim Reeves croon to us in his comfy cardigan. I mean, check this one, can you imagine Jim Reeves singing 'I remember you-hooo' to a reggae beat? Nor could we. We were tired of people telling us we should be grinning our bright, white teeth because *Love Thy Neighbour* was on the telly. Tired of suffering in Babylon.

'Babylon is a bitch.' One more time it left my mouth.

Our supporters started to stamp their feet. They didn't call me King Stir It Up for nothing (although it was a close-run ting – some people wanted to call me King Drink It Up because I loved to pose with a mic in one hand and a bottle of Guinness or Red Stripe in the other).

I looked over at Desmond, who stood next to our speakers, or houses of joy as we name-checked them. He looked at me. I nodded my head. The excitement of the crowd sizzled higher because they knew we were getting ready to drop our exclusive killer tune. We always made our exclusives on dub plates, which were one-off acetate versions of a popular tune that had already been released on vinyl. There was only one killer tune, kung-fu-chopping shit on the street that year – 'Police And Thieves' by my man Junior Murvin.

'Forward,' I yelled out, giving Desmond the signal.

Then Desmond did those wonderful things with his fingers caressing the turntable.

He flicked once. The dub plate dropped.

Flicked twice. The mid-range dropped.

Flicked a third time. The treble dropped.

Desmond's fingers hovered over the controls for the bass line.

Man, you could've heard a mouse tiptoe across the floor, it was that quiet.

Desmond moved his fingers. Dropped the biscuit.

Whoooooosssssh.

The B-line skated. Swept the floor. Hit the crowd. Man, the place just erupted into an atomic explosion of feet, hips and emotions.

'Forward,' I yelled again.

Man, you should've felt my heartbeat, it was almost ping-ponging inside my soul. I brought the mic to my lips ready to annihilate our competitor, Mount Zion. I started toasting out lyrics to the melody of 'Police And Thieves':

'One time, we trashed our opposition.'

The crowd threw back, 'Oh yeah.'

'Two times, we smashed our opposition.'

'Oh yeah.'

'Three times, we mashed our opposition.'

'Oh yeah.'

One of our supporters in the middle of the crowd blasted out, 'Someone call a doctor, because there's a fever in Hackney tonight.'

The room corked up to mass hysteria. Our supporters began banging drinks cans, blowing whistles and horns, and took out their red, gold and green handkerchiefs and waved them furiously in the air. When Mount Zion's supporters joined in the uprising I knew that our rivals were dead. I began to skank and dance, ninja-man-style, legs and arms kicking the air. What a feeling. There I was, twenty-two years old, with a one-month old son, centre of the party.

And that's when it happened.

Just as Desmond let loose with an echo chamber that reverberated around the room the entrance and fire doors burst open like the mouth of hell. A high-pitched scream ripped the air. I stared hard at the doors to see what was going on.

Well, kiss my sweet black rah-rah.

Charging through the hall was the whore of Babylon herself – the police. A whole brick wall of them. I held fast to the stage and shook my head. I had seen this all before. The police raiding up the place and interrupting our positive vibe was a regular business.

'Police raid. No one move,' one of them shouted.

No one move? He must be mad. Everyone moved. It felt like the floor and walls moved as well. People just scattered, pushed, shoved. The sound of platform shoes skidding on the board floor filled the air as everyone ran. As people tried to flee, two of the boys in blue ran over to our houses of joy. They took out their truncheons and started to mash them up. Every blow hit me hard in the heart. No wonder some of the community called the defenders of the law another name – Beast. The blood just boiled in my head and I got real mad. No way was this the first time Babylon had mutilated our houses of joy, and I knew that it wouldn't be the last. I always figured that they did it because they believed it was one way of cutting out our tongues. Silence the music and you don't hear the people. They must've been high on something stupid because no way was that going to suppress the bass line of the black community.

One of the Babylon raised his head and drank in the air like he had just finished doing his gal. He looked at me and yelled, 'Oi, chocolate drop, get up against the wall.'

I cast my eye at the mess he'd made of our beautiful speakers. It just weren't right, man, weren't right. I flared my nostrils in rebellion and defiance. Spread my legs. I started to stare him out. I held my mic out defiantly to the side. His eyes swung between my mic and me like he was thinking two against one. He decided to take us on. He rushed towards me, truncheon held high. He held his wooden snake over my head like he was back trying to capture one of my ancestors in West Africa, you check me? But his hand didn't fall. Man, I didn't have time for this kind of botheration. I just pick up my feet, kissed my teeth and brushed past him, like the nasty-hearted little mosquito he was.

I jumped down from the stage and moved to the wall, where the Babylon had a whole heap of us already lined up. I knew the procedure. Spread your hands, spread your legs, hands flat against the wall. Sometimes, as a young black man in England, you felt that the wall was your second home, you check me? As I fixed myself up to the wall a young white girl, with chin-cut hair, was making a carnival-load of noise as the police tried to push her against the wall. She looked like one of those student types who loved spending the night getting dizzy on weed and black music. I looked at her and shook my head. What's the sense in miaowing in the middle of a pack of dogs?

'No one move, I said.' The voice came from behind. Sounded like it was stuck in the air.

I shifted my head around to the side and saw a tall, thin, plain-clothes Babylon standing on top of the bar. Pug-dog face, and the way my man held his body you could tell he was playing at being Jack Regan from *The Sweeney*.

The lights went up. His voice boomed, 'Right, you people, I have a search warrant for these premises . . .'

He started waving this piece of paper.

'Man, I bet it's a dry-cleaning bill,' a voice to my right side whispered. I turned my head and saw that I was standing next to a small man. His dark brown profile was cocked to the side underneath a puffed red, gold and green tam on top of his dreadlocks, with a wicked smile propping up his cheeks. He had one of them bookie pens behind his ear.

'Oi, you with the tea cosy on your head, shut it,' a policeman yelled behind us.

'Jack Regan' continued, 'The sooner we get this search over with the sooner you people can go back to mugging old ladies and doing voodoo and whatever it is you people like to do of an evening.'

'This is pure harassment,' I growled to the man in the hat beside me.

He lifted his eyebrow. A truncheon poked me in the back. I heard 'Jack's' feet hit the ground as he jumped down from the bar. His feet clipped against the wooden floor, getting louder as he got closer. I knew my bollocks were his next dish of the day. His hand shoved into my pocket. Shit, man.

'Excuse me, "sir",' he said, ' would you mind telling me what this is . . . ?'

I turned around, slowly, to give myself time to think. I looked at the long spliff he held between two matchstick-style fingers. I had a long look at it myself before I replied, all innocent like, 'It looks like some herb – one of your people must be trying to fit me up . . .'

Before I could finish he pointed at me and shouted to one of the uniformed cops, 'This one – possession of a controlled drug and assaulting a police officer . . .'

They took my name and address – I told them I was Bob Nesta Marley and I lived at number 1 Babylon Street, Tunbridge Wells. As the Babylon patted everyone else down and asked for details, two of them just grab me up, quick time. They started dragging me to the back of the building. Sweat carved up all over my body because I knew the police only took you into the back for one reason. We reached what I knew was the manager's office. The two Babylon dashed me inside. I shoved my head down quick time to guard against the first blow.

Know what happened? Nothing. So I lifted my head real slow and peered forward. My gaze came level with a chest covered with a white shirt opened at the neck. I lifted my head some more.

Well, kiss my sweet black rah-rah.

There was 'Jack Regan' sitting in the manager's chair pulling hard on my spliff.

'This is fucking good gear, mate – have you got any more?' he said as I straightened up.

I looked at him, like the rat he was, but I said, 'I don't know – what's in it for me?'

You might say I was an idiot-boy even dreaming of doing business with these people. But what else could I do?

He took another long puff and blew the smoke out across the office. At least he didn't seem to be interested in my bollocks any more.

'Well, I expect I can be a bit flexible on the charges when we get down the nick . . .'

I kept my mouth shut.

' . . . and obviously I'll pay for it – I mean, I'm not a fucking criminal, am I?'

I fished out a few ounces that I was holding in my sock for later. He pulled a couple of oners out of his wallet, passed them over and then he stumbled out of the chair and I was dragged back into the hall.

They slung some of us into the back of their devil vans. I ended up next to the white girl who had been mouthing off earlier. When I heard which police station we were being taken to shivers took control of my skin. Officials called it Unity Road police station. We name-checked it as the Abomination.

The Abomination, someone once pulled me up and told me, was an example of the high point of Georgian architecture, a bit like *The Harder They Come* became a classic piece of Caribbean cinema. The police station was preserved by those folks looking after 'English heritage', which I suppose explains why, in 1976, it didn't take too kindly to preserving anyone of African heritage. Which must explain why so many brothers were dragged in with a full head of teeth and slung out with a fistful missing. Which must explain why I was so scared, as I shivered and paced back and forward in one of its cells.

I was too frightened to sit down. Too frightened that if they came for me I wouldn't be prepared. You'd have to have no eyes, ears and be plain living in another country not to know what happened in Unity Road. I mean, check this one – last year, a brother had bolted into the station pleading for protection against two National Front bald heads who were chasing him, all the way from Hoxton. The brother got something all right – busted and banged up for two years for carrying an offensive weapon. As for the fascists, they're still chasing anyone they don't like, any chance they can get. We all knew it was only a matter of time before someone went into Unity Road taking in air and came out with their next home the dead house. Let me tell you plain and straight, that somebody wasn't going to be me, you check me?

I heard a scuffing sound coming from outside, in the corridor. I stopped pacing. I jerked my head towards the blue metal door. The sound got closer. Then I heard the jangle of metal hitting metal. I knew that sound. Babylon's musical notes. Cell keys. They were finally coming for my raas. No way, man, were they putting me down without a fight. I started swinging around, searching for anything to help save my skin. Only tings I could see were a grubby plastic bucket that I'm sure used to be white and the rumpled, grey blanket on the bunk. The jangle of the keys got louder. Before I could say 'number one record' that bucket was in my hand. The bucket didn't smell too good but it was tough enough to do some damage. I hoisted the bucket up like a trophy. The key rattled in the door. I pushed out my chest, head and the arm that held the bucket. This was one black man Babylon wasn't going to take without a mighty rumble. The lock started to turn as the bucket shook in my hand. *Please God, please God, whatever they do, don't let them mash up my mouth or mic hand.* The door pushed partway open. The strong electric light from the corridor swept inside. Man, I got ready to charge. Next thing I know, a small man was shoved inside as a voice behind him said, 'And keep the noise down until feeding time.'

Tings were moving so fast I decided not to take any chances. I pelted the bucket with the speed of a West Indian fast bowler at the man's head. His eyes grew wide when he saw the bucket coming for him. He clutched the red, gold and green tam on his head and ducked, like he'd had one too many rums. The bucket bounced against the wall behind him.

'What the raas you doing, man?' the squatting man asked, but didn't raise his head.

From his words and accent I knew that he was a brother. Relief made my legs wobble as I stepped back. I stared at his tam-covered head. He pushed his face up and peered at me. I realised it was the same man – the one Her Majesty's officers had referred to as wearing a tea cosy – who had been lined up next to me by the wall at the club.

His face was the size and shape of a Trojan single. I knew, just as when the needle drops into the groove of the vinyl, this man's voice was going to be big and loud. He grinned, showing a gold side tooth and making his beard twitch.

'That is no way for a king to treat one of his loyal subjects,' the man said as he cocked his head to the side.

I got my breath back and moved towards the bunk. I flopped down on to it.

'You ranked tonight, man. You won the clash hands down,' my new cellmate said as he picked himself up and moved towards me.

I was grateful for the praise, but I didn't want no chatter-chatter, I just wanted out. He sat down beside me and said, 'Slave name is Stanford, but all man just name-check me as Houdini.'

That intrigued me so I asked, 'Why the brothers call you that?'

'Because I and I always just disappear, like a puff of ganja, when the police come knocking at the door.'

I listened to him say 'I and I' and knew that my man Houdini was a fully fledged member of the Rasta community. The dreads' distinctive way of living came with its own distinctive language, which to my ears seemed to be a whole string of I words. I mean, check this, they never pointed to themselves and said 'I', it was always 'I and I' or 'I-man'. Anything that was pure and natural was 'Ital'. When everything was cool and bouncy they said tings were 'Irie'. Even though I was no dread, I used their words too. We all did. Maybe it was our way of developing a language against Babylon. A language of resistance.

Anyway, I certainly wasn't feeling irie as I looked back at Houdini and said, 'Well, it looks like from tomorrow they'll have to find you a new name.'

'Even the great Houdini himself cock it up every now and then.'

He shuffled his backside forward, pulling part of the blanket away from me. He bent over and pulled off one of his shoes. I looked at them. Nodded at his style. Funked-out tiger-print platform heels. He reached inside and pulled out a packet of Marlboro. He twisted to the side, did his shuffling motion again and pulled a lighter from his other shoe. He pulled out a fag and offered me one. I took it. I didn't smoke – well, not tobacco – but figured it would make the time go. As I took the cigarette I asked, 'They searched me all over so how come they never find these on you?'

'They just gave me a light touch. The Babylon were in a hurry, you know, just in case they missed last orders at the pub.'

I smiled at his joke, but knew it couldn't be true because the light coming through the window testified to it being anywhere after two in the morning. I smoked that fag like it was my best friend. The nerves inside me made the smoke leave my mouth in a shaky pattern.

'Don't worry, man. No shame in being a virgin,' Houdini said as he shuffled closer to me.

'A what?'

'Every black youth has to know that they will have to enter the house of Babylon one day.'

He was right. The police used the suspicion law or sus, as we called it, to stop and search anyone they thought was suspicious. Well, as far as the Babylon were concerned, every black man who walked the street was suspicious, so they pulled us in left, right and centre. It was happening to all of us. When it rains it rains on all of our roofs, you check me?

Houdini eased down to lie flat on his back on the bunk. I followed him and rested beside him. I stared at the ceiling. In the middle were some graffiti someone had written (how they got up there God alone knows). *The Abomination* was printed in large red pen. We both soaked into our cigarettes. I shut my eyes. Then this funny ting happened. I started to feel like we were two friends lying in the seductive sands on Maracas beach in Port of Spain in Trinidad. Instead of the peeling ceiling I saw the mellowest sky. Instead of the words *The Abomination* I saw the peaceful sun. The Mighty Sparrow's – that's the King of Calypso, Bernie, if you don't know – voice belted out 'The Congo Man'. That was my father's best tune.

I relaxed farther into the baking sand.

'So which part of London you hail from?' Houdini asked, his words floating up with the smoke into the sky. I didn't want to talk. I just wanted to savour the cool sea that my feet tipped into. But I wanted the time to go by, so I answered him.

I was born in 1954 and grew up in Notting Hill, or North Kensington, as it was name-checked back then. West London was the place where the Trinidadian and Grenadian communities decided to settle where they came to England. I lived with my mother and sister in a room in a large house. The house on the right side was used for Sunday service and the house on the left was a brothel. Well, it must have been either that or there were all-night domino sessions going on. My father, who lived in Shepherd's Bush, was a well known calypso singer that everyone name-checked as Demon. Demon because he could make people dance until their feet dropped off and his real name was Nicodemus. Demon lived for two things in life – music and women, in that order. The first jam he took me to was a basement shabeen, called the Sugar Apple. The woman Demon lived with – Charmaine – said it was no place for an eleven-year-old, full of bad people and loose women. Fancy telling that to an eleven-year-old. Man, I was sitting pretty in my party clothes long before Demon finished shaving. And that's how my education started. I soon began to visit the record shops on the All Saints Road on my way home from school. Mummy didn't like that.

'Them people down there is no good,' she would yell at me. I knew what she meant. Prostitutes, pimps, drugs. But there was a community as well. And the community I was interested in was the musicians. I started liming with a group of lads who wanted to set up their own sound system. We didn't have any cash, so we saved hard. Did part-time work after school. We use to jam under the Westway, the flyover near where I lived. When I was fifteen and Demon was getting ready to leave this world he said one thing to me: 'Remember that music isn't a living, living is music.' From that moment on that's how I lived my life.

'And that's how I'm going to bring up my little boy Jeremiah. He don't live with me, but I'm going to make sure he learns the true way of life.'

When I finished Houdini turned to me like he wanted another bedtime story.

'Your sound system hire yourself out to big boys only or you deal with us smaller people?' he asked.

'We take the music to whoever wants to lace the bass.'

He smiled at that. Yeah, I was starting to like this brother.

'You free this Saturday evening?'

'Who's asking?'

'Community group I know are holding a function to celebrate one year of being on this earth and need someone to dread up the festivities.'

'Where are this group holding up?'

He told me the address, which was between two of the big roads that ran through Hackney – Queensbridge and Kingsland.

'I'll need to check back with the boys, but let's put a provisional in.'

'Come down and check us tomorrow and see if we're the type of place you want to rest your houses of joy.'

As I started to answer a key rattled in the door. We both shot up. I looked around for the bucket. The cell door was pushed back. A policeman entered with a face as cold as a dog's nose.

'Right, you and you, up and out, your brief's here.'

I left that cell quick time. As we entered the reception I saw an older white man in a large black coat hustling the same young woman who'd been shooting her mouth at the police at the club towards the exit door. The man looked like someone had spun the wrong tune on his radiogram.

'How many times do I have to tell you not to be in this part of the city, much less be seen in one of those places,' the man said as he dragged her closer to the exit.

'OK, Daddy, I won't go to one of those dances again.'

Her voice faded as I checked the man at the front desk. He was black and looked more like he was ready to sit down at a dinner party than stand up in some Hackney police station. He was a stranger to me, but obviously not to Houdini, who hailed out, 'Mr lawyer, man, I have to thank you for coming.'

The lawyer shook Houdini's hand and then stretched his out to mine.

'Good to meet you, Mr Stir It Up.'

'Name's Isaiah Scantleberry.'

'Mr Scantleberry, good to meet you. My name is Kwesi Abjani and I will be acting on your behalf.'

'But I don't have . . .'

'No worries, man, no worries, runnings is cool,' Houdini's voice smoothed from behind me like he was rubbing my back.

The sergeant placed our belongings on the desk as he said, 'Boys, no charges will be pending. Just keep your noses clean in the future.'

'Thanks,' I said to the lawyer and Houdini.

We left the police station and entered the early February morning air.

'Gentlemen, I will take my leave of you,' the lawyer said, and walked away.

'How did you get me a lawyer?' I asked as I hunched my shoulders, trying to keep warm.

'Told you my name was Houdini. Couldn't leave the King inside someone else's castle.'

A big grin splashed over my face.

'Thanks, man.'

I put out my hand and touched skin with his hand. We started to walk down the lonely London street together. Houdini did that bump-and-walk move that some of the brothers favoured, which was an upward side twist of one buttock and then a stride. So Houdini was a man who liked everyone to know his style.

'So how did you manage to get a lawyer here so quickly?'

'The Liberation Republic, of course.'

'The what?'

Doing the rounds of London with our sound system I usually heard about all the dips and holes in London. But I never heard of no Liberation Republic.

'The Liberation Republic is the community group I was telling you about. You did say you'd check us tomorrow.'

I nodded. So said, so done. The opportunity for more work was always good. Wasn't it?

So the next day I fixed myself up for my visit to the Liberation Republic. My yard was a one-room in a house off Stoke Newington Green in Hackney. The house behaved like it was the bad man of the street – big and scary. A house that did what it wanted. Check this out – one night I'm sleeping in my bed when I hear a loud crash from above. Had a girl with me. The girl started shaking me, telling me to get up and investigate. Investigate at three in the morning? I turned to the girl and asked her if she thought she was stepping out with Shaft? I just threw the blanket back over our heads. Next day it turned out that part of the roof had collapsed. No one ever turned up to repair it. The landlord never turned up to do shit, so we never gave him shit. Only ever paid for electricity and gas.

I stood in front of my full-length mirror putting my threads on as I bubbled with the distorted, electric-guitar madness screaming from the Isley Brothers' 'Summer Breeze' playing on my radiogram. Man, that tune was raucous. I was decked out in a pair of black bell-bottoms or trumpet trousers as I liked to name-check them, because after they left your knees they flared the same way a trumpet does. I fastened the second button from the top on my red silk shirt that I bought in Kensington Market.

Although I was slipping into some of my best rigs let me be upfront and honest – I resented leaving the paraffin warmth of my yard to go somewhere called the Liberation Republic, or, to give it its official title, the Organisation of Black Communities.

Organisation? Don't make me laugh. Like black people could ever organise anything. I know that should be Whitey's line, but truth is truth. Black people in this country had a problem keeping any organisation going. Sure, there were some great ones, like the Claudia Jones organisation that you knew would still be there when your head was sprouting grey hair. But I had taken my good intentions to too many of these community shuffles to have much faith in them. Memories of meetings where spirits were high in the morning, people are making noise and marching in the afternoon, partying with victory in the night and come morning light all man have split to do their own ting or decided commitment's just too big a load. The day black people get their shit organised is the day the National Front carve up the streets of Hoxton, waving their Union Jacks with James Brown-style drops and spins, singing 'Say it loud, I'm black and I'm proud'.

But the opportunity to spread our reputation with a new posse was a chance we couldn't miss, so I straightened my shirt, fixed my lips, as the final guitar chord did a whirl, a back flip and screamed one last time in the room.

A bang at the door made me turn around. I smiled. It could only be one person – my boy, Sean.

'Sean, what's happening, man?' I asked as I opened the door for him to come inside.

He stretched out his hand to mine and we touched skin. When you first looked at Sean all you saw was your typical seventeen-year-old white kid. He was always decked in the latest fashion, shoulder-length blond hair, height that said he was going to be a six-foot-plus man. But cast your eye over him twice and you saw a chin that was down and knew that in a few years time his shoulders would follow. I kissed my teeth when I saw the purple bruise under his eye. His father was back. I hated to see Sean hunched over like that. You wouldn't believe it but when a smile stretched that boy's eyes they could light up your world.

Sean eased up into my life long before I ever saw him. The first night I moved into my room I soon got to know Sean and his people a bit too well. Man, that night all I could hear were

licks passing, fist on flesh, hard, solid, for a good five minutes.
I had to cock my hands over my ears to escape the boy's tiny
cries and the man's grunts of 'you fucking ponce', 'you little poof'.
Man, them English people could curse. That went on, on and off,
for about a month. Then it stopped, just like that. My ears picked
up from the other neighbours that the man always left, either
doing bird in prison or to put his jack boots under some other
woman's bed. Then he'd be back. Some nights, when me and the
boys were drinking stouts and slamming bones, I couldn't tell the
B-line coming from the vinyl from the man's bully-boy fists next
door. The woman of the house I sometimes heard. Always knocking
into things and stumbling around. Reminded me of one of my
uncles who couldn't pass a day without kissing at least two bottles
of throat-breaking white rum. He drank but he didn't get that irie
high from it no more, you check me? I think it was the same
with her next door.

The first time I actually saw Sean he was sitting on the steps
that led to the main door. I had been enjoying a soak in my
scratched bath when all of a sudden the electricity cut off. No
electricity, no hot water. I kissed my teeth because I had to get
out of the bath and go downstairs to put 50p into the meter near
the house's front door. With my bath towel wrapped around my
unmentionables, I passed Sean's slouched figure on the bare
wooden steps. As I fumbled to put the coin into the meter all of
a sudden he shouts at me, 'Mister, do you want me to show you
the 50p trick?'

I looked up at the same time as the light, coming from the
panel of glass above the front door, touched his blue eyes and
lit up the two bruises evenly spaced under each eye. I will admit
I caught my breath. The same hands that had boxed him up felt
like they were doing the same to my belly. He didn't look like
no teenager, he favoured them boys in the playground who have
no friends. And if I'm upfront and truthful I didn't want to be
his friend either. I was a carefree musician and didn't need any
trouble. Just one look at him told me that there was a bellyful
of trouble brewing in his guts. But I thought of my son Jerry

asking questions as he grew older and people turning their back on him – no sir, I wouldn't like that. So out of respect to my son's future education I answered the boy.

'What trick?' I asked suspiciously, but kept my tone light like I was talking to a five-year-old.

He flew down the stairs like I was giving him back his life. I took a mini-step back, just so he understood that me and him weren't getting into no lifetime commitment ting. I let him have the coin. He took the 50p from me with his large, long hand. The last time I'd seen hands like that was on an Indian tabla player in Trinidad. With hands like that he should have been whacking his old man back. Respect can be a real shit sometimes. He took it from me and pushed it into the slot on the meter. Instantly the electric lighting from my room paved the upstairs landing. He grinned mischievously. I raised my eyebrow because I ain't seen any magic yet. He turned back to the meter and then thumped it with his palm. The 50p popped back into the money slot with quick silver cheekiness, like it was saying, 'It's show time again, Daddy-O.' The boy pulled it from the slot and handed it back to me.

'Great trick, ain't it. Electricity for life for one fifty p. This coin will become your best mate.'

He was right. Me and that coin got real tight, but nowhere near the closeness that Sean and I got. When he found out I was a music man, his eyes catch a fire like he'd been waiting for me all his young life. That's when he started knocking at my door and banging into my life. Since his mum's only interest was the molasses juice in front of her, I let him tag along. He would always be chatting about music – 'What's that rhythm?'; 'What's that instrument?'; 'What's that groove?' I had a companion who wanted to know more, more, more, so I decided to become his teacher. First stop in his education was a visit to 007 Shanty Town, a record shop under the arches that ran from London Fields to Mare Street. We'd rifle through LPs, extended versions and singles. Then get the owner to play a selection. Sean would have to identify the music style. He learnt double quick. He became a master at telling his roots reggae from rock steady, his madhouse funk from sweet-talkin' soul. Soon he started showing me the kind of music he really liked. He began to take me to the Roxy Club in Covent Garden where some white kids were playing this type of fast, furious, underground sound. People were name-checking it as punk. I liked the outlaw emotion of the music, but wasn't sure it was for me, but Sean certainly got an irie high on it. In the daytime he hung out with a group of white kids who fancied themselves as musicians. He played the drums with pocket money he earned from odd jobs and sang. He kept saying he was going to get a gig at the Roxy some day. I believed him.

Don't ask me why I took that hurt boy into my heart because I'm not sure I really know. Maybe I realised that he was married to music same as me. Maybe he was just keeping the spotlight blazing until my Jerry came of age. Whatever the reason he was soon accompanying me and the boys to our gigs. Maximus and Desmond didn't take it well having some white boy in the sound.

'Can't bring no white youf inna the place,' Maximus would say.

But I just dashed their worries aside with, 'How you going to explain to God and his boy, the Angel Gabriel, when your time comes, that you decide that music have a colour?'

The boys just shook their heads, but let it be.

'Did they lock you up?' Sean asked me about my stay in the Abomination as he stepped into my yard.

'You can't lock the King up,' I said, pushing out my chest.

'Wish my old man was banged up again.'

'Want me to send the Babylon around and plant some gear on him?'

His mouth quirked up at that. I moved my hand to ruffle his hair. The richness of his hair made me think about my own son at home with Marcia, my ex-girl. Marcia was threatening to go to Canada, taking my own flesh and blood with her. No way was that going to happen. No way. She could take her skinny money-grabbing self, but not my boy.

'What was it like?' he asked as we moved to sit on my single bed.

'Dirty, rough . . .' I nearly said fuckress, but I held it back. Cursing in front of a boy aged seventeen wasn't right. A musician with standards, yeah, that's a first.

'So when's our next gig?'

'Wednesday night, over at the Cool bar in Tottenham.'

Sean sighed with disappointment. He had this eagerness to do it every night, every hour, every minute. I understood. We were young. Didn't want to rest. Wanted to go on until someone pulled the plug.

'Got any plans today?' I asked.

'Nothing much. Just going to the Wine House to fill up mum's supply of sauce.'

'Fancy a trip?'

'Where we going?'

'Not far. Down the road to a new kingdom called the Liberation Republic.'

The address I'd been given – 16 Cecil Rhodes Square – was only a twenty-minute stride from our place, so me and Sean took our sweet time and walked through Hackney. We passed through the bustle, smells and shouts of Ridley Road market and picked up a bag of herbs along the way. Passed tower blocks that were built before anyone realised the only way a coffin could fit in the lift was to put it standing upright. Passed three-storey houses that looked like villas sunbathing in the Italian sunshine. On the surface Hackney looked battered, but underneath it was one of the warmest places I knew. Other parts of London blew hot and cold, but in Hackney there was always something going on. It was a musician's paradise. People wanted your music to uplift their souls. Man, after hearing us you couldn't help but walk tall again.

We passed a new tower block that was being built – people said it was going to be called Parkview – and entered Cecil Rhodes Square. The place looked like World War II had finished just before the crack of dawn. Some houses were lived in and others were abandoned. Some were boarded up with their own floorboards and had LEBOFF scrawled on the front door in thick black ink, which meant the London Electricity Board had disconnected the electricity. One house had no roof and the only thing keeping the brickwork together was quick-drying hope. As we strolled on, a wonderful Muddy Waters-style blues riff from Marc Bolan's 'Get It On' licked from an upstairs window of a house that had a 'PROPERTY IS THEFT' sign standing lopsided against its bottom step. A classic squatters' dwelling. There were a few on the street I lived on.

'Do you think it's that house?' Sean asked, pointing.

I followed the direction of his finger. The house was big, brash. It was tilted so high in its four-storey pride that I wasn't even sure it was touching the ground. It watched us with large jutting windows that were underneath all this funky and fancy patterned plaster held together by the brickwork. I pushed the black metal gate and my trumpet trousers blasted in the breeze as we climbed up the chipped stone steps. From the street the house might be parading itself as the funkiest dread in the neighbourhood, but up close it was still slogging it out with nature in round ten. The crumbling brickwork, the green mould stains near the leaking pipes and the black speckled fungal damp. We reached the red door. The knocker was shaped into a fist. A black fist. Shining with gloss, as smooth as the purest rum. Nice touch. I liked that. I was tempted to touch my closed fist to it, you know, one brother to another. Instead I gripped it, pulled it back and let it fall.

The same time I heard another bang. It came from underneath us. I peered over and saw a brother, not as tall as me, but big, coming out of the side door of the basement floor. A woman followed him. She had her back to me, wore a hat so I couldn't catch her face. She put her hand out and grasped the man's arm. I'm sure it was a white hand. That surprised me because I didn't think brothers who came to a joint like this would be playing tricks with no white chicks. The sound of footsteps inside the house drew me back to the main door. The footsteps sounded dainty and small like a child's eager to play outside. The door opened.

Well, kiss my sweet black rah-rah.

One of the most delicious sisters I had ever had the pleasure of ingesting my eyes over opened the door. She was pure bouncy, bouncy, you check me – a bit on top and even more below. Her face pulled back into a smile that would change the atmosphere of the whole square if she stood in the middle of it.

'Who you looking for?' she asked. Even her voice was sweet.

I let one of my flirty, flirty smile take over my face.

'We're here to check Houdini.'

Her gaze dipped low, slow enough for her brown-sugar eyes to caramelise over me. Brother, what a feeling. She eased the door back. As Sean moved to my side, the smile jumped clean off her face. The idiot that I sometimes am, I didn't spot what the problem was. I soon found out when she let us inside.

The house weren't in good shape, but that weren't no big surprise considering it was Hackney. The air was musky and damp, the flowered wallpaper was faded and peeling, the staircase looked like it should have been condemned years ago and the red and black diamond floor tiles plain hurt my eyes. But you know what, I felt like I was strolling into the first day of summer. That house just drew me in. Natural light flew in from windows and opened doors. Fresh chatter dived and rose in a blend of rhythms. And children's laughter. Nothing like children bubbling away to make you think the world's gonna be all right.

The woman turned around and said, 'I think Houdini's in the Sweet and Dandy.'

She pointed to the room, although it looked more like an extension to me, facing us at the end of the hall. As we got nearer I heard music, talking and banging. The Sweet and Dandy restaurant was five plain tables and mismatched chairs on top of a scratched wooden floor, a makeshift counter with a radio throbbing on it and boxes stacked in two corners. But the smells kissing my nostrils and taste buds made me understand why it was name-checking itself as something grander than it was. I inhaled, real strong.

The tune on the radio changed to the brooding, synthesised introduction of Stevie Wonder's urban parable 'Living For The

City'. Every eye in the place looked up to stare at us. The stares shifted and pinned to Sean, hot and hostile. Man, suddenly that room felt tight and ugly.

Well, kiss my sweet black rah-rah.

You'd think I was back in a cell at Unity Road police station with a gangload of Babylon lined up ready to beat my skin up. I found Houdini. He sat at a far table playing dominoes. He looked like he was ready to punch me up too. He bolted from his chair with the energy of a warrior ready for what the world's going to give. He skinned his teeth at me, a smile that was no smile at all. He called out, 'Must be a great day when the King can join us.'

He walked over to us, but wasn't watching me. His eyes carved into Sean.

'Let's take a walk.'

He didn't wait for us, but moved into the hall. He stopped near the front door, his hand on the handle. Looked like he was ready to go somewhere.

'King, make me and you have a word.'

I smiled at Sean and moved towards Houdini. He cocked his head to the side, like he had never seen me before.

'What's with the zamo?' he asked, the balls of his feet lifting with each word.

'The what?'

'The zamo, man.' He flicked his head and tam towards Sean. 'The white boy.'

Suddenly I understood why he was calling Sean a zamo. Zamo was the name of a popular brand of bleach. So that's why the smile catapulted from the woman who'd opened the door.

'That's just my spar Sean.'

'Spar?' The word wrung from his mouth like a rotten batch of ganja grazing the enamel on his teeth.

'Yes, spar.'

'King, you must be dead, because there is no such ting as a white friend. A white devil, a white Satan, yes, but a white spar? Never.'

'I don't want no fussing and fighting, so if it's going to become one big callaloo, I will take me and my little devil and peacefully leave the Republic.'

His lips moved in a little smile at my use of his own insult, but he stood his ground.

'No, man. Just tell the zamo to go about his business and go away. This is the Liberation Republic. The place that bredren and sistren come to get away from the stress of Babylon. The rule is no white people, you understand?'

He pointed to a large poster stuck on the walls above our heads. It read 'The Liberation Republic Manifesto'. Point number one said, 'Africans only.' You know what, when I thought of Sean I didn't see white, all I saw was the memory of purple bruises underneath hunched blue eyes.

I remembered the white woman I thought I'd seen outside, so I asked him, 'So, if all white people are born in hell, how come I saw some brother outside with a white woman with her pale hands all over him?'

It'd been a long time since I'd seen anyone's face run with shock the way his did. Quick time, he settled his features back into their customary merry-making pose.

'You must be mistaken because there's no white women here. Everyone here is one of us.'

'Same way Sean is one of us. Me and the boys. Our music machine.'

He rubbed his beard with forefinger and thumb.

'OK, man. Just remember that I and I don't deal with no white people, you understand?'

I nodded. As I always kept Sean close to me that wouldn't be a problem.

Houdini rubbed his hands together and grabbed my arm.

'Let me show you what happens in the Republic.'

His hot feet back in gear, he took me – ignored Sean, who trailed after us – on a tour of the house. The tour was twenty minutes of rooms that dedicated themselves to what Houdini called 'black self-reliance and pride'. The two reception rooms on the ground floor were used as a supplementary school that specialised in ensuring that the next generation knew their three Rs inside out and everything about the greatness of Africa. The first floor doubled up as a centre that helped people fill in job applications and interviews and gave free legal advice. The top floor was disused, with a mashed-up bathroom, and two rooms where much of the plasterwork on the ceiling had fallen and just been left on the floor. As we moved back to the Sweet and Dandy restaurant, I noticed that the basement floor was shut off by a padlocked door. I asked him what was through there. He squinted his eyes and rasped, 'Nothing, man, nothing.'

Well, every man is entitled to their hush-hush moments so I left it alone.

'Winnie, meet King Stir It Up,' he called to the woman bent behind the counter.

When she lifted her head I saw that it was the sister who'd let us in.

'So what can I tempt a king with today?' she asked when she reached our table.

'Sean?'

His eyes scanned the menu board.

'What's Guinness punch?' he asked.

'A liquid that will take you to heaven and back,' she replied, smiling at him.

'Three punches for me and my spar,' Houdini said, bracing out his chest.

I noticed he left the 's' off spar, but the three told me he had included Sean in the order.

'So how did you get the house?' I asked.

'When the Babylon started to pull their nasty dread moves on us on the street, we knew we needed somewhere that the community could go for legal advice. We knew a couple of lawyers who would do it for free, like my man Kwesi, who bailed us out of the Abomination. Now Hackney is full of empty houses, so we just took possession of the place.'

'What about the landlord?'

'What landlord? The whole of the square is under a CPO . . .'

'A what?'

'Compulsory purchase order. The council want to flatten the square to make way for three tower blocks. So the place ain't worth nothing to nobody, so no one ever turned up looking for rent. On Saturday we are having a celebration to mark one year of the Republic's life and we wanted some music. But not any old ting, we wanted a rebel sound to show who we are. Only one man has the voice we're looking for and that's the King.'

I didn't say yes, I didn't say no. Just let it mellow in my mind. I looked over at Sean. He nodded his head. I turned back to Houdini.

'OK, man, we'll give you a rebel sound you'll never forget,' I promised.

Houdini and I touched skin. So said, so done. Houdini smiled, head thrown back, gold tooth twinkling. At that moment I swear, as God is my witness, the house whispered, 'Come here, man,' and invited me into its embrace that was strong and true. Being a man who adored public displays of affection I lapped it up. But being a man of the world I should have realised, right then, that even the most tender embrace can become an everlasting suffocation.

So a week later, on a fresh-eyed Saturday evening, at the start of March, me and the boys took our new houses of joy to the Liberation Republic. We weren't going to be on until around eight, but we got there for six, enough time to set up and partake of some of the celebrations.

Houdini and a few men helped us unload our van and took us up the front stairs. We set up in the first two rooms on the ground floor. Like the shutters on the window, the white door that divided the two rooms was folded back. In the middle of the room were rows of chairs, enough to seat forty people. A group of four women laid food and drinks on a table in front of the fancy fireplace. All Caribbean gatherings have two things – always food, always music. And I'm not chatting about no soggy cucumber sandwiches. I mean real food. You know, saltfish and plantain frittering and frying up the air, Guinness and rum punches spicing the very soles of feet. Maybe we just learned long ago that having a beat of flavours and the fragrance of music was the best way to forget your troubles.

We decided to set up at the back of the room. As we got our equipment ready, the floorboards bounced as people started to arrive. The people arriving were some serious brothers and sisters. One look at the revolutionary threads they were hijacking told you they took their role in the Black Consciousness movement seriously. Some bowed down to Mother Africa through their dashiki tops and head wraps that were soaked in the colours of red, gold and green. Others paid homage to the Black Panthers through their slimline trousers and waist-length leather sporting jackets. Every head in that room was crowned with a type of natural – some small, others big like they were saying the day for black world domination was coming soon, man, coming soon.

While Maximus and Desmond set up the decks, me and Sean put out the houses of joy. Now there were three ways we could place them – each one on its own in a corner of the room so that the pulse took all sides, two side by side or two stacked on to each other. This was a dread celebration so we decided to go tall and stack two on to each other. After pushing the last speaker into place, I wiped the sweat from my face and looked at the other end of the room. There was a long table underneath the large bay window. On the front of the table hung two posters. One was a plain white paper that had 'Black Power' painted on it in black ink. The other was a picture of Malcolm X. One chair was positioned behind the table. About an hour later the crowd began to drift to their seats. The audience sat straight. They kept their eyes on the table like they were at a picture show. Something was ready to happen in that room. It was like they were getting ready for a bass line to drop. Me and Sean moved over to the food table. I took hold of a saltfish fritter. As I bit into it a voice boomed from the hall outside, 'It's been four hundred years.'

The crowd twisted sideways to stare at the entrance to the

room. I realised the B-line had dropped. I pulled the fritter out of my mouth.

'You heard right, brothers and sisters, four hundred years.'

We still could not see who it was. The door pushed forward. The crowd strained their necks up.

Well, kiss my sweet black rah-rah.

The man that I thought I had seen with the white woman on my first visit to the Republic came in the room. He was large, compact and showcased a TWA, (teeny-weeny Afro). He wore a classic Black Panther look – leather coat, pullover, but no beret. His cinnamon dark brown face was cut short, a little bit chubby with a lived-in beard and moustache. A man who obviously liked a big plate of rice, peas and chicken on a Sunday afternoon. The fritter fell back with my hand as I felt the power of a war drum coming in the room. His eyes swept the crowd. He lifted his foot the same time he spoke. Man, his voice was something else. Beautiful, quiet like a spring of cool water, but with the power to create a flash flood of change.

'Four.'

He stamped his foot in a long stride forward.

'Hundred.'

He took a second step.

'Years.'

His third step beat on the ground, creating a tempo that pulled the skin of the tension in the room.

'Four hundred years.'

Those three words whizzed around the room in a single stroke of sound. Man, I never heard a ring shot like it before in my life. The saltfish fritter slid from my hand on to the table. It took him three steps to reach the table. He took two steps to face the crowd. He shuffled his feet apart. He shook his shoulders. He surveyed his people. He stared at them with you-better-listen-up eyes. He raised his hand, palm down, towards the audience and restarted his oration.

'Four hundred years is a long time. So don't berate yourself for being tired. Don't berate yourself for not getting the qualifications that you want. Don't berate yourself for having to shelter your family in one room ...'

I leaned forward.

'Four hundred years of slamming you down. Four hundred years of telling you your nose and hair is ugly. Four hundred years of letting you look in the pot but not taste the curry.'

That got a murmur. Can't put food in front of black people and tell them not to touch it.

'Alabama. South Africa. Mozambique. Angola. Rhodesia. Yes, people, we are tired.'

There was a collective murmur of approval from the crowd.

'As if four hundred razor-sharp years wasn't enough, where do we find ourselves now? I said, where do we find ourselves now? Where? Huh, in the blue-eyed jaw of Babylon. When I was young' – his voice dipped to a whisper like he was reading to me while my head lay softly against a pillow – 'my grandma would tell me all about Babylon, but I didn't listen to her. Babylon was a place in the Bible. Babylon didn't exist. But one day I packed my bags, I took that ship and I landed inna Ingland. The first time my teacher ignored my raised hand in the class I knew I was in Babylon. The first time I see water come out of my auntie's eyes after the police mash up her son I knew I was in Babylon. The first time a woman told me she couldn't get a job as a dinner lady at her daughter's school because the headmistress said she didn't know what the other parents would say when they heard she had touched their children's food, I knew I was in Babylon.'

The crowd muttered angrily.

'It's time, people.

A time to let the word out.

A time for them to feel our licks.

A time for the unrecorded truth.

A time to beat the blue-dressed legitimate 666.

A time for anger.

A time for our collective cry.

A time for you to stand up.

A time to make the pigs squeal and die.

It's time, people.

Time. Time. Time.'

The audience jumped up and joined in his cry. His voice struck out above them.

'When your children are being sent to a school for the educationally subnormal, where do you come?'

'The Liberation Republic,' the audience belted out.

'When the system won't give you a job, where do you come?'

'The Liberation Republic.'

'When you want the Babylon to stop harassing you on the street, where you going to come?'

'The Liberation Republic.'

It was only after the final cry that I realised I was on my feet, sweating and shouting with everyone else.

The dancing started the same time the sun went down and the heat in the room went up. Usually at dances and blues parties we knew exactly what the crowd wanted – some currents, old-time classics and exclusives to make everyone feel good. The riff that the speaker's message had scattered earlier in the room made it hard to judge what vinyl to spin. We turned to Sean and told him to watch the crowd and make the decision.

He nodded his head and whispered, 'Hard jam and heavy.'

So that's what we did, flung out some pure roots rocker tunes, mashed with some big-time funk. The crowd took up the challenge of the solid beat, heads down, Afros glistening. I decided against any toasting as the crowd didn't need another voice milling among the turbulent voices already in their minds.

Now this will sound like I'm some kind of idiot-boy, but I could feel this drumbeat sticking up under my shoe like it was only meant for me to hear. I knew what it meant – the main dude himself was finally coming to clasp my hand. Houdini brought him over to me.

'Houdini, introduce me to our newest member,' the man who had riled the crowd with his speech said.

'King, meet the ranking man of the moment, Shakespeare.'

We touched skin. His hand gripped mine, warm and solid like he'd been my spar for years.

I didn't bat an eyelid at his name. I knew it wasn't the name given to him when the priest threw water over his head. Most black people had a home name and the one on their birth certificate. We didn't usually ask what someone's official name was because what mattered was who they were now. Only time you usually found out was when someone was getting married or buried. But I was curious about how he got his name. So I asked him.

'People say I have a way with words.'

His voice was soft. Although he put his words together official-like, his Caribbean-styled accent was strong.

'Your speech was irie, man.' I just had to praise him.

'Thank you. I don't see it as a speech, more a banner for our times.'

I caught Sean's face looking at him, dew-eyed and dopey like he was waiting for his mum to wipe his nose.

'And who's this?' Shakespeare asked, his eyes following mine to Sean.

Crap. I hope I wasn't getting into a 'no honkies allowed inna da house' speech.

'Sean.' My boy's voice came out as a squeak as Shakespeare took his hand.

'Glad to meet you, Sean.'

Looking at Sean, I understood what they meant by someone's face lighting up. Look like he had a pair of matches sizzling behind both eyes.

Shakespeare turned his wonderful self to me.

'Let me get you something to wet your mouth as a thank-you for consenting to do the music at our celebration.'

He bought me back a red label.

'So how do you like the way we stir it up in the Republic?'

I chuckled at the way he used part of my name. I didn't want to insult him, but like I said before, I weren't a man much for organisations.

'Looks like you people are doing an irie job.'

'That sounds like a man who won't commit himself.'

'Commitment is never easy for a musician.'

He laughed, full and open like he didn't care what anyone thought about him.

'So you just going to play music for the rest of your days?'

'Music's my life.'

'And what about the life of other people? Have you never thought that you could use that voice of yours to really stir it up?'

There was this slice of provocation in his breath that made me take a step back towards the wall.

'We need people like you. People with voices that others want to hear. People who are willing to take that stand on the higher ground. People who are not going to let anything knock them down.'

My back touched the wall. This man had some powerful juju juice that I knew could seduce and reduce me to what he wanted.

As I opened my mouth a shout sounded by the door. We both turned the same time as a youth, inches smaller than Sean, about sixteen, staggered into the room. As God is my witness, you should have seen this boy. Blood all over his small face, one coat sleeve torn up and who knows what happened to his left shoe. And the tears, man, the water rolling from that boy's eye. While the music kept turning everyone just froze. The boy didn't need to open his mouth to tell us what happened.

'Where's Shakespeare?' the youth cried.

Shakespeare left me and rushed to the youth.

'What happened?'

'The Babylon attacked us and now they have Rufus.'

Houdini helped the boy to a chair.

'Tell me slowly what happened,' Shakespeare said.

The boy took a large breath and then the force of the words just dashed out of his mouth like he'd been holding them as long as he'd been running.

'We were coming back from a mate's and all of a sudden a

vanload of Babylon come out of nowhere. They just push us up against a wall and said that our cigarettes were drugs. So Rufus tells them that if we are smoking herb they'll have to take it up with Benson and Hedges. They didn't like that and pulled out their sticks and started licking us in the head. Then they grab up Rufus and say that he fits the profile of someone who did a robbery that evening. We told them that we were at our friends', but they didn't believe us. Told them we could produce our friends as witnesses. They told me to piss off and bundled Rufus into their van. I didn't know what to do so I came here.'

'You did the right thing, son.' Shakespeare crouched down by the injured boy's chair. He ran his hand over the boy's face and stilled it near the cut oozing blood.

'Houdini, bring the first-aid kit.'

Our eyes met and Shakespeare nodded briskly at me. He looked at Sean and smiled. I was grateful for his quiet acceptance of Sean.

Shakespeare stood up and breathed so hard I'm sure the trees bent outside.

'Have you told your parents?' he asked the boy.

'No. I'm frightened my mum might not believe me and beat me. She just doesn't understand.'

'Don't worry, son, I'll speak with her. Don't blame her. She thinks she's protecting you.'

Houdini came bustling into the room and set about cleaning the boy's face. I could feel the anger vibrating from him. It finally burst out of him.

'Second time this week. Second time that two of our children have been attacked on the street. Can't go on much longer. Can't go on. Any time they want to stop us they do what the hell they like.'

'It's time, people.' Shakespeare looked directly at me as he shouted, 'Time to stir it up.'

He clenched his right fist over his heart. Tight. As screwed-up as the anger breathing retribution from his body.

The people were angry. The music was angry. Shakespeare

pulled me and Houdini aside and whispered, 'We can't let this go on. We have to hold an emergency Black Fist meeting now.'

'A black what?' I asked.

Shakespeare looked directly at me.

'You have to decide what the gift God has given you is really for.'

Then he turned his back on me and left. I could feel Sean looking at me. I looked at him and saw his fading bruises. Saw the blood smashed against the other boy's chin. Both beaten by those who should have protected them. That wasn't being sentimental, that was dealing with the reality of life back in 1976. I had two choices – finish our gig and forget the Republic or follow Shakespeare and Houdini.

'What's the Black Fist?' Sean asked.

'Let's go and find out.'

We followed Shakespeare and Houdini as they walked towards the padlocked door to the basement. Shakespeare pulled out a key and unlocked the padlock. Houdini and Shakespeare climbed down a set of stairs. Me and Sean followed. Each step I took I kept trying to remember that responsibility isn't a musical word. My foot hovered over the last step as the tune in the main room changed to the Trojan classic, Dandy Livingstone's 'Suzanne Beware Of The Devil'.

# TRACK 16: COVER VERSION

The tape clicked off.

LT and Bernie sat, wired, in the silence of his bedroom. They both continued to stare at the Dictaphone on the bed. The humidity was rampant in the air. Too thick to ignore, too thick to enjoy. Bernie was the first to break the silence.

'Did your father mention any of this to you?'

LT shook his head. Ran his hand over his face. His hand came away covered in a sheen of freezing sweat. Suddenly, knife-point cramps stabbed into his left calf muscle. Twisted the muscle right. He sucked in his breath. Screwed up his eyes. He swung his legs over the side of the bed and jammed back on to the pillow. The mattress moved as Bernie left the bed. He felt her kneel at his bended legs. Felt her lean close so that one of his knees touched her right shoulder. Felt her fingers massage his calf muscle with the sedative and soothing power of Dorothy Ashby's harp on Stevie Wonder's 'If It's Magic'.

'Did your father ever mention the Liberation Republic or the Black Fist?'

He opened his eyes and gazed at her bowed, blonde head.

'The King loved to tell stories. Lived his life by telling stories. But he never told tales about a house in Hackney. He always maintained official politics was a fool's game. Sure, he helped the community, but he never got any deeper than that.'

Her fingers were gentle. The pain got softer.

'We've got three names – Shakespeare, Sean and Houdini. Did the King ever mention them?'

'Everyone knows about Houdini.'

Her fingertips became light.

'How come?'

'Because he's dead.'

Her fingers stopped moving. She pitched her face up to stare at him, her question set in her eyes. He answered her.

'Stanford Fellows, or Houdini as everyone called him, was found dead at the Notting Hill carnival in 1976.'

'The carnival?'

Her fingers began moving again in a distracted, uncoordinated rhythm.

'The tension between the police and the community exploded at the carnival that year. I was still a baby, but there were all these rumours that whispered the police killed him.'

'What reason would they have had to kill him?'

'Reason?' he shot at her. 'Weren't you listening to the tape? The police didn't seem to need to justify fucking people up.'

He winced as the pain took up its twists and turns again. He gritted his teeth, but kept talking.

'From what I understand, Houdini's death made people take a stand. The Writer in Residence of Ladbroke Grove was set up in honour of him.'

'Isn't that the competition . . .'

'That I'm taking part in. The King was one of the original organisers of it, but I never realised he knew Houdini.'

'What about Shakespeare and Sean?'

He shook his head, like he had done it too many times before. He eased his leg out of her hands. Stood up. Hobbled to the window.

'Your father obviously hasn't finished telling his story, so there must be other tapes. Did he have any other domino sets?' Bernie asked as she joined him by the window.

'Yeah. Two more. One he called his 'any time, anyplace' set. Small enough for him to carry around, so he was never surprised if he found himself in a game. The other he just called Susie after the woman who gave it to him.'

'Whoever committed the burglary at his home can't have found them, if that's what they were after, because they tried to get into your place. So someone must have those domino boxes and his best jacket. Do you know who he might have left them with?'

LT rubbed his finger and thumb over his L-lettered earring as he thought.

'He kept life close to his chest. He never had a woman living with him, never had a best mate. He was everyone's friend. He was a man who put his arm around everyone's shoulder.'

'OK, let's agree that until we find out who has the other two tapes we don't tell anyone about this.'

He nodded sharply in agreement. Limped back to the bed. As he moved, the phone on the bedside table started ringing. He picked it up. Listened. He nodded his head once and put the phone down. He wiped a damp palm over his mouth.

'What is it?' she asked, moving towards him.

His body trembled as he sat down on the edge of the bed.

'What's the matter?'

His eyes brimmed with tiredness as he said, 'That was the coroner's office. There ain't going to be an inquest.'

'What did they say?'

'That the King died of natural causes. Well, that's the end of that,' he said wearily. 'Now I just want to bury my dad and move on. They said they are going to release the body, so I can go ahead with the funeral as soon as possible.'

'Do you really believe that he died of natural causes?' Her words marched angrily over him. 'And even if he did, don't you owe it to him to find out why he died in a place he hated? Why his body was found under a pile of black rubbish bags? Why he felt he had to leave you secret tapes to tell you about whatever happened in 1976? To find out who he met on the day he died?'

'You know what they say's the difference between a violinist and a dog?' he shot at her. 'A dog knows when to stop scratching.'

Bernie's heavy sigh bounced in the room. She sat down heavily beside him. Her arm brushed his shirt. He so wanted her to put her arm around his shoulders so he could melt into the comfort of her beautiful violinist's fingers on his skin.

Her arm didn't move, but her mouth did. 'If you're going to challenge the findings of the coroner's office you're going to need to get a solicitor.'

'Solicitors like their milk and honey and my cupboard's bare.'

'Don't worry about the money, we'll work it out. The top of our priority list is to find out what happened to your father, which means we are going to do everything and anything to discover the truth. I know you're tired but we're going to need to hit the streets right now, asking questions and finding out what happened.'

He looked back at the phone.

'Hackney's a big place,' he finally said.

'Where your father died isn't.'

A rush of tepid evening air pushed inside Joe's Café as Bernie and LT came through its door. LT was nervous. He hadn't been to Hoxton since he was eight years old. Hadn't been since he found himself praying for his life inside the doomed darkness of a skip. The café was on the side of Hoxton that hadn't been gentrified, near the Estates. The side that multiplied his memories of running through the night.

He shrugged his right shoulder, throwing off the bad times as he swept his eyes around the café. No punters inside, just a woman behind the counter. They moved towards her. She was about Bernie's height and age, with cropped, spiky, tar-black hair and skin kept smooth by the daily beauty treatment from the steam puffing from the urn beside her. Her lips were sewn together into a hard line, just in case customers took her for a pushover.

'We're about to shut,' she told them. The bite and belt of her voice marked her as a woman who kept people at a distance.

'What do you remember about an old man who was found dead in Gazoo Lane yesterday?' LT asked.

She rested her hand next to the saucer with 'Tips' written in red ink on it.

'He weren't that old. He could give you a run for your money.'

'But how was he behaving?'

'A bit jumpy, but who ain't around here?' Her hand touched the edge of the tips saucer. 'He sort of leaped up and left after looking at the telly.'

'What was on the telly?'

The woman shuffled her neck forward. Looked LT over.

'You're Lord Tribulation.' Her tone was flat. Not a fan. 'The dead guy was listening to that minister lady slag you off. You look like him. You his boy?'

'Can you remember anything else?' LT asked, knowing she already had the answer to her question.

'Yeah.' Her hand retreated from the tips saucer. 'He didn't pay his bill. Two pound fifty plus ten per cent.'

LT took the hint and put the money into the saucer. Then they left.

LT and Bernie stood in the east-side corner of Hoxton Square. The square teemed with people, sitting outside, drinking their last shot of the August evening air.

'Let's hope that people are a bit more friendly and forthcoming than the woman in the café,' Bernie began, her hands jammed in her jacket pockets. 'I'll check this side and the north side and you check over there and the south side.'

Concern and uncertainty deepened the shadows of her eyes as she looked at LT. He lifted his eyebrow at her and said, 'Are my boxers around my ankles, or something?'

'Look.' Her voice was soft. 'I know this isn't easy for you being back here, but we need to find out what people saw.'

LT gazed at the green in the middle of the square. The memories came back. So did the pain. A tiny cramp flickered across his calf muscle. Then left him. He straightened his back. Straightened his shoulders and said, 'Let's do what we've got to do, but don't ever ask me to come back here again.'

They moved at the same time, in opposite directions, searching for the truth. LT wasn't hopeful. He knew that the majority of the people would tell him that they hadn't seen anything. That was a basic by-law of the street, especially where death and violence were concerned. 'Never complain, never explain', that was the East End motto, and although Hoxton had pushed itself up in the world, LT suspected it would be no different. Ten minutes later the eagerness of his movements began to drag as no information was passed his way. He took a breath as he watched Bernie come out of Martha's 'eat all you can for £7.95' vegan restaurant. The wind picked up, making Bernie's chest bow forward, like her violin was strapped to her back. She stood with the same defiant elegance she wore the first time he had seen her in the school canteen. She made him feel so horny, back then. And now. Who would have thought that sex and death would make for such an intense coupling? As he started turning to resume his search he saw her hand plunge into the side pocket of her rucksack. She yanked out her mobile. Held it to her face. From the churning movement of her lips he knew she wasn't happy. The call was quick. Over in tens seconds. She dropped the phone back into her bag. Leaned against the café window. Ran a finger in a circle under her collarbone. Took short breaths as she closed her eyes.

'You all right?' he called out.

Her eyes popped open as she heard him. She pulled her back off the window. She didn't meet his eyes as she nodded. Pushed her bag securely on her shoulder and briskly moved on. LT set his face forward and continued with his search. Five minutes later, dizzy from watching everyone he spoke to shake their heads at him, he stood outside the last building on the west side of the square. Demetri's Cabs, which backed on to Gazoo Lane. It was a run-down building that tried half-heartedly to keep up appearances, but as its main business was always parked on the street it did not try too hard.

'Did you find out anything?'

He looked to his side to find Bernie standing next to him. He shook his head.

'I didn't find out anything either.' Her voice was deflated. Tired.

'Who was that giving you aggro on the phone?' he asked.

'Nobody.'

Her eyelids fluttered down, half covering her eyes. That made him curious because he knew she always looked life straight in the face.

'Boyfriend?'

Her eyelids slowly folded back up as she sniffed and shuffled her index finger under her nose.

'So that was your dealer, was it?'

She ignored his remark, set her face like she didn't appreciate anyone taking free rides on her back and said, 'If anyone saw anything it would be in here as it backs on to Gazoo Lane, where your father died.'

They walked inside. The interior looked a bit better than outside but not much. Worn, washed-out blue lino and peeling pastel-green painted walls. Two brown plastic chairs were left for customers to sit to the right of the rough wooden counter. The place was empty. No one in the chairs. No one behind the counter. Suddenly a door behind the controller's counter was pulled wide. A woman came inside. Her understated beauty struck LT as soon as he saw her. Rich red hair nestled over a face that was long, slim, with skin that women in the beauty parlour next door only ever dreamed about. Her body was maybe too thin, but subtle, doing a great job of the tracksuit she wore. The only thing getting in the way of her having the full package was that nervy twitch in her nut-brown eyes.

Bernie sent him a look that said, 'I'll take care of this.' That was fine with him as he was happy to keep looking.

'We're wondering if you can help us,' Bernie said.

The woman eased towards the counter with tentative steps, like she'd learned the hard way to think before you took that next move forward.

'It will be a half-hour wait.'

She had an accent. Heavy. Sounded like the Kosovans who lived next door to LT.

'We don't want a cab. We just want to ask some questions about the body that was found in Gazoo Lane yesterday.'

The woman's body tensed. She took a step back.

'We aren't here to make any trouble.' Bernie's voice was gentle. She sat down in one of the chairs. Her hand slipped into her pocket.

'Please take a seat.' She continued like it was her home.

The woman reluctantly grabbed the other chair. Pulled it to the other side of the room. Sat down. She pinned her legs together. Folded her arms.

'I did some reporting from Kosovo during those bad years,' Bernie began.

The woman's scattered breathing added a fragile edge to the transient room.

'I saw what happened to the people. To the children. The women.'

The woman rubbed her long finger over her bottom lip. Back and forth.

'This man' – Bernie waved her hand in LT's direction – 'needs to find out what happened to his father.'

The woman's finger dropped from her lip as she croaked, 'I didn't see anything.'

'That's what people said in Kosovo. Then one day someone spoke out. Told the outside world.'

'I need the money from this job . . .'

'I know, to send to your family back home.'

The woman nodded, making her hair swing over her face like a curtain that wasn't sure whether to remain drawn or stay opened.

'My friend needs to send news back home to his grandmother about what happened to her son.'

LT looked sharply at Bernie. He'd never discussed his grandmother with her.

'Tell me what you saw,' Bernie carried on in her coaxing tone.

Silence fell in the room like it was nobody's friend. The woman ran her tongue over her bottom lip. Then the top. She pulled her tongue back inside. She looked at Bernie. Shifted her brown eyes. Pinned them hard on to LT, like she was trying to find out what type of man he was. Finally she pushed her hair out of her face and started speaking.

'Someone tell me that your father was a musician, is this right?'

LT nodded his head once. A small smile fluttered against her lips.

'Before I came to this country I use to play the piano.' She clipped her words off as if she had said too much.

LT returned her smile and said, 'I can tell by your fingers you were good. I'm a singer and my friend plays the violin. I'm Jerry and my friend is Bernie. What's your name?'

The woman ran fretful eyes over him, but she gave them her name. 'Jane. Jane Blake.'

'All we want to do, Jane, is find out why my dad isn't going to be singing any more.'

The woman looked down at her fingers, nervously arching in her lap. She slowly raised her head and said, 'I was upstairs at the window. I see a man. I see a big car. The man, he move to side to let car go by. I did not see more. I close curtains.'

'Thank you.' Bernie edged slightly out of the chair. 'Would you be willing to make a statement?'

The woman shot up. The chair rocked back on its legs. She began to pace, shaking her head. Bernie got up, slowly and calmly walked over to her. The woman turned her back.

The woman's body shook as she cried, 'I can't. My papers aren't even my own.'

'If you do this, this man can bury his father in peace. Just like you were finally able to bury your people in peace.'

The woman wrapped her arms around her stomach as she continued to shake her head.

'All I want you to do is to think about it,' Bernie continued. 'We're not going to tell Immigration about you or involve the police. We just need to know that if my friend's solicitor contacts you, you might be able to speak to him.'

The room filled with an uncomfortable silence. The woman kept her back to them, her shoulders shaking to the beat of her quick breathing. Finally the woman spoke but didn't turn around.

'If he calls I might not be able to tell him anything.'

'If that's what you decide to do that's what you decide to do. But I don't know what my friend is going to tell his grandmother when she comes over to bury her son.'

Bernie moved towards LT. When she reached him she whispered, 'Let's go.'

'But . . .'

'Come on.'

As Bernie opened the door, LT moved to the counter and picked up one of the cab's business cards. He placed it in his pocket as he followed Bernie. As he reached the door he glanced back at the woman. She remained with her back to them.

When they got outside LT started walking.

'Where are you going?' Bernie asked.

He didn't answer her. Just kept walking. He turned the corner. On to Gazoo Lane where he now realised the King might not have been alone when he died.

The sun did the dying moves of a one-for-the-road dance behind a cloud as Bernie stood next to LT in Gazoo Lane. The area where the King had met his death was cordoned off with red-and-white tape.

'Why didn't you pressurise her to help us?' LT asked Bernie as he looked away from the place where the King took his last painful breath.

'Two ways you can get people to help you. You either back them into a corner so they have no alternative or you leave them with guilt sitting on their shoulder. That woman's been living in a corner for such a long time we couldn't push her back in any farther. But thoughts of an old woman weeping over her musician son's grave might make her step out. If she doesn't we've always got this.'

She pulled her digital Dictaphone from her pocket. Pressed 'play'. The air filled with the stumbling voice of the witness from the cab office telling her tale.

'You were taping her?'

'We need as much help as we can get . . .'

Her voice was cut off by the roar of a car at the entrance of the lane. They both swung around. Silver-blue Benz. His manager sat in the driver's seat. Window yelled LT's name.

'Shit, this must be urgent. Window never comes looking for me. He must have got on the street grapevine to find out where I was. I'm going to have to go. Will you be OK getting back?'

'I'm a big girl now. Don't worry about me. Don't forget what we agreed – we don't tell anyone about those tapes.'

He nodded and rushed towards his manager's car.

'Window?' he asked anxiously as he dipped down to the driver's side.

'Remember those big, black clouds we talked about regarding the arson attack and your concert? There's one coming our way. Get in.'

LT jumped in the passenger's side. The car peeled down the street, past the white van that was parked outside the beauty parlour.

The man stepped out of the white van. He held back as he watched the woman with the short blonde hair reach her car. As soon as she got inside he started moving. Towards the cab office. He pushed the door. Walked inside. The woman behind the counter looked up. He reached the counter and said, 'I'm making enquiries about the incident on Gazoo Lane yesterday.'

The woman's face paled to a shattered sheen of white. He leaned over. Flattened his large hands on to the counter. Her eyes flicked nervously to his hands, as if the last time someone had put their hand on her it had not been a pleasant experience.

'I've been sent to find out if anyone here saw anything.'

He said the words insolently. Slowly. Curled his hands into fists. Her nostrils flared as she erratically sucked air into her body. Her red mask of hair tumbled over her face as she rapidly shook her head, mumbling, 'I did not see anything.'

Her words were half swallowed, caught way back in her throat. He moved his fists to the edge of the counter, one inch from her wide-open eyes. His knuckles stretched the skin on his hand as if they were the hardest material on God's earth.

The phone rang at the same time as his fists shot out. Her mouth flew open to scream. But it never came. Never made it into the room because his hands got to her throat first. His fingers locked into her flesh. Circled. Tightened. He dragged her forward until the tip of her chin scraped the top of the counter. One of his hands left her throat and swiftly twisted into her hair. He jammed her head down, squashing one side of her face on to the splintered surface of the counter. He pressed down hard at the same time as he forced out his words.

'Make sure that's what you tell anyone else who comes knocking at your two-bit door asking questions.'

He held her for three seconds more. Then he let go. Pushed his body straight. He left her gasping for breath. The phone still ringing. Her face still on the counter.

Window cut the engine of his Benz in an anonymous alley a few minutes' drive from Gazoo Lane. The shadows in his eyes were heavy as he looked at LT.

'I've moved up the worry scale, haven't I?' LT asked.

Window kept his hand on the steering wheel, as if he knew they weren't going to be staying long.

'Eyes and ears are telling me that the word rats are putting on their tap shoes ready to make a big song and dance in the press about this youth, the arson attack and your music.'

LT let his hand glide over the pocket with the record contract in it as he said, 'What kind of media show are they getting ready to stage?'

'My people couldn't give exact details, or even when, but it sounds like we're going to need some help on this.'

LT's hand stopped moving.

'What kind of help?'

'I've talked to my brief, who says if the shit comes our way there are two ways to dodge it. We can keep a low profile and say nothing. The problem with that is silence can make you look like you're hiding something under your du-rag.'

'Option two?'

One of Window's hands left the steering wheel. Switched the sat nav on.

'Find someone to advocate on your behalf. Someone the media trust, we trust. Someone who's well use to balancing themselves in both worlds.'

'You've always done right by me, Window, what do you suggest we do?'

His manager twisted the key in the ignition.

'Let's go for a ride.'

Beresford Clarke, OBE, sat in the main room of his house and listened to a cut from Steel Pulse's classic '78 debut album, *Handsworth Revolution*.

Track 6.

'Ku Klux Klan'.

The lead singer, David Hinds', wrenching and wailing vocals and the band's militant roots sound made it a killer anthem of its time. A time Beresford remembered well.

The front doorbell sounded. He threw his head back against the sofa. Sighed. Being available twenty-four-seven, as the youth called a day in your life, was the price he paid for being a high-profile figure in the black community. Not that he was complaining. But sometimes, yeah, just sometimes, he wanted to be able to kick up those rhythmic stones and play the whole of *Handsworth Revolution* with no interruptions. In all the years he'd been a community activist he hadn't been able to do that. He grabbed the music system's remote. His hand hovered over the stop button, then shifted to the pause instead and pressed down. Maybe, just maybe, whoever it was didn't need that much time. He eased up from the sofa. Left the main room. Took his time walking down the stairs to the hall on the first floor.

He activated the video screen on the security system. He peered at the faces. Both he knew. One much better than the other. He moved to the front door. Opened it. He smiled, cleansing the weariness from his brown face. He held out both his hands towards the man with a tattoo on his neck and breathed, 'Alexander.'

LT watched as Window grasped the hands of the older man. Two revelations fought for top billing in his mind. The one he finally dealt with first was that the man standing in the doorway was also the man who had defended him on the television when the Minister of Culture was denouncing his music. His teeth pinched his bottom lip as he tried to remember the man's name. Clarke. Somebody Clarke. The first name kept slipping and sliding but he couldn't capture it. He also couldn't understand how Window knew this man. His manager's name prompted the second revelation to sneak in and take up position in his mind. That Window was really an Alexander. He'd always seen him as a Wesley, or a Steadman, even maybe a Marcus, but an Alexander? No way.

'Beresford Clarke, but just call me Beresford,' the man introduced himself to LT in a well-rounded baritone.

Both his hands came out to grip LT's hand and forearm. His grip was warm and welcoming. LT thrilled at the way success clung to Beresford Clarke like an aroma that was illegal to purchase. He was a few inches shorter than LT, but the way he tilted his shaved head made him look like he was looking down on LT, not LT looking down on him. Just like his voice, his weak-tea, honey-sweetened toned face was rounded with a gold stud living it up in his left earlobe. There were no lines on his face, making him look like he was on the crest of forty, but the slight tang of bay rum that he used as an aftershave placed him more realistically in his fifties.

'Come in, gentlemen.'

They stepped into a thin four-storey house in the East End's Isle of Dogs. The house breathed the same rhythmic calm as its owner, with its pastel-coloured walls and wire-brushed oak floors. They took the first flight of stairs to the main room. The room was simple and uncluttered. Ornaments and keepsakes – pictures, wood carvings, two strong cases of books and one strong case of music, a Guyanese flag – were all staged around the edge of the room. The middle had the feel of a wide-open beach that you had all to yourself and could do anything you wanted on.

'Please take a seat,' Beresford said as he pressed the music system's remote control.

He took the high-backed wicker chair opposite them. Crossed

his right leg over his left. LT coughed nervously then said, 'I want to thank you for defending me on the telly.'

'No problem. I was sorry to hear about the King.'

'Did you know him?'

Beresford gently smiled.

'Everyone knew your father. Even saw him play with his sound system once or twice when I lived in Birmingham. A real monarch of the stage.'

Beresford shifted his eyes to Window and cocked his eyebrow as a teacher does to a naughty child.

'I can tell by the way you're pulling your cuffs down that this is business. You did that the first time I met you. Do you remember? You kept pulling down the cuffs on that uniform you wore in that borstal in Birmingham. You and that boy you were sharing a cell with. What was his name? Ah, yes, Barry.'

LT expected Window to look embarrassed that pieces of his life story were being laid bare, but his head was dead centre straight with ease, as if occasionally hearing about your mistakes was one of the only ways you could appreciate the person you had become.

'So what can I do for you?' Beresford asked as he unlocked his legs and shifted forward in the chair, injecting another infusion of his bay rum aftershave into the room.

'You know how much I respect you,' Window started. 'And you know there's no one on this earth I respect more. The only reason I'm here today is because you took the time to sort me out in those days in Birmingham during my stay on the Handsworth Road. You should be asking me favours, not the other way round, but I need a big one.'

Beresford remained silent, but his deep brown eyes kept smiling.

'The grapevine's saying that this business with the children injured in the arson attack and LT's music is going to explode. I'm good at what I do, but I don't do cameras. Plus LT's words would sound much better if they came from the mouth of someone they trusted . . .'

'Someone like me?'

Beresford leaned back into his chair. He crossed his legs, left over right, and continued, 'I'm not sure. One of the reasons I came down to London last year was to find some peace and quiet. Not that I've got that, but I don't do the media thing myself much any more.'

LT could see this wonderful man and his great aura slipping away, so he dived in and said, 'This is my last chance. If the media crucify me I won't get that record deal. I won't win the competition. The King might be gone, but I still want him to be proud of me.'

Beresford's eyes probed him. They lifted to the du-rag on his forehead.

'You know why I'm going to help you? Because I like a young black man who knows his history. Not many people of your generation I suspect know who Emmett Till was.'

Heat flooded LT's skin. He was embarrassed that he was part of the pack that didn't know. He shifted his gaze away from the older man.

'So how are we going to play this?' Window asked.

Beresford unfolded his leg and turned to Window.

'Like I used to tell you when you were young, always get in there and fight your demons. You don't do that they never disappear, and when you're least expecting it they sneak up and bite you where the hurt lasts for years.'

'Can we take the Minister of Culture down in the first round or is she going to keep getting up?' Window asked.

'Don't know much about her. Met her a few times, but it's hard to get to know any of these politicians. They never look you in the eye. They're too busy looking up at the next rung of the political ladder. Plus next year's the election and maybe she just wants an issue to remind the voters that she's still around. We'll soon find out. Alexander, you take care of making sure LT gets that record deal and I'll deal with the press.'

He turned to LT. 'What about arrangements for the King's inquest and funeral? Are they all in hand?'

LT sighed, leaned back and told them about the call from the coroner's office.

'So are you going to challenge their findings?'

'Bernie said that I should . . .'

'That's not Berlina Ray by any chance?' the older man interrupted.

'How do you know her?'

'She interviewed me for some work she's doing for the Notting Hill carnival committee.'

'The big problemo for me is I'll need to get a solicitor and they don't come cheap. But I think we've found a witness who can help us.'

Beresford rubbed his finger and thumb across his chin. Then he shuffled forward in his chair.

'If you need a solicitor don't worry about the money. I know someone. She's good. Quick. I'll help you get through this.'

LT nodded, grateful for any help he could get.

Suddenly Beresford pushed out of the chair. Took soft steps towards LT. He crouched down by the younger man. Gripped his shoulders with his hands and said, 'Do you believe in who you are?'

His voice was low. Soft. LT nodded, mesmerised by the soothing resonance of being read a bedtime story.

'Do you believe in what you're doing?'

LT nodded again.

'OK. What I need you to do is to concentrate on arranging your father's funeral. Dress in black. Be seen around town. Play up being the grieving son, which of course you really are. If and when the media decide to create some noise I'll be ready for them and we'll create the biggest bang of all.'

That night, for the first time in years, Bernie listened to one of her favourite violin compositions. Mark O'Connor's sleepy fiddle on 'Misty Moonlight Waltz'. She kept all the violin music locked away in a drawer under the kitchen sink. She just sat there. On the sofa, in the main room. Her knees tucked under her chin. Arms wrapped around her legs. She listened to the music, hoping it would lull her to sleep. Praying that the phone wouldn't ring again, with a call like the one she'd received when she was with LT earlier that day. Five minutes later her eyes wavered. Closed. One minute later the phone tipped her lids open again. Her arms tightened around her knees. She let it ring. Just as she had the last three times it rang. The answer machine clicked on.

'Berlina, it's Irinia. You haven't returned any of my calls, darling, and I did not appreciate the way you spoke to me when I rang you earlier. This is serious. It isn't going away. They called me today. They want you to ring them. The phone number is . . .'

She unwrapped her arms as she listened to her mother read out the phone number. She calmly got up. Walked over to the answer machine. Bent down. Unplugged it. She straightened up and looked at the small transparent packet of coke by the phone. Ghost diamonds, that's what her dealer called this batch. Potent. Send you to a universe you never knew existed. She'd had it once before and had been out of action for a number of days. She needed it now because she couldn't face Jerry with what she'd eventually have to tell him. She picked the packet up. Switched the light off. Left the violin rocking in the deep black of the house.

# THE CROWD PULLER

Black. That was what LT wore for the next five days. A son mourning his father. Be seen around town, that's what Beresford had told him. Keep your profile going, that's what Beresford had told him. So he went to gigs. Prepared for the Writer in Residence of Ladbroke Grove competition. A few photographers took shots of him, but soon stopped when the stern looks thrown at them from people said, 'For Christ sake, boys, can't you leave him alone, his dad's just died.' And the black cloud Window had talked about didn't appear in any papers. Maybe Window's people had got it wrong.

Now he stood once again in black, on Wednesday morning, watching the King laid out in his open-topped coffin in the Church of African Harmony and Fulfilment in Notting Hill. He smiled at how well turned out his father looked in his coffin. He wasn't wearing his best jacket like he'd requested, but yeah, this was what a king should look like for his final performance.

'Even when you're in your coffin, son, you still got to be ready to perform.' That was what the King had told him. His smile turned bitter-sweet as he remembered the day the King had given him those words of advice.

Notting Hill carnival, 1985.

A year exactly after that awful night in Hoxton.

The first time the King had let him play Mas, or masquerade.

The King's float always dressed up as Jab-Jabs, or pretty devils, as some called them. The King loved to play Jab-Jab because it was an outlaw figure poking fun and harassing anything conservative. They dressed up in white satin trousers and shirts and wore a chain around their waist. From the chain they hung six small silver bells, three at the front and three at the back. On their heads they wore helmets with horns on. On the back of their trousers they pinned a tail. Then the King smeared both of their faces with thick, black grease. They resembled European court jesters and mischievous devils. The King made him suck three red gobstopper sweets so that his tongue was dyed a vibrant red. For most of the day they would be on the float with the parade of other bands, winding and twining along the carnival route, abandoning themselves to the music. Whenever the road march song, the most popular calypso tune of the year, played, the crowd jumped up to its infectious melody and chanted the chorus as they moved along the street. Every now and then LT and his father would jump off the float and leap near the crowd, threatening to cover people with grease and poking out their red tongues. Leaping around, they would then torment the crowd with the chant:

*'We're gonna mash the place down*
*Jab-Jab*
*Make the street our town*
*Jab-Jab*
*Take away your nine-to-five frown*
*Jab-Jab*
*Win your soul face down*
*Jab-Jab.'*

The crowd had loved it, playing their part by rearing back in mock horror when it looked as if they would be smeared in grease. When rain started to fall and kept falling he had been disappointed, thinking that it was time to pack up and go. But the King had just grinned at him and said, 'Even when you're in your coffin, son, you still got to be ready to perform.'

The perfume of the oriental lilies in the vases on either side of the coffin drew LT back to the church. He turned around and still could not believe how many people had turned up for the funeral. The seats were all taken; the aisles were lined with familiar, half-familiar and unfamiliar faces. Window had employed three large bouncers to man the doors against any possible press intrusion and over-eager fans. The only person he couldn't see was Bernie. He hadn't heard from her since they'd trod the pavements of Hoxton together. The sound of his Aunt Glad crying and wailing for the benefit of the congregation shook the church, diverting his thoughts from Bernie. Rumour had it that his aunt complained when members of the family didn't die for a while.

LT took his place in the front row, next to May. The pastor rose to his feet. The congregation followed him, holding on to their hymn sheets, ready to start serenading the King to his place of rest. The pastor twisted his mouth and nodded his head disapprovingly towards LT. LT nodded to one of the men from the undertakers. The man moved to a tape deck placed at the foot of the coffin. He pressed 'play'. The church began vibrating to the delicate, wailing falsetto of Junior Murvin singing 'Police And Thieves'. The King said he wanted this memorable 1976 reggae classic to be played at his funeral before all the personal eulogies began. Nothing like hearing a Lee 'Scratch' Perry legendary Black Ark record label production to remind everyone that life was for living. The congregation read the lyrics to 'Police And Thieves' on their hymn sheet and started singing. Their bodies and vocals swayed to the unifying reggae beat. Some of the older members of the congregation started to drop some stylish footwork, moving the tempo of the church from sombre to hot. As the final chords of the song died, someone shouted out, 'Play it again, Sam.' The voice ended in a croak as someone prodded him with an elbow, reminding him it was a funeral, not a dance hall.

The mourners settled back into their seats. LT knew the next section was going to be hard because it was time for him to do his eulogy. He took a swift breath into his body and stood up. He stopped next to the King's coffin and faced the congregation.

'There was this old bloke who lived in the King's block. Mr Rosenberg,' he began, the words wobbling on his lips. 'He was Jewish and he always called the King 'a mensch'. I never asked my dad what it meant, but I think it meant he was the Man. You know, the kind of man who makes everyone turn their heads when he walked into the room. The kind of man whose jokes made everyone laugh days after he'd told them. The kind of guy whose style will be cutting through this earth long after me and you have left it. A mensch who don't need no headstone for everyone to remember him. He stood for things, believed in things, fought for things and hoped for things. Some of those things won't mean much any more, some of them I don't agree with, but he worked for them anyway. He always tried to do the right thing, and if he failed he at least had the decency to feel bad about it, and we all know how unusual that is these days. Sometimes when people say someone will be greatly missed they're lying or they're wrong, but in this instance, and not just because I'm his boy, they will be right.'

Tears formed in his eyes.

'The King loved telling stories and jokes that took the piss out of musicians. I'm going to end with one of his favourites. What's the difference between a musician and a trust fund?'

LT's gaze swept the crowd. No one attempted the punchline. He took a deep breath and gave it to them.

'The trust fund eventually matures and earns money.'

A quiet, dignified ripple of laughter shook the crowd. LT stood with his head bowed for a few moments before climbing back down again and taking his seat.

After LT did his eulogy there was an open-mic spot where members of the congregation were invited to share their memories of the King. LT sat, shattered, mind grieving while one well-meaning mourner after another shared their sometimes humorous, sometimes serious stories about what a great guy his dad had been. The final speaker, Beresford Clarke, stood up. He moved past the microphone that other speakers had used and walked up into the pulpit so everyone could see him. Beresford paused briefly.

Cleared his throat. Surveyed the mourners. Then, in a deep, gentle voice, began to narrate his story.

'I remember when we came to this country some people use to say go back to your own cemetery.'

The congregation pushed out a hesitant laugh.

'Many of our brothers here today have been remembering King Stir It Up the man. That is right and proper. But I want to remember another King Stir It Up – the man who spent his life working on behalf of his community. He fought for the liberation of our people. Liberation from mental slavery and self-hatred. He knew our history and he understood how that determined our future. For in the hands of King Stir It Up the microphone was a weapon. A weapon of change...'

The doors of the church flew open. The mourners shifted and turned. LT did the same. A collective gasp went up when everyone realised who the new mourner was.

LT stared with shock and disbelief at the man walking down the aisle. A man who everyone agreed was a living legend of the music industry.

Sean Sparkle.

His rangy, six-foot frame took the aisle with ease and confidence. Everyone knew what Sean Sparkle looked like because he always dressed in white. Today was no different. Today's white was an eye-catching Navajo white blended with a mint cream linen suit, slimline trousers and double-breasted jacket with each button done up – and a very pale face. His shoulder-length blond hair flowed in the same style he'd worn since his Ibiza days. LT swallowed deeply as he followed his progress. Sean Sparkle didn't look up at Beresford as he moved over to the coffin. His blond hair shook from behind as he gazed down at the King. The sound of the congregation whispering skated in every pew. Sean Sparkle shook his head, turned around and moved towards LT. He smiled at LT with glistening blue eyes and sat next to him.

*Oh my God, oh my God*, LT chanted in his mind. He could not believe that his dad – yes, his dad – had known this man. Not once had the King mentioned knowing Sean Sparkle. Not when they heard one of Sean Sparkle's songs. Not when they watched the news report about marijuana being found in his bag at Heathrow. Not when a rap band he produced won four Grammys. Sean's ringed hand touched LT's shoulder. Jesus. Sean leaned his mouth close to LT's ear and whispered, 'I'm really sorry about the King.'

LT couldn't reply. Instead he nodded. Beresford coughed loudly from the pulpit and raised the pastor's glass of water to his mouth. He took a strong gulp and put it down. His eyes stretched back over the church as he resumed his oration.

'The King knew everybody and everybody knew the King. I did not know the King very well but he touched me like he touched so many other people. Today, when we see so many of our young people trapped in a swamp of apathy, drugs, criminality and self-destructive behaviour, we need to remember his commitment more then ever – and start applying it to where we are now. Let us remember these words from one of his songs, "We're killing ourselves in the line for the concessionary when we should liberate our minds – by any means necessary!"'

As Beresford came down from the pulpit, there was a scattering of applause. LT turned to Sean and asked, 'Do you want to . . . ?'

'No,' he replied quietly, his head down.

The two undertakers near the coffin repositioned themselves, getting ready for mourners to file past the coffin for their final view of the King. After viewing him, some mourners whispered in LT's ear how well turned out the King was. That almost made him cry. He finally sobbed when he viewed the King for the final time on his own. He sat back down, his breath and tears exploding in his chest. Sean Sparkle put his arm around his shoulder.

'I remember when you were . . .' Abruptly his words stopped. His arm fell away. He thrust to his feet.

'I'll see you at the wake.'

Then Sean Sparkle marched along the aisle and was gone. LT watched after him, wondering why he seemed so upset. Wondering what he'd been about to say.

The sound of the undertakers getting the body ready for cremation made him turn back to the front. He heard Aunt Glad grumble from her seat on the other side of May. She was very disapproving of a cremation. The burying of a member of the Caribbean community was an art in itself. At the graveside a close relative or friend of the family was chosen to lead the hymns. While people sang, male members of the congregation, rather than the gravediggers, took it in turns to shovel the loving earth on the coffin. But the King had always wanted to be cremated. After seeing a Hindu family cremating a loved one while visiting his grandmother in Trinidad, that was how he said he wanted to go.

As the coffin took the King on his final journey LT still wondered what Sean Sparkle had been about to say.

After a morning spent mourning, people liked nothing better than to relax the afternoon away filling up their bellies. The tables in the community hall were packed with people enjoying the Caribbean cooking and a selection of drinks. From the laughter booming from certain parts of the hall, the rum punch seemed to be the favourite beverage. The beat of hardcore 1970s reggae from the sound system set up in the corner boomed in the room. LT was exhausted. He had spent an hour working the room, making sure the mourners were OK.

Now, as he stood in the main doorway, he watched a group of older men and the three bouncers Window had employed play dominoes. They were playing cut-throat, which meant they were playing as individuals rather than as partners. The banter flowed constant, thick and low across the table, as the game heated up.

'You playing Jamaican style.'

'No sir, me is an Englishman now.'

'Rupert, you suppose to have your glasses on.'

That bought a group laugh, except from Rupert.

'I go force you.' A player wearing a pork-pie hat banged his domino down.

'I'll show you who needs to visit the eye doctor,' the one called Rupert said.

He lifted his last domino high into the air. Waited until every eye was fixed on it. Then slammed it down. He pushed the domino into formation and yelled, 'Dead.'

Rupert started laughing, showing his immaculate pair of false teeth.

'Shuffle that boneyard good,' he called out in his triumphant nasal voice.

'Jerry?' a soft voice called out beside LT.

He turned to find Sean Sparkle standing hesitantly near him with his hands shoved in his front pockets. His face was pasty and his eyes red, as if he'd been crying. LT looked at him, surprised that he'd used the name Jerry. Only the King, Bernie and various family members called him that.

'Mr Sparkle,' LT began, taking a step towards him. 'I really appreciate you coming to the funeral. I didn't realise that you and the King were friends.'

'He did some session work for me a few times back in the eighties. He weren't really a mate of mine, but he was a character, so I just had to come and pay my respects.'

They both fell silent, not sure what to say.

'Look,' Sean began, one of his hands coming out of his pocket, 'the King came to see me a week ago. He left this with me and asked me to give it to you.'

He held out a small, box-shaped parcel wrapped in blue metallic paper. LT took it.

'What is it?'

'He didn't say. Look, I've got to do an interview so I've got to shoot. If you need anything just get in touch. If not I'll see you at the Ladbroke Grove competition. Hope you get that treble medal.'

He passed LT his business card, then turned to leave. As he reached the entrance, Bernie came through it. He didn't stop as he passed her.

Bernie looked over at LT and asked, astonishment filling her voice, 'Was that who I think it was?'

'Well, well, well.' LT crossed his arms over his black double-breasted jacket. 'If it isn't the woman who comes and goes as she pleases.'

'I didn't realise I had to clock on and off. I do have a life, you know. So was that Sean Sparkle?'

She moved towards him with the speed of her question.

'Yeah.'

'How did he know the King?'

'He said they worked together briefly back in the day. He said the King left this for me.'

He held out the wrapped box for her to see.

'That was Sean, wasn't it?' Her voice was breathless. Excited. Low.

'I just told you that...'

'No, Sean from the King's tape. Isn't Sean Sparkle's production company called 50p Trick?'

'Yeah. So?'

'The Sean in the tape met the King when he showed him his fifty p trick. And there was that old fifty p in the King's bag.'

'The King never once mentioned knowing Sean Sparkle.' His words stopped as he looked at the box in his hand. He swallowed. 'Do you think this is...'

'One of the King's domino sets with a tape in it?' she finished for him.

Their eyes met. Disbelieving brown meeting triumphant blue.

'Great, it finally looks like our luck's turning,' Bernie said. 'I've got our witness on tape and now we might have the second instalment of the King's story...'

'Excuse me, kids, sorry to interrupt.'

They both turned to find Beresford Clarke. He smiled at them.

'Good to see you again, Berlina. I just came to say goodbye. Take care, son.'

He shook LT's hand and left them.

'We need to unwrap this box and find out if the tape's in it,' Bernie said. 'Where's your motor parked?'

He told her. They marched to the entrance. Hit the sunlight outside. A voice roared, 'There he is.'

A crowd of about twenty people started to converge on them. 'What the . . .' he started.

Microphones and cameras were pressed into LT's face as Bernie was pushed to the side by a stout man. The man flung a question at him. 'What is your response to confirmation that the teenager who committed the arson attack was listening to your song "Gasoline Ghetto" as he threw the petrol bomb?'

It took LT a full five seconds of shock and bewilderment before he realised it was the press. But five seconds was all it took for them to stake their turf around him. For them to circle their questions about him.

'What is your response to the allegation that the suspect lit the fire using one of your designer du-rags?'

'What would you like to say to the family of one of the boys injured in the attack who is now on a life support machine . . . ?'

'They have charged the suspect with attempted manslaughter. Do you think your music should be in the dock as well?'

He got dizzy on a turntable of question after question being fired at him. The cameras seemed to flash with increasing hostility. His hand tightened around the box Sean Sparkle had given him. The scrum pushed him closer to the wall of the community centre. He could not see Bernie.

'Oi, what the fucking hell is going on?' a furious voice shouted.

LT twisted his head and saw the three bouncers and his Aunt Glad storming out of the entrance of the community centre. As his aunt and the bouncers struggled through the crowd another question was fired at him.

'The Minister of Culture says you should stop performing your inflammatory and violent music – any thoughts on that?'

Suddenly his aunt emerged in front of him. She pushed the male reporter who had asked the questions backwards. 'This is a funeral, young man, not the damn carnival.'

'Steady on, Grandma. We're only doing our job. Why don't you go and shine some shoes?'

LT watched his aunt hitch up the elastic of her skirt one inch higher. He winced because he knew what was coming. Gladys

'The Crusher' Scantleberry had been her nickname at school. She reared back, sending her wet-look wig flying as she landed an uppercut on the reporter's jaw. The crowd scattered.

'Get in,' a voice yelled.

LT swept his eyes through a gap in the crowd towards the direction of the voice. He saw Beresford Clarke in his flamenco-red Jaguar XJS. Revved up. Passenger door open. Ready to pull out.

He did not even think. He ran over to the car and jumped in.

# TRACK 19: PUNK BEAT

Beresford drove through the last stretch of the Limehouse Tunnel and entered the Isle of Dogs, or the Island, as locals called it. The part of East London that demonstrated what the East End used to be and what it had the potential to become. After the death of working life on the docks in the late 1960s, the Island had become an isolated wasteland that time had almost forgotten. That had all changed in the late 1980s when the cramped City realised that the Island was virgin territory begging to be had. So regeneration began with huge buildings cast in glass and steel, abandoned warehouses becoming fashionable riverside apartments, a new railway system to rival any other part of London and the country's tallest building – Canary Wharf – reflecting its mirror roof over the capital. Some proclaimed that the new development gave the Island a new sense of lived-in warmth, while others whispered that the parade of Porsches that drove by the council estates only made the cold chill of poverty blow stronger.

LT shivered in his magnolia seat. The punk beat that had swooped on him while he'd waited to identify the King's body was back, driving its bass notes in his head. The wind slicing in from the open window played cat-and-mouse on his face. Since finding refuge inside Beresford's wheels he had been too stunned to speak. He was grateful to Beresford for not trying to fill the car with the pitter-patter of meaningless words. Without asking, LT stretched forward. Put the radio on.

'You sure you want to be doing that, son?'

He found a national station, one he rarely listened to. The news came on. He listened.

War.

Death.

A maybe war.

A definite death.

Him.

'Musician Jeremiah Scantleberry, who uses the stage name "Lord Tribulation", was involved in further controversy today after an incident in East London. Mr Scantleberry, who had been attending his father's funeral, is alleged to have assaulted journalists. Sources are also saying that the teenager who injured two children in an arson attack last week, who cannot be named for legal reasons, was listening to Lord Tribulation's controversial song "Gasoline Ghetto" when he committed the act. Sources also say that one of the boys injured in the attack is now on a life support machine . . .'

Beresford took one hand off the steering wheel and switched the radio off.

LT gulped as the three-chord riff inside him dug deeper.

'Did you hear that? They're saying my music made him do it.'

Beresford said nothing.

'The kid was probably pumped up on God knows what new drug they're stressing everyone out with on the street. When you're in that state you'll do anything. You don't need music to help you pull a trigger.'

'Take a breath, boy.'

'I need to call Window and May . . .'

His hand rammed into his trouser pocket for his phone.

'Leave it.'

'But the funeral and the record company . . .'

'You need to get your head back on your shoulders before you speak to anyone. Window's speciality is sorting out disturbances, so he'll take care of the funeral.'

LT shoved his hand into his jacket pocket, feeling the box that Sean Sparkle had given him.

'I don't believe these fucking people. Since the concert last week they've been hounding me. Don't they have any respect for someone's grief?'

'You want the long or the short answer?'

LT drummed the back of his head against the seat.

'If this messes up my chances of winning the Writer in Residence of Ladbroke Grove competition and getting into the Paradise Records stable, it don't matter how high I jump, there ain't going to be any other great leaps for me in the music industry.'

Beresford leaned the car into a tight right as he spoke.

'OK, son, this is how we're going to play it. We need to be in control of this situation, so when we get to my place I'm going to make some calls and arrange a press conference for tomorrow. We want them to feel uncomfortable so we'll hold it at the Marcus Garvey Community Centre in Notting Hill.'

The car leaned into a tight left as he continued. 'Let's hope that just hearing the name Marcus Garvey will make some of them think twice about the type of questions they'll ask you. You want still to look like the grieving son, so make sure you're still wearing black. And wear that Emmett Till du-rag. That will make you look like a black man who is confident about how he walks in life.'

LT nodded. He turned his head to the side so the wind could lessen the heat burning his face because he still didn't know who Emmett Till was.

Regina Carter's mournful and haunting violin on the track 'Reflections' played in the background as Bernie picked up the phone for the fourth time and dialled the number her mother had left on her answering machine five days earlier. The connection clicked on. One ring. She slammed the receiver back down. Closed her eyes. Her finger rotated in the groove above her collarbone. For five days she'd lived in a coke-fuelled haze, stayed away from Jerry and convinced herself that everything would go away. That everything would be OK. Who the fuck was she kidding? After what had happened at the funeral today, it would never be the same again. She didn't have an alternative. She had to do this. She picked up the phone. Dialled the number. Got past the first ring. A voice came. A voice she hadn't heard in fifteen years.

He picked up the phone. He knew who it was.

'What took you so long?' he asked sarcastically.

'Stop screwing around. Did everything go according to plan at the funeral?'

He stretched back into the single sofa.

'The King is finally buried and it looks like the press are ready to do the same to the son.'

'I still don't understand how the coroner's office came back with a natural death conclusion.'

A little smile twisted the corners of his lips. He was glad that she couldn't see him because she'd want to know what he was smiling about and he wasn't ready to tell her the truth yet. The truth made people behave in unpredictable ways and he couldn't afford for that to start happening to her.

'Have you found the jacket yet?' she asked.

'If I had don't you think I'd have shown it to you? Don't worry. While the boy's pushing the media off his back with one hand and holding out the other to grab that recording contract, I'll just find that opening and get it. But now we've got two problems.'

'What?' Her voice shook and rasped in his ear.

'A face from the past made an appearance. That punk Sean Docherty or Sean Sparkle as the world knows him.'

'I thought he didn't live here any more.'

'He lives in Los Angeles, not Mars, so the news of the King's death was bound to reach him. Besides, he's a judge at this year's Writer in Residence of Ladbroke Grove competition.'

'Do you think he told the boy anything?' Anxiety coated all eight words.

'Unless he wants to know what the colour scheme of one of his posters looks like on a cell wall at Brixton prison, I don't think so. Remember, he's got so much more to lose than you or I.'

'And the other problem is . . .'

'The grapevine is saying the girl has the witness on tape . . .'

'I don't want anyone hurt . . .'

'Welcome to the real world.'

'I mean it. There's already a stink of death. If there's another one we don't know who might smell it.'

He cut the call without reassuring her. The whole of his successful life was at stake and he was going to do what he needed to do to protect it. If she didn't understand, that was her problem. He punched in a new number. Began to speak.

'It's me. Tomorrow follow the girl and this is what I need you to do . . .'

When LT got back to his flat, the rain was gushing from the gutters and Bernie was at his door. Her hair was damp, face fretful and body still clinging to its mourning clothes. His eyes blinked in a rapid chopping motion over her as he shook his head. He walked past her. Put the key in the lock and said, 'I don't need any company at the moment.'

She followed him inside.

'Where's the tape?' Her voice was tired, as if someone had been banging on her door all night long.

'What?'

He stopped by a lone album that was propped up against the wall. The Rolling Stones' *Sticky Fingers*. Unlike later editions it had a real brass zipper on the trousers on the front. Another gift from the King when he learned he was dying.

Bernie kicked the door shut with her heel as she said, 'The box of dominoes Sean Sparkle left with you. You forgot all about them, didn't you?'

'No I haven't,' he ground out against her accusation. 'But forgive me if I've been a bit preoccupied, thinking of how to avoid the roasting on top of the righteous bonfire the press are stoking up for me.'

He searched inside his pocket and dragged out the wrapped box.

'Did Beresford tell you anything more about the arson attack?'

Her quiet question surprised him. He hitched his head back so he could really look at her. Her eyes shone in her lonesome face like freshly watered blue grass behind a black picket fence.

'No. Why?'

'Nothing.' She gulped the 'g' sound into her body like a smoker on their last drag. Then she continued in a hot rush. 'Come on, then, let's see if the legendary Sean Sparkle gave you that tape.'

She took the lead and moved into his bedroom. The evening light shifted in the room. They sat on the bed. Left side facing the door. He started to pull the metallic blue paper from the package. A rush of anticipation left Bernie's mouth when she saw the box he held in his hand. Small, plain brown, no patterns or frills.

'This was the King's any time, anyplace domino set.'

He slid the lid back. Black tiles, white dots. He half turned and tipped the dominoes on the bed. He saw the Dictaphone tape straight away. It was balanced on top of the double three and the double four. He picked it up. Just like the first tape, it had a label with black writing:

'Revival Selection: 1976, Volume 2'.

'Where's the King's Dictaphone?' Bernie asked.

He told her where to find it on the bedside table. As she moved around the bed he settled back on to a pillow. Bernie's weight pushed the mattress down as she joined him on the bed. She handed him the Dictaphone. Eased herself back. He placed the tape inside the machine. Pressed 'play'. Put the Dictaphone in between them on the duvet.

The King's voice pulsed into the room.

'You ever been through a door and realised you shouldn't have done it? You should have gone the other way? That's what I should have done when I went down those basement steps. When I went through that door that took me into the life of the Black Fist, I went through a door that spun my whole world out of control . . .'

DISC 2

# 'POLICE AND THIEVES'

**PLAYLIST**
1. REVIVAL SELECTION: 1976, VOLUME 2
   (EP: Extended Play)
2. TOO HOT TO HANDLE
3. IT'S LIKE DIS, IT'S LIKE DAT
4. SNOW LIGHTS
5. RAW & UNCUT
6. RIDE THE RAILS
7. THE LIBERATION REPUBLIC
8. BLUE BEAT
9. THE PIANO PLAYER
10. DOWNTOWN, UPTOWN RIFF
11. MURDER MUSIC
12. SELL OUT
13. GHOSTS
14. 'EXODUS'
15. REVIVAL SELECTION: 1976, VOLUME 3
    (7" SINGLE: A-SIDE)
16. 'IT HURTS SO GOOD'
17. REVIVAL SELECTION: 1976, VOLUME 3
    (7" SINGLE: B-SIDE)
18. WHO'S THAT GIRL?
19. WHO'S THAT GIRL? ('76 CLUB REMIX)
20. TRUTH JIVE
21. MOST WANTED
22. RHYTHMIC RUSH
23. KILLER TUNE
24. DROP THE BISCUIT (FEATURING BERNIE)
25. BONUS TRACK

# REVIVAL SELECTION: 1976, VOLUME 2
## (EP: Extended Play)

'Welcome to the Black Fist,' Shakespeare whispered with pride as he turned the light on in the basement of the Liberation Republic.

The small room put me in mind of my own bedsit the first day I moved in – musty, damp, with cracked white walls. The floor was concrete and bumpy and so hard that you knew if you tripped and hit your head no way were you getting up for a week. It had this real funny smell. A smell that hadn't touched my nostrils in years. At first I couldn't place it, but when my eyes got use to the light I saw what the smell was.

Books, man, books. Books everywhere. Relaxing on chairs, stacked high on the floor, embracing back to back on the three tables. A large bookcase took over the whole of one wall. It housed the collection of a single titled magazine – *The Black Fist*. So that's where I'd heard the name before. I'd seen brothers selling it outside Ridley Road market on a Saturday. There were posters covering the walls. At the time I didn't have a clue who the people in the posters were, but later on I found out. The biggest ones were a portrait of Huey Newton, the founder of the Black Panthers, sitting in a wicker chair holding a spear in one hand and a rifle in the other, and a red-and-black poster of Che Guevara. The Che Guevara one had Spanish writing on. Well, I think it was Spanish. Of course, I couldn't read it. That's when it pinged in my head – what the raas was I doing in a room surrounded by books with words I couldn't read? Time for me and my boy

Sean to go. As I started to open my mouth to say 'Adios', Houdini exploded.

'Enough is enough, man. We have a right to be here like anyone else. Can't even walk the street without the Babylon stopping us with their stupid sus law. We're two per cent of this country's population, do you know how many times we get stopped – forty per cent of the time. I can't take the pressure no more.'

He snatched his tam off his head. He began pacing with this strange two-step dance. You know, one, two back, one, two forward, like he was a chained man. His locks did some kung-fu kicking madness in the air. He stopped with a jerk.

'You see me.' He pointed to his chest. 'I'm their worst nightmare. A black man with a purpose. You see these.' He pointed to his pumping feet. 'That's what frightens them, a son of Africa on the move. A bona fide, rent-book-holding resident of Hackney. All right, I bought the rent book off someone else, but that don't matter. A son of Africa who ain't letting nothing or no one block his way.'

'Sit down, Houdini,' Shakespeare said wearily, with a tone that told you he had seen it all before.

Houdini's locks fell flat as he flopped into a black plastic chair. He was still vex as he wrung his tam in his hand.

'Take a seat,' Shakespeare told me as he pointed to the chair nearest to me. I picked up the two books on the chair – *Soledad Brother: The Prison Letters of George Jackson* and Frantz Fanon's *Black Skin, White Mask*. It makes me feel shame now to admit at the time I hadn't heard of either of these books. I placed them on the floor and pushed myself into the chair. Sean leaned back against the door. Shakespeare sat down at the far table, which had piles of papers on it and a telephone.

Houdini's eyes rooted on to the chair I was sitting in. Still looking at my chair, he half rose and asked Shakespeare, 'Shall I call . . . ?'

Shakespeare stopped his words with one look. Man, the look was so sharp I almost ducked my head, afraid that my throat might get cut. Houdini collapsed back in the chair. Whoever they were chatting about hadn't been at the celebrations, which made my curiosity leap high. But I didn't ask, because you know what, I might have placed my skin in a chair, but I wasn't intending on staying long.

'So what's the Black Fist?' Sean asked Shakespeare.

I threw that boy one of them 'wait till you get home' looks. The blood drained from his face. Shit, I'd forgotten about what his old man did to him.

'We are an organisation that operates within the Republic,' Shakespeare eagerly began to answer Sean's question. 'We produce a monthly magazine that attacks the bourgeois lifestyle and corruption of the system. I'm the Minister of Action and Houdini is the Minister of Information.'

'We are the way, man, the way,' Houdini added, fixing his tam back on his head.

Shakespeare got real comfortable and slid his arms across the table as he said, 'If the community is being treated wrong, we highlight it. If there's a battle to be waged, we fight it. If there's a right to be wronged, we're at the vanguard of it. I write the articles and Houdini organises distribution. We have one missing ingredient.' He looked directly at me. 'We need a griot.'

'A what?' I fired back. Griot? Didn't sound too healthy to me.

'A griot. A poet in the tradition of the African storyteller toasting out the good and bad news.'

I looked at him like he was Clint Eastwood with his poncho flicked back, pointing his six-shooter at me.

'Man, those long words you just flashed out – bourgeois and vanguard – they ain't part of my dictionary.' I shook my head to emphasise every word.

Shakespeare picked up his chair and brought it over to my table. He sat next to me. So now we were best friends?

'You chant out positive messages, right?'

I didn't want to nod, but I did.

'You preach to the community when injustice is reeking havoc, right?'

I nodded.

'You shout about the rottenness of living in Babylon's corrupt embrace, right?'

I nodded.

'Then you're a griot. Our griot. Our Minister of Illumination.'

I felt like I was at the labour exchange being confronted with a job that no man on earth wanted to do.

'I ain't no poet, man.'

He just settled himself and his chair closer to me. 'Look, let me tell you what we plan to do, then go away and think about it and make your decision. It's time for us to organise a mass demonstration on Unity Road police station. We want you to write and read a poem to the crowd . . .'

Brother, he went on and on, pushing into my face the type of world my son would be living in if I didn't get off my raas and stand up to be counted. But you know what, no way was I going to do it. As he told his parable, I chanted in my head – responsibility ain't a musical word, responsibility ain't a musical word. Over and over until I thought I'd won the battle. But he got me in the end. Got me where every musician loves to be tickled – in the heart of their vanity.

'*Your words can make the world change.*'

Seven words, that's all Shakespeare said to me. Seven words that made me feel that God had a purpose when he put me on this earth. Sounds stupid, don't it, but I had met so many people who just didn't know a backside what they were doing with their life. No one had ever said that to me before. Sure, people had come up to me, patted me on the back, congratulated me on my lyrics with the usual appreciative words – cool, dread, bubbling – but no one had ever said that my lyrics could change the world. Man, that just made me feel as high as a coconut tree on the banks of the River Thames. How could I shut my eyes and dream sweet dreams at night knowing that without my warrior cry we might never make it? Sean and my Jerry might never make it.

So, on a coat-hugging Wednesday evening in March, I took

Sean back with me to the Liberation Republic to become the Minister of Illumination of the Black Fist. When we arrived the Free Rufus Williams Defence Committee was in full swing. Kwesi, the lawyer, had been to see Rufus in remand to find the young brother battered this side of hell. After hearing this people were angry and wanted to take to the streets straight away. But Shakespeare calmed tings down and told people that if Rufus was to get back home to his mum we had to do tings right. So we began to organise the demonstration on Unity Road police station. I was surprised that we enlisted the help of a few white radical groups. Although they helped us, Shakespeare made a point of reminding them every so often that this was a black ting, a black struggle, their help was important but we had to be at the vanguard of the resistance. (Yeah, I was even using words like vanguard now.) I was surprised that we had food and drink to keep everyone going. When I asked Shakespeare where the money came from he just smiled and said, 'Where there's justice, there's bread.'

Man, I still wasn't convinced that I was any poet. It sounded too serious. I'd signed up to the bouncy, bouncy style of living – touch, enjoy and roll on. But the way Shakespeare asked you to do something, with his solemn eyes and beautiful voice, who could tell him no? So between helping to organise the demo and late-night gigs I tried to write a poem. Now, you think that I, being a man who was used to writing his own lyrics, would find it easy. Brother, it was so hard. It made the nerves crackle right on the bottom of my feet. I tried everything to find inspiration – writing during the break at gigs, listening to music, taking walks. But them blasted words wouldn't come. There was one day left and I still didn't have no poem. And every time Shakespeare asked me how it was going, like an idiot-boy, I said tings was irie. Tings were cooler in hell. The evening before the demo I went back to my yard and put anything on my radiogram that would give me inspiration – U-Roy, Marley, Otis Redding. When that failed I went to the few books I had and must have read the lot – Linton Kwesi Johnston, Gil Scott Heron's *The Revolution Will Not Be Televised*. But nothing worked. Exhausted and frustrated,

I heaved myself on the bed listening to the Sellotape I used to keep the draught out of the windows creaking against the wind. It was like my mind just dried up. Like the ABC was some foreign language to me. I must have lain there for well over an hour when I heard a scraping sound near the door. I jumped out of bed. Underneath the door lay a book with a white piece of paper on top. I bent down. Picked it up. The paper was loose so I held it in one hand and the book in the other. I looked at the paper, which had black writing scrawled in the middle.

*I thought this might help you. S.*

I smiled. I should have known of all people my boy Sean could read me and know when I needed help. Mind you, I hope he hadn't nicked it from the library. I looked at the small brown-covered book and read the writing.

*Songs of Experience.*

William Blake.

I kissed my teeth and nearly threw the book straight back down to the spot where it had entered my life. What did Sean think he was playing at? I needed the divine intervention of God and he was expecting me to read some dead white man's poetry. The one and only time I had heard Blake was aged twelve as our English teacher went off into the twilight zone and read one of his poems to the class. She had been so wrapped up in reading 'The Fly' that she never noticed how the thous, thees and arts made us doze in the afternoon sun. I crawled back on to the bed with the book, eased back and started flicking through it. Sure enough, 'The Fly' was in town. I almost closed it and put it down, but I thought of Sean taking his time to bring it to me, so I kept on skipping through it. When I got to this poem called 'London', that's when it happened. That's when the words leapt out at me, Bruce Lee-style.

'In every cry of every man.'

The first time I read it this ache appeared just under my heart. I read it again. The ache got stronger. I must have read that line over a dozen times before I realised what I was feeling was this tremendous hurt. Like some chick that I really loved had stood me up, while I stood in public in my best threads. Just like living in Babylon had let us all down. I understood that if we didn't do something quick time, Rufus Williams would embody the cry of not just every black man, but every man. I scrambled to find my paper and pen and started to write my poem. A poem I gave a one-word title to.

'Why?'

Friday, 20 March. The day of the demonstration dawned with a warm current that testified to what everyone were saying, that it was going to be a heat-licking summer that year. I got rigged out in full rebellious, roots regalia – black beret, black leather jacket, white T-shirt with a huge printed black fist pounding on the front and a walk that proclaimed maximum self-esteem as my middle name. If there was one thing the system didn't like it was a man who looked like they couldn't take him down. The march took the Kingsland High Street like a revolutionary blade with an edge that people just hadn't seen before. I finally understood what brother Gil Scott Heron meant when he said that no way could the revolution be televised, it had to be live. The type of energy and emotion that we were raising you couldn't feel on film, you had to feel our dread moves pulse beneath your feet. We yelled out the slogan 'Free Rufus Williams. Down with Sus'. We held up banners and placards in the colours of either red, gold or green with messages swaying from 'Rufus Williams Is A Schoolboy' to 'Free Rufus Now'. I was at the head of the march with Shakespeare to my left, Houdini to my right and Sean behind me. Both Shakespeare and Houdini shouted through megaphones. As the black railings of the pavement hemmed us in, people stared at us. Black as well as white. One old black woman, who put me in mind of Grandma, was staring at me, with her blue headscarf tied as tight around her chin as the expression of disapproval pinching up her lips. I met her eyes and her gaze said one thing: 'Why the sweet Lord Jesus are you young people making it hard for the rest of us?' What you have to understand is that our parents just didn't get it. They landed in England, suitcases in one hand and hopes and dreams in the other. They thought that all you had to do was work hard and tings would be irie. A bit like when Jimmy Cliff sings in 'You Can Get It If You Really Want', all you have to do is 'Try. Try and try'. Bare bollocks – as them English people would say – us young black men could search from dawn to dusk and still find no work.

'Free Rufus Williams,' I yelled out defiantly, straight at her. Her lips puckered out and I knew she was kissing her National Health teeth. The woman hugged up her shopping bag to go one way as my feet took me another.

When Unity Road police station came in sight there was almost a collective eruption in the crowd as feet quickened in their haste to get there quickly, in their haste to let their anger out at the foot of Babylon. (Well, that's how it looked to me.) We had been given permission for the march as long as we didn't interfere in police business, which meant not going on to Babylon's property. A single Babylon stood at the top of the stairs, four steps up from the road, like a blue dog defending his yard. The crowd erupted at the bottom, their shouts getting louder. I began to shake because I knew that everyone was waiting for me, the Minister of Illumination, to address the crowd. Being no stranger to performing before an audience, it may seem strange that every nerve ending I had felt like it was on fire. You know what the problem was? I had never performed without my lifetime companion – music. Houdini nudged me and I looked at him. He raised the megaphone and I remembered that I needed to say my poem through it. I took it, looked up at the policeman, whose gaze went straight over my head. So he thought I was invisible, did he? The blood boiled in my head. I flicked my eyes above him to look at the windows and saw faces watching me from every pane of glass. That should have made my nerves itch, but the funny thing was it made me grow large, knowing that I had the attention of every Beast in the block. The crowd had stopped moving, but I could feel that eternal skank rhythm that resonates hardest when your back is against the wall. I turned my back on the Abomination and faced the crowd (I like to think like a

Mandingo warrior who the catchers ain't going to get). I raised
the megaphone to my lips and pushed my first ever poem out.

'Police arrest him – and you want to know why?
Coz he was just another brother passing by.
He's up against the wall but are they quite sure?
Yeah, they've got it right – he's black and he's poor.

Sit him in a cell while they devise an offence,
But he's definitely black so there'll be no defence,
A lady's got robbed and he can take the blame.
And he looks a bit like him, see they all look the same.

Up in court and the jury's been picked.
They're all white, just like their verdict,
Standard tariff, a five years in jail,
But just to make sure the judge add another one on as well.

That's how it is and they make no pretence,
Being black in this city is a criminal offence.
But are we going to grovel and bow to their police?
I'll tell you this people – no justice – no peace!'

I blasted out 'no justice – no peace' again and again and then
the crowd rocked the police station as they joined in. No point
being King Stir It Up if the crowd didn't check my positive vibe.
For a first performance it was irie.

As I chanted, I tried to find Shakespeare in the crowd. I will
admit looking for his approval. I immediately went to the place
at the front where he had been standing, but was surprised to
find him gone. I tried hard to find him in the swaying colours
and people. I finally found him.

Well, kiss my sweet black rah-rah.

He was near the student movement section, standing between
a couple taking a photograph and a young woman. White woman.
She wore a black cap, like those Chinese communists, and a face

I knew I had seen somewhere before. I couldn't place her.
Shakespeare was talking to her and the way his mouth was moving,
like he had too much spit in his mouth, I knew the words jetting
from his tongue weren't good. The woman's head moved back
with the pressure of his words biting in her face. Then she reared
up and opened her mouth and bit him back. I couldn't figure out
what the raas was going on. Man, I was vex. Vex that his attention, like everyone else's, wasn't on me. There I was, at the gateway
to Babylon, having moved people with my dread verbal vibrations, and there was Shakespeare, going at it (as Sean would say)
with some white gal. It felt like the ultimate slap in my face. No,
I was not pleased. Not pleased at all.

When we got back to the Republic after the march finished I
was on a mission to find out what had happened to Shakespeare.
I pulled him up when we got to the Black Fist office and asked,
'So how did you like my first poem?'

'The best, man, the best.'

His palm clutched my shoulders.

'I was surprised you noticed because you looked deep into it
with the white chick.'

His hand stopped moving.

'What white woman?'

His hand dropped away.

'The one you were munching up.'

'Oh, her. That was nothing. I can't even remember what it was
about. Who cares about any woman when the King stirred them
up.'

He put his arms around my shoulders as his words wrapped
around me. Then he fell into that wonderful Shakespeare trick of
his, using his words to praise me. Being the typical man that I
am I let his words soothe me and forgot about the woman in the
crowd. None of us would forget, though, that when his trial came
up five months later Rufus got sent down for four years.

April drummed into May with everyone humming Billy Ocean's
'Love Really Hurts Without You'. May drummed into June with

everyone humming the Real Thing's 'You To Me Are Everything'. Yes, everyone was in the mood for the cool runnings from a good love song. Life grooved into a pattern of jammin' with the boys at night and organising with the Black Fist in the day. The Liberation Republic soon became a second home for me and Sean. Shakespeare even let us use the small room next to the Black Fist's office to store our equipment and turn into a makeshift studio where we could rehearse and make tapes for our exclusive dub plates. I even left my record collection there. I'm sure Houdini and Shakespeare got fed up with me boasting about my records and their amazing covers. Soon the boys and me were doing impromptu (man, now I was a poet I had some big words behind me) jammin' sessions in the Sweet and Dandy. And that was the problem, because you can't serve two masters. I knew that Desmond and Maximus weren't irie about my involvement in the Republic. Sure, they came and jammed with us there, but the politics they stayed well away from. Their big gripe was that the Republic took me away from the music at our most important time of the year.

The run-up to the Notting Hill carnival was crucial. The carnival jumped up on the last Sunday and bank holiday Monday of August. Didn't matter where you went – Harlesden, Brixton, Peckham, Clapton – everyone was chanting that Carnival '76 was going to be the One. The One that no one would be able to ever forget. There's no greater pleasure in life – including the ting you and your woman does between the sheets, believe me – than jumping up in the open air and watching the year's steam and stress evaporate from your soul. A lot of the white kids understood that your doctor couldn't prescribe that kind of medicine and started to join us. The run-up to the carnival was a sound systems paradise. '75 had been the first real year when us sound systems had flexed our rhythms and rides on the streets of Notting Hill. Clubs wanted you and parties wanted you. Sometimes the demand got so heavy that we had to turn work down. But Shakespeare had a way of drawing me in, making me feel that without me the Black Fist just became two fingers.

But I did have some doubts about how much time I was spending there.

It was during one of those getting ready for carnival moments that some personal trouble arrived. We were rehearsing in our space in the basement when a cool breeze butted my back. I noticed Desmond and Sean's faces turn low as they watched over my head and I knew that the door had opened. From their downbeat expressions I knew whoever had come wasn't welcome. I turned, not surprised to see Marcie, my ex, standing in the doorway, wearing her white go-go boots, holding my five-month-old son, Jeremiah, like he was a weapon. She moved towards me in that ultimate party-gal walk of hers – bouncy, bouncy hip sway with a flick of her heeled toes. I looked at her downturned bottom lip and knew I was in for a heavy ride. Wasn't it St Paul himself who said that love was free, so I was just in the habit of taking it. Only when I met Marcie did I realise that love, like everything else, has a price. I had met her one night after a gig in Lewisham. She had adored my performance, so I sweet-talked her at the bar, took her home and had a memorable time. But that was it. No everlasting words jumped from my lips. Before I could say kiss my sweet black rah-rah, the girl tell me how she was having my child. How one of her friends makes wedding dresses (discounted for us, of course). I backed off. Told her I would take care of my child, but me and she were yesterday's news.

'So this is where you're holded up, while your son is hungry,' she said in her heavy Jamaican accent. Don't ever go out with no woman who come straight from Caribbean because they didn't beat around no bush like the girls born in England. They just take out their knife tongue and hack straight to the point. Purebred Caribbean sharks.

'What do you want, Marcie?'

'I tell you what your son wants, he needs a father who is going to put milk in his mouth and food in his belly.'

I reached for my Jerry and tugged him out of her arms. He looked up at me with my father's black inquisitive eyes and I cuddled him close. I didn't want the boys to see me getting lashed up, so I took them outside and stood next to the railed green area in the middle of the square. Marcie took a defiant stand next to me and I wasn't sure what was more harsh, her or the wind raking me over.

'I send money every week.'

'What, you think a few shillings is enough? You're just one big stupid-arse joke. Get a proper job.'

'Oh, is that why when you heaved yourself into bed with me you tell me to move aside so you can start screwing my wallet?'

She grabbed the baby out of my arms.

'Look, I don't have no time to play any stupidness with you. I'm telling you straight, that if you don't pull your low-ranking shit up, me and Jerry will be in Canada by September.'

I took a step towards her. She'd been threatening to leave for Canada for months.

'You ain't taking my flesh anywhere, you hear me.'

She just kissed her teeth and turned her back on me. Then she got into the car that waited for her with a brother at the wheel. I didn't feel jealous that she had found lovin' elsewhere, but it hurt that some other man was looking after my son. That hit low. I watched the car reverse and speed away, knowing I would have to make a decision about my son soon or he could be lost to me for ever. That's when I started thinking that maybe Marcie was right. Maybe I was giving too much of my life to music and the Black Fist.

Then June 16th happened, squashing all my doubts.

We were all playing some bones in the Sweet and Dandy with the newly installed black-and-white TV blaring in the background. The news flashed on, flinging words and pictures that made us stop. I don't remember what the exact words of the newscaster were, but black children had been killed by police in Soweto in South Africa. One image stuck with me – a young man carrying the body of a dead child. We were stunned. Shocked. Pissed at the world. That one minute our children could be peacefully calling for their rights and then the next their lives were extinguished at the hands of the legitimate police. Things changed in the

Republic after that. We became hardcore, militant. Houdini wanted Sean gone. I knew what he was feeling, but Sean was my boy. I was grateful (at least then) to Shakespeare for talking up for Sean and letting him stay. But Houdini wasn't happy, no way.

We all got frightened and thought that Soweto could happen on the streets of London. So we developed a new strategy. Every time any of us witnessed police harassing a brother in public we would stop and watch. Once a few of us stopped it gave other people the courage to do the same. The first time we did it, the Babylon tried to move us on, but we told them to show us the law which said walking the Queen's streets was illegal. They didn't like it, but there was nothing they could do. It made them jumpy. It made us hold our ground. The air in London ran thick and tense. By the start of July the heat in London was screaming. The weatherman on the BBC gave some technical explanation why we were having it. He was wrong. You want to know what that hot weather was? It was tempers between the police and the community rising to fever point. Only two ways a fever can go – it either breaks or boils over.

I was playing to a packed crowd a week later, on the fourteenth night of the heatwave. We were playing the Four Aces, off Kingsland Road, which had at one time been Dalston Theatre. The crowd were mashing up the place with their funky dread moves. The way they moved was flinging heat into my face, making the sweat peel with the same ease of the lyrics leaving my mouth.

I was absorbed in what I was doing but I knew exactly when Shakespeare entered the hall. I sensed the changed beat long before I saw him. I hitched my head back and scanned the crowd. I found him, shuffling from the back, through the crowd towards the side of the stage. I was surprised to see him. Houdini often came down, but never Shakespeare. I always suspected that he liked crowds but he didn't like the squashed heat of them ramming into him. I kept my eyes glued to him, expecting him to come to the front of the stage. Instead he went to the side and walked up to Sean, who lounged back by one of our houses of joy. I saw him slip something into Sean's hand. He didn't look at me, like he was in a hurry to be somewhere else.

After the gig, as soon as the lights went up, I was off that stage and moving towards Sean.

'What you have for me?'

'Ah?' in that airy-fairy way most men got when they drank that one jar too much. I reminded myself to have a word with him later. Bring up his old man to remind him that drink was a pleasure, not to blot out suffering.

'What did Shakespeare give you?'

He dug into his pocket and pulled out a piece of paper. He handed it to me the same time as he took the last dregs from his bottle.

*Need you at the Republic*
*Alone*
*Bring the van.*

'Take me with you. I can't go home. My old man's back,' Sean said.

I glanced back down at the note, my eyes stuck on the word *alone*. I looked back at Sean and the dance of alcohol whining from him and knew that if he didn't come with me tonight, in a few years' time he'd become a replica of his old man. It ain't easy when home is the place you're most afraid to go. I scuffed my tongue over my top teeth. Yes, I felt a responsibility for him. And now I was living a life where responsibility was the ultimate musical word.

So I took him with me five minutes after the crowd went home. We dropped the boys off and drove on towards the Republic. When we got there, Sean jumped out of the van and moved directly to the back doors to unload the houses of joy. I told him to leave them, we'd deal with them after seeing Shakespeare.

We both took the stairs two at a time, unlocked the door and moved inside. We made our way down the steps to the basement.

The mingling of voices drew us on as we neared the door. A door slammed, the creak in its echo telling me that it was the door that led from the basement to the garden and the side steps to the front. The voices stopped. I pushed the handle down and entered. Shakespeare and Houdini sat on chairs near each other, cast in the murky, low yellow light that told me the bulb was going to blow soon. I noticed a third chair kicked back like someone had moved out in a hurry. On the seat lay a black cap. The scuff of Sean's feet made Houdini twist his head towards us. The smile that began to paste his mouth jerked back when he saw Sean. He shot out of his chair, making it wobble on its back legs. Houdini looked well vex.

'Man, you was meant to come alone.'

He kissed his teeth as he strode towards me. Shakespeare didn't move an inch, assessing me and Sean. Vexation kicked up inside me as well. After a hard night plugging the stage I didn't need no verbal licks from no one.

'My boy goes where I go,' I said, throwing my words straight into Houdini's blood-filled face.

He kissed his teeth for a second time and then spun to face Shakespeare.

'This is fuckrees, man. This ain't going to work. No sir. No way.'

Shakespeare spread his palms out as he said, 'Let's just cool it down and rest.'

Me and Houdini stood there, gunslingers in a stand-off, both not wanting to back down. 'This isn't the time for unfinished business,' Shakespeare whispered from his chair. 'Sean, take a seat,' he continued.

I was surprised that Sean followed the command instantly. Like he'd been doing it for most of his life. I sat down.

'We're in danger of losing the Republic,' Shakespeare said.

That made me sit up, fast.

'What you saying, man?' I asked.

'Let's just say that our financial backer has pulled out.'

'What financial backer?' I chucked my question at him. But Houdini jumped in instead.

'I told you we should've never got involved with them, man,' he said.

'Involved with who?' I asked.

My head swung back between both men. Shakespeare stood up like he needed to stretch his mind. As he moved, the spice of his aftershave shook up the space.

'In order for us as a people to be free we need to be independent. We need to own our own property. We can't be held hostage by a landlord. One day we're in and the next we've got to pack our bundle and get out. Isn't that how it's always been for us? So the Black Fist took a stand and decided to buy this house outright. After what happened to our children on June sixteenth I knew we had to take a stand.'

'But where did you get the money from?' I asked

I looked at the cap on the empty chair and knew whoever owned it was also the money man.

'Stupid gal had to mess it up,' Houdini mumbled.

Gal? A woman?

'What woman?'

Shakespeare looked at Houdini with eyes dipped in heat. Houdini fought back with, 'You might as well tell her to come out.'

Suddenly the door connecting with the garden opened. In stepped a woman. A white woman. The same one I had seen talking to Shakespeare at the march on the police station. The same one I'd seen with the older man at Unity Road police station. The same one (no one had to tell me) that Shakespeare had been talking to at the basement door. She was slim, with brown hair that swam around her ears. Her hands folded over the waist of her banana jeans and bottle-green corduroy jacket. Her face wasn't my style but I could see how some men might check it over more than once.

'King Stir It Up and Brother Sean, meet Anne, our financial backer, otherwise known as the Black Fist's Minister of Monetary Well-being,' Shakespeare said.

I stormed to my feet, my head hurting with the motion.

'Someone better start speaking to me, man.'

Don't get me wrong, I didn't have any problem with white women, but the Republic had made me think it was wrong. Plus, tangling with a white woman could only mean trouble.

She said nothing, like she was under strict instructions to be quiet.

'Easy, man. Anne has done a lot for us. Anyway, we don't have any time for introductions, just listen to me,' Shakespeare said.

I closed my mouth.

'OK, King, this is how it is. Anne was in the process of helping us to buy this house. As this place was under a compulsory purchase order the landlord wasn't bothered. Then last week the compulsory purchase order was lifted, so the council aren't going to flatten the square any more. Now the landlord isn't so keen to sell. The price of the property went up considerably. At the same time Anne's assets froze up.'

'Don't look at me. The bank ain't going to lend no broke musician any money.'

Shakespeare ran his hand through his Afro. He took a deep breath and said, 'There is a way out.'

None of us said a word. It was as silent as when the crowd waits for that bass line to drop. Shakespeare dropped the B-line.

'This house is one of many owned by the landlord. So losing this one is no big deal to him. He's willing to let us buy this house for the nominal price of one pound if we do two jobs for him.'

'A pound?' Houdini's voice rang out, saying the same words that were clapping in my skull.

'You know what they say, Shakespeare,' I started, 'if it's too good to be true . . .'

'Don't you think I've told myself that? But there's no other way forward.'

'So what does he want us to do?'

'That doesn't matter. All I need to know is whether you're in or out.' His voice switched chord gears and slipped into his beautiful beat. 'Just remember, when you make your decision the loss of the Republic will not just hit us, it will devastate the whole community.'

Immediately Houdini said, 'I'm in.'

I thought a bit longer. If Shakespeare wasn't telling us what the job was it must be some serious doo-doo. But we could lose the Republic.

'Tell me a bit more about this job.'

'OK, all we have to do is collect something and put it somewhere. Just this one thing and the Republic's ours.'

Sounded simple. But as I should know from my dealings with Marcie, it's the tings that start out simple that become the most crazy. But you know what I did? I nodded my head anyway. Shakespeare went to his desk. Pulled out what looked like some black clothes. He kept them gripped in his hand as he calmly said, 'We're going to Hoxton.'

Man, I nearly fell down dead there right away. Telling us we were going into Hoxton was like telling us we were going into hell. Hoxton was the capital city of the National Front. Only racists and mad people went there.

'No way, man,' I said, standing up.

'Do you want us to lose the Republic? Watch our children be mowed down on the streets by state-sanctioned gunfire?' Shakespeare shot all over me.

I didn't say anything. Just kind of like put my head down a bit.

'All we've got to do is one simple, quick job. Collect something, store it away. Then we're back here and the Republic is ours.' His voice was back to bedtime-story man.

The image of that young man carrying the dead child in Soweto came to me. I looked up at Shakespeare and nodded.

He went over to Houdini and gave him one of the things he had in his hand. I still couldn't see what they were. He walked over to the girl Anne and did the same thing. He walked past Sean and came straight over to me. His hand shot out, so I took what he held out to me. I gazed at it. The ground began to bubble under my feet when I realised what it was.

A black ski mask.

The tape clicked off. Bernie's voice clicked on.

'Why would they have needed ski masks?' she asked.

The darkness hunched over the bedroom. LT didn't answer her. Instead he looked down, dazed, at the clothes he was wearing. Black tie, black pants, black jacket. Why was he wearing black? He remembered. It had been the King's funeral that morning.

He reached across, hand shaking, to the lamp and put it on. He settled himself back on to the pillow and glanced across at Bernie on the bed beside him. He steadied his breathing, but couldn't steady his hand.

Bernie carried on talking.

'Why would a group of black radicals go into Hoxton of all places in 1976? Didn't the National Front have a stronghold over Hoxton back then? I thought you said that your father never went into Hoxton?'

Finally he answered her.

'As far as I can remember he never went there before the incident in '84, The place was lower than hell, not just to him, but for most Black people.'

Bernie played with the black butterfly clip in her hair as she lowered her voice and asked, 'I know you don't like thinking about 1984, but can you remember how the King reacted to being in Hoxton that night?'

'That's a fool's question because he behaved like any black

man would. Scared. Fucking outraged.' He stopped talking. His tongue did a full circuit of his lips as he thought back to that night. It darted back inside. Settled back into its groove ready to talk. 'I do remember that as soon as we hit Hoxton Square he got really jumpy. I just thought it was because of the National Front following us.'

She stopped playing with her butterfly clip.

'Something definitely happened in Hoxton before 1984. Whatever it was, we need to find out about it.'

He looked up at the record covers on the ceiling. A storm of annoyance thundered inside him. He was annoyed with his old man. He'd grieved for him this morning, said goodbye to him this afternoon, and now the King didn't even have the decency to wait three days before his resurrection. Beresford was right, he should be concentrating on his career.

'Bernie, I don't want any dealings with Hoxton. All I want to do now is make sure I'm ready for the big time knocking at my door.'

'You're just scared that you might find out that the father you thought you knew maybe didn't exist.'

'I didn't realise that I was lying on a black couch and paying you by the hour.'

'Takes a man to take a stand,' she sneered the quote from Public Enemy's 'Revolutionary Generation' at him.

That made the anger blow up in his face. The words ripped from his gut.

'The King is dead.' He thumped his chest. 'Do you know what that means? It means my call-and-response partner isn't coming back. When I win the Writer in Residence of Ladbroke Grove competition he won't be calling out, "That's my son." When I get that bloody record contract he won't be shouting out, "That's my boy."'

He bowed his head. Took three breaths. Deep. He saw the image of the King's empty flat. The rhythm of his father's home ripped out by intruders. The King's record collection gone. All the physical memories that LT was meant to have, taken. He remembered what the King had said on the tape – 'Responsibility isn't a musical word.' The King might have once believed that but that was not how he'd taught LT to live his life. He pulled his head back up.

'OK, Miss Marple, how are we going to do this?'

She didn't smile at his joke.

'We've got a new name to add to our list – Anne. Did he ever mention knowing an Anne?'

'Never saw the King with a white woman in my life. Don't get me wrong, he didn't have a problem with them. As he used to say, when you're deep inside a woman the colours you see ain't nothing to do with the colour of her skin.'

They looked at each other. Their eyes caught. Assertive brown meeting retreating blue. He knew what she was thinking. The same thing he was. About the last time they had made love on this same bed. Bernie pushed herself off the bed. Hitched her neck tall as she moved to stand by the door. Leaned, back straight, against the wall. Tilted her chin to the left. Avoided his eyes as she started talking.

'We're going to have to view this Anne as a ghost. Because she was white they obviously made sure no one knew she was connected to them. The Black Fist would have ruined their radical African-conscious credentials if people knew they were associating and taking money from a blue-eyed devil. Which means it's going to be hard for us to find her. So we urgently need to find that last domino box with the tape. Let's assume that he left tapes number one and two with people he trusted – Sister Begum and Sean Sparkle. Who else does he trust? What about the other members of his sound system?'

LT ran his fingers through his 'fro as he said, 'Desmond "Blood" Jay now lives in Florida and Maximus died back in '98.'

'Who else, then?'

LT's hand dropped from his hair. He eased back on to the pillow.

'The only other person I can think of is May.'

'What's your life like tomorrow?'

'Hectic. Beresford has organised for me to play the ultimate black role model at a press conference at the Marcus Garvey centre in Notting Hill at eleven tomorrow morning.'

'After you're finished meet me outside. We'll start with the King's boy, Sean Sparkle. The King didn't say that Shakespeare gave him a black mask, but he was certainly there. Then we'll visit May. While you're at the press conference, I'm going to check the local archives to see if they have any documents about this Liberation Republic.'

He nodded with the slow swing of reluctance. She flicked her chin to the left. Tilted it. Caught his eye. Smiled. She posed on the wall like the fresh-faced musician he'd once known.

'You haven't even asked a girl if she wants something to drink.'

Her words were slow. Easy. Doing that low, throaty voice technique that only she and Al Green seemed to know.

He looked back at her, surprised. Since she had come back into his life she hadn't asked him for anything. So why now? He left the bed. Took three strides to reach her. Looked down at her. Couldn't read the emotion on her face, but couldn't look away either. Just like when he kept pressing the repeat button on his MP3 so he could listen to his current favourite track – just one more time. Except it was never one more time.

Repeat. Play.

Repeat. Play.

That was how he kept looking at her now. He eased his head towards her face. Let his lips hover over her partially opened mouth. He spoke, his quiet words brushing on to her lips.

'Let's see if you want something hot or cold.'

He lowered his mouth. Fused with her lips. Kissed her in a massaging motion. Her mouth picked up his rhythm. Together, they didn't rush it. Took it easy. Then he felt her stop. Close her mouth. He pulled his head up and said, 'I think you want something hot, but maybe not today. I'll get you something cold. Lots of ice.'

Then he left the room. As soon as he was in the kitchen a puff of air pumped out of Bernie's mouth. She rushed over to the bed. Grabbed the Dictaphone. Pulled out the tape and shoved it into her pocket.

### 'MY LIFE OF HELL WITH RAPPER'

The next morning LT cursed his former girlfriend Mel as he read the headline on page 4 of one of the two tabloids that came through his door. Now he realised why Mel had yelled at him, 'A poet can survive everything but a misprint,' the last time he'd seen her. It was a story about him, where Mel wasn't pulling her punches and was packing in her lies.

'Today the woman who shared the life of notorious rapper Lord Tribulation talks for the first time about what she knows.'

'I felt I had to speak,' former convent-educated Melanie Fitzpatrick told us. 'He'll do anything to get to the top. I know what he's like. When he heard about that poor kid on the life support machine, I bet he was laughing. Then he would have gone straight on the Net, checking what it had done for his CD sales. That's what he's like – he's sick and dangerous . . .'

LT furiously skimmed down, then growled 'Bitch' when Mel said he had a shrine to Karen Carpenter in his bedroom. His eyes rushed over the remainder of the article. Stopped when he reached the final line – 'Always forgive your enemies – nothing annoys them so much'. No one needed to tell him that his former girl-friend was quoting from Oscar Wilde.

He dashed the paper on to the floor. He was annoyed with himself. Annoyed that he'd forgotten the advice given to him by an old-time musician. 'When you're in the public eyes, son, and you've got to let a woman go, always do it gently. Don't tell them it's over, just say you need your own creative space for a while or you're really gay and you can't fight it any more . . .'

He picked up the other tabloid as he sat on the sofa. He wasn't surprised to see that its headline on page 5 had also gone for the jugular.

### 'TEEN'S FANTASY DEATH WISH FIRED UP BY RAPPER'

A photograph of Aunt Glad throwing a punch outside the funeral accompanied the headline. Underneath was a story by reporter Tad Williams about the alleged connection between LT's music and a young boy finding himself on a life support machine.

He tossed the paper on top of the other one on the floor. He grabbed the broadsheet. It had also followed the scent of his blood, but via the 'let's have a dialogue' approach.

## 'RAP: TOO HOT TO HANDLE?'

LT flicked through the newspaper until he got to the comments page and saw that the editorial was written by the Minister of Culture, Clarissa Hathaway. His eyes scanned quickly, catching words like 'defective', 'dangerous' and 'destructive'.

He shoved up, standing tall and furious. He screwed the newspaper into a ball. As he headed for the front door he pushed the ball deep into his pocket to remind him what he had to do at the press conference.

Bernie skipped past the white van parked behind her car and entered the former Victorian school that housed the local archive centre. It cast its austere but simple Queen Anne façade over the smaller houses, no doubt a deliberate move by the Victorians to let the community know it meant business in its efforts to civilise the working classes. She climbed the narrow stairs to the second floor. The main archives were housed in a rectangular assembly hall and adjacent classrooms. She approached the counter that stood opposite a stepped gallery at the other end. Behind the counter sat a woman, humming at a small desk with a computer. Bernie caught the tune – Cole Porter's 'Love For Sale'. The woman swung her swivel chair to face Bernie. She peered at her over thick, black-framed glasses and asked, 'May I help you?'

Before Bernie could answer the woman stood up and moved towards the counter. She was a few inches shorter than Bernie, with her whole mid-forty life defined by her comfortable green mohair cardigan which was buttoned to her neck. She smiled at

Bernie. Her head swayed slightly, as if she couldn't get Cole Porter out of her head.

'Yes,' Bernie answered as she smiled back. 'I would like to view any material that you have concerning 1976, especially anything to do with an organisation called the Liberation Republic.'

The woman's head stopped mid-sway.

'That name doesn't sound familiar, but I'll go and find out.'

She left the counter and disappeared inside the middle classroom on the right.

Three minutes later she was back. Her thin mouth was compressed into a harassed line. The two top buttons of her cardigan were undone.

'Is there a problem?' Bernie asked as she leaned on the counter.

The woman's fine fingers did a jig on her chin.

'I can't understand this. Let me just check the computer.'

She retreated to her desk. The tap of her fingers was hard as she consulted her monitor. Two minutes later she was back at the counter. She undid another button on her cardigan.

'I'm sorry, but it would appear that the section of the archive you want is unavailable.'

'Unavailable?'

The archivist's button-brown eyes fluttered at Bernie.

'Yes.'

'How can it be unavailable?' Bernie continued probing.

The archivist's fingers twisted in the two remaining buttons.

'It would appear that 1976 is currently being . . .' She paused. Freed the buttons. 'Recatalogued and classified.'

'Is that normal practice?'

'Yes. But . . .' She did not finish the sentence. Her teeth pinched the inside of her bottom lip. As the blood recoiled from her lip it resurfaced on the skin of her face.

Bernie didn't speak. She let the woman take her time.

'We usually do it in year order and the last year to be recatalogued was 1967.'

'You looked surprised, like you didn't know?' Bernie persisted.

The archivist carefully elongated her neck. Did up the buttons on her cardigan.

'Well, I'm usually in charge of all recataloguing. But it must have happened when I was off with the flu.'

'How long will it take?'

'It can take up to two months.'

Bernie swore and shook her head. Her fingers danced in her hair until she found her baby butterfly clip. Black with sprinkles of glitter on it above her right ear. She unclipped it. Moved it half an inch. Clipped it back. She thanked the woman. The woman shuffled back to her desk. Slipped back into Cole Porter's world. Bernie turned towards the exit. Her steps were sharp as she realised that someone was trying to erase all traces of the Liberation Republic.

LT stood at the entrance to the main hall at the Marcus Garvey Community Centre, contemplating the best way to make an entrance in front of the waiting press. The emotions he felt inside ranged from anger to terror, but he couldn't show the media that. He chose his walk – upright 'n' glide. He reminded himself to never rush it. Always take it easy.

He entered the room.

As Beresford walked beside him in a tanned, tailored suit.

He took it easy.

As the fifteen members of the press turned in their chairs to stare at him and his Emmett Till du-rag.

He took it easy.

As he passed the large posting advertising the exhibition 'Exodus: The Story of Black London 1948 – the New Millennium'.

He took it easy.

As he reached the long table facing the audience with its two chairs.

He took it easy.

He sat on the first chair and Beresford sat next to him. Beresford did his gentle smile as he turned to LT and whispered, 'Don't forget, you look upset and bewildered while I answer all the questions. I know it will be tempting to try and answer some, but if you mess up here your career will be over by lunchtime, so let me take care of it . . .'

LT nodded. Beresford eased his smile away and faced the press. He started.

'Ladies. Gentlemen . . .'

He read a short statement expressing regret for the injuries both children in the arson attack had suffered, disclaiming any responsibility, quoted some 'socially conscious' lyrics from LT's music, absolutely condemning violence and giving a long list of anti-racist and pro-peace gigs LT had performed at. Then he asked whether there were any questions. The first question shot their way.

'If Lord Tribulation is whiter than white – if I'm allowed to say that – why did the police find this arsonist's room festooned with pictures of him?'

A camera flashed like gunfire.

'Presumably you mean alleged arsonist?' Beresford countered. 'Unless you're one of those journalists who thinks bothering with the formality of a trial is political correctness gone mad?'

Beresford leaned back in his seat, locking his fingers together in front of him on the table. 'I'll ask you a simple question instead – are you responsible for the actions of your readers? Is Paul McCartney responsible for Charles Manson because Manson claims to have drawn his inspiration from "Helter-Skelter"? Are the people who wrote the Bible taking the rap for the Spanish Inquisition? Let's be sensible here, shall we, people? Lord Tribulation is an artist – that's all, OK?'

'Can you explain,' a nasal voice called out, 'how a boy who is scoring A grades, is a gifted violinist and comes from a good family decides one day to firebomb a house whilst listening to a song that explicitly talks about burning buildings down?'

Beresford sighed. Leaned forward and said, 'We live in complex times. Who really knows what's going on in that boy's life? I understand that he set the fire using a bottle of rum, which suggests that he has an association with alcohol.'

'Can I ask Lord Tribulation . . .' the next question began, point-edly, 'what does this line he wrote mean: "I've got my gat and don't forget that . . ."?'

'"Gat" means,' Beresford interrupted again, 'the same as it meant when Raymond Chandler used it the 1930s. It's slang, as you well know, for a certain type of gun. Lord Tribulation uses it as a metaphor for our times. The song "Gasoline Ghetto" is a story. In stories characters do things and sometimes they do bad things, but you don't hold the author accountable. Are you saying that Shakespeare should be banned because of the body count in his plays?'

A restless ripple ran through the reporters.

'I've got a question for Lord Tribulation,' a strident voice began from the middle of the pack. 'Can you tell me what the point of him being here is? He seems to have taken a vow of silence, uncharacteristically so, seeing as how mouthy and aggressive he was outside his father's funeral . . .'

Beresford saw his chance and took it. He rose to his feet, using his hand to gently guide LT up as well.

'You've had your answers, ladies, gentlemen. Please remember that this is a very traumatic time for Lord Tribulation as he has just laid his father to rest. So if you have any other questions please do not hesitate to contact me.'

They moved from the table and began to walk past the press. One young reporter stood up as they got abreast of him and fired off a question. Beresford stopped. Smiled. Dipped his head low and whispered in the reporter's ear, 'You're not holding the whip on the plantation any more, son.'

He pulled himself straight and guided LT past the barrage of continuing questions. They entered the corridor and moved into the cool and quiet of a back room. It had no furniture and was filled with closed and half-opened boxes that were pushed to the far side of the room.

'Thanks,' LT said.

Suddenly he realised he didn't need to show the world he could take it easy, so he collapsed back into the wall, shifting the air in a steady rhythm into his body.

Beresford pulled out his calm smile.

'No problem. They've had their bite at you and will leave you alone. With the state of the world today something else is bound to shift you off the news top ten. What's happening with Paradise Records?'

The room filled with LT's frustrated sigh.

'A brick wall at the moment. They contacted Window. Everything's on hold until they speak to their people upstairs. Four days to go to the bank holiday carnival and my life's looking like shit. I can't afford for the smell to reach the noses of the judges of the Writer in Residence slam-down.'

'Well, I'm one of those judges and life is only smelling sweet from where I'm standing.'

LT smiled gratefully at Beresford.

'Son, here's some good news. I've found you a solicitor who will assist you in challenging the coroner's findings. These are her details.'

Beresford pulled a card from the top pocket of his jacket and passed it to LT.

While LT looked at the card the older man continued, 'Why don't you call your witness and find out if she's willing to make a statement to the solicitor.'

LT pulled out his mobile. Scrolled through his address book. Found the cab office number. Punched 'call'.

'Can I speak to Jane Blake?'

The answer he got made him fill the room with a string of swear words.

'What is it?' Beresford asked, taking a step towards LT.

LT leaned the back of his Emmett Till du-rag into the coolness of the wall.

'She don't work there any more.'

LT found Bernie outside the community centre, leaning against her Caribbean blue Mini.

'What happened?' she asked, pushing herself forward.

'Beresford was good. He made them feel like they were in the zoo, not me, so I think they'll leave me alone now.'

Bernie leaned back, deflated, on to the car and told him about what had happened at the archive centre. He eased back next to her and told her about the witness from the cab office.

'But the solicitor has requested a summary of the coroner's medical report,' LT finished.

'Have the police contacted you with any new information about the burglary at your father's?' she asked.

'I've called them more times than I did my last girlfriend. It's either "sorry, sir, there's no progress" or they don't even bother to pick the phone up.'

'So at the moment all we've got are Sean Sparkle and May,' Bernie confirmed.

'Who shall we leave our calling card with first?'

'Mr Sparkle. Didn't you say his place in London is in Notting Hill?'

LT took out the card Sean Sparkle had given him. He nodded at her. They set off on foot, past the white van that was parked on the opposite side of the street.

# IT'S LIKE DIS, IT'S LIKE DAT

They travelled up through Ladbroke Grove until they stood outside Sean Sparkle's London residence. Number 13 St William's Gardens. Including the basement and attic, the house was a six-storey, white Georgian-style townhouse. Each floor stood on top of the one under it with the grace of a freshly iced wedding cake. To LT it looked like a mini-sized mansion. From the tales the King had told about growing up in Notting Hill LT had no doubt that back in the sixties and seventies this magnificent house would have been either divided into bedsits cramped with families, many of them migrants, or a brothel. But once the mid-1980s hit, huge amounts of cash had started to heal the wounds of urban deprivation and replace it with the cosy feel of gentrification and fashion. Some said nothing much had changed because Notting Hill was still doing what it did best – squeezing as much money out of everyone for accommodation.

Bernie pressed the intercom next to the door. LT shuffled his feet, nervously.

'Don't forget what I said.' LT checked Bernie from the corner of his eye. 'Mr Sparkle is a legend. He's influential . . .'

'Nothing like using the death of a loved one to keep that networking alive.'

The blood shot to his face at her comment.

'Just go easy, OK?'

'And remember what I said, don't mention the tapes.'

A male voice on the intercom asked them what they wanted. They had agreed to say that LT was taking up Sean's invitation of calling him up if he needed any help. The telecom clicked off. They were left standing in the gutsy heat for a few minutes. Then the door eased open.

A small man, doing his last lap of his thirties, wearing designer T-shirt and shorts, greeted them. They followed him through the large, sparsely furnished hallway. The walls were lined with framed photographs and pictures of Sean Sparkle receiving awards and with some of the artists he'd worked with and made. LT searched for one of him and the King. He found none. The man left them at the entrance of a room that looked like a white marble temple anointed by hidden uplighters. The room ran to a huge bay window with four slim panes of glass, two of which cuddled together as French windows leading to a small walled garden. A long gallery divided the north wall. The man they were looking for sat in the middle of the room. Wearing his customary white. On a low-back sofa with his hands clasped behind his head. His eyes were closed. His face serene and calm as he listened to the composition that pumped from the hidden music system. Japanese taiko drums. Cymbals and bamboo flutes yelped from one speaker, while drums and human shouts charged from the other. The drums pulsed beneath LT's feet. The toes inside his right trainer began to lift, fall, lift, fall.

Sean Sparkle's eyes bloomed open as the final, climactic drumbeat rolled across the room. He looked at them. Gave them a laidback smile. He unfolded his legs. Stood up. Moved towards them with the ease of a boy wandering across a midday beach, not a man who would soon be knocking on fifty's door.

LT put his hand out for the customary handshake, but Sean Sparkle pulled him into his embrace. 'Good to see you again,' he breathed, so close to LT's ear he could hear the undercurrent of Californian vowels mixed with his still-strong London accent. Sean broke the embrace but kept his arm around LT's shoulders. He pulled LT into the room.

'Who's your friend?'

LT introduced Bernie, using her full name.

'Classy name for a classy lady.' Sean caressed Bernie with his cheeky eyes.

Bernie gave him a full smile, but her eyes were frosty blue.

'Let's go up and have some real peace and quiet.' He nodded towards the gallery.

As they moved up the stairs, Sean said, 'Don't worry about all that tosser stuff they're writing about you in the newspapers. They love it really. Look at me – I've done all the bad-boy things. Now they're giving me lifetime achievement awards. Wankers.'

The space in the galley was a soft and wild Moroccan style. Mauve, geometric-patterned cushions, saffron rug and walls painted in the hue of tangerine drama. A simple wall-to-ceiling door leading to a roof terrace was coyly opened, as if hiding a belly dancer shimmering under a palm grove. Bernie and LT sat on the sofa, while Sean sat cross-legged – meditation style – on a large floor cushion.

'So what can I do for you kids?'

LT gave a loud cough, trying to shift his nerves.

'I wouldn't be disturbing you if I didn't think it was important, but you being a famous star and all, I just didn't . . .'

Bernie's voice cut over him.

'Jerry's challenging the coroner's decision that his father died from natural causes.'

The cheeky look in Sean's eyes faded as he said, 'Like I said at the funeral, I didn't know the King that well, so how can I help?'

LT and Bernie looked at each other. Their eyes caught. LT turned back to Sean. He did his awkward cough again, dipped his voice low and said, 'We know why you called your company 50p Trick.'

The peace of the day drained from Sean's face. His eyes moved over LT and Bernie with indecision. Suddenly he jumped up. Moved to stand at the terrace doors. He turned his back on them. He jerked his hand through his hair. LT got up to stand beside him.

'I'm not trying to create any problems. I'm just looking for answers. We know he was the one who gave you your leg-up into the music industry.'

Sean's eyes brooded on to the terrace as he spoke, his accent now a complete son of East London.

'He cared for me. Looked out for me. Protected me when the world wouldn't. He saved my life. I never told him that the day he saw me sitting on the stairs was the day I decided to die. I was getting ready to go back upstairs, run a bath and end my life. I've always been such a fucking drama queen. After I'd been with him for a while he wanted me to stand on my own two feet. Become independent. He said he didn't want to be part of my limelight. That's not why he played music. So over the years we discreetly kept in contact. I always sent him money to make sure he lived a comfortable life.' He moved his head gently, like a bird in the morning wind, towards LT. 'How did you find out about me?'

LT shifted his eyes away from Sean so he couldn't see the lie.

'Once he knew he was dying he started telling me stories about the old days and of course your name popped up because you held an important place in his life.'

'Tell us about the Liberation Republic,' Bernie shot out, taking up the role of questioner.

Both men turned to face her. Sean Sparkle thrust his hands into his front pockets.

'We used to go there before and after gigs. Then we had our small studio there. Those were good times. People would come around and listen to us jam. The King really believed in what they were doing.'

'Were you involved with their politics?'

Sean laughed, with a joy that was not reflected in his eyes.

'Are you joking? White people were blue-eyed devils. No whites allowed, that was rule number one on their ten-point manifesto. But I was tolerated because I was the King's boy.'

'So who were Shakespeare, Houdini and Anne?'

He swallowed. Looked at the rug. His hands came out of his

pockets. Curled at his sides. His hair flopped back from his cheeks as he raised his head.

'Shakespeare was the leader of the Black Fist.'

Bernie pushed with her questions as she leaned forward. 'Who were they?'

'I suppose you'd call them the militant wing of the Liberation Republic.'

'So who is this Shakespeare?'

Sean Sparkle's gaze hit the rug again.

'I didn't know him so well. Sort of remote guy. Kept to himself. You got to remember I was white. No way was I going to be part of Shakespeare's inner circle.'

'What happened to him?'

There was a two-second silence before Sean replied, lifting up his blond head.

'The word was that he got killed playing freedom fighter liberating Zimbabwe, which was then Rhodesia.'

'What about Anne?'

Sean flicked his tongue on to his bottom lip. 'I don't remember an Anne.'

'White . . .'

'No white women allowed.' For the first time Sean's voice was hard. Angry.

LT's stare collided with Bernie. The words in her throat dried up. LT turned to Sean and said, 'Look, Mr Sparkle, we'll level with you. We know that on a night in July back in '76 you went to Hoxton with my dad, Shakespeare, Houdini and a white woman called Anne. We know they were all wearing masks. Where did you all go?'

Sean swiftly turned back towards the roof terrace and rasped, 'How did you find out about that night?'

'Like I said before, the King started telling me stories.'

'I don't know where they went because the King sent me home. I didn't ask them where they were going. Do you know why? When you live with a man who beats the bollocks out of you, you learn not to ask questions.'

He swung around. Faced them. Looked at them like he was back cringing under the falling force of his father's fist.

'We know they left the Liberation Republic with ski masks . . .'

'Kids,' Sean Sparkle interrupted. 'I'm sorry, but we're going to have to cut this one short. I've got to be on the radio in half an hour.'

He swiftly moved towards the door as he spoke. Bernie and LT followed him. When they reached him, the cheeky expression was back on his face. He shoved his hand out to Bernie. She took it.

'Always refreshing to meet a pretty lady before you face the outside world.'

He turned from her. Embraced LT. Tightly. Whispered in his ear, 'The King would be so proud of you, he would.'

LT whispered back, 'Did my dad leave his best jacket with you?'

Sean shoved LT away from him. LT stumbled. Sean's hand covered his mouth. His chest shook with the uneven pattern of his breathing. He looked at LT, eyes shining like sapphires. Then his hand fell away from his mouth.

'Sorry, son, I didn't mean to do that. Must be tired. Like I said, kids, I got to go.'

He turned from them. Retreated into the room. Shut the door quietly in their faces.

LT dragged in a smooth smoke from the apple-flavoured tobacco in the large Turkish water pipe positioned on the floor of the café. He peered at Bernie across the table and asked, 'Did you see how he reacted when we mentioned the best jacket?'

They sat in the roasting, sweet-pepper perfume of Ahmed's Turkish café on Portobello Road. They had ordered small cups of sweet coffee and a water pipe, or shisha as it was referred to on the menu. LT had his own water pipe at home. Sweetened tobacco was the only drug he allowed himself. It cooled him down. Helped him to think. And after visiting Sean Sparkle that was what he needed to do.

He passed the water pipe to Bernie. She pulled some smoke into her system. Exhaled and said, 'The last time I saw someone look like that it was a torture victim being threatened with deportation from this country.'

'Whoever did over the King's place must have taken it because there was nothing in that denim jacket he left in his bag.'

She pinched her nostrils, sniffed softly and said, 'I'm not so sure. There's something going on with this jacket that we're missing.'

They stopped talking. Just passed the water pipe between them. Got lost in the residue of apple-molasses tobacco surfing their bodies and their own thoughts.

'Let's just think about what we've got so far,' Bernie said five minutes later through a punched zigzag of smoke from her mouth. 'We know something went on in 1976. That something has to do with a radical black group, with a white woman, going to racist Hoxton on a night in July. We know Sean Sparkle is involved. Know that he's scared shitless of whatever is in your father's best jacket. I think he's lying about not going to Hoxton. And because he's lying, I don't think we should believe him when he says that Shakespeare is dead or his denial that he doesn't know who Anne is. We do know that the King met someone on the day he died. We got three candidates – Anne, Shakespeare and Sean Sparkle.'

She passed the water pipe back to him as she asked, 'Do you think Sean was involved in your father's death?'

He sucked, grateful for the sweet taste that settled in his mouth as he looked for an answer. He found it.

'No. He definitely knows something about something, but no, I don't think he hurt the King. On the tape the King talked about him with such affection. I never understood how the King existed on the money he had. Or how he could afford a private hospital room. But Sean must have been helping him over the years. That doesn't sound like the rhythm pattern of someone who would want to kill him.'

'Which leaves Anne and Shakespeare.' Bernie stood up and added, 'Come on, we've still got work to do.'

His lips did their last dance with the water pipe. Then he followed her to the back of the café. To the Internet section. They

paid the woman sitting at the first computer and took a seat at
a workspace in the corner. Bernie took the seat opposite the screen
and LT sat at her side. As her fingers hit the keyboard he asked,
'You're a woman with her nose to the ground. What do you know
about the music biz and the Internet?'

'Do you mean downloading material?'

Her fingers kept moving as she spoke.

'No. Artists networking and cutting out the record companies.'

'I'm no expert, but the word is that the record companies didn't
take these networks seriously. Or downloading. Now they have,
people are saying it's too late. The artists have got their foot in
the door and are already leaping forward. Why?' She raised her
head with her question.

'Window thinks I should hook up with some Internet network
called music@yourfingertips.net.'

'Yeah, I've heard of them,' she carried on as the screen changed.
'Run by a bloke called Barry Gibson. Very successful, although I
believe he started life as a member of a very rough family . . .
here we go.'

They looked at the screen as the hits came up for the Liberation
Republic. Twenty hits.

'Don't hold your breath. Most of these won't be what we're
after. Actually, I'm surprised that there's that many as there's very
little material about the black radical movements in Britain in
the 1970s.'

She was right. The first dozen hits ranged from a club in Brazil
to a site for motivating the population to take control of their
lives.

'Let's refine the search.'

She added the word Hackney. Two hits. She smiled as she activated the first site. The screen lit up. A 'Sorry – site no longer
available' notice. She hit the second site. The same notice came
back.

'Just as I thought. Those shadows are back and covering their
tracks. We've got to find that next tape, which means a visit to
May.' She exhaled as she leaned back in the chair.

She started to get up, but his voice made her stop.

'Can we do one more search?'

'What?'

His fingers touched his du-rag.

'I need to find out what happened to a boy called Emmett Till.'

May Branigan, or Auntie May, as most people called her, lived in an azure-painted Georgian house in Hackney that was nick-named True Blue. But the colour of her home wasn't how it acquired its affectionate name. May ran a beauty parlour, or as she called it 'a community of uplifting spirits', from the two lower floors. Customers agreed that you went in looking a mess and came out feeling true blue.

Bernie and LT approached the front door. His steps were heavy. Weighed down by what he'd found out about Emmett Till. By flashbacks of himself in that skip in Hoxton all those years ago. He shook off the horrific images thrown up by the Internet. Shook off Hoxton. Pressed the doorbell. The powerful, gospel sincerity of Jimmy Cliff singing 'Many Rivers To Cross' fluttered from inside the house. LT wasn't surprised. Auntie May loved every last song on the soundtrack to the film *The Harder They Come*.

The music cut off. The door opened. May stood there wearing a turquoise head wrap that accentuated the gloss of her teak-coloured face.

'Well, if it isn't tribulation on my doorstep! Come in, son, come in.' Her lips spread with affection as she looked over at LT.

The house was scented with the flavour of crushed mangoes massaged with the aroma of oils ranging from olive to carrot and the heat of blow-dryers rising from downstairs.

'Let me get you something to wet your soul.'

She turned her back on them, ready to go to the kitchen, but LT's voice stopped her.

'No thanks, Auntie, we just want to ask you something.'

She took them into the front reception room. As with many people from the Caribbean of her generation, the front room of her home was reserved for special guests. It was a room that LT had seen many times before in the houses of other relatives. He could close his eyes and itemise the contents without having to look – waist-high glass cabinet containing glasses that were rarely used; a transparent coffee table in the middle; settees with crocheted covers over the headrest; photographs of family and friends; a 3D picture of the Last Supper presiding over all inside. The only touches of modern living in this room were the plain-patterned white wallpaper and the vanilla-scented candles on the mantelpiece of the black marble fireplace.

Bernie and LT sat on a gently reclining suede settee. May remained standing. She peered closely at LT's face.

'Your skin looks really terrible, boy. What you washing it with? Sandpaper? I have just . . .'

'May, do you have one of my dad's domino sets?' he interrupted her.

May kept running her gaze over his face. Finally she straightened and said, 'One minute, I have it right here.'

She scurried, laughing, out of the room.

'Thank God for that,' LT signed to Bernie.

When May re-entered, she held a small brown package in her hand. LT smiled as he took it. His smile and satisfaction receded when he realised that it was not a box of dominoes but one of May's legendary home-made soaps.

'This will do the trick,' she told him triumphantly. 'Use morning and night and your skin will soon be back to your old shine.'

He read the writing on the label: 'Soothing cocoa butter moisturising soap. Washes away demonic spirits'.

His hand tightened around the soap.

'May, I don't need . . .'

'Yes, you do . . .'

The kiss of his teeth rang across the room as he shoved up.

May stumbled back. LT knew he had crossed a line by kissing his teeth. You just didn't do that to the older folks. Bernie stood up. Stepped between them. Faced May.

'Auntie, put your feet up,' Bernie coaxed as she swept her hand

towards the single sofa nestled by one corner of the fireplace.
May cut LT with her eyes as she sat down. Her hands smoothed
her cornflower, petal-print skirt. Bernie sat back down. Turned to
her. LT held his ground in the middle of the room. Bernie fixed
that wonderful smile she had used when she had played the violin
to now play Auntie May.

'Do you know where the King's dominoes are?'

May's lips tightened as red rose up on her cheeks to massage
under her skin. She opened her mouth once but no words came
out. She tried again and this time the words came with a trembling smile.

'The way he held his dominoes was the most beautiful thing
that I've ever seen. He caressed them in a way that told me he
cared about them, and I knew that if his hands ever touched me
he'd care about me.'

'Of course you cared about him, which means he trusted you
of all people with his dominoes.'

May's hands rubbed against each other as if they were feeling
the dominoes.

'I know how much he loved them bones.'

'Can you get them for us?'

Her hands and lips twisted.

'He left them with me. Told me to give them to you.' She
avoided looking at LT.

'Please get them for me,' he breathed out in relief.

May twisted her hands some more. He took a large stride
towards her.

'You have still got them?' His tone was low.

She finally peered up at him, her words coming out in a high-
speed run.

'Well, yes and no. See, there's this exhibition called "Exodus:
The Story of Black London 1948 – the New Millennium" that's
opening at the Marcus Garvey centre in Notting Hill on Sunday
as part of the carnival celebrations. The exhibition is going to
have all kinds of things – clothes, photos, records, films – to
show the public. They asked people if they would give them their

things on loan, so I thought it would be a great final tribute to him to share his beloved dominoes with other...'

LT leaped over to the fireplace. Banged his fist down on the mantelpiece. Two of the candles tipped over and fell to the carpet. He swung back towards the two women.

'Tell me I'm not hearing this, May.'

Bernie stood up as she said, 'Easy, Jerry.'

'You had no right to do it, Auntie, no right. He left them to me.'

His voice grew louder with each word. May jumped to her feet. Rushed her five-nothing frame right up to him. Stood in his face. She didn't yell, but quietly said, 'You didn't even stay long enough at the funeral to collect his ashes.'

The anger staggered out of him. He leaned on the mantelpiece.

'Can we get them back from the exhibition?' Bernie asked.

May didn't answer. Instead she left the room and came back with a number scrawled on a piece of paper. She handed it to LT and said, 'This is their number. They might give them back to you.'

He took out his mobile. Punched in the number. Five minutes later he terminated the call.

'What did they say?' Bernie asked.

'That they were disappointed and the rest, but they'll send them to me in the post.'

'Maybe we should go and get them,' she suggested, her voice laced with impatience.

'Can't. They have all the exhibits at a depot somewhere, so they'll send them out from there. We'll just have to wait.'

He turned to May and asked, 'Did he give you his best jacket?'

'Don't know nothing about no best jacket. The King was a person who never wear jackets too often. He liked to go with his chest open, to impress the girls.' May ended on a small chuckle.

LT leaned down. Kissed her on the cheek.

'Thanks. I'm a bit busy so we'll be off.'

As Bernie got up, Auntie May looked hard at her face.

'Your skin's good but the shine from your eye is missing. I've got just the thing for you.'

She left them. Came back with another soap, wrapped in pepper-mint-green paper. In her other hand she carried a blue rucksack. She handed the soap to Bernie. Bernie read the label: 'Gentle mango and strawberry exfoliating soap. Rejuvenates past sorrows back into joy'.

LT noticed that, instead of smiling, Bernie had this awful expression gutting her face.

'You all right?'

She twisted her gaze away from him as she whispered, 'Yeah. Just been a long couple of days.'

'And this, my boy,' May started speaking, making him turn away from Bernie, 'is for you.'

She handed the blue rucksack to him. He unzipped it. Looked inside. The liquid in his mouth dried up.

'Oh yeah. Thanks.'

'What's in the bag?' Bernie asked as they retook to the street. She pushed the soap into her pocket.

'The King's ashes.'

Her mouth formed into an 'Oh'.

'So what do we do while we wait for the dominoes?' he asked.

'I think I know someone who might be able to help us find out more about Anne and Shakespeare.'

'Who?'

'My mother. She was involved in all that radical stuff back in the seventies. At least she was until her heritage came knocking at the door. She might know something about the Liberation Republic and the Black Fist.'

As they approached Bernie's Mini, LT's mobile started ringing. He hustled the mobile from his pocket. Nodded his head as the caller spoke. He gently lowered the phone. Glanced at Bernie anxiously.

'That was the King's solicitor. He wants to see me at four. I didn't even know that the King had a solicitor.'

LT stood outside the King's solicitors and was surprised. Surprised that they were in Chancery Lane and not in an office above a shop, dealing with personal injury and immigration problems. Plain-bricked. Three storeys high. Immaculately kept, with a sign that said 'Notary Public and Family Law'. After leaving Bernie, he'd rushed home and donned a two-buttoned, finely tailored pinstrip suit. Thin, clipped down with respectability. No du-rag. On his back was the blue rucksack holding the King's urn. He wasn't sure what to do with it, but leaving it at his place on its own didn't seem right.

He pushed the transparent entrance door. Walked inside. It was pale, almost cold, with grey-white marble floor tiles and antique white walls. Soft cushioned leather chairs were positioned near the receptionist. He walked over to her. She looked up. About fifty, slender, restful face, with kind grey eyes.

'Mr Scantleberry, Mr Richards is expecting you.'

He didn't ask how she knew his name. Her roving look told him she'd seen his face in the newspaper. She picked the phone up and made her call.

'Mr Richards is ready to see you. Take the lift to the second floor.'

As he turned away her voice pulled him back.

'I was sorry to hear about your father. He was a good man. Always bringing me bottles of rum to take home for my Ted.'

He nodded and moved to the lift. Mr Richards' PA was waiting

for him when he reached the second floor. He was shown
into a large office, with a wooden floor, door and bookcases.
The wood gave it a colonial feel. LT looked up, expecting
to see a ceiling fan whizzing overhead. Mr Richards was
seated behind a desk so small that LT knew he was a man who
prided himself on his efficiency and neatness. The solicitor stood
up. Medium height, small boned with rosy cheeks that said he
was looking forward to his retirement, waiting just around the
corner.

'Mr Scantleberry, it's a pleasure to meet you.'

His voice crackled like an old seven-inch single. They shook
hands. He waved for LT to take a seat. He pulled the lapels of
his jacket closer together then resumed his seat.

'Can I just say that I was surprised to get your call,' LT began.
'The King, I mean my dad, never told me about having a solicitor.'

'Your father was an old-fashioned man. Part of the generation
who believed in taking care of their death while they were still
enjoying their life.'

The solicitor opened a drawer. Pulled out a document wallet.
Manila. Official. He opened it up and pulled out a white envelope. Nothing special, it could have come from any stationery
cupboard.

'I'm not sure if you were aware that your father was a man
of means. He left you something quite substantial.'

He passed the envelope to LT. LT took it and immediately felt
the weight of something inside it. He hesitated. He wasn't sure
of the protocol.

'Please, go ahead,' Mr Richards said gently.

He slid his thumb under the sealed edge, opening it. He put
his fingers inside. Felt something cold, maybe metal. He grasped
it. Lifted it into the warmth of the room. Two keys. Standard Yale
and mortar locks. He looked at the solicitor.

'I don't get it . . .'

'There's also a piece of paper inside.'

He placed the keys on the desk. Pulled the piece of paper from the envelope. It was folded in two. He opened it out. Read it. An address.

16 Cecil Rhodes Square.

As the afternoon rolled to a lazy 4.15 p.m. mood, Bernie sucked up the final line of coke as she hunched over in her car. She was parked a few metres from her mother's house in Chelsea. She leaned back. Let out a hard laugh. No, not mother. Irinia, with its long, flowing Russian vowels, that's what her mother liked to be called by everyone, including her. When she was eight, Grandie, her affectionate name for her grandmother, whispered, over her cocoa and cream crackers, that it was really Irene, named after her great-grandmother, who had been a Lancashire lacemaker. But her mother liked her illusions, so she kept calling herself Irinia. Bernie laughed again. Softer. Longer. Great, the coke was kicking in. No way could she go inside that house on her own.

She wiped the residue of powder from under her nose. Got out of the Mini at the same time as a white van pulled up across the road. Began striding down the cobbled street. She reached the small, Portland-brick house. Pressed the bell on the six-panel olive-green door. Squeezed her nostrils. Exhaled.

A tall woman, in a smock dress, in which red won the battle of the patchwork of colours, opened the door. Her blonde hair was a texture of silk and fluff from years of experimenting with dye. Her eyes were her daughter's – bright, meddlesome blue.

'Darling.' Her mother pressed her lips to her cheek. 'You haven't been answering my calls.'

'I thought you'd be too busy with all your charity work to spend time worrying about a lost cause like me.'

Her mother lifted her carefully shaped eyebrow at Bernie's comment. But she said nothing, so Bernie stepped into the hall. She was always disconcerted by the fact that the interior of the house reflected the interior of Irinia's mind – cluttered, a mish-mash of styles and devoid of any music. The hall was tight, with neutral walls, a glamorous nineteenth-century chest of drawers and a gold-plated mirror that looked as if it came from page 70 of the Argos catalogue. The substantial drawing room carried on the theme with its classical Turkish carpet, art deco lighting, smattering of family furniture that had come up through the ages and frilly red curtains that Mae West would have gloried in front of.

Irinia perched herself on the double-ended tiger-print chaise longue. Her fuchsia nails flashed as she patted the space next to her. Bernie peeled the rucksack from her back and sat down. Close enough to smell the gin in the glass her mother held, but far enough away to give the impression she wouldn't be warming the cushion for long.

Instead of the dramatic tone Irinia often used, she began speaking in a manner that was dead serious.

'He rang to tell me you called him and said you refused to meet him.'

Bernie hugged her bag to her rolling middle.

'Bernie, you can't just pretend this isn't happening,' her mother pressed on. 'What about Jeremiah? I know you've been seeing him again. I saw your face in a photograph in the newspaper this morning outside his father's funeral. You've got to tell him . . .'

Bernie's voice jumped across Irinia's as she bit out, 'Didn't you do all that banner-waving stuff in the seventies?'

Irinia sighed, giving in to her daughter's desperate need to change the conversation.

'Didn't everyone, darling?'

'Do you remember a character called Shakespeare?'

Irinia laughed. Solid and free.

'I knew a Lord Byron. Real romantic. I did him on Saturdays and Sundays and your father had me all to himself during the week.'

Bernie let the last sentence pass over her.

'What about somewhere called the Liberation Republic?'

Irinia pulled some gin from her glass.

'They all fancied themselves as liberation republics, but not one of them called themselves that.'

'It was in Hackney, before we moved there.'

'We lived in squats in Notting Hill and, of course, in Europe.'

'What about a white radical called Anne?'

The lines on Irinia's face deepened as she thought.

'No, I knew an Annabelle and an Anita. And, of course, an Anna Marie . . .'

'But no Annes?'

Her mother shook her head as she savoured more gin.

'If you remember anything else, let me know.'

She leaned over. Kissed Irinia's warm cheek.

'Bernie.' Her mother looked at her with the eyes of a parent. 'We need to talk.'

'I don't want to do this.' Bernie reached down. Grabbed her bag.

Her mother's hand circled her wrist. Tightened as if she were teaching her how to cross the road all over again.

'This is getting worse. He tried to see him . . .'

Bernie clasped her hand to her mouth in shock.

'But he didn't manage to talk to him. Sniffing a bucketful of Californian cornflakes up your nose is not going to make it go away.'

Bernie's hand tightened around her mouth.

'You can't hide anything from me. I am your mother. Just like I was your mother fifteen years ago . . .'

Bernie furiously shook off her mother's hand. Shot up. Yelled out, 'Yes, you were my mother fifteen years ago and we agreed what I had to do. It's not right to ask me to break that agreement now.'

She hooked her bag on to her back. Left, with the tap of Auntie May's 'rejuvenates past sorrows into joy' soap slapping her thigh from inside her jacket pocket.

Irinia Ray lifted the curtain and watched her eldest daughter storm across the street. A shiver of sadness moved through her as she lowered the curtain. She moved across the room. Stopped by the phone. Picked it up. Dialled. She sat at the writing bureau.

'It's me. She's just been here. She's angry. Hurt. Give her time to cool down. What I suggest you do is contact her tonight. This is her home phone number ...'

Bernie knew her mother had been watching her as she rushed through the quiet street back to her Mini. Her vision was hazy, with small dots, or snow lights as they were nicknamed by cocaine users. She knew Irinia was right, that she'd have to deal with this shit that had dive-bombed back into her life. But not yet. As she reached the car Vivaldi's Concerto no. 3 in F minor started to play. Her mobile ringtone. She swore. Pulled it out. She looked at the name and number on the screen. LT. The one person she did not want to speak to at the moment. She debated whether to answer it. She answered it.

'What happened at the solicitor's?' She got in first.

'You won't believe ...'

An arm locked around Bernie's throat. A man's arm. Her attacker heaved her up. Slammed her into his hard body.

'Bernie?' she heard LT's voice coming through the phone.

She tried to yell, but the words caught somewhere deep in her throat. She was dragged backwards. Quickly. Her foot ricocheted against the car door. The phone toppled from her hand. She flailed her arms and legs wildly. The arm increased the pressure, diminishing her access to her airway. She twisted her right foot back, kicked, trying to connect with the body behind her. The arm twisted her neck to the side. Pain danced inside her head. Her mouth fell open, gasping for breath. Her attacker grunted with the zeal of a shot-putter. Jerked his arm up. Her feet left the ground. Her head fell backwards, her eyes connecting with the soulless sky.

'Get bloody on with it,' the man carrying her growled.

The heat from another figure appeared in front of her. He got between her legs. No fucking way, she thought. She bent her right knee. Pulled it up to her chest. Kicked out with the ball of her foot. The powerful front kick hit the chest of the person in front of her. A high grunt split the air.

'Bitch.' The word whacked her in the face at the same time as a fist hit her belly. Pain smashed over her. Tears convulsed from her eyes. Hands were thrust in her pockets. Searching.

'Hurry up,' the voice next to her ear snarled.

The hands kept searching.

'It ain't fucking here.'

'Check the bag.'

Suddenly the man behind her let her go. She tumbled to the ground. Her hands came out to break her fall. But she wasn't quick enough. The side of her head hit the road. Dazed, she tasted grit as her mouth flopped open. She felt something sharp touch her back. She knew what it was. She had felt knives before in her line of work. Fear and her saliva pasted the ground under her lips. The knife sliced through the rucksack straps. Her bag was torn from her back. She heard shuffling. Scraping. The contents of her bag landed on top of her back. A hand began to move on her back, through the items, searching. Suddenly it stopped.

'I got it. But there's this tape as well. Should I leave the tape?'

'No, let's take it as well. It might put the smile back on the face of Mr . . .'

The name slammed through the blistering fog of Bernie's pain. It was the last thing she heard before she lost consciousness.

The man on the bench by the river swore as he looked at his watch. His people were twenty minutes late. Two things he hated in life were time-wasting and having to dodge questions when people asked about his past life. Time-wasting he could not do much about, but recounting the chronicle of his early adult life he had down to a pat. He took out a cigar from his inside pocket. Slim, aromatic, Cuban. He lit up. Inhaled. He heard the footsteps behind him. They were here. The men he'd been expecting stood in front of him, their breathing harassed in the early evening air. No words were needed. He put out his hand. The more muscular of the two men placed in it the digital Dictaphone, with the initials B.R. engraved on it. His hand clenched over it.

'We found this as well.'

The man held out a small tape. A Dictaphone tape. He noticed the label on the front. He read it.

'Revival Selection: 1976, Volume 2'.

Beresford was woken up from his evening nap by the continual screech of his intercom. The music coming from the music system was still on.

Steele Pulse's *Handsworth Revolution*.

Track two.

'Bad Man'.

He eased up. Got to the video intercom in the hall. He saw the distorted, panting face of LT on the screen. He shook the sleep from his body and rushed to the door.

'What's wrong?' he asked as he let the younger man in.

'I tried Window, but I couldn't get him. I didn't know who else to . . .'

'Slow down and let's get you sat down.'

He took LT into the main room. He cut the music as LT started pacing.

'Something has happened to Bernie.'

'Tell me slowly.'

LT stopped pacing, looking at him with beseeching eyes.

'When I phoned her today she suddenly stopped talking. I could hear grunts and feet scraping like a scuffle.'

'Do you think someone has hurt her?'

LT nodded.

'Have you tried to contact her again?'

'Yeah, but it's a constant engaged tone.'

'What about hospitals?' Beresford said it softly.

LT shook his head.

'Do you know where she was going today?'

'I think she went to see her mum, who lives in Chelsea.'

'I'll try the hospitals there.'

Beresford moved to the phone. Made the calls. On the third call he talked longer. LT stopped pacing. Beresford put the phone down. He looked at LT.

'She's in the Chelsea and Westminster hospital. She was attacked earlier today.'

LT rushed into the cubicle in the accident and emergency department. Beresford followed, more slowly, behind him. On the bed, curled on her right side, lay Bernie.

'Bernie?' he called softly as he approached the bed.

She didn't move. His hands shook as he reached out to touch her. Fear and rage made his hand hover over her head. He took a deep breath and let his hand fall. His shaking fingers fluttered into her hair. Caressed the strands. The heat from her body sucked at his fingers, pulling his hand deeper. He heard her groan. He yanked his hand away.

'Bernie?'

She groaned again. This time she rolled over. His breath pulled back in his chest when he saw the left side of her face. A scraped red bruise ran like violent blusher across the whole of her cheekbone to the corner of her eye. The skin under her eye was raised and puffy.

'I bet it doesn't look as bad as the time I got held up on the Syrian–Lebanese border.'

Her voice was small. Rasping.

'What happened?' Beresford asked as he walked to stand by LT.

Bernie's blue eyes shuffled over Beresford. She drew back into the bed.

'I got jumped outside my mother's.' She clutched her belly as the last word left her lips.

'Do you want me to get someone?' LT's voice shook.

She shook her head. Her top teeth gripped her bottom lip.

'Just my pumps.' Her body expelled a sharp lisp of air after each word.

'Should you be doing that?' Beresford's voice took on the tone of Daddy.

Her gaze clipped into him again. Then she swung herself to the side of the bed, the tips of her toes grazing the floor. LT grabbed her trainers, peeping from under the bed. He straightened and turned to Beresford.

'Thanks for the lift and help. I'll check you tomorrow.'

'You sure, son?'

LT nodded. Beresford looked over at Bernie. Nodded his head and left.

LT hunkered down by her feet. He carefully eased on her trainers. As he straightened up he saw the expression on her face. Her lips began to move. She had something to say. So did he. He knew they were going to do their classic Double D minor Rap routine, speaking at the same time. He got his words out first.

'Right, that's it . . .'

'We need to talk . . .'

'No more Starsky and Hutch . . .'

'But I've got to tell you . . .'

'I'm contacting the boys in blue . . .'

'The men who attacked me said a name . . .'

'Let them sort this out . . .'

'They said Beresford Clarke.'

'You what?' His hands sprang off her.

She rushed to her feet. Wobbled. Steadied herself. She gazed at him with hooded, blurred blue eyes.

'At least, that's what I think I heard,' she said, the syllables of each word laced with pain.

'You think? Before you go-tell-it-on-the-mountain, baby, you better be sure about the version of the good news you're preaching.'

'Just before I lost consciousness, I'm sure that one of the men said Mr Clarke.'

'If I pick up the telephone directory, do you know how many Clarkes I'm going to find? The bloke who attacked you might've been chatting about his shoes, for all you know.'

'I know what I heard.'

'What you think you heard.'

'What do you really know about him?'

'I'll tell you what I know about him. Since the press have been spitting in my face he's the only man prepared to wipe their muck off. Me and Window went to see him, not the other way round. He brought me all the way here so I could find you. He was concerned about you. Don't you get it, that man has been like a father to me.'

'He's got under your skin, so you aren't going to listen to me.'

'I'm listening all right, but the lyrics you're spinning are from the wrong tune.'

She grabbed on to his arms and in a trembling voice said, 'If Beresford has been behind this, I'm scared. Scared for you.'

He felt the texture and resonance of her beautiful violin hands immobile on him. For the first time since she had come back in his life, her fingers were at rest on him. Even when they had made love, the day the King's body had been found, her hands had kept moving, seeking, never staying in one spot for too long. Since then she'd kept her hands to herself. Now they remained still. Soft. On his skin. Exactly spaced apart as she used to place them on the fingerboard of her violin. The pads of her fingers lightened. Dropped away from his arm.

'OK, if you don't want to believe me . . .' she said, and stumbled to get her jacket, slung on the end of the bed. She picked up her bag. Winced as she straightened up.

'They took my Dictaphone. The one with the witness statement on it. Did you tell anyone about the witness statement? Beresford?'

He shook his head angrily at her and said, 'No, so there's another bit of your Beresford puzzle that doesn't fit.'

She shifted her eyes away from him. He knew that look. She was holding out on him.

'Cough up the rest, Bernie.'

'They also took the King's second tape.'

'But they can't have because it's at mine . . .' He stopped. Stared hard at her, finally catching the truth in her eyes. 'What the fuck did you take it for?'

'To keep it safe. You're always losing things. Can't remember where you put things. You couldn't even remember where the King's bag was that Sister Begum gave you.'

'Well, thanks to your wonderful organisational skills we're now minus a tape.'

She moved towards the cubicle exit, groaning in pain. He sighed as his shoulders softened. He knew that whatever happened in his life, Bernie Ray would most probably be the most amazing woman he'd ever known. He took long strides. Reached her.

She passed her bag to him. He took it. They walked out of the cubicle.

'And do you know what the bitch of it is?' she said.

He put his arm around her and shook his head.

'The bastards took my coke.'

'Maybe it's time for you to let it stay gone.'

She huffed at that. Then asked, 'What did the solicitor say?'

'That I'm now the owner of 16 Cecil Rhodes Square, otherwise known as the Liberation Republic.'

# TRACK 6: RIDE THE RAILS

Bernie opened the door of a two-up, two-down Victorian terrace off Stoke Newington Church Street. LT was surprised that she lived a ten-minute bus journey from his home.

'I didn't realise you lived back in Hackney.'

'Just under a year now, although I've owned this place for longer.'

'How did you get your hands on a piece of Church Street?'

'Mummy bought it back in the seventies when Stoke Newington was one of those places you never mentioned you came from. I got it on my twenty-first. Completely falling to bits. A bit like me back then.'

He opened his mouth to step through the door of the past she'd opened, but she cut him off.

'Don't want to talk about it. I've already been dropped on my head today, I don't need it happening again tonight. What we do need to talk about is Beresford . . .'

Now it was his turn to cut her off.

'Bernie, you can keep singing that song, but you know what, girl, my radio ain't on.'

She looked at him as if she was going to say more. But she turned and put the dimmer light on in the hall instead. He was surprised that her home wasn't all wooden floorboards. Instead it ran with a carpet the colour and bounce of a Bacardi hurricane cocktail. It felt peaceful. Graceful. A retreat. Huge necklaces hung from door handles – onyx beads, green glass beads, jagged amber. He wondered whether hot pink topaz was looped over the handle of her bedroom door. She took him into the lounge, which was minimalist, with a sofa, music collection and plasma TV. In each corner was a different stringed instrument. Instruments he'd never seen before. Must be from her travels around the world.

As she dug in her pocket and placed the soap Auntie May had given her by her telephone she asked, 'Cup of something?'

'Spring water. From the fridge.'

She disappeared into the kitchen. He didn't follow her. She might not want to talk about the past but he was going to take his opportunity to find out. Best way to find out about a person was to look through their music collection. He moved to the shelves on the wall by the TV. They went from the ceiling to the floor. CDs were stacked high, vinyl kept low. He couldn't see it all but he ran his eyes across to get a good impression. Reggae, classical, jazz funk, soul. Old skool rap. A world music section that ran from the manic, Afro beat of Fela Kuti to the soft Welsh harp of Catrin Finch. What told him most about her was what he didn't find. No violin music. So she really had put her violin to rest. Funny she should have all those stringed instruments.

'Like what you see?' she asked as she re-entered the room.

He turned to face her. She rested the two glasses she carried on the glass table. They passed each other as he took a seat on the sofa and she went to the music collection. She flipped out a Stevie Wonder. He didn't need to ask to know it was the epic double album *Songs In the Key Of Life*. As well as having a passion for Public Enemy they both shared a hot-tempo appreciation of Stevie Wonder. An appreciation they had both picked up from their fathers. She put on their track, 'Pastime Paradise'. She floated to the table. Took her cup. Sat next to him. Must be all that medication they gave her, he thought, because no way would she usually be getting that close to his body heat. They rode the rails of the synthesised drums and swaying strings of the song. When they were young they did this little play with the words. Parts of the lyrics would slip into what felt like a one-word poem. She would recite one word, he would say the other. That's how they worked it out. Now the song dived into the poem. Suddenly he couldn't help it. In unison with Stevie Wonder he called out the first word.

Bernie threw back the next one.

That's how they went on.

Him

Her

And Stevie

Just like it use to be.

Then instead of following the song's next line they invented their own words, just as they used to. By the pucker of her mouth he knew she was going to throw the first word.

'Tribulation.'

'Inspiration.'

'Temptation.'

'Flirtation.'

'Sensation'

'Gyration.'

'Adoration.'

'Elation.'

As each threw a word, their faces got closer. Now their lips were less than an inch apart. He leaned his mouth into her. She leaned into him.

Together they whispered, 'To the peace of the world.'

Their lips melted into a fifteen-year-old hungry kiss. She drew him down with the softness of her hand around his neck. His hands started to go under her top, feeling the emotions deeper than her skin. The phone started ringing. They ignored it. He lay over her. Her hands scorched his back. The song crested in a Hare Krishna gospel crescendo. The answer machine hissed on. A man's voice. Formal, as if he knew her but didn't know her well enough.

'Berlina, we need to talk about . . .'

Frantically she pushed LT off. She flopped off the sofa. Ran to the answer machine. Clicked it off. She kept her back to him as she said, 'Thanks for bringing me home, but you need to go.'

'Boyfriend? Sounds a bit old for you.'

She didn't answer him. Wouldn't look at him.

He stared, puzzled, at her back for a few seconds. Shifted his gaze to the answer machine. He got up. Hit the door. Stopped. Didn't turn around as he said, 'I don't have the right to interfere in your life, but do something for me tonight. If you've got any Daddy C in the place don't take it. Get some rest to repair that beautiful face of yours. See you at my place tomorrow, eleven thirty sharp.'

He wasn't happy about going, but he left.

The door closed. Bernie looked down at the answer machine. A finger sawed inside the dipped groove in the middle of her collarbone as she thought about her violin key. Thought about who had it now. She leaned the bruised side of her face against the cold wall. Her life was catching up, not just with her, but with Jerry as well. And she didn't know what to do.

He took out the Dictaphone he'd purchased in the shop that evening. Old. Bulky. The exact fit for the tape he had in his hand. If he was still a God-fearing man he would pray to the Almighty right now for this not to be what he thought it was. He placed the Dictaphone on the small table. Hunched over. Pressed 'play'. The King's voice burst into the room.

'Welcome to the Black Fist,' Shakespeare whispered with pride as he flicked the light on in the basement of the Liberation Republic . . .

He wanted to scream. To crush the tape under his heel. But he knew he had no alternative but to listen to it. To find out whether what the King would say had the potential to make his hard-fought-for achievements come off the rails.

That night LT couldn't sleep. He stood, chest bare, nipple ring twinkling in the dark, as he watched the canal drift by. But it wasn't the canal he saw. Two other images took up his mind. The first one he knew was true, the second he could swear wasn't. When he'd tried catching sleep tonight the first image had flashed in his mind. An image the Internet had told him was true.

Mississippi.

The summer of '55.

A fourteen-year-old boy.

Emmett 'Bobo' Till.

Displayed in an open casket, at the bequest of his mother, so everyone could see how hatred mutilates the world. Then the image had twisted into him, suffocating in a skip, with a demon wearing a halo singing 'Redemption Song'.

Sweat spreading like a new skin over his body, he'd got up. Poured his favourite summer drink – pineapple and coconut water. Swallowed it in a few gulps. Then he'd gone back to bed. That was when the second image came, the one he knew just couldn't be true.

Hoxton.

August 17th.

The King lying dead.

Beresford Clarke dragging his body.

The image was hazy. All wrong. He knew it couldn't be true. Not Beresford Clarke. Everyone said he was a saint. Even good old Queen E was going to tap her sword on to his shoulders soon, if the rumours circulating were true.

A police car screeched past the block, bringing him back to reality – the image of the canal in front of him. He shook what Bernie had said about Beresford from his mind. Strolled back to bed. Lay down. Tried to catch some sleep. But those two images jumped under the duvet with him. At 3.30 he got up when the cramps came and his nose started bleeding. Mixed another shot of his favourite summer drink. Didn't try to sleep any more.

# TRACK 7: THE LIBERATION REPUBLIC

'Tell me the address again,' Bernie said to LT the next morning as she sat in the warm currents of his sitting room.

She'd arrived five minutes before the time agreed. Twenty-five minutes after eleven. But he was dressed and ready to go, wearing a light blue du-rag with the Emmett Till headline he just couldn't let go. She wore a tan-coloured suede baker's-boy hat low over her face to hide the bruise. But he saw it and it looked worse in the freshness of the morning light. Tender. Swollen. Her eyes were the murky blue of pain.

'16 Cecil Rhodes Square.' He lounged against the sitting-room door with the rucksack that contained the King's ashes at his feet.

She pulled out her electronic organiser and tapped away.

'Got it.'

She smiled. Her head dropped closer. The smile came off her face.

'Can't be.' The tone of her voice was like she was swearing in the back row of church.

'What is it?' He stepped towards her.

She flipped her head up. Avoided his gaze. Pushed her organiser into her pocket.

'Nothing.'

'Bernie?'

'It's nothing.' She looked up at him, tried to revive the smile on her lips, but failed.

'I'm going to find out soon enough, so spit.'

'My bruise is killing me. Come on, let's hit the road.'

As soon as Bernie's Mini swerved into what had once been Cecil Rhodes Square LT knew exactly what she hadn't been saying. Cecil Rhodes Square no longer existed, except on maps of London before 1990. The square stood on part of the estate once owned by the Rhodes family. In honour of its most famous member and the 'founder' of Rhodesia, the Victorians had named it after Cecil Rhodes. The fuss about the name didn't start until over a hundred years later. By the mid-1980s some of the multiracial community were outraged that one of their most memorable squares was named after, as they shouted it, an oppressor of black people. The struggle had been long, but in 1990 the council had rubbed Cecil out, making it plain Rhodes Square, in honour of other members of the family.

Of course, it would never be just plain to LT because it was the same square where the teenage arsonist had thrown his petrol bomb.

'Is someone having a laugh?' LT said as the car passed the burnt-out shell of number 12.

Abruptly, he said, 'Stop the bloody car.'

Bernie did not respond. She carried on driving.

'I don't want to be here. What do you think the papers are going to say when they find out I've come here of all places? Get the headline now – "Murder Rapper Goes On Macabre Journey".'

'Of course they wouldn't write that, it's far too long for a head-line.'

He leaned back into the primrose leather seat. Bernie grinned, letting the car crawl so that she could read the numbers on the doors.

'There it is.'

LT leaned forward. Whistled. The King was right. This house had style and presence. A four-storey Victorian monster. The type of house that growled its presence and stood its ground for all to see. It had a grand sweep of stairs that led to the front door and stairs that led to the bottom as if for lesser beings to travel on.

'How the fuck did the King get his mic hands on this?' he said to himself.

As Bernie parked the car she said, 'Now I understand what he kept looking at when I was with him at the hospital. He kept staring out of the window. I assumed that he was looking at the boy who eventually set the fire, but he wasn't. He was looking at the house with the black-fist knocker. He was looking at the Liberation Republic.'

They hopped out of the car. LT slung the rucksack with the King's ashes on his back. Bernie led him up the stairs. They stood in front of the great door. Stared at the door knocker. An ebony black fist. Bernie's hand reached out. Lifted the knocker, as if it were an old friend, and held it.

'Welcome to the Liberation Republic,' she said, as if she were a master of ceremonies addressing an audience.

'What if someone's living here?'

Bernie let the knocker drop hard on to the door. They both waited. She knocked again. No sounds from inside.

He slotted the key into the lock. Twisted. Pushed. The draught of cold air greeted them as they stepped inside. The house was nothing like the King had described it. Now it was fully restored to its late Victorian glory. As soon as they stepped inside something in the passage drew them in. LT wasn't sure what it was. Its narrow length? The serene whiteness of the walls? The plasterwork that resembled tiaras? The way the staircase stretched with a lover's yawn that dared them to step up and discover all the fantasies that lay ahead?

'How on earth did the King get his hands on what had once been the Liberation Republic?' he asked as his eyes glided around.

She didn't answer his question. Instead she said, 'Let's explore.'

They started upstairs. As on the lower floor, all the rooms had been restored. Fireplaces, toe-hugging carpet, ceilings that looked as if they had gone up the day before. Back downstairs they entered what must have been the Sweet and Dandy café. Now it held only one table and three chairs in the middle of the room. The extension gave a panoramic view of the huge garden in the back.

'If this was the café,' Bernie started, 'then this' – she moved out of the room to the hall – 'must have been the door that led to the Black Fist office.'

LT hesitated. Gulped. His mouth was dry. Indecision was an indulgence he had dumped years ago. In his business 'what if...' was a question for those afraid to step through the door.

'What's the problem?' she asked as she stared at the emotions stabbing new lines into his features.

'No problem.'

He hitched the rucksack closer to his shoulders and calmly walked towards her. Like most human beings, the door had aged with time. Bernie pushed her palm against it. It opened.

They looked down from the top of the stairs. It must have been a normal five-second walk to the door at the bottom but from where they stood it looked a long way down. A long, dark way down.

'Be careful. The steps might be rotten,' he said, taking the lead. This was his house so he was going first.

He gripped the banister. Tried out the first step. He let his toes touch it, testing the pressure of his weight. He flattened his whole foot on it. The step creaked like a cat's cry in the night. He tried the next step. And the next.

'I think the steps are all right.'

With renewed confidence he walked down. His foot hit the third from last step. The step sighed. Groaned. Gave way. His foot shot through the wood. His other leg was already lifting, ready to move forward. His weight catapulted forward. His hand skidded along the banister. He tightened his hand to stop it moving, but he kept moving forward. Bernie grabbed his rucksack. She hung on to it. Hauled him back. The swift reversal of direction made his trapped foot twist back. A splinter pierced his shin. He cried out. Bernie cupped her arms around his waist. She held him steady until his rocking stopped.

'You all right?'

'Just hold me so I can get my foot free.'

Her grip tightened around his waist.

'Be careful. Don't wrench it out.'

He arched his trapped foot down. Wriggled it from side to side as he slowly eased it up. His foot came loose. He leaned heavily into Bernie. She pulled him closer. They stood there for a while like that. He wasn't sure why, but they did.

'Shall I check your foot?'

Their past flashed over him. Made him shiver. He eased away from her.

'I'm fine. Let's just get on with this.'

He took the two remaining steps slowly. Bernie joined him at the door at the bottom. Similar to the one upstairs, but closed.

'Shit,' he swore as he tried both keys in the lock. The door didn't budge.

'Let me have a go,' Bernie offered.

'Been moonlighting as a magician?'

She rolled her eyes at him. Opened her bag and pulled out a credit card.

'Tools of the trade,' she said, colliding with his suspicious stare.

She gently inserted the side of the credit card between the lock and frame. She eased the card from side to side. They heard a click. She turned the handle. The door opened.

She pushed it wide and said, 'After you.'

His shin tingled as he moved forward and stepped inside. Dust flicked into his face, making him cough. He put his hand over his mouth. He couldn't see. The room was dark, permeated with particles of damp. Suddenly light flooded the room. Startled, he pivoted on his heels. Bernie stood by an old light switch near the door. In strong contrast to the rest of the house the room was four walls of flaking white paint, a concrete floor and empty, as if someone had locked it years before, turned their back and forgotten about it.

'There's nothing here.'

She didn't answer him. Instead she moved slowly into the room.

Her eyes roved up and down, over walls, ceiling and floor. She hunched down at a spot just past the middle of the room. She peered at the floor.

'Look at this.'

He looked down at the spot she indicated on the floor.

'What?'

'See this.' She pointed at the floor. He looked hard.

'This is a shoe print,' she continued.

'People have been known to leave them as they travel in life.'

She ran her finger over the print. She held her finger up to show him. It had dirt on it. 'This is fresh. Someone was here recently. The doors weren't forced. Someone else has got keys.'

She pulled herself up. Rubbed her finger on her trousers.

'I think we should go to the Bill and tell them everything,' LT said.

'And what is everything? That you've inherited a house that needs a spring clean in the basement? That your father left you some tapes that say he went out with some friends one night to Hoxton in 1976?'

He closed his eyes, his lack of sleep finally catching up with him. The words puffed wearily from his mouth. 'You know what, I'm exhausted. Not only have I got my dad on my back, I've got you as well.'

She turned and walked towards him with determined strides.

'Let's go upstairs. We need to talk about Beresford Clarke.'

'Like you just said, if we went to the police, what evidence have you got to show them about Beresford?'

She pulled her lips into a tight line. He shook his head as he kissed his teeth. He turned away from her and hit the stairs. As soon as he reached the next floor his mobile started beeping. He pulled it out. Two missed calls, one text message. He scrolled down the missed calls and listened.

'Shit, it's Window,' he said to Bernie as she stepped back upstairs.

He called his manager. He shook his head a couple of times during their conversation. Then clicked off the connection.

'Thanks to being stuck in a basement I almost missed the call from the record company. They want to see me tomorrow. I've got to go.'

'You can't go now.'

'Watch this space.'

He headed for the door.

'You can't just leave.' She ran towards him. 'You don't even need the record deal now. This house must be worth a few grand short of a cool million. We still need to talk about Beresford.'

He stopped. Flicked around.

'You don't get it.'

She slammed her palm against the door to stop him from opening it. Their eyes caught. Outraged brown clashing with distressed blue. Neither one of them was prepared to back down. That's when they both started banging out words, at the same time, in their Double D minor Rap.

'Nothing, including you, Bernie, is getting in my way.'

'We've got the house now so all we need is to get the tape.'

'Take your hand off the door, Bernie.'

'Don't you dare run out on me.'

'Run out on you?'

His words torpedoed into her. Her hand fell. She staggered back. Stopped talking.

'Run out on you?' he repeated. 'Is this from the woman who ran out on me fifteen years ago and got rid of my kid?'

Bernie's eyes got bright. Her shoulders dipped as if her backbone were going to break. Then she straightened up. Breathed deep through her nose. Her chin tipped to the left side. Her hands curled up as if she were ready to play an imaginary violin. Instead her hand moved to the door. Opened it and she was gone. He didn't call her back.

Half an hour later, LT sat cross-legged in the middle of the floor of the main room of the King's empty home. He felt strung out and mad. Mad at himself. His mind picked up a furious ska riff. His thoughts pitched into the blues swing of the drum on the second beat. Fourth beat. Second. Fourth.

He hadn't meant to say it to Bernie. Wrong time. Wrong place. But life was no neatly fitting jigsaw puzzle. Fifteen years ago, when Bernie hadn't turned up for school, he'd done his best to find out what had happened to her. When he checked with the school office they told him her family had moved away. Gone. He'd been devastated. Hadn't been able to play music for three long months. Then he'd found out while he waited for a bus, on Kingsland Road, outside the Caribbean takeaway, why she'd gone. A group of schoolgirls from another school had been whispering about not getting 'caught', as they put it, not like that girl 'Bernie' who'd gone away to 'get rid of it'. For months this grand feeling of remorse had stuck close by him. Now the feeling was back. He loathed it. Made him feel like he'd done something wrong. Thirty years old and the junk from fifteen years ago still had him nearly blubbing. Crying over what, he did not quite know. Fatherhood? A family? A son to pass the musical bow on to? Why were people always going on and on and on about the stuff that never happened rather than what had? And if he was truthful, that's what he hated – he tested the word out. 'Hated.' Yeah, that was the right word – about Bernie's return. She put him slam bang in the shit of 'what if . . .'. And the biggest 'what if . . .' she had left with him today was 'what if someone had killed his father and they got away with it because he'd decided to put his career first?'

He tucked his head to the side and watched the bag with the King's ashes. The smile fell from his lips. He knew he owed it to the King to find out what had happened to him. His gaze skidded around the silence and emptiness of the room. The ska riff hardened in his head as anger seeped into his body. He took out his mobile. Called a cab. The controller asked him his destination. Four words. A place he had never been before. A place the King had.

'Unity Road police station.'

He clicked off, knowing it was time to ask Her Majesty's finest what answers they had about the burglary at the King's home.

The cab came ten minutes later. Female driver. Blue baseball cap with a red-coloured ponytail sticking out the back. She'd learned her trade well and didn't say much. In fact she drove the cab as if she couldn't wait to get LT to his destination. The heat of unanswered questions blowing from LT was stifling. He told the driver to push the window down. All the way. He sucked the fresh air in. It didn't help. He caught the eyes of the cab driver in the rear-view mirror.

Nut-brown eyes.

Red hair.

LT leaned forward with disbelief when he realised who it was. Jane Blake.

The witness from the cab office, who obviously now worked for a different cab company. She caught his eyes in the mirror. The strain in her eyes intensified. Now he realised why she was driving the car so fast, because she had recognised who he was.

'Well, well, well,' he bit out bitterly. 'If it isn't the piano player from Hoxton.'

'Please, I don't want any trouble . . .'

'I don't want any trouble either but I've got it anyway. My dad is dead and you were one of the only people who could help find out about it.'

Her hand tightened on the steering wheel as her words pushed out defiantly. 'I've got troubles of my own. I need to stay in this country, you understand? I don't need any more problems with people . . .'

Suddenly she stopped talking. Shook her head. Drank in air as if it were fire entering her body. Then she picked up her words again in a hushed, pained tone. 'I understand what you're feeling. My father was killed by people too, but I couldn't get any justice in my country. Maybe you can get justice, maybe you can't, but don't look to me because I can't help. That's how it is.'

Her arm stretched out. Put the radio on. Terminated their conversation. He slumped back in his seat. Swore loudly. He was annoyed. With himself, yet again. For sympathising with her because he couldn't blame anyone for trying to move forward instead of back.

DJ Lady Hectic's *Big Afternoon Talk-in Show* on Station Debt-E-Nation FM flipped into the car.

'People of the metropolis, we're waiting for your calls. "Is rap music a crime against humanity?" That's our big subject today. Should artists, like Lord Tribu . . .'

'Kill it,' LT growled at Jane Blake.

She turned the radio off. A claustrophobic silence fine-tuned its rhythm inside the car until they reached the police station. From the picture the King had painted in his tape, Unity Road police station had changed over the years. It still wore its Georgian physique well, but now it was touting itself as a friend of the community. The rows of jolly and cheerful multicoloured beds of flowers to the side of its entrance said it wasn't the worse thing on earth to end up in one of its cells. Now its relationship with the community was 75 per cent wholesome, 25 per cent touch 'n' go. With its quota of coppers from ethnic minorities filling up, the 25 per cent was sure to fade. LT jumped out of the cab with the rucksack. He turned to Jane Blake and said,

'Wait for me. Don't worry, this is about me, not you, so please wait.'

She looked at him from under her cap, chewing her bottom lip. But she turned the engine off. LT slipped the rucksack on to his chest. He walked into the station. The only life in the reception was a family. Mum, son and baby in a three-wheel pushchair. They had ASBO scrawled all over them. Mum was chucking out words at the boy as if she had completed a creative writing class. The son took it. From the red of his ears he had already taken the back of her hand. LT moved past them to the main desk. The sergeant looked up at him. Female, late forties, a tan she picked up twice a year in her holiday home in Portugal. She didn't smile, just said, 'How can I help you, sir?'

LT leaned the rucksack into the edge of the desk.

'I need to talk to someone about a burglary I reported at my dad's place.'

She straightened her back as she picked the phone up and began to talk. She put the phone down.

'Someone will be out to see you shortly.'

Five minutes later the steel door behind the sergeant opened. A big, muscular policeman came through it. In his large hand he held a beige file. He leaned on the counter and let his squinting grey eyes snap into LT.

'How can I help you, sir?'

The baby in the pushchair let out a cry.

LT repeated what he had told the sergeant. Big Cop sighed, flicked a page in the file in front of him. He closed it, looked up and said, 'Sir, we are still looking into it.'

'How long will that take?'

'As long as it takes, sir,' the policeman answered with a tone that almost said that burglary wasn't a crime any more.

The ska blue beat pounded back in LT's head. Not just the drums this time, but the savage high-handed strum of the guitars. He knew what he had to do. He just hoped that the King understood.

'Why don't you tell my dad that?' he said defiantly, drawing back from the counter.

'I beg your pardon, sir?'

LT unzipped the rucksack on his chest. He shoved his hands inside. The baby stopped crying.

'Tell it to my dad,' he shouted.

Then he slammed the urn containing the King's ashes on to the counter. Both police officers jumped back. The sergeant was the first to realise what the urn was. She gasped, her hand stroking her throat. LT felt the movement of the mum and son behind him as they sprang to their feet. A shocked silence tightened in the room.

LT zipped up the rucksack.

'I've made it easy for you. When you've found the evidence, don't bother ringing me, just tell my dad.'

He swung around and walked past the family. The boy's eyes were shining with respect. He looked at his mum as if he finally knew what to do with her when she took her last breath. LT walked out of Unity Road police station towards the waiting cab without the King.

# TRACK 9: THE PIANO PLAYER

Jane Blake stopped the cab in the twisting afternoon light touching Ernest Bevin House. LT got out. He thought about trying to persuade her to see his solicitor as he gave her the fare. But what the fuck, if she didn't want to talk there wasn't much he could do about it. She took the money. Ignited the engine and drove away.

When he got to the fourth floor he found Beresford lounging outside his flat, one foot kicked up against the wall like a young man styling himself for any passing girls. LT looked at him and remembered what Bernie had accused him of.

'What are you doing here?' he asked suspiciously.

Beresford smiled. Pulled his foot off the wall and pushed his hand into his pocket. He pulled out an envelope.

'The solicitor says she's been trying to contact you with no joy. So I drove over to her office and picked this up for you. It's a summary of the King's post-mortem report from the coroner's office.'

The suspicion vanished as LT took the envelope. They entered the flat. Walked to the main room. They both remained standing as LT opened the envelope. What he read pushed him into the single sofa next to him.

'What does it say?' Beresford asked quietly as he took the sofa near the Northern Soul record collection.

'It says that he died of heart failure most probably induced by the drug he was using to treat the tumour in his stomach.

A possible side effect of the drug is heart failure. It's rare but every now and again, especially under extreme stress, someone gets unlucky.'

LT's voice trailed off as he stared at the letter in his hand. He carefully folded it and placed it on the arm of the sofa.

'It doesn't look like you're going to get very far challenging them with this kind of medical evidence,' Beresford said.

'The woman in the cab office saw a car near him at the time of his death. I mean, for fuck's sake, if he just keeled over, how did his body end up under a load of rubbish bins?'

'That's not the job of the coroner's office. Maybe this car was just passing by?'

'No way,' LT replied fiercely, his head rocking from side to side. 'The King wouldn't have gone into Hoxton unless someone made him. And I know that someone was in that car.'

'The only people who are going to be able to help you are the police. And they're going to find it pretty hard going without a statement from your disappearing witness, son.'

'Son?' LT shook his head. 'You want to know what kind of son I am? My dad leaves me a house worth mega milk and honey and what do I do? I dump him at Unity Road police station.'

'What house?' Beresford asked sharply.

LT told him about the Liberation Republic. LT watched as Beresford ran a finger across his bottom lip. For the first time he saw all the years this man carried imprinted on his face. Reminded him of the time the doctors told the King he was going to die. He didn't want the first time Beresford came into his home to be filled with bad memories, so he injected a light spring into his voice and said, 'But at least Paradise Records want to see me tomorrow.'

The finger dropped from Beresford's lip, but he didn't smile at LT's news. Instead he stood up. Walked over to a section of LT's music collection stacked on shelves on the right side of the room. His hand went to the shelf level with his chest. His index finger half flipped out an album. Vinyl. The Mighty Diamonds.

'Is this your seventies reggae stash?' he asked, keeping his finger and eyes on the album.

'Yeah.'

Beresford pushed the Mighty Diamonds back into place. Then his fingers started fanning through the albums.

U-Roy.

I-Roy.

Dilinger.

Steele Pulse.

His fingers stopped. Caressed the album cover.

'So how did you find out about this Liberation Republic?' the older man asked, his fingers still flipping.

LT eagerly opened his mouth to speak, then stopped. He remembered what Bernie had said about telling anyone about the tapes. Then he saw her bruised and beaten in a hospital room. He desperately needed to talk to someone about this. He glanced at Beresford. Thought about what Bernie had said about hearing Beresford's name. No, he corrected himself – about hearing the name Clarke. He knew she was wrong because this man had acted like a father to him. And if there was one thing he needed in his life at the moment it was a father. But what if . . .

'Did you grow up in Birmingham?' LT asked the older man.

'No, in Guyana,' Beresford answered as his fingers stopped moving. 'I came to England when I was ten. I stayed with my aunt in London. I left London in 1973 to stay with my uncle in Birmingham. Why?'

He turned to face LT with his finger still touching an album cover. LT studied the older man, looking for a lie, the same way he did when he went to record company meetings to find out whether they were stringing him along. He always knew when those record execs were taking him for a fool. The way their eyes never quite caught his. The way they laughed at his jokes that one second too long. The way they kept looking at their watches as if he was just another nobody in a queue always rapping at their door. Now he studied Beresford, looking for the same signs. In his eyes. In his easy smile. In the way his hand touched the record cover. LT slumped back, grateful that the only signs he saw were of a man who looked comfortable in his home.

'Nothing. It's just you've been so good to me and I didn't know very much about you.'

'Well, I hope I passed the Lord Tribulation entrance test.' Beresford turned back to the shelf. His fingers resumed their rapid movement through the album covers.

Bob Marley.

Bunny Wailer.

Peter Tosh.

Big Youth.

Junior Murvin.

His hand stopped at the same time as he said, 'So, you were telling me how you found out about this Liberation Republic . . .'

'The King left me some . . .'

There was a bang on the front door as Beresford pulled the Junior Murvin album off the shelf. LT groaned at the sound of the door.

'The one thing I don't need now is company.'

But he left anyway. He reluctantly opened the front door. His lips tightened when he stared into the eyes of the person standing in front of him.

Nut-brown eyes stared timidly at him. Jane Blake twisted her baseball cap nervously in her hand.

'I thought you didn't do justice?' LT emphasised the *you* as his hand gripped the edge of the door.

Her shoulders rotated forward as if she were in the midst of the spray of a cold shower.

'I feel bad. Feel I did the wrong thing.'

'You and me, baby.'

She took a mini-step forward.

'Please, I wish to help now. I didn't tell you everything that I saw.'

His grip tightened on the door as his eyes shot over her. He wasn't sure but he thought he saw sincerity in her face. The way her lips pressed together. The way her eyes stayed level with his face. His hold softened. He pulled the door back. She took the invitation and came inside. He banged the door shut and moved ahead of her. She followed him into the main room. Beresford still stood by the vinyl collection, clutching the Junior Murvin album in his hand. He lowered the album when he saw her.

LT didn't offer Jane Blake a seat. Kept her standing there by the single sofa like she owed him something. She held herself with a pose that was respectful, shy, frightened.

He turned to Beresford and said, 'This is . . .'

'Your star witness,' Beresford whispered.

'She wants to help me now. Claims she's got more to say,' LT said sceptically.

'Do you want to make a statement?' Beresford asked Jane Blake.

'I want to tell the truth.'

That strained look blew full force into her eyes. Beresford smiled as he spoke to LT.

'Jeremiah, why don't you make us some tea and I'll explain the intricacies of the legal process to Ms . . .' He cocked his head towards her.

'Blake.'

As Beresford asked her to take a seat, LT left them, closed the door and strode towards the kitchen. For the first time that day a true smile banged a summer-breeze riff on to his lips.

'Please take a seat, Ms Blake,' Beresford said.

As she followed his command he moved over to the single sofa. Instead of sitting down he placed the Junior Murvin album on it. He turned and moved towards the cab driver. He eased his body down next to her. A blue cushion was wedged between them. He crossed his legs. Right over left. He shifted to face her.

'Can you tell me what you saw the day Jeremiah's father died?'

'Like I tell your friend, I see a car moving towards his father. Then I close the curtains. Didn't want to see any more.' She gazed down at her cap. Resumed speaking, her accent heavy, her voice pinched and low. 'What I didn't tell your friend was then I hear this screech of tyres, so I open the curtains again. The car was still there, but I couldn't see your friend's father any more. A man got out of the car. I couldn't see his face. He was big, like you. He bend down. Then he move forward and I see him dragging the other man on the floor, you know, by his legs. I couldn't see any blood on your friend's father so I don't know if he fell, if the car hit him, I don't know. The other man drag him to the bins and threw his body there. Pushed him under some bin bags. Then he get back in the car and drive off. Now I shut the curtains.'

'And this is the statement you're prepared to give a solicitor?' Beresford's question was quiet.

She nodded.

'This is the right thing to do,' he said, as he picked up the blue cushion as if he were removing a barrier between them.

'When shall I see this solicitor?' she asked as she placed her baseball cap in her own lap.

Beresford drew the cushion into his own lap.

'Are you absolutely sure you want to do this?' he asked as he gripped the cushion with both hands.

She nodded. Smiled. He smiled back. Leaned into her. His mouth stopped by her ear. His breath brushed her profile. He whispered, 'OK, this is what you have to do . . .'

His hands punched forward, slamming the cushion over her face. Her head bounced back with the suddenness and force of the move. He hiked his right knee on to the sofa by her hip. Braced his body weight forward. Pressed down. Shock encased her in a web of stillness. He felt the bone in her nose through the cushion. Felt the erratic swing of her bead-shaped eyelids. Then she moved. Her chest jerked. Legs kicked. He increased the pressure. He whipped his head towards the closed door. Listening. Silence. Then he heard the sound of LT's trainers grazing against the lino in the kitchen. He twisted his head back to his victim.

He leaned down into her.

'Did they do this to you when they raped you in Kosovo?'

Her head twitched in terror.

'How many were there? Did you keep a count?'

He pushed down harder.

'Did their hands feel like mine do now?'

He kept the pressure the same.

'Now I am a man who deplores that type of behaviour. But I understand why people do it. It's like telling someone to mind their own business and keep quiet, but instead they decide to play the hero. When my friend came to see you – I'm sure you remember him, big hands, big knuckles – you told him you saw nothing. So let's keep it that way, Ms Blake. You saw nothing.'

He tilted his head towards the door again. Listening. LT whistling a tune. 'Polly Put The Kettle On'.

He swivelled his head back and down to her.

'When I take this cushion away, let's keep it really simple. You're going to walk out of here. And keep walking. And walking. Any time you feel tempted to do the right thing just remember what my hands felt like. What their hands felt like.'

The whistling stopped in the kitchen.

Beresford eased his knee down. Leaned back. Pulled the cushion from her face. She crumpled forward. Spluttering. Coughing. Her baseball cap hit the floor. Beresford pulled himself up. Stood over her, the cushion still in his hand.

'You need to go now,' he whispered gently, as if delivering the final line of a parable.

Jane Blake jumped up, wheezing air into her bent body as she rushed to the door. She clawed at the handle. Threw the door open. She collided with LT, who stood on the threshold holding two mugs of tea. She kept her head down. Heaved past him. One of the mugs flew from his hand.

'What the . . .' LT started as he watched her run to the door.

The cooling wind swept inside as she pulled the door open and rushed outside.

'Where you going?' LT shouted as he rushed into the path left by her shadow.

The tea in the mug in his right hand splashed in lines in the air as he moved.

'I couldn't stop her,' Beresford called behind him.

LT stopped. Turned around.

'What the f-ing hell happened?'

Beresford briskly walked to him.

'Her mobile went off. I've got no idea who it was. Then she bolted for the door. I couldn't stop her.'

'Shit, shit, shit.' LT banged his hand against the wall with each expletive as the ska beat came back, riding high inside his head.

Beresford stood in exactly the same place his desk had been back in 1976 in the basement of number 16 Rhodes Square. The Liberation Republic. The Black Fist office.

'Shakespeare, why here of all places?'

He kicked his head up at the sound of the voice of the woman who came into the room.

'No one has called me that in thirty years, so I'll remind you not to use it again,' he said.

Her eyes swept over him. Down his arm.

'You found the jacket,' she said when she saw what he was holding.

Her breath shuddered. She sought support in the wall. His grip tightened on what he was holding.

'I thought it was. But it isn't. Forget that for now because we've got more urgent problems.'

'What problems?'

He moved out of the space where his desk had been.

'That boy not only knows about the Republic, he owns it.'

'How?'

'The very gracious and very dead King Stir It Up never sold it, like he said he would. Instead, it's become a family heirloom. That's why I asked you to meet me here, because I came here yesterday and, surprise, surprise, my key still fits the basement door.'

She began pacing and talking at the same time.

'We need to get rid of this house. Burn it down. Bulldoze it. Anything.'

'One fire on a street can be bad luck. Two fires, now that's just suspicious.' His voice softened and dropped as he continued. 'Look around you, there's nothing here that can touch us.'

'Don't do one of your bleeding-heart community speeches with me.'

'Such vulgarity. What would Mummy and Daddy say after spending all that money on your education?'

Her face burned red. He still knew the quickest way to hurt her.

'What about Berlina Ray's witness tape?'

'My people got it. But . . .'

He let the word hang in the air. He was enjoying the pinched expression around her eyes and mouth.

'But my people also found another tape she was carrying. A tape of the King telling tales about '76. Luckily all they know so far is that one night the King and his comrades took a trip. They have no idea where we went. And they won't have if we can get the last tape the King left. But I think I know where it is.'

'Where?'

For the first time she came into his space.

'The King was always a man who loved to pour his heart out to the ladies. And his current lady is someone called May Branigan. I met her at the funeral. Sweet lady. I'll take care of her, you concentrate on getting your end sorted out.'

'My end's already moving.'

He turned to the door. Opened it.

Her words stabbed his back. 'If we don't find it you can't hurt the boy or his friend. You've already hurt her once.'

He didn't turn around as he answered her. 'You know what my grandfather told me when I was ten and they put me on that ship leaving Guyana to come to England? "In life hurt lurks around every corner, boy, and what people are telling me is England is full of corners." If the boy and girl haven't learned that one yet, that isn't my problem.'

He flicked his head to look at her out of the corner of his eye.

'Sir Beresford Clarke. Sounds grand, doesn't it. Not bad for a boy who was born next to a field of sugar cane. Now I know that knighthood will soon be mine, thanks to your wonderful influence, my friend, nothing and no one is going to stand in my way. If I haven't found the jacket or the tape by bank holiday Monday the best place to deal with the boy and Berlina Ray will be at the carnival in three days' time. So many things can happen in such a crowded place.'

He stepped outside, walking way from the Liberation Republic.

LT inhaled the apple tobacco vapour from his hand-held powder-blue Turkish water pipe as he leaned back against the pillows on the bed. He checked the radio clock on the table. Minutes to ten. It had been a bitch and a twister of a day. His eyes caressed the keys and unsigned record contract on the table near the clock. Two pieces of his life lying peacefully side by side. The King's death. His career. He wished he could say it had been a toss-up which one he dealt with first, but that would be lying. Tomorrow's meeting with Paradise Records, he suspected, was going to be one of his final sniffs at stardom.

His teeth bit into the wooden mouthpiece. Inhaled another long lug. As for where he'd left the King, he wasn't thinking about that one. There was a bang on the front door. Hard.

'Sod off,' he yelled.

He was tired. Tired of people. Then his mind began to rationalise. If it was the press it wouldn't do to be photographed looking like the worst kind of shit. Whether you were at the supermarket or in the doctor's surgery, appearance was everything. He'd learned that one when he'd been sitting on a bus and heard a girl whisper, 'He looks a bit of an ug mug in real life.' He sprang off the bed and rushed to the mirror inside the wardrobe. He checked his appearance. Tired, but still one up on the ordinary man. He grabbed a pen and a blank du-rag and wrote across the top 'No Comment'. There was another bang. He tied the du-rag around his head. His chest was bare and he decided to leave it that way because it made it look like he was indulging in some late-night lovin'. When he reached the door he sketched a smile. He opened it. His lips froze when he saw the one person who could break his concentration – Bernie.

She stood, shining and soaked from the rain, back unbreakably straight, cutting her eyes at him from head to toe. He looked at her mouth, slightly dry, but moving, and he knew she had something to say. She crossed her arms over her middle.

'That wasn't fair what you said to me today. I was fifteen, you were fifteen. Too young to know better.'

She followed him inside. He looked at her and in some ways wished it was the word rats instead. At least they didn't expect the truth, only a story. He headed for the sitting room but stopped when he realised that she was going into the bedroom. Shit, no way was this going to work out in there.

'Shouldn't we go in here?' he said, indicating the sitting room.

She didn't answer. Just disappeared into the room she'd chosen.

He swallowed as he followed her. He remained by the door, wondering what she was going to do. She reached the edge of the bed. Bent down. Pulled her boots off. Pushed them away. Eased on to the bed and stretched out. That surprised him. He'd thought she'd want that emotional distance. He walked over to the window. Opened it. Wide. He unlocked his lips and caught the breeze. He moved back to the bed, keeping his eyes away from her. Fluffed his pillow and then stretched out beside her. He relit the charcoal on the top of the water pipe. Passed it to her. She took it and as she inhaled he began to speak.

'What's your favourite album cover?'

They both tipped their heads back to look at the record covers on the ceiling.

'Pink Floyd's *Dark Side Of The Moon*.' Her words left her mouth with the spiralling smoke. 'My father would play it all the time. The cover was black with a prism in the middle. On one side you had white light and on the other a spectrum of the rainbow. It was like our minds have this amazing light show going on inside.'

'I got two all-time favourites.' He pointed to the ceiling. 'Public Enemy's *It Takes A Nation Of Millions To Hold Us Back* and Smiley Culture's *Cockney Translation*. Of course, *Cockney Translation* isn't an album. My copy is the extended twelve-inch dub remix.'

He felt the apple tobacco push her farther into the bed. Suddenly he felt the fear of what she might say, so he kept on speaking.

'Public Enemy's album came out about the time I first saw you. I love the way that Chuck D looks so defiant and abrasive behind the mock prison bars. I loved the red on black, the black on yellow. The ultimate golden age of rap. Now Smiley Culture's a bit more relaxed. Your typical dodgy London scene – dodgy red Vauxhall Nova, dodgy bridge. When I use to sing along, I would toast, "It's Lord Tribulation with the mic in me hand." His song was the first time I really heard that mix of Caribbean and British ting getting it on. Was that the trouble, Bernie, you just weren't ready to have a kid with that type of mix?'

He kept his eyes on the ceiling.

'Hardly. Do you know how many black men in Britain have white partners? Hardly taboo.'

'But back then maybe your mum and dad just weren't ready. We all know your mum couldn't stand me.'

She laughed. 'Are you joking? My parents thought they were hipper than me. Why else do you think they sent me to the local comprehensive? They prided themselves on having the trends before they hit mainstream. Bringing a grandson of dual heritage into her set would have been the ultimate representation of chic for Mummy.'

'So why, then?'

She heard the yearning in his voice.

'Don't get romantic. Being up the duff and still at school was no fairy tale.'

He didn't know whether this was true but felt compelled to say it. 'I would have stood by you.'

'Let's be honest, the only thing you wanted to stand by was, as you put it, the mic in your hand.'

'But you could have kept it. It wasn't as if your family didn't have the readies.'

She took a slow, deep suck on the pipe.

'It wasn't about money, it wasn't about you, believe it or not, it was about me. I wasn't ready and still don't feel ready. Let's just say that the glow of my future was a stronger call, and even at fifteen I understood that the light would begin to dim with a baby on my back.'

'If the light was so bright, where's your violin?'

The duvet cover tightened as she moved.

'I moved on, Jerry.'

She bent over and put the water pipe on the floor. As she raised herself up, she said, 'Let's talk about Beresford Clarke.'

He rubbed an agitated thumb and finger over his T-lettered earring and said, 'One of the things I loved about you was you never gave up. But you know what, I'm starting to hate it now.'

'I've been thinking about my attack. How my attackers knew I had that witness on my Dictaphone. You never told anyone, nor did I, which means someone must have heard us talking about it. The only time I can remember us talking about it in public was at the funeral. If I remember . . .'

'Fucking ifs again,' he rammed out as he twisted towards her.

'Beresford was the only person near us. In fact, as soon as I said the words he interrupted us.'

He dug his arms into the mattress and shoved his back straight.

'He came over to us to say goodbye, for heaven's sake. If you'd bothered to come to the church you would have heard the wonderful words he said about the King. I never heard anyone talk about the King that way. Besides, when the witness from the cab office was here today . . .'

'She came here?' The disbelief in her voice ricocheted around the room.

He nodded his head rapidly at her and answered, 'She came pleading at my door, now wanting to hold my hand and give me some new information. Beresford, who you insist is public enemy number one, tried to encourage her to give a statement. But she flipped out when she got a phone call and ran off.'

'Why didn't you try to stop her?'

'You ever tried to stop a woman before?' he belted out, pissed at the angry tone she shoved his way. 'Besides, I wasn't in the room at the time. Beresford was with her explaining what would happen when she met the solicitor . . .'

Bernie leapt off the bed, cutting off his words.

'Can't you see it? She was in the room alone with him. How do you know her mobile went off? That's what he told you, but how do you know that's what happened?'

She strode towards him as the sound of her words became harder. 'You said she looked distressed when she left. He must have said something to her. Maybe even threatened her . . .'

'Stop this now,' he yelled out as he jumped off the bed, swinging his arm, sending the water pipe tumbling backwards.

'Is that what you see when you look down your middle-class nose at me, Bernie?' he carried on, his voice getting louder. 'A man whose only purpose on this earth is so that everyone can take him for a ride?'

He touched the bottom of his palm against his forehead, as if the best idea he'd ever had had just come to him. 'Fucking hell, stupid me, of course, you're right, because you of all people would know. Took me for that mega-ride fifteen years ago. The one person I thought I knew and I got it bollocks wrong. But you know what, I learned from my mistake with you. I've spent the last fifteen years learning how to read people. Learning how to see the good and bad in people. And when I look at Beresford all I see is good, just like my father.'

A fist banged twice against the wall and a voice boomed from next door, 'Keep the soddin' noise down before you wake the bloody baby.'

They stood looking at each other in the shattered silence. The cry of a baby pierced the wall. It was the one sound neither of them wanted to hear. The one musical note from their past they weren't sure they could ever fully deal with.

Bernie spoke, her voice choked, her words simple. 'I did what I thought was best and I can't understand why no one will believe me.'

He watched her pick up her boots. Move to the door. At the threshold she turned back to him and whispered, 'If you get the domino set in the post tomorrow you will let me know.'

She didn't wait for his reply, but turned and left. LT dropped to the bed and looked at the King's vintage denim jacket, now on the floor. He knew he wasn't going to sleep again tonight because the punk beat was back. The images were back. Emmett Till and Beresford Clarke.

At 11.30 the next morning, LT blew down the stairs wearing an uptown smile and clothes he hoped the record company would see bulged with the hard-on of success. The words 'Who's The Daddy?' blazed in black letters across his white du-rag. He'd gone back to wearing his trademark du-rag and ditched the Emmett Till one. Just as he'd ditched any thoughts of Beresford Clarke being a snake in the grass. He swung down the flight of stairs leading to the second floor. He just missed the postman, who appeared from the right-hand corner of the third-floor balcony and moved upwards. To the fourth floor. In his hand he held a bundle of letters and two parcels. One parcel was addressed to:

Mr J. Scantleberry
44 Ernest Bevin House

# TRACK 11: MURDER MUSIC

LT sat in a hard plastic chair in front of a wooden desk in the room he knew Paradise Records set aside for discussing 'artistic differences'. Window sat beside him, shadows reclining in his eyes. Helena and Carlton faced them, in comfortable chairs, behind the desk. There were no champagne flutes. No offerings of gear. No 'welcome to the clan, my man' smiles. On the walls around them were framed photographs of bands and musicians who had been yesterday's next best thang and today's one-hit wonders. LT looked at the two record executives and knew that everything had shifted – he needed them, but did they still need him?

'Lord Tribulation, good to see you again. Thanks for coming,' Carlton greeted him, extending his hand across the table.

LT shook his hand, the twinkle of Carlton's cufflinks suggesting they were the only things having a good time in the room. Carlton shook Window's hand. LT looked directly at Helena. She wore a formal DKNY ruffle-fronted blouse and her hair was held back, locked into place. But he was not looking at her clothes. His eyes were fixed to the paper she had pinned to the table with her fingertips. The contract.

Her purple-tipped nails caressed the paper in tiny, light circles.

'I see you understand that a contract can be such a beautiful thing,' she spoke softly. 'The first contract I ever did was with a girl band, the Come-On Girls.'

She eased the contract into her hand as she stood up. Moved

across the room to stand near a large colour photo on the wall. Three girls, one black, two white, posed with a ready-to-go look.

Helena picked up her oration with the tone of someone giving a master class.

'Style, music, sex appeal. The girls were wrapped up, on the express to success. So we sat them down. Kissed them on both cheeks. Welcomed them to our family. When you enter our family we take the time to explain our rules. The problem with the girls was that they never quite understood those rules. Never quite understood that being drunk at three a.m. was fine, but getting snapped chucking up in a West End gutter wasn't. Never quite understood that you can hump whoever you like, but telling a reporter you were waiting for your humpee's divorce to come through wasn't. Never quite understood that it was fine to say that you were suffering from nervous exhaustion, but not OK to say you were going into rehab.'

Each word hit the room with such a savage downstroke that it shook him up. Sure, he hadn't kidded himself that this meeting was going to be easy, but he thought they would fall into a quick cycle of explanation, reassurance, shake hands on it and put ink on to kissable paper.

'Talk to me, LT,' Carlton said, quiet but with an edge that demanded a response. 'Unpick for us your thoughts on this arson attack and the alleged connection to your music.'

LT gathered a smile on to his face and shuffled his arms on to the table. He had agreed with Window that he would do most of the talking. It was his music, and if anyone was going to defend it, it would be him.

'Some unhappy kid. The world's full of them . . .'

Carlton cut over him. 'But you can see from our perspective it does not look good if one of our products is associated with hurting children.'

'It could have been any music that he was playing. I bet when the police checked his MP3 it was loaded with all types of artists. It's just unfortunate that it was my tune that happened to be coming through when he did what he had to do.'

Carlton crossed his arms over his chest.

'We really want to sign you, but is the risk going to be too big?'

He felt Window move in his chair next to him, but he shuffled his arms farther forward, ready to answer.

'This is how I see things from my angle. I'm unique. My sound is unique. My following is unique. Now I'm impressed with you because I click with your future plans. I know that you're going to take care of me. Most probably give me the best deal I'll come across in my life. But if you don't want me you need to let me know now because every day there's a new hand banging on my door. Everyone wants to get their hands on the man who's going to be crowned the Writer in Residence of Ladbroke Grove for a record-breaking third year in a row in two days' time. Such as the successful Internet network, music@yourfingertips.net.'

He paused when he saw Carlton and Helena both suck in their breath as if an evil spirit had floated into the room.

He carried on.

'Believe me when I say that I regret the injury caused to another human being, especially a child, as much as anyone else. But to associate my music with this act would be wrong. Look at me. I'm not just a music man, I'm *the* music man. No one else has got the white-black, middle-class–working-class, out-of-towners–urban mass that I have following me. When I come to Paradise Records that clientele will be grooving behind me. This is a unique opportunity, at a unique time. The world's ready. Are you ready for the world?'

He stopped, watching indecision high-kicking across the faces of the man and woman opposite him. Helena bit her lip. Smoothed her hand over her fringe. She dipped her eyelids to Carlton. Nodded her head. Smiled and said, 'Let's get some refreshments and maybe complete this in another room.'

She pressed a button on the desk. LT suspected it was the one they usually used to call security.

'Maxie, darling, get some drinks ready for the Ivory Room.'

They all got up and moved towards the door.

'We're really excited about working with you,' she said to LT, back to being the flimsy and fly woman he'd met at their first meeting.

'We've already got a series of gigs lined up for you and possible TV appearances,' Carlton added.

They went on like that, back and forth, good news piling on top of good news, as if they had found him at the roadside and given him back his otherwise worthless life. The Ivory Room, the place where the first meeting had been held. The three men took a seat on the corner leather suite, while Helena fussed at the door.

'Maxie, darling, can you bring that crisp, new copy of the contract in.'

LT grinned and relaxed for the first time that day. The shadows in Window's eyes remained rooted, cautious to the end. The door opened and a young woman, with purple hair and roller skates, wheeled herself into the room. She handed the paper to Helena and rolled out.

Muffled noises drifted up from the street. None of them paid any attention. Their eyes were glued to the contract Helena had positioned on the table, as if it were her newborn baby. Carlton got up to open a drawer, looking for a pen.

The voices from outside became thicker. Louder.

Carlton closed the drawer and approached LT.

The voices from outside were joined by loud whistles and chants.

Carlton placed the pen in LT's hand.

The chanting from outside grew into angry shouts.

As Helena got up to place the contract into LT's hand one of the shouts from outside bounced loud and clear into the room – 'Stop murder music now.'

They all froze, allowing another shout to dominate the room.

'Attack rap, not our children.'

Helena whipped the contract away from LT and marched over to the window. She jacked up the glass and leaned out.

'Oh, balls,' she rasped.

Carlton and LT jumped up to join her. They jammed their heads out of the window. A lively crowd of women bustled furiously

on the pavement outside the record company. In front of them
stood a block of photographers and cameras. Two women held
up a long white banner with a black-scrawled slogan that read:
'MAMM – Mothers Against Murder Music'.

Now they were all shouting together, 'Paradise selling hell,'
again and again. Helena and Carlton turned and looked at LT. He
looked at Window, who remained seated, with a sombre expression that read 'this is just how life goes'. LT looked down at
Helena's hand holding the contract. She held it high, as if she
wanted him to see a beloved relative that one last time before
they went kicking and screaming to the electric chair. She folded
it into two. Into four. Then passed it to Carlton.

LT's eyes followed the contract, his heart filling with a profound
sense of loss. The same loss he'd felt at the King's funeral. The
loss of knowing he might never get a chance at the big time
again.

Bulbs flashed, journalists jostled and cameras fought for position
on the pavement outside Paradise Records' headquarters. The air
was filled with the shouts of 'Stop murder music now' from the
thick crowd of female demonstrators. All cameras were focused
on the front row of the demonstration, where fifty-two-year-old
Magdelana Delaney stood. She gazed with ferocity and determination at the three TV cameras focusing on her.

She held her hand up to the crowd. The demonstrators grew
silent. She looked at the cameras and said, 'I would like to read
out a statement on behalf of Mothers Against Murder Music.
Today we want to ask Paradise Records' shareholders not to sign
a contract with an artist who sings songs with titles such as
"Gasoline Ghetto". Last week a boy of fourteen petrol-bombed a
house as he listened to the destructive lyrics of this song. This
song contains lyrics such as: "Fire it up in the morning / Send
that match way high / Burn down the system / Die baby die."'

Her face panned across the cameras. She gave it five seconds
then began speaking again.

'As you will all be aware, two young children were seriously injured in this attack. We want to ask Paradise Records how it can contemplate signing a musician who advocates that our young people should attack each other. We want to ask Paradise Records how it can contemplate supporting this gratuitous, senseless violence. We want to ask Paradise Records how it can call the burning of children entertainment. We have come here to safeguard the futures of our children. Safeguard the futures of the next generation. We will be here every day, outside this building, until the shareholders of this record label understand that we as mothers are outraged and refuse to be quiet while this type of music murders the family values that we all stand for. We will continue to make noise until this stops.'

The demonstrators took up her cry and started to blow their whistles.

Magdelana Delaney stopped talking and pandemonium broke out as journalists started to fire questions at her.

Auntie May danced at the sink in her sky-blue kitchen as she made her most popular facial scrub. 'Spirit of Youth. Drives stress lines and wayward spirits away.' Made of olive oil, oatmeal and honey. Manuka honey. And her secret ingredient. The ladies could not get enough of it. It was so popular a well-known high-street chain wanted her to sell it in their stores. But she was not going to do that. As soon as you got involved with the big guys life lost its tantalising flavour. Her hipline bounced to the soundtrack of *The Harder They Come*. Best soundtrack in history. That's what she told people. That was why she played it every Saturday from 1 to 2 p.m. Toots and the Maytals' 'Pressure Drop' came on. Hands covered in Spirit of Youth, she spun around. That Toots Hibbert voice sure knew how to make people feel they were at a gospel revival. She began spinning, feet skating, head rolling, hips winding as she took her revival across the kitchen floor. People hadn't called her 'Bass Boogie May' for nothing when she was a young woman.

She was so deep in the music she did not hear the front doorbell. She heard it on the second ring. She stopped dancing. Kissed her teeth in annoyance. She debated whether to answer it. Women were always having emergencies. She went to the door. Two men stood on her doorstep. One held a package, the other a clipboard. Both wore black baseball caps, creating a shadow over their eyes.

'Package for May Branigan.'

'Who's it from?'

'We're just the delivery boys.'

The younger one held out the clipboard and pen in his glove-covered hands. She sighed. Reached over to take the package. The man clutched on to it.

'It's too delicate for a little bird like you, love, let me bring it in.'

The last person to call her 'love' was the King. Her lips spread in a bitter-sweet smile. She opened the door wide to let them in. They came inside. She closed the door. There was a sharp noise behind her. Puzzled, she turned quickly around. She stopped moving when she noticed that the package and clipboard were on the floor. She pushed her face up to look at both men. They looked at her. Towered over her. She still couldn't see their eyes. Her fingers rubbed against her throat. She took a step back.

'What's going . . .'

They rushed at her at the same time as Toots Hibbert's breathless voice began to boil over. She managed a half-twist to the door, but they caught her. Each grabbed an arm. Lifted her. They carried her into the kitchen. Stopped in front of the sink.

'OK, lady, just tell us where the tape and jacket are.'

May opened her mouth but her tongue wasn't moving. They lowered her feet to the floor. She stood breast high with the sink. The arm of the man on her left shot out, like a cobra, on a trajectory to the cold tap. He twisted it on. The bowl with the facial scrub mixture began to fill up.

'One more time, old girl, where are they?'

May shook her head, transfixed by the running water. As swift as a blow, a hand grabbed the back of her head. Slammed her head into the bowl. Shock made her stop breathing. Her eyes opened wide. Grains of oatmeal and sweet water swam over and into her eye socket. Up her nasal passage. Down her throat. Into the depths of where her fear bubbled with the speed of a waterfall in reverse in her gut. Then she started breathing, the fear coming out of her mouth as screaming bubbles. The water from the tap above pounded her head and neck. That was when she started to gulp. Huge. Frequent. Flooding her lungs with liquid. She tried to move her legs back. Hands slammed her legs forward again. The fingers of her right hand dug into the hard muscle of a leg. The leg shook them off. She clutched warm air.

Fingers roped in her hair. Her head was jerked out of the water. Rocked back on her neck. She drew in a wild whoosh of air. Coughed. Coughed again, this time vomiting over her chin.

'Where are they, bitch?'

'No, no, no,' she rasped.

Tears scraped a path through the honey and oatmeal on her face. The hand tightened behind her head. Toots and the Maytals' high-energy chanting of 'pressure, pressure, pressure' smacked the room.

They smashed her head so hard into the bowl this time that her front tooth stuck into her bottom lip. This time, when the water filled up her body, it squeezed her head and chest. A pressure so strong she thought her spinal column was going to break. Her chest was going to cave in. Then the pain started to drift. Her mind began to float. Float back to the time she first stepped out with her husband Charlie on Grand Anse beach in Grenada. '62. Orange, mauve, dying blue sunset and cotton-wool-soft sand. He kissed her on the lips as they held hands. She opened her mouth . . . .

Her head was pulled back. That was when she screamed because she knew Charlie was never coming back. They held on to her when her legs would not.

'Shall we do it again?'

'Can't fucking kill her.'

'She don't know nothing anyway. Let's turn the place over.'

They dropped her. She tumbled to the floor. The voices were

above her. They left her tangled on the floor. Her right hand curved limply against her thigh. She drifted into unconsciousness at the same time as the track on the stereo changed to Jimmy Cliff's 'Sitting In Limbo'.

In the Minus One club, Window, his wife Evie Campbell and their nine-month-old son watched LT as he watched the replay of Magdelana Delaney denouncing him on the big screen.

'Turn it off,' he growled.

Window shut the screen down.

'Two days to go to the competition and carnival and I'm stuffed. I wanted to get on the stage with a copy of the record contract blazing on my T-shirt.'

LT was angry and he didn't care who knew it. He wished the King were here. The baby fussed in his mother's arms as Window poured LT a glass of chilled water. LT took it. Drank from it. Then his words spluttered. 'What the backside am I meant to do now? Sing on the street corner and hope the Salvation Army give me a deal?'

Window sighed. Then he smiled at his son.

'Like I've said from the beginning, there's always Barry and his Internet network. He's one of us. From the street. He'll look after you.'

LT kissed his teeth loudly at that one. Going Window's route was like admitting defeat.

'Who the big-F hell are Mothers Against Murder Music anyway? How did they find out I was signing the contract today?'

Window leaned on the bar.

'There's no such thing as confidential in the music bizz.' Window shook his head. This has happened in the States before and the musicians survived. So will you. I'm going to call my lawyer to find out more about these people and where we stand. You sit back and relax.'

He started to walk away, then turned back and said, 'Good news. The young boy in hospital is out of danger.'

Yeah, it was good news. It probably wouldn't bring Paradise Records back haggling at his door, but it was good news. As soon as Window left LT felt uncomfortable. He always felt nervous in the presence of Window's wife, Evie Campbell. He looked over at her as she settled the baby into its carrycot. She was a few inches shorter than him, with shoulder-length natural-coloured extensions and a dark brown face that glowed from stern to soft. As well as being Window's wife she was also the older sister of Jackie Jarvis's boyfriend, Elijah 'Schoolboy' Campbell. They had all been inmates of St Ignatius school together. Even back then she had been on the do-gooder trip that would define her existence in later life. He was mistrustful of anyone who said they put the well-being of the community above their own health.

He judged her expression. Decided she was coming over all soft, so he said, 'Can you believe these people?'

She folded her arms over her chest and looked at him. He realised he'd misread her.

'So you're just a little piggy and they're all big bad wolves beating down your door?' Her question thundered towards him.

His eyes bulged in surprise, then flicked down in annoyance.

'I'm just a music man doing my shuffle.'

'So you're innocent?'

'I didn't realise getting on to a stage meant entering a court-room. I never claimed to live an innocent life.'

'Blameless? Is that a better word?'

'Blame means I did something wrong and I didn't.'

'What about artistic responsibility?'

He let out a small humourless laugh.

'The only responsibility I've got is to make sure my followers get their dollars' worth. I'm an entertainer, a showman, that's what I do. When I put the mic to my mouth people don't expect to hear a party political broadcast on behalf of the Tribulation party.'

'So some of your lyrics like, "If they want you out of town, go ahead angry brother burn the place down", don't make disaffected young men feel enraged enough to turn to violence?'

He stretched his neck, feeling his own rage.

'Oh, I get it, all that trouble in the Middle East is down to people listening to my music. Better get on the blower and let the cops know that the mastermind is sitting right here.'

'You wear a du-rag with Emmett Till blazing on it. Do you even know who he is? Or when you raise your fist on stage like the three black Olympians in Mexico in 1968, do you know who they are? Or have some of our most iconoclastic images just become a way for you to own a fast buck?'

Iconoclastic? What the fuck was that? Didn't sound like no musical word to him. He watched her purse her lips, in annoyance or to hold back more words, he didn't know. What he did know was he was tired of being the current bogeyman.

'Everyone else is taking potshots at me, so now you're at the head of the queue don't hold it back, girl.'

She shook her extensions back.

'OK. Don't you think that you're just taking a genuine black artistic literary tradition, which has transcended the middle passage to take the message of the African griot to all the four corners of the world, and trashed it into some fake, misogynistic, consumer-chewing, pimp-prancing song-and-dance routine, whose only call and response is sell-out, sell-out, sell-out!'

He pulled himself off the stool, rising to what he saw as her insult and bare-faced condemnation of him.

'Are you calling me a clown?'

'Why don't you look in the mirror and answer that one yourself?'

The heat started to burn inside and he knew he was angry. Screw-'em-all angry.

'And yeah, you'd know all about selling out, Evie. Nice Wapping warehouse tucked neatly back from the community. You might chat different now, dress different, but don't think any of us have forgotten that you were born on the same dirty council estates as the rest of us. Just because you got Window wrapped around your little pinkie as Mr Lover Man don't make you any better than me.'

The silence was charged. Only when he stopped did he realise that his finger was stabbing at her. He saw her eyes go behind him. Felt a shadow pass over his back. He twisted around to find his manager looking at him with seething fury. LT realised that he'd crossed a line. Doing a word slam with Evie was fine. Doing it in front of Window's kid was not.

'Window, I . . .'

'You need to leave because I'm not sure I can be representing you no more.'

LT stopped his ride five minutes away from his home. In the type of backstreet that no one ever learns the name of. He leaned his forehead on the steering wheel. For the first time in years he acknowledged that he was bent over with the weight of a defeated man. No way was he going to get through this without the mighty Window holding his hand. No King, no Window, no career. Sure, he was still in line to hook up with the Writer in Residence prize for the third year, but then what? Going back to the darkness of basement clubs? He pushed his head up, back into the afternoon light. His car phone rang. He punched it on to speakerphone.

'Look, if this is the fucking word rats I'm not . . .'

'It's Rochelle, May's daughter. Can you come to the hospital?'

'What happened?' LT's voice was as tiny as the unconscious woman who lay in the bed in St Luke's hospital.

May's middle daughter, Rochelle, sat by the bed, holding her mother's hand. He knew Rochelle from their days at St Ignatius. The joker at the back of the class. Always keeping everyone happy. Now he saw her tears for the first time.

'Looks like intruders got in. Tried to drown her. Ransacked her beautiful house. Tipped her records all over the place. They didn't even take anything.'

'They didn't take anything?' He said the words slowly.

She shook her head. He rubbed his hand over his face. He left her ten minutes later when her voice began to fade.

He took weary steps out of the ward to the communal area. Guilt pushed him up against the wall next to the lift. He should have warned May. Told her what was going on. 'You can't serve two masters at the same time,' that was what the King had chanted. He'd been serving himself for such a long time the silhouette of other people didn't even fall into range of his radar. The lift shuddered. Opened. He closed his eyes. He heard footsteps. Felt a shadow warm him.

'I heard about May,' a voice whispered in front of him.

Bernie.

She was back to wearing all black, except for the baker's-boy hat which did its job of hiding the bruise on her face from the world. But not from him.

'Bastards nearly drowned her,' he said as the guilt screwed him deeper into the wall. 'Nothing was taken so they were obviously looking for something.'

'The tape and jacket?' she asked as she leaned next to him. The sigh she gave made it sound as if she was really grateful for the chance to stop for a while.

'Made a real mess of her home. Threw all her records around the place.'

'Records?' She pushed off her contentment and the wall.

She shuffled around to stand in front of him.

'Funny thing to do, throw records around.'

The guilt eased up on him. He came off the wall. Took a step sideways so he wasn't in her space.

'Who the hecking hell knows. All I know is I need to get that tape quick before someone else gets hurt. As for this jacket, only the Devil and his disciples seem to know about that one.'

'So the dominoes didn't arrive today?'

'We're talking Royal Mail here. Most probably still in some fucking sorting office in Glasgow.'

'What you going to do?'

He gazed at her wearily and said, 'I don't know. Everything's a big turd of a mess and do you want to know why? Because I'm one big selfish bastard.'

'Why do you think that?' Her voice was soft. Reassuring.

'I should have warned May. Made her go to her girls and stay for a while. But I was too busy widening the spectrum of my own limelight. Someone just accused me of stealing all those classic black history images so that I can just become a pimp-prancing superstar. That's what I've become, a black man who didn't know who Emmett Till was. A black man who didn't know who Huey Newton was. A man who stuck his Black Power fist in the air with no idea where it came from. And the biggest shit was the King realised it all the time and was just laughing at me. The idiot son who believed that Fidel Castro and Che Guevara were members of a rumba band.'

'I think that you're wrong about the King. I don't think he was laughing, I think he was proud and had big hopes. Maybe he left those tapes because it was his way of helping to push you on a road you didn't realise was in front of you.'

They brooded in their own silence. She came out of hers first.

'I heard about the righteous-mothers-from-hell brigade. What were they called?'

'Mothers Against Murder Music,' he answered.

Bernie pushed her hand through her hair as she thought. Then she said, 'I'd never heard of them before. I usually hear about those types of groups long before the general public know they're on the scene. Does that mean it's tits up with the record company?'

He wiped his hand over his du-rag.

'You know what, I don't give a shit about that any more. I'm tired of rolling over every time they decide they want to tickle my belly. The only thing I want to do is find that tape, so all this shit can stop. Then on Monday win the competition because it's mine, baby, mine.'

The last three words echoed around them.

He started walking away from her. She called out, 'Where you going?'

'To check my post to see if the domino set has arrived. Be ready for my call if it has.'

LT's strides were swift and eager as he neared the front door of his home. He just hoped that the dominoes had arrived. As he stuck the key into the lock he felt someone behind him. Bollocks. He was no fighter. The muscles in his back stiffened. He heard a scuffle of footsteps. Whoever it was set a chill over his back.

'Lord Tribulation?' a cockney voice behind him asked. Old-time cockney, not the hybrid Caribbean–London patter the kids used nowadays.

Suddenly his arm was expertly forced up his back. He was shoved, face first, against the door.

'You're nicked, mate!' the voice breathed, dirty by his ear. 'Wait till we get you down the station – I've got a nasty feeling you're going to have an accident with another type of door – a cell door, you know what I mean . . . ?'

No way. LT pushed back hard. The policeman dropped his arm. LT swung around, mouth ready to confront the officer with a string of words about his civil liberties and shit. He relaxed, clipping his words back, when he saw it was no policeman. Elijah 'Schoolboy' Campbell. The least likely person to be a member of the Metropolitan Police force. But then again, maybe in today's modern police service, a young black guy with a record like Schoolboy's would be fast-tracked for promotion. Schoolboy stood next to a white carrier bag.

'Hey,' LT said simply, looking at the smaller man in front of him.

Schoolboy had skin of smooth pine and shoulder-length locks that were tied back. Must be a sign of his new lifestyle because he'd always worn them loose and untamed in the past.

They leaned over and embraced.

'Tribulation, boy, long time no see – and what's this I hear that you've taken my place as the estate's number-one bad bwoi? Inciting the youth to go around setting people on fire. You should be singing country and western like my mum used to like – it's a lot safer, man, I'm telling you.'

A laugh, a mixture of sadness and merriment, pushed up from LT as he remembered what the King had said about Jim Reeves on the tape. When his laughter drained away he said, 'Jackie said you were coming back. What's life like down in the West country?'

Schoolboy had cleaned his fingernails, left London's underworld to go and work with a friend in the restaurant business in Devon. Well, that was what some people said. Others said he'd been doing time in an open prison by the sea. Whichever tale was true, Schoolboy had left the capital's badlands in one big hurry.

Schoolboy's dimples stood tall on his cheeks as he spoke.

'Good. But you know me, I could never go through life without my dose of London's inner-city sizzler. Also checking up on my sister.'

LT's face tightened at the mention of Schoolboy's sister – Evie Campbell.

'Look, before I forget,' Schoolboy picked up the white carrier bag and held it out to LT. 'Jackie said the police left this for you.'

LT took it from him. Looked inside. Some of the blood retreated from his face.

'Thanks,' he said, tightening his hands on the handle of the bag that held the King's urn.

'Come in for a bit. After the day I've had I could do with a bit of company.'

As he leaned his key towards the lock one of his feet hit something on the floor.

'What the fuck's that?' he said as he stepped back.

He bent down and saw a box-shaped parcel. As he grabbed it he yelled out a jubilant, 'yesss.'

He tucked the parcel under his arm. Quickly unlocked the door.

'I see the Royal Mail hasn't changed much,' Schoolboy grumbled behind him.

'Fancy leaving that on the balcony. Anyone could've nabbed it. I should know, I use to be the door-stop-nicking-king, back-in-the-day.'

LT didn't answer as he moved urgently into the main room. He flicked the light on. Threw himself on to the nearest sofa.

He placed the bag with the King's ashes gently on the floor. Then he tore the paper from the parcel. Looked down at the domino set. Read the attached letter.

'No way,' he yelled as he shot to his feet.

'What's the matter, G?' Schoolboy asked, arms folded as he leaned by the door.

LT waved the domino set at his friend.

'They sent the wrong one.'

'The wrong what?'

Schoolboy strode over to LT.

'Friggin' box of bones. Look at the label. It says Mr Franklin Ross, not Isaiah Scantleberry. And this box is from some kiddies' toyshop. The King's domino box was made from Middle Eastern wood.'

Schoolboy reached him.

'Slow it down, G. You're all erratic.'

Instead of answering LT jerked his wrist up and checked his watch. He hit the room with a few more swear words.

'They'll be long shut,' he slammed out.

'What's going on?'

He looked up at his friend.

'Tomorrow's the exhibition, and if I don't get the dominoes now I know someone else will figure it all out and get them.'

'What exhibition?'

'I've got no alternative. I've got to get that domino set tonight.' He looked at Schoolboy with pleading eyes. 'I know you've been out of the burglary business a long time, but I need you to help me organise a snatch before tomorrow morning.'

'What kind of job do you want doing?' Schoolboy asked.

They stood on the balcony in the brewing darkness.

'Nothing too heavy, just a simple snatch. Quick in-and-out job.'

'But?'

'But it may involve alarms.'

Schoolboy let out a huff and said, 'You're not talking financial institution?'

'What do I look like to you?'

'A man who's almost wetting himself.'

LT's heavy breath rocked against the open air. His conscience just would not let go. His conscience told him it was wrong, but reality told him it was right. He might sing about a life lived outside the law, but he had never broken the law in his life. He shook his conscience off. Thought of May. Thought of Bernie's face. Saw the King on a slab in the mortuary.

'Whoever you get, tell them that I'm coming with them.'

Schoolboy's eyes searched him for a full ten seconds.

'You really want to do this?'

'After seeing May in the hospital . . .' He just shook his head.

He saw the puzzlement in Schoolboy's face at the mention of May's name.

'Let's just say this is really personal now,' LT continued.

'Ain't you got enough problems?'

'That's why I'm doing it. My dad's dead. A pack of old girls waving umbrellas are after me. Record company have put me on their undesirable list. My manager I think has dumped me. What have I got to lose? So you got someone for me?'

'Could mess up your chance with the competition if you get caught and busted.'

Schoolboy took a small red ball from his pocket. Began bouncing it against the balcony.

'What's that?'

'Ryan's, Jackie's boy. Made me take it away from him. She's got me playing Daddy.'

'Do you have a name for me?'

His friend cocked his head to the side and studied him. He tucked his lips in with what LT knew was regret. Regret at what he didn't know. He pushed the ball back into his pocket.

'Yeah, I've got just the geezer for you. Meet me back here tonight at eleven thirty. Bring your wheels. A torch. Gloves. Make sure you're garmed in a hooded jacket that flops over your forehead and zips up well over your nose.'

'I'm really sorry to disturb you, but we need to talk,' Bernie said as she looked at Window standing in the doorway of his Wapping duplex, holding his son.

He stepped back as he said, 'Come in.'

She moved inside the fashionable warehouse home.

'Let's go out here,' he said as he took her through the lounge.

They stepped out on to a balcony overlooking the sleepy, shifting river. Window hugged his son on his right shoulder.

'I always bring him out here just before his bedtime. The air lulls him to sleep. But you ain't come up here to talk about my son, but about my boy.'

'He may not still be your boy from what I hear.'

Window soothed his son's back with his large hand.

'We just got a bit tangled up today. We'll straighten it out come the morning light.'

She clutched the rail. Let the river breeze knead her face.

'From what I understand you know Beresford Clarke better than most,' she said.

'The finest man you'll ever meet.'

The baby yawned, a quiet push of air in the moving night.

'When exactly did he arrive in Birmingham?'

'Girl, that's like asking when did God create the earth. In this life no one ever asks when did they arrive, only what they did when they got there. And Beresford was a man who changed the community. Gave his life up for our community.'

He transferred the baby to his other shoulder.

'Was he there before 1976?'

A troubled light shone in Window's eyes as he answered.

'I see where you're going. So now he's all mixed up with that '76 shit that's been stinking up LT's yard. Wrong man, girl.'

'Let me be straight with you. The day I got beaten up and my Dictaphone was stolen, one of the muggers mentioned the name Clarke . . .'

'That's a popular name. I could touch my fingers with the names of ten other Clarkes I know.'

She carried on as if she hadn't heard him.

'Then the witness from the cab office comes to Jerry's yesterday, the same time Beresford's there. Then she's running for her life.'

The baby whimpered but his father said nothing. Bernie looked at the baby. She touched his curled hand with her finger. Caressed him.

'What did you feel like when he was born?' Her voice was quiet, as if they were standing in a maternity ward.

'Humble. Immense. My gut kept tugging and pulling.'

'Well, my gut keeps pulling and tugging every time I hear the name Beresford Clarke.'

He turned on his heels, making her finger fall. He took slow steps back inside. Took the baby into his room. Laid him down. Kissed him. Tucked the covers up to his soft chin. Closed the door and joined her in the hallway.

'I don't know the answer to your question. But I know someone who does. They call him the Major. You'll need to go to Birmingham because he's a man who likes to see who he's doing business with. Head for the Handsworth Road and you'll find him. Just mention my name.'

Bernie sat hunched over her computer under the sidelight in the lounge. A half-empty glass of white wine – Australian, sweet – sat next to the keyboard. She typed 'Mothers Against Murder Music' into the search engine. A thousand and ninety-five hits. She whistled. For an organisation that had just appeared that day they had been very busy. She hit the first site. Their website. The main page. No pictures. Just the strapline 'Stop murder music now' and a menu.

*About us.*

*Our campaign.*

*How to join.*

She pressed 'our campaign'. Now she got pictures. Photographs of them demonstrating outside Paradise Records with quotes.

'Parents need to take responsibility for their children's listening.'

'Stop murder music now.'

'The record companies are as guilty as the artists they sign.'

At the bottom of the page MAMM thanked the many people who had already pledged money to the campaign, including their main sponsor, whom they did not name. Bernie flicked her eyes back to the photographs. She noticed that one face kept appearing. Dead centre every time. A woman with a determined but stilted pose, who tried to look forty but was kicking ten years more than that. No name. She pressed backspace. Waved the cursor over 'How to join us'. Pressed. Scrolled down, looking for a name. It came at the bottom. Magdelana Delaney, campaign organiser.

Bernie tapped in a new search. Magdelana Delaney. Over ten thousand hits. An important woman. She clicked the fourth site – Magdelana Delaney, biography.

'Magdelana Delaney has been a leading pioneer in advancing the life chances of children in Britain's inner cities. She is most noted as the managing director of Teen Life, a partnership between the City and London schools to offer valued work experience to disadvantaged youngsters. Before devoting herself to charity work she was an active member of London's feminist movement and other radical groups ...'

Bernie stopped reading. She knew it might be a long shot, but she might have found another ghost from 1976 – Anne.

'Only two rules make a successful burglary. Getting in and getting out,' Schoolboy whispered to LT. They stood in an alley around the back of the Marcus Garvey Community Centre in Notting Hill, the building where LT had faced the press two days earlier. They stood under a back window. The window that was going to get them inside. The night breeze was thick. Chilled. Held on to LT's skin with the tenacity of a warning.

Schoolboy flicked his wrist up. Checked his watch. Thirty-four minutes past midnight.

'We got ten minutes to be back here.'

LT didn't argue. Schoolboy knew his former trade. LT's eyes fretted over the museum.

'Not still worrying about the security, are you, because there ain't none,' Schoolboy said confidently.

When they had arrived, Schoolboy had conducted a thorough check of the outside of the building, looking for surveillance equipment. He had found nothing.

'How can you be so sure?'

'Look, if the council were bellyaching about whether they had enough funds to keep this place going one more year, they sure ain't ploughing no dosh into no security system. Plus didn't you say it's full of gear belonging to black people?'

LT nodded.

'Definitely no security,' Schoolboy said.

Schoolboy got down to business and took a screwdriver from his back pocket. He tipped on to his toes. Leaned into the window ledge. Frozen rivers of rust were randomly striped across the metal. He pushed the screwdriver between the window and ledge. He heaved himself into his task. The window eased up from the frame. He shoved the screwdriver back into his pocket. Used his palms to push the window higher. Enough space for them to slide through. He turned back to LT.

'Rule number three . . .'

'Thought you said there were only two rules.'

'Rule number three is always listen to the leader.'

LT nodded his head.

'I'm going in first and then I'll pull you through.'

Schoolboy braced his hands against the windowsill. He let out a stout groan as he shifted his upper body weight on to his arms. He clambered up the wall, his feet dragging against the brickwork in a slalom motion. He shifted his hands so that one gripped the inside of the windowsill and the other remained outside. He did the same with his legs until he rode the windowsill like a seasoned jockey on a Grand National favourite. LT saw him move his mouth to the count of three. Then he swung his other leg over and dropped down inside. LT held his breath, convinced an alarm would go off. When it remained silent he started to breathe. He was startled by the sound of a car engine coming from the neighbouring street. In panic he flattened himself against the wall. Flashing headlights lit up the entrance to the alley. The pounding music from his killer tune, 'Gasoline Ghetto', came from the car's interior. He closed his eyes. Forgot to breathe. The music died in the distance as the car drove by.

'Where you gone?' Schoolboy's voice whispered above.

LT pushed himself forward. Schoolboy leaned out of the window and stretched his arms down. LT didn't need to be told what to do. He grabbed his friend's arms and pulled himself up. Schoolboy tugged him through the window. LT landed on a tiled floor. He adjusted his eyes to the dark. It was a small, rectangular room. He saw his reflection in the long mirror that took up the whole of one wall. He looked like what he was trying to be, a silhouette creeping unnoticed in the night. Opposite the mirror were four cubicles with frosted glass doors. From the sweet smell he knew it was the Ladies. He turned his torch on.

Schoolboy groped in his pocket, looking for his own torch. He swore.

'I still got Ryan's ball,' he said, realising his hand was in the wrong pocket.

He checked his other pocket and dragged the torch out. Following his friend's example, he flicked it on.

Schoolboy pulled the arched metal handle of the door. Eased it open. He leaned his head out and shone the torch to the right. To the left. Then he stepped out. LT followed. They stood next to a curved staircase. LT hoped it was not too far up to the next floor. Through the darkness they could make out a counter, like in a canteen, and tables and chairs. The centre's café.

'Which way?' LT asked.

'Up the stairs. Turn your torch off.'

Darkness enveloped them. LT groped for the banister rail with his hand and fumbled for the first step with his foot. Within seconds they hit the next floor. LT realised they were in the room where the press had grilled him with questions. Schoolboy flicked his torch back on. LT followed suit. They waved their torches around a long room that displayed exhibits on the walls and on podiums. The main exhibition hall. Schoolboy whispered, 'Check the walls first, middle next. You take that side and I'll take this.'

They started work, shifting their torchlight against pictures, a gallery of album covers, musical instruments and carefully staged clothes. LT moved to the middle of the room to investigate the exhibits standing on podiums. His torch went up, searched, then came down. He did this six times before he found what he was looking for. On a waist-height podium, near the side of the room nearest the stairs they had come up, was the King's box of bones.

'Yes,' he breathed, his first smile of the night breaking his face.

'Found it,' he called to Schoolboy.

He shone his torch on to it. Rectangular, with an ebony border and polished so many times every knot in the wood stood out. LT laughed. Strong, high, as if life had just begun.

'Sh,' Schoolboy hushed him as he reached his side.

The laughter died on LT's face. Schoolboy spun around to face the entrance on the other side of the room. He pushed his head forward. Cocked it to the side.

'Shit,' exploded from Schoolboy's lips.

'What is it?'

Schoolboy spun back to LT and said one word.

'Run.'

Schoolboy ran. LT could not move. He stood transfixed. Shocked by the distorted shadow that was nipping at the entrance of the room. Then he heard the growl. Deep. Rough. A dog. The second growl made him move. He swung around, looking for Schoolboy. He could not see him. Could not see which way he had gone.

A bark boomed at the entrance. LT knew he should not look, but he could not help himself. In the doorway stood a twenty-four-inch-high, powerfully built Rottweiler. The dog lifted its top lip in a snarl that showed its scissor precision teeth. LT sprinted towards the stairs. In his haste he moved both feet at the same time. A mistake. His front foot accelerated with a speed his back foot didn't show. His front foot dived under his back foot. They tangled up like disgruntled lovers. His balance tipped to the left side.

He stretched out his left arm to grab an exhibit to break his fall, but his fingers found thin air. He heard the dog's panting breathing as it ran towards him. He kept falling. An inbuilt reflex made him close his eyes. He kept falling. The panting grew louder. He kept falling. A musky scent mixed with lemon shampoo skidded over his nose. A hard body barrelled into him. Breath touched his neck. Jesus. He started to scream. A hand clamped over his mouth. His eyes flew open and wide.

'Sh,' Schoolboy whispered in his ear.

Schoolboy dragged him backwards and said, 'Shift it.'

Schoolboy let go of LT's mouth. LT dropped to his knees as the domino set dropped from his hand. He looked up at the same time as the dog found them. Schoolboy fiddled in his pocket. He took out something round. The dog reared up. Schoolboy threw what he was holding across the room. When it bounced, LT realised it was Ryan's ball.

The dog twisted and ran after it. They bolted for the stairs.

Jumped down. They hit the café floor. They twisted round the corner towards the Ladies. Schoolboy got there first. Yanked the door open. They fell inside. Schoolboy rotated back to the door, his hands groping over it.

'Fuck, no lock.'

Schoolboy slammed his back against the door.

'I left the dominoes behind,' LT said.

'That's where they're going to have to stay for now because Rover outside ain't moving. We can't get out at the same time because he'll be in here before we manage it. You'll have to go first.'

The dog's bark on the other side of the door made LT move. He leaped up. Gripped the windowsill. Used his feet against the wall to push his body higher. Hitched up one leg. Straddled the windowsill. He turned his body to look at his friend.

'Go on, jump,' Schoolboy told him. Voice strained as he rocked his back against the door.

LT jumped. He landed under the window in a blast of cold air. He heard Schoolboy count, 'One . . . two . . . three.' Then he heard a rush of feet. A growl. Schoolboy's fingertips appeared, clutching the windowsill.

'You ain't touching me, you bastard.' Schoolboy said the last word as if he were hitting something. A whining filled the air. Schoolboy's breathing got rougher, louder, as his hands now appeared in their entirety. His right leg came over. Then he cried out, 'Shit.'

His head and shoulders shot through. He scrambled up, pulling his upper body out. Swung his left leg through. Jumped down. He landed in a crouched position. He took a couple of breaths and then straightened up.

'Look what it did to my trainers,' he said.

LT looked down to see a set of teeth marks on the tip of Schoolboy's right trainer.

'Do you know how much they cost me?'

'Screw your trainers. Are you hurt?'

'By that pussycat, no way.'

LT turned around and hit his hand hard against the brick wall as he yelled, 'I'm well and truly stuffed now. Tomorrow's the exhibition. How the hell am I going to make sure someone doesn't get the tape before me?'

At 7.15 the next morning, Bernie listened to The Smiths' 'Heaven Knows I'm Miserable Now' on her MP3 as she settled back against the train seat on her way to Birmingham. She didn't have much time. She had to find the so-called Major, still had to check out any information about Magdelana Delaney and be back in London for the exhibition's grand opening at 1 p.m. The train started moving. She shut her eyes.

The exhibition, 'Exodus: The Story of Black London 1948 – the New Millennium', opened its doors to the public at one in the afternoon on the first day of the Notting Hill carnival. Sunday, 27 August. Children's carnival day. Under barn-like beams and within bare, red-brick walls the exhibition displayed a varied collection of objects that celebrated the existence of London's Caribbean community – hundreds of photographs, which included shots of fresh-faced Jamaicans standing on the quayside with the *Empire Windrush* in the background, a wall that had been turned into a tapestry of album covers, tailor's dummies dressed in different styles of clothing and artefacts that ranged from steel pans to dominoes.

The opening had attracted plenty of people. There were the great and the good, such as the mayor, who was posing for photographs for the local press. There were people who made it their first stop on their way to the carnival. There were groups of teenagers from the local comprehensive, or the Academy of Excellence as it was calling itself these days, some who looked genuinely interested in the displays and others who appeared sullen, as if the local authority had press-ganged them to make up the numbers.

And there was Lord Tribulation.

He was staring at a framed black-and-white publicity still of Jimmy Cliff in the film *The Harder They Come*. Jimmy Cliff's character, with serious face and handgun, leaned into the camera lens, his outrageous, slick, rude-boy stance insolent. The clothes dared to blend styles in a way that makeover programmes told you to avoid – an oversize white baker's-boy cap, leopard-print shirt, pinstripe slacks and mock-croc shoes. What made the photograph popular with LT was that it was mounted on the wall directly in front of the white podium with the King's last box of bones.

LT looked around. He swore under his breath. Too many people around for him to go for the smash-and-grab option. But what other option did he have? He left Jimmy Cliff and strode towards the domino box. As he took the final stride towards it a group of four men, all tall, all dressed in black, came into the room. Shit. He stepped back. The men looked official. One of them got out a walkie-talkie. The group of men went out and came back in, shielding someone. The men peeled back. The group shifted, Red Sea-style, revealing Clarissa Hathaway, Minister of Culture.

Clarissa Hathaway, there as guest of honour, had a phalanx of aides and hangers-on busying themselves around her as she got ready to make the opening speech. LT stood with the rest of the audience, thankful that none of the press had recognised him without his du-rag on. They wouldn't be able to resist an opportunity to get him and the minister to pose together.

'Did you get them?' a voice whispered by his side.

LT looked sideways and down to find Bernie next to him. The disarrayed sweep of her hair made her look tired.

'If I had do you think I would be standing here listening to the Minister of Crapation?'

She leaned close to him and said, 'I thought I'd found Anne.'

'What?' He looked at her face and could tell it wasn't good news.

She explained her initial hunch about Magdelana Delaney.

'But it was a no-go. She was definitely in Canada burying her father on August bank holiday 1976. Besides, she was part of a radical lesbian group that didn't have any dealings with men.'

The minister coughed, ready to begin. Bernie and LT shifted to listen to her.

'I'd like to welcome everyone here today and it's a great privilege to be asked to open...' The Minister of Culture paused briefly while checking her notes. '... this important exhibition, not only for the black community but for the communities of London. As you all know the preservation and acknowledgement of all cultures is at the top of the government's lists of priorities. I'm delighted that the government and the council are working in partnership with the local community. Without further ado I now declare the exhibition, "Exodus: The Story of Black London 1948 – the New Millennium", officially open.'

Everyone clapped. Then began to drift off. LT knew that there was enough confusion and noise for him to try to steal the box of bones. He left Bernie. Picked up speed towards the podium. Looked left, looked right. His hand shot out. Heart pumped up. A hand clamped around his wrist. Shit. He twisted around and relaxed when he saw that the hand belonged to Schoolboy.

His friend whispered, 'You can't just take it like that. This ain't *Carry On Thieving.*'

Schoolboy dragged him to the side.

'If I don't get them I'll never find out what happened to the King,' LT replied, eyes still on the domino box.

The minister's entourage swept past towards the exit with the minister in the middle.

'You just rock 'n' roll and enjoy the exhibition, man – I'll get your bones for you,' Schoolboy said.

He smiled, his dimples popping, and walked away.

LT wandered through the exhibition, his nerves biting him with each step. He saw Bernie standing next to a framed black-and-white photograph. He sighed, knowing that a week ago he wouldn't have known what the photograph was. It had taken Emmett Till and his father's tapes to push him to find out more about the Black Power movement. The photograph showed Stokely Carmichael, in a suit, loosened tie, mini-'fro and dark glasses, making a speech at a Black Power conference at the Roundhouse in Camden in 1967. Also seated at the central table was Michael X, the former British Black Power leader. Bernie raised her eyebrow in a question. She didn't need to tell him which question she was throwing across the room at him. He shook his head.

Suddenly a bluster of voices projected from the other side of the room. He turned to find two groups of teenagers squaring up to each other. Baseball caps were turned backwards. Hoods pulled down. Other youths came flying through the halls like multicoloured bees, hurrying to support one side or the other. LT watched as a short kid at the back of one of the gangs pulled a framed poster of Bob Marley with the tag line 'One Love' and threw it towards the heads of the opposition. The other group scattered as the glass shattered on the floor. Visitors screamed and fled, some running with little children in pushchairs, as the fight developed. When a photograph of Nelson Mandela in Trafalgar Square landed at LT's feet he realised the youths were using anything they could get their hands on to win the battle. Bollocks. The domino box. He ducked his head, weaving forward, trying to get to the King's box of bones. But a security guard swooped in front of him and yelled, 'Everyone out.'

LT turned to him, pleading, 'But . . .'

'Out now, sir.'

LT fled the building with the rest of the scrambling crowd. As he stumbled to the kerb he heard police sirens splitting the air. Security guards began to wave the crowd well back from the building. As they moved Bernie appeared at his side.

'What the fuck are we going to do now?' she asked harshly as they found a corner to stand in.

Frustration clogged LT's throat, blocking the words that were bubbling in his head.

'Quite a row, weren't it?' a voice said behind them.

They twisted around to find Schoolboy, arms folded, a cocky grin dancing on his face. His eyes darted around, doing a quick scout of the street. Then he unfolded his arms, allowing something to drop from the sleeve of his jacket. He caught it and pressed it into LT's hand like a wrap of cocaine. Without looking, from its shape and hard feel, LT knew it was the box of bones. In one easy move, he dropped it into the long side pocket of his trousers. They stood in silence before LT whispered, 'That fight turned out to be quite a lucky break, then?'

'It was a break, OK – but there was nothing lucky about it . . .' Schoolboy's voice sank lower. 'It was me that promoted the fight . . .'

'You?'

'Yeah – I told the Portobello Kids that the Grove Boys were dissing them up. Well – that's got to mean trouble, hasn't it? Although I must admit, I didn't think it was going to be that bad.'

'Thanks, mate. Bernie, we're out of here.'

LT started walking, but Bernie called, 'Wait for me by your car.'

Now he began running, eager to find the tape.

Bernie looked at Schoolboy. She remembered him as one of the crowd who could fight their way out of anything back in their days at St Ignatius.

'You don't remember me but . . .'

'I remember you all right.' His tone was offhand, not friendly.

'Look, I need you to do something for me . . .'

'Why should I help the woman who cut out on LT all those years ago?'

'Because he won't believe that there's someone dangerous living in his pocket.'

He held his head back, looking at her suspiciously.

'Go on.'

'I think I know who might have been involved in his father's death. This person said they lived in Birmingham from 1973, but I found out this morning they didn't get there until September 1976. But Jerry's not going to believe me. I need to show him some concrete evidence. I'm frightened he'll get hurt.'

He hitched his gaze at her and studied her for a full ten seconds.

'OK. Where does my shadow fit into all of this?'

'I know you're out of circulation. But I need you to do a job for me.'

'What kind of job?'

'It involves a house. A house on the Isle of Dogs. Walk me to Jerry's car and I'll tell you the rest.'

An hour later LT's four-by-four pumped music and speed as it crossed back over Hackney's borders. It did a smooth right into Queensbridge Road. When Bernie left Schoolboy and got to LT's car he was already behind the steering wheel, the tape on the dashboard. As soon as she buckled up the car peeled out towards East London.

'This isn't your usual route,' Bernie said as the wind fanned her face from the open window.

'We're not going back to mine.'

The car swerved left.

'But I thought we were going to listen to the tape,' she said, her tone loaded with anxiety.

'We are. I thought we could do with some authentic atmos this time.'

The worry lines around her eyes deepened as she realised he was taking them to the Liberation Republic.

The house streamed with belts of light when they entered. LT pushed the door, closing out the world.

'Choose any room you like, except downstairs,' he said as they stood in the hall.

Bernie looked up the stairs and then down the hall.

'Let's go into the Sweet and Dandy.'

He followed her to the far end of the hall, to the extension that had once been the Liberation Republic's drinking and eating hole. The room was surprisingly cold, as if its single back window had been open since 1976. They sat down on the chairs at the single table. LT dragged the tape from his pocket. He studied the words the King had written on the label: 'Revival Selection: 1976, Volume 3'.

He pulled out the Dictaphone from his other pocket. Opened it. Slid the tape inside. Closed it.

He looked up at her. She looked back at him.

'Ready?' he asked.

She nodded.

He pressed 'play'.

The King's solemn, downbeat voice wavered into the room.

'I sometimes think about what life would have been like if we never went on that journey that night. If we never did those jobs for our landlord in that hellhole called Hoxton. If we never decided that the price of our principles was one pound. But we did. And, God forgive us, it changed our lives for ever . . .'

# REVIVAL SELECTION: 1976, VOLUME 3
### (7" Single: A-Side)

So me, Houdini and Anne jumped in the back of the van on our way to Hoxton. Sean took the driver's side and Shakespeare sat next to him. Houdini sat on the edge of one box of joy and me and the girl sat on the other, opposite him. I moved my eyes so I didn't have to look at him or the girl. Man, I was scared. Scared of the black mask shaking in my hand and of going into Hoxton. What if a gang of NF bully-boys found us? . . . Shit, I didn't want to think about that. As the engine started that's when I felt them. Those damn seven little devils beating their Satanic drums beneath my feet. I tried to shift my pumps but they stayed with me, as the van hightailed it through the streets. If someone had flung open the back doors right then I would have jumped out, letting the van go one way while me and my good intentions went the other. Know what kept me in that van? The Cause, grabbing up the front of my shirt, reminding me what was right and wrong.

'Put your masks on,' Shakespeare ordered from the front.

Houdini put his on straight away. He tucked his locks into the top of his jacket. Then Anne did the same. She bunched her hair up into the mask, like she was touting dreadlocks. Her grey eyes stared at me from behind the mask. I gripped mine, not moving it towards my face.

'What's wrong with you, man? Put it on,' Houdini said.

Man, what choice did I have? I shoved its raas over my head. The heat and the mask encased my face with a vengeance. How long we drove I couldn't tell you. The van began to slow as my heart started to pound up. All of a sudden the van shuddered to a stop, making the house of joy I sat on skid. The engine kicked off. Shakespeare whispered to Sean, who nodded. Shakespeare got out and came around to the back of the van. The doors were pulled open and he leapt awkwardly inside. He was carrying something in his hand. My eye shot down to it.

Well, kiss my sweet black rah-rah, quick time.

In his right hand he held a long stick. A baseball bat. I knew we weren't going to be playing no ball games that night. Fucking hell, I hoped we weren't preparing for no ruck with them National Front, baldhead bastards. The only rough play I ever did was on the stage. Violence, no sir, that wasn't my ting. I shot up from the speaker.

'Sit down. Please, brother, sit down.' Shakespeare's voice was calm.

His words pushed me back.

'Sometimes in life in order to realise the dream you have to step over the boundary. The biggest thing in our lives is the Cause. You saw what they did to our children last month in Soweto. We've got to break the cycle, man, break the cycle. When we wake up in the morning we think about the Cause. When we shut our eyes at night we think about the Cause. Everything else comes after that. When we go inside no one speaks. Just do what I tell you to do.'

His quiet, soothing voice eased me down. I straightened up. I didn't even know where 'inside' was, but I was ready to go.

He swivelled on the balls of his pumps and jumped outside. Thank the Lord that Sean stayed in the van. We followed Shakespeare like Indians who'd strayed into cowboy country. We jumped out into an alleyway. On the wall that faced us, carefully written, like someone had taken their sweet time, were the words 'Wogs Out'. Hoxton was full of bad lyrics, bad smells and buildings that looked like they had finally given up the will to live. It looked like a bit of London that even the bin men didn't go to. A rat saw us and jumped in a hole.

'Don't forget,' Shakespeare whispered, 'that this end of town don't take kindly to sons of Africa. So just do what I tell you to do. Then we'll be gone from here before you know it.'

The heat started to kind of choke me up, making it hard to breathe through the mask. Shakespeare took long strides down the street. So we followed him, his three soldiers of the revolution. Past a school. Past a 'Keep Britain White' slogan on the wall. Past Gazoo Lane. We stopped in front of a tall, narrow house, you know, one of them plain-looking Georgian homes, next to a café called Joe's.

Shakespeare took the first steps towards the house and once again we followed. He thrust the stick at me and automatically – maybe you think I was an idiot-boy – I held it. His hand shifted inside his jacket pocket. He pulled out something metal. I couldn't see what it was. When he moved it to the front of the door I knew it was a key. He pushed it in and it clicked as he turned it. The door opened. Real quiet, like the times I use to slip out of my mother's house when I was a youth to go to some blues party at night.

I couldn't see too good, but there were three doors in the passage – two in the right wall and one straight ahead, facing us, at the far end. My hand moved along the passage wall. We stopped when the wall became a door. We heard a snore. Heavy, but real gentle. Our bodies strained back in a collective gasp of breath. I still didn't know what the raas I was doing here.

'Just remember what I said. Follow me,' Shakespeare whispered as he took the stick from my hand.

Real slow he opened the door. He pushed it back. He stretched his arm out. One of his fingers flicked and a burst of light traumatised the room.

Well, kiss my sweet black rah-rah three times.

Inside the simple room was a family. Yes, you heard right, a family. And do you know what really got my eyes popping out of my head? They were a black family. Lying in two single beds. A woman and a man in one and a small boy and a gurgling baby in the other. I thought Shakespeare said that the job was collecting something and storing it away. What the hell did that have to do with a black family?

But I kept my thoughts to myself. It didn't take long for the man's eyes to shoot open. When he saw us his eyes grew big like black car headlights.

'What the . . .' the man let out in the thick, Jamaican accent of someone who hadn't been in the country too long.

His booming voice woke up the woman and children. He leapt up, in underpants and vest. The woman and children huddled together, wrapped in the cloak of the paraffin warmth coming from the two-burner heater and the protection of the camphor smell of mothballs. Sometimes you just have to harden your heart and this was one of those times. Nothing was higher than the Cause. Higher than the Republic. Higher than global freedom. I believed that with my whole being, but something inside me – God forgive me – was pleased that Sean was in the van. I didn't want him witnessing that the price of freedom was nasty, unavoidable, right.

The baby let out a phlegm-clogged whimper that shook the room. It looked at the man. The man looked at the baby. And that's when it happened. That's when the bass line dropped.

The man charged forward, straight at Shakespeare, his eyes glued to the stick. Me, Anne and Houdini scattered like unwanted pamphlets on the wind. Shakespeare stood firm, the rock that he was, and let the man come at him. The man kept coming until he was almost on top of Shakespeare. That was when Shakespeare made his move. He lifted the stick quick time, stuck it out straight and caught the man just above his navel. The man groaned, you know, one of them groans that says no one can help him with his pain. Then he fell heavy to the floor. The woman jumped up, with a bellow of rage so big I just step aside. She leapt towards Shakespeare's bent figure. As her rage took her closer I saw the frying pan in one of her raised hands and the baby clutched in the other. Houdini flew in front of her. She brought the frying pan up, then chopped it down. The pan touched the side of Houdini's head. Dazed, he pushed the woman back. Her body wobbled backwards and that was when it happened. The baby flew from her hand.

The small body moved in an arc up high, then it was like gravity held it still. For one second, two, I don't know, but then it started to drop. Jesus. The woman's anguish tore up the room as she twisted her head and watched her child fall. We all watched. I watched. I couldn't move, man, not one bone, not one joint. The baby screamed high as it skydived to earth. It hit the rumpled covers on the single bed where the young boy huddled. The baby sank into the softness of the bedding. The young boy scrambled towards its brother or sister – shit, man, we didn't even know if it was a boy or a girl – and tenderly pulled it into his arms. He rocked the baby, soothed it through his own tears.

'You know what you've got to do, brother.' Shakespeare's voice took the air, muffled by the mask or by a genuine disgust, I wasn't sure. 'Do what the landlord says and get out. Now. He needs his property back. Pack your stuff. Go. All the other tenants in this house have left. Nothing is worth the safety of your family. Besides, believe me when I say you don't want your family to be living in this neck of town.'

Shakespeare moved towards a black-and-white photo of an older couple on the mantelpiece. Dressed in 1950s threads. The woman looked like my grandmother on my mother's side. Shakespeare looked at it. Then he raised the stick and knocked it to the floor, making the glass shatter. I didn't like what he did, not one bit, but I kept my mouth shut. He turned to look at the man's face as he still held his belly. The man's eyes crumbled.

'Pack your stuff and get out.'

'Hold up, hold up,' Houdini cried out.

Shakespeare swung around and moved swiftly towards him. He hustled him to a corner while the family grabbed their belongings.

'Man, you can't send them out into Hoxton. What about those NF fuckers?'

'What do you want me to do? Drive them to a new location?' Shakespeare's finger started poking Houdini in the chest as he said his next words. 'Remember the Cause. We've got a job to do. They'll be all right.'

So said, so done. Half an hour later we watched the family as they hightailed it through Hoxton's murky night. Was I proud of what I did? Most probably not. Was I sorry for what I did? At the time, most probably not. See, in that thirty minutes I learned that if you want the bigger things in life you sometimes have to tread on the smaller things. Not stamp on them, just a tread, so in a few days they will be all right. But if we lost the opportunity to buy the Republic we wouldn't be all right in a few days, it would be lost to us for ever. But still the taste in my mouth felt like I'd been downing Red Stripe for three days without brushing my teeth. Since my time with the Republic everything had been black and white. Good or bad. For the first time I was living in a world of confusing grey.

'I think I'm going to be sick,' Anne suddenly said, flopping against the wall.

I just kissed my teeth. The stupid gal shouldn't have been involved in our business in the first place. Shakespeare rushed to her and helped to pull off her mask. She bent over, her hands slipping to her knees. The girl fought to get her breath back. Shakespeare whipped off his mask and hunched down next to her.

'Are you all right?'

She nodded, her breathing becoming easy. He put his arm over her shoulders and helped her to stand up. Then he let her go. Let us all go. Made sure we were standing with our eyes wide open on our own two feet. He turned to us all.

'Now the house is empty, we can get on with the second job.'

'What second job?' I said. 'Man, you said there was only one. That all we had to do was collect something and store it away.'

'It is really one job. The thing we have to collect has to be stored here. But the only way that could happen was if the house was empty. Now it is we can go and get the stuff. We're halfway there. We've almost got the Republic. Come on.'

He headed for the door before I could lick him with any more words. Idealistic fool that I was, I followed him.

Our second job took us to Broad Street, which was between the Regent's Canal to the north and London Fields to the south, a ten-minute drive from the house. The van stopped. We jumped out, masks now tucked in our pockets, at the top of this creepy, deserted street. One of them streets that looked like Jack the Ripper country. Although the heat was still churning, I felt cold. Someone once told me that victims from the Great Plague in, I think, the seventeenth century were buried in London Fields. Felt like them ghosts were dancing in my shadow. I shivered.

'Shakespeare, what we doing here?' I asked, wanting to get the hell out.

'Just follow me.'

So we did. A cat whined high into the night. Jesus, what the backside was I doing here? I kept flicking my head back like I was expecting some nutcase to jump out at me with an axe in their hand. We kept walking, with the Regent's Canal in the distance getting bigger. We reached the end of the street, looking down on the canal. The water was creeping, murky, full of rubbish and God alone knows what other cast-offs of life. There was a long boat in the water. I think they call them narrowboats. The dark disguised its colours. It was about ten times as long as it was wide, with a long cabin stretched across it with three evenly spaced windows. At both ends was a space for people to get on and off. And I wanted to be off. Now. But we were all in this together.

Shakespeare turned to us.

'Me and Houdini are going down to collect some boxes. When we bring them up, King, you and Anne take them to the van.'

They quickly walked down some steps to get to the towpath. As they reached the boat a man came out. He was about Shakespeare's height, with a cap, but I couldn't see his face. Didn't want to see his face. He pulled Houdini, then Shakespeare, on to the boat. They disappeared into the long cabin.

I twisted my head away from them and looked at the girl. First time I really checked her out. She looked back at me. She smiled, I did not. What the raas was there to grin your teeth about?

'So what are you doing slumming with a bunch of brothers? We all know that Whitey always wants some kind of payback,' I whispered.

Her hands gathered around her middle. Her eyebrow cocked back just the way that exclusive girls school had taught her, along with the other girls, to judge the working man from a distance. Well, that's how it looked to me, brother.

'You might not believe this, but I have as much invested in winning the class struggle as you. I know what you're thinking – posh girl wants a little bit of rough – and you would be right and wrong. Sure, I've got access to money, I'm not going to deny it, but taking a walk on the wild side, no way. I want equal rights as much as anyone else.'

Equal rights? Man, I just kissed my teeth. Like she knew anything about equal rights.

'So if you've got access to bread why have we just busted up a family, not just any family, you know, a black family, to buy the Republic?'

'Do you remember the first time you saw me?' I nodded, remembering her from the dance and the police station. 'Well, that man with me was my father. A self-righteous man who believes in two things in life – money and family honour. He wanted me to follow in the family tradition of lawyers. Now, the problem with me was that I had a different type of honour in mind. Daddy didn't take to that. Told me on more than one occasion that if he caught me on the wrong side of town he was going to stop my allowance.'

Now it was my turn to cock my eyebrow. An allowance? Can you imagine your family paying you money when you're old enough to work? I let out a little laugh.

'Go ahead and scoff because you're right, why should I have access to an allowance while everyone else has to work? It disgusts me as much as you. Until I realised that I could use it, money literally from Daddy's pocket to help the common man. So we used my allowance as the down payment towards the house. We were so nearly there when Daddy found out what I was doing.'

'How did that happen?'

She brushed her fringe out of the sweat on her forehead.

'We've all got a weakness. Mine is that when I've decided on a course it's hard for me to pull back. After the night at the police station Shakespeare told me to cool it and not go to the demo on Unity Road. But I went. Someone took some pictures that fell into Daddy's lap. He gave me two choices – join the family law firm or do my thing without his help. Well, you know which one I chose. So he stopped my allowance.'

She paused, seeing Houdini and Shakespeare each struggling off the boat with a box close to their chests. When they got to us their breathing tugged at the air. They handed us a wooden box each. They were heavy. As Houdini and Shakespeare went back to the boat me and Anne struggled to the van. Sean helped us put them in the back. We did that three times. Ten minutes later the van was loaded. I knew we were going back to Hoxton. Sean kept a lookout for the skinheads while we put the boxes in the house. Man, we moved like the Devil and his demons might appear at any moment. Once inside, Shakespeare told us, 'All the boxes have to go down to the basement.'

The door to the basement was located on the far side of the hall. Shakespeare took out another key and went to the basement door. He unlocked it. He shoved the door to the side. It smelt dusty, dank, but we took the boxes down and placed them in the middle of a room that looked just like other basements I had seen – bare, concrete floors and lonely. Me and Sean picked up the final box. That made me sigh with relief. We were nearly there. We both puffed hard, trying to keep the heat from our faces. Suddenly Sean missed his footing. My hand shot out to steady him. The box tumbled and smashed. The contents banged against the steps. I got a funny feeling in my gut. The other three rushed to the top of the stairs. We all looked down.

Do you know what was on the stairs? Guns. Big and small. Seven badass bullet-pumping machines. I ain't ever seen a gun in life, but I knew what they were. I'd watched enough Clint Eastwood films to know. Alongside them were two bottles of liquid, which didn't look like Coca-Cola, you check me?

'No way, Shakespeare, no way,' Anne cried out.

'I didn't know,' he replied. First time I ever seen Shakespeare with his mouth laid open.

Anne swung around to him with anger burning from every pore she had.

'What, you didn't know that the job entailed carrying arms and explosives? I heard stories that the canal was used as transportation for arms because the authorities are too busy checking the ports and airports. But I never believed it.'

'Who is our landlord?' Houdini asked.

'I've only met him once . . .' Shakespeare started.

But Houdini didn't give him a chance to finish. 'You fucking crazy, man? Say all this stuff is for the National Front? Say he's one of them?'

'It can't be . . .' Shakespeare jumped in.

'How the backside do you know?' Houdini screamed. 'What if all this stuff is going to be used to kill and injure our people?'

Well, let me tell you, that was enough for me. Blew my grey confused mind. I rushed up the stairs, pushed past everyone, ready to leave that house. I called Sean's name as I got to the door. Instead of Sean I felt Shakespeare's arm grab me up. He swung me around.

'You can't leave,' he shouted at me.

'Man, I'm already gone.' I shoved for the door.

He just grabbed me up, quick time, and slammed me against the wall. Wrong move. Sean was on him like a child on his Christmas present. He flung him against the wall. Pinned him there. I rushed over and dragged Sean off.

We all just looked at each other, bodies shaking. First time in my life, me a toaster and I couldn't speak. I couldn't utter one word. Shakespeare shook himself off the wall and started speaking.

'None of us were expecting this. The landlord is Jewish, so there's no way it's going to be used by those evil fascist thugs,

OK? We need to ease it up, cool it down. Forget what you saw and remember what we're doing here. We're on a mission. A mission to save our people. If we don't save them, who will?'

His words touched me. Reminded me that I was here to uphold something bigger than me. You ever found yourself in a situation where everything your mum and dad taught you about right or wrong just has to go out of the window? What's right and wrong when you're living in dread times? I mean, was it right that the police could just grab you up any time, shove your arse up against the wall and do whatever they want to you? Was it right that at a job interview first thing that happens is you're shown the door because your skin's too dark? Was it right that we should lose our base and the opportunity to keep helping the community just because we decided not to move a few boxes?

A few boxes that might belong to the National Front?

That question burned inside me. Shakespeare would never do that. Go that far. Would he? I pushed it deep where I didn't have to deal with it.

I nodded my head at Shakespeare. The others nodded their heads too. He smiled, real gentle. Then spoke, quiet, like a tiny waterfall seeping from the damp walls of the house.

'Good. We're all in this together. I'll sort out the broken box. Then we're out of here. Gone. No need to ever look back. But when we leave, the Liberation Republic will be ours.'

We were on our way back when the confusion between Shakespeare and Houdini started again. I sat with Anne on a house of joy as the van took off. Houdini shuffled his feet against the floor. As the journey went on his feet got quicker. Suddenly they stopped. He crawled and gripped the partition behind Shakespeare's seat.

'No way we should have done any of that, you understand?'

Shakespeare swivelled his head to the side.

'Just sit down. We'll talk tomorrow when the air is clear.'

'No. I need to chat now.'

'Sit down.' Shakespeare's voice drove downwards.

'Say the National Front get hold of those guns? Is that the

price you're willing to pay so we can keep a house? Because that's all it is, man, a house. No one's life, black or white, is worth that.'

'I said sit down,' Shakespeare growled.

'No.' Houdini grabbed the back of Shakespeare's jacket. Real hard, like he was never going to let go.

Shakespeare tried to break free but Houdini only tightened his grip. I jumped forward and gripped Houdini. I tried to drag him back, but he shook me off so hard I toppled backwards on to the floor. I looked up dazed, and saw that Shakespeare and Houdini's hands were moving in some mad-arse struggle. Sean looked around, and when he saw me on the floor his hands lifted from the wheel like he was going to jump in the back to help me.

'Keep your eyes on the road,' I shouted at him.

Sean turned back at the same time Shakespeare shook Houdini off. Houdini fell back with me on the floor.

'I'm calling the shots.' Shakespeare's voice was hard.

Houdini slumped back and whispered, 'I didn't know that the struggle would be so hard.'

No one answered him. What could we say?

Shakespeare fixed his clothes and said, 'There's only one other obstacle. When we sign for the house someone needs to have their name on the papers.'

We looked around at each other. Anne spoke first.

'I can't sign the ownership papers for the house. If Daddy finds out he'll find some way to get that house off me and will make it his personal mission to smash the Republic.'

Then Houdini.

'I can't sign them either because no Rasta wants to own any part of Babylon.'

Then Shakespeare.

'And me, well, you know that my mission is to help the brothers and sisters in southern Africa. One day I'm going to go down there and become one of the freedom fighters. If something happened to the house and I wasn't here nothing could get sorted. It wouldn't be fair.'

They all turned to me. No way, José.

'I don't want that kind of responsibility . . .'

Remember what I said earlier about responsibility not being a musical word? I tried to tell them that but they wouldn't listen to me. Shakespeare carried on talking, making sure that responsibility was going to be the first word on my tombstone.

'All you need to do is put your name to it. If anything should ever happen we just need to know that someone we can all trust and who's near by has the legal rights to the house.'

So said, so done. The next day we went about our business as if nothing had happened the night before. That was until news reached us that a black family had been attacked in the street not far from Hoxton by the National Front. No one needed to tell me that it was a man, a woman and their two children. The man was beaten badly and in St Luke's. They had left the woman and children alone – well, that's if you consider spitting on people not a crime. Anguish crippled me, but we just kept our mouths shut. Didn't look in each other's eyes for a few days. But it stayed between us, just like where those explosives and guns might end up did.

A week later, with the heat still killing us, I became the sole owner – on paper at least – of a house that gloried in liberation and was bought with money from the destruction of other people's lives. Well, that was how I saw tings. We didn't breathe a word to another soul. We didn't celebrate. We just got on with preparing our next issue of *The Black Fist* with the headline 'Solidarity Brothers and Sisters'. But it was there between us. Just because I didn't speak about my Jerry living with that bitch Marcie didn't mean that he wasn't with me all the time. The big problem with holding stuff in is that when it comes out it don't smell too good. Every man has their way of digging deep to try to ditch the pain. Mine was music. Any offers of gigs that came our way I encouraged the boys to take. I even distracted myself by trying to get to know Anne and showing her my record collection and favourite record cover. I flung myself into preparation for our appearance at the Notting Hill carnival.

The only person who showed that his conscience seemed to be heavy was Houdini. The look in his troubled black eyes reminded me of a story my grandmother told me the first time my father took me to visit her in Trinidad. She lived in a wooden house that stood on stilts. I would help her work in her garden, and when the sun got too strong she would take me to sit under the house. That was where she told me the story about a fisherman and a dog. Instead of going to his yard when he was hungry the dog went to the neighbours and grabbed up a chicken or two. When the neighbours realised who was the culprit they began to complain to the woman who owned the dog. The woman tried and tried with the dog – giving it a few lashes, putting pepper in its nose to teach it right from wrong – but the dog wouldn't mind its own business. After an attack just before Christmas the woman had to make a decision. She called a local fisherman to take the dog away. The fisherman strolled with the dog to Maracas beach, put him in the boat and took him out to sea. When they were in the rough waters of the Caribbean, he put the dog in a sack with stones, tied the top and threw him out to sea. I looked in Houdini's stare and knew what the dog's eyes must have looked liked just before the beautiful Caribbean sea took him.

We threw ourselves into what Shakespeare was calling 'liberation summer' and took no notice of Houdini. Big mistake. The trouble started 21 July – man, it was still roasting – when Houdini got arrested by the police for a fracas in the bookie's. We all have our weaknesses. Mine was my boys, Sean and Jerry. Anne's was her father. Shakespeare's . . . well, I wasn't sure what his was, but he must have had one because everyone does. Now, Houdini's was gambling. He went everywhere with that bookie's pen behind his ear. The Babylon kept him for a day and night. When he came back he held his face like he was a different man. He was even more insulting towards Sean. But you know what, for the sake of peace I just bit my tongue.

August arrived and the tension with the police stoked up. Preparations for the carnival heated up. Then the incidents started happening. First one was a pile of leaflets that someone left in the Sweet and Dandy attacking the Black Fist. 'Enemies of the community and state,' they proclaimed us. No one knew how they got there. Next an angry member of another black organisation from South London came to visit Shakespeare, asking him why he had sent them a letter. The letter was hot stuff. A letter that was headed 'The Black Fist will only work with organisations that pay them £100 allegiance money'. It was signed by Shakespeare. An outright forgery, but the other organisation didn't believe us and refused to have any dealings with us. The word spread and soon other black organisations took the same line. We couldn't believe it. We felt left out in the cold (although the sun was still eating our skins). We were in no doubt that the state was trying to not only discredit us but put a wedge of mistrust between organisations. And if I'm truthful they were succeeding.

On the first day of the carnival Shakespeare declared that we needed to meet to discuss the issue. So we decided to meet in our office after I came back from the festivities. My sound system's performance that day was irie. There's only one place every sound system wants to kill the crowd – the All Saints Road. We mashed our opponents. So that night I was walking tall. After I dropped Sean home I went back to the Republic. I decided to kill two birds with one stone. While we were having our discussion I would also make the tape for a new dub plate of 'Police And Thieves' to kill the crowd at the carnival the next day. If I had known what would happen in the Black Fist office that night, as God is my witness, I would never have gone.

Shakespeare, Anne and Houdini were waiting for me in the basement. Shakespeare sat at his desk. Houdini and Anne sat well away from each other, like their teacher had sent them to sit in the corner. The atmosphere in the room was choking, like it was filling up with smoke. I took a seat, but I didn't take it fully.

Shakespeare stood up and started pacing.

'The state is waging a war of counter-intelligence against us.' None of us said anything.

'Our problem is trying to find out how they are managing to do it.'

'What do you mean?' Houdini asked, cocking his head to the side.

'I find it very strange how those defamatory leaflets were left in the Sweet and Dandy.'

'Maybe the Babylon broke in and left them,' I said.

Shakespeare just shook his head.

'No, there was no evidence of a break-in.'

'What you trying to say, man? That one of our own did it?' Houdini asked.

'No way,' I put in.

'The only way,' Shakespeare insisted. 'I've spoken to Winnie and she said she never saw anyone leave anything in the café. Therefore it must have happened when the café was closed.'

'But who?' I asked.

'Someone who has access to the building the same way that we do.'

'But that's all the other organisations. You think we got a pig squealer among us?' Anne spoke for the first time.

'Not only do I think, I know.'

Suddenly Houdini stood up. He began to pace. Sweat rolled under his hat like amber beads. He looked at Shakespeare and said, 'How you know that, man?'

'Let's just say we have our own system of finding out our enemies' plans. One of the young sisters works as a cleaner in Unity Road police station. Lots of information to be found on a screwed-up piece of paper in a bin. She say . . .'

Suddenly Houdini shot out at me, 'It's that damn boy. I know we should've never let the little devil in.'

I didn't need to ask who the little devil boy was.

Man, I just galvanised myself out of my chair and shouted back, 'Your chatting fuckrees, man. Sean would never do that.'

'Exactly,' Shakespeare backed me up. 'See the problem is our sister found out that the Babylon are running an informer called Man Friday. An agent of oppression who is a black man.'

Let me tell you, that stung the room. We all looked at each other. But do you know what, I felt like I'd had enough. I was angry. Anger can be such a twister of an emotion that I spent most of my life staying the hell away from it. Only two people ever got the hiss of anger to steam from me – Jerry and Sean. Plus, I'd just come back from a roots-rocking time at the carnival and wasn't in the mood to discuss no agent of oppression. So I said, 'You know what, people, I'm going to make the tape for my dub plate. Then I'm going to go home. Then I'm going to put my head down. Then I'm going to get up. Then I'm going to have a irie high time at the carnival.'

I walked towards the adjoining room where we had our makeshift studio and went inside. I was going to shut the door, but I felt so choked up that I left it open. I got down to making the tape for my dub plate. As I set up the equipment I could still hear them arguing. I switched on the record button. The tape started to run but the voices next door got louder. You can't make a good tape for a dub plate with that kind of noise interference. So I stood up to close the door. As I touched the door Shakespeare and Houdini came tumbling through it, grappling with each other. I stepped aside, quick time.

'I know it was you,' Shakespeare squeezed out as Houdini dragged him by his T-shirt.

'No way, man,' Houdini croaked as he pushed Shakespeare against the wall.

'I know they recruited you on the day you were arrested.' Shakespeare managed to thrust them back into the middle of the room.

'What we did was wrong, man, wrong.'

Now they started throwing punches. Who threw first I didn't know. But I couldn't stand by and let two brothers who had been so close try and damage each other. I jumped in, trying to pull them apart. Instead we got caught up in this three-way tangle and started spinning around the room. I felt this pressure between us. Suddenly Houdini started falling backwards. Towards one of our spare houses of joy and the equipment where the tape was still running. His arms waved in the air while his legs bent back. I rushed forward. But, as God is my witness, I couldn't reach him. I watched him fall and fall and fall. His head clipped the side of the house of joy, then he twisted into a heap on the floor. His chest rose, pushing out his ragged breathing that came in little spurts, in and out. Then, all of a sudden, his breathing stopped.

There was a gasp from the doorway. We turned to find Anne standing there with her hand over her mouth. I rushed over to Houdini. Hunched down to him. Felt his chest. No heartbeat.

'Check his pulse,' Shakespeare said. First time I ever heard his voice lose control.

'Where the backside is his pulse?'

Shakespeare shoved me aside and felt Houdini's neck. He kept his fingers there for what felt like a long time. He took his fingers off. Looked at us. He didn't need to say the words. Just the haunted depth of his gaze was enough.

I stood up, quick time.

'What are we going to do?' Anne asked, slowly walking into the room like she was afraid.

'We have to call an ambulance.' My voice was plain crazy.

'He's already dead,' Shakespeare whispered.

He jumped up. Began pacing in a way that spun the crazy wheel in my mind even more. Halfway across the room he just stopped, like he'd hit a glass wall. He swooped around. He said, with his eyes shining with the seven bells of wisdom ringing in his mind, 'We can't inform the police because no way will they believe it was an accident. In fact, they'd love nothing better than to see us all rotting in Brixton and,' he turned to Anne, 'Holloway.'

She shook at his words. The girl was really scared.

'We don't have an alternative. We'll have to get rid of the body . . .'

LT lunged towards the Dictaphone. Clicked the stop button. Bernie snapped her head up to look at him.

'What are you . . . ?' she began.

He grabbed the Dictaphone. Jumped up. Shuffled away until his back was against a wall.

'The tape hasn't finished running,' Bernie said as she jerked to her feet, confusion pulling her neck high and long.

'Yes it has,' he gritted between his teeth. His hand tightened on the Dictaphone.

Her baffled eyes read his face.

'Don't do it,' she pleaded. She stepped into the shaft of melting daylight coming through the window.

He kept his eyes on her face as he pressed the eject button.

She took a step towards him.

He pulled the tape out of the Dictaphone.

She took another step.

He held the tape lightly, as if it were burning his hand. It made a clattering sound as he dropped it on to the tiled floor.

'You can't do this.'

He put his palm against the wall to balance his weight. He raised his right trainer and held it over the tape.

'Jerry . . .'

'I can't let anyone hear this. He was my dad. My King.'

His foot wavered above the tape as she soothed, 'I know you're going through one of those "I'm on a spaceship" moments. You're in shock. I know it must be hard for you to deal with the implications of what your father has just revealed, but . . .'

His heel moved down as the words shook from him.

'There is no way I would have started any of this if I'd known what he was going to say. What he'd been involved in.'

'You didn't start this, they did. OK?' She shook her head. Moved slightly out of his space. Lowered her voice. 'Go ahead, do it. Do you really think it's all going to float away? That you're going to wake up in the morning, yawn and say it was all a weird dream? That they're going to leave you alone?'

His heel jerked to a different rhythm. Indecision.

'They've already got one tape, so they must realise there are others. And the one person they are going to suspect has them is you.'

The sweat on his palm made his hand slip on the wall. He heaved it back, not taking his eyes from her. She walked towards him, face up. Reached him. Placed the fingers of her left hand on his chest. Over the exact spot where the high-tuned dynamics of his heart pulsed. She pulled her fingers away, one by one. Then she bent and confidently picked up the tape.

The air that shoved upwards as she straightened seemed to slam him into the wall. He took huge gulps of oxygen into his bloodstream.

'I promise you that I'm not going to share this with anyone,' she whispered.

When he eventually looked at her she was back in her spot, at the table, waiting for him.

'I'm scared.' The honesty in his voice was painful for him to hear.

'So am I.' She clung to that last word as her eyes flicked away, as if she were talking about something else.

She looked back at him. 'If we don't listen to this tape, they'll keep hurting people until they get what they're looking for. And maybe your father's going to finally tell us what his best jacket is.'

He thought of her lying in the hospital with her beautiful,

bruised face. Thought of May still in an unnatural sleep. He pulled
his back off the wall and slowly moved towards the table, holding
the Dictaphone. He eased down. Passed the Dictaphone to her.
She put the tape back inside. He leaned back into the hardness
of the chair as she pressed 'play'.

# TRACK 17: REVIVAL SELECTION: 1976, VOLUME 3
## (7" Single: B-Side)

That night I didn't even try to sleep. I knew that if I shut my eyes I would see the body hidden inside one of our houses of joy in the bowels of the Liberation Republic. The body? Can't believe that's how I'm now name-checking someone who was my friend. Before I left the house we agreed a plan that was simple. Hide the body and find transport. Me and Shakespeare understood the street but neither of us knew how to dispose of a body. I'm a music man, aren't I? All we knew was the body had to be gone, quick time. Anne was a mess, so we left her shaking in the basement.

We ran up to the Sweet and Dandy and collected some plastic bags and Sellotape. We hightailed it back downstairs to cover and tape him up. Only way we could both do it was to put him belly down. No way we could look at his face. When we'd finished he looked like a plastic mannequin. We rolled him up in a length of old carpet from the attic. Then we pushed him inside one of our houses of joy. When we stood up we were both breathing hard, dripping in the heat of the night.

Shakespeare walked over to Anne, who was still trembling against the wall.

'Tomorrow we need your car.'

Just like that he told her, as if he was asking her to go to the shop and buy him a pound of sugar. Well, my girl didn't take it too good. She went berserk.

'You're crazy, I'm not driving him around in my car . . .'

She shook, in tears, as she turned towards the door. Shakespeare's arm shot out, like a spear being thrown through the night. His hand grabbed her by the throat and pushed her up against the wall. I didn't like that but I kept my legs where I stood.

'If we go on trial for this man's life . . . they may have the rope back by then. Maybe you want to feel a noose tightening around your pretty posh schoolgirl throat, but I don't. He can't stay here and you're the only one with a car. Now you go and get it then we can drive him somewhere nice in the boot, drop him off and then we can forget all about it.'

She was having trouble breathing and I think she was scared she was next, but she managed to splutter, 'I can't get the car until tomorrow . . .'

He let her go. She massaged her neck, broke down and crumpled to her knees on the floor with her head in her hands. That was when Shakespeare knelt down beside her, put his arm round her shoulder and whispered, in that soothing voice of his, 'Listen, comrade, we're all in big trouble here and none of us are feeling good, OK? We can't undo what's been done but we can avoid going to prison for it – because us going to prison isn't going to bring him back, is it?'

Her sobbing tore up the room.

'Bring the car here tomorrow, early. It's bank holiday so there'll be no one around and all the police will be in Notting Hill making sure all those black folks behave themselves on the Queen's precious streets. We'll put our friend in the boot and when it gets dark we'll find a nice place to let him rest. Don't worry about any police because they aren't going to stop a nice white girl like you.'

I left the house and didn't meet anyone's eye as I rushed home. I was sure she was going to do it. These rich white people are very resourceful and they keep a stiff upper lip – that was how they built an empire, isn't it? Well, that and killing people.

Later that night, while demons made me toss and turn in my bed, there was a bang on the door. I couldn't move. What if it was the Babylon? What if they had found out what we'd done? The door shook harder this time. I eased out of bed. My heart was trying to escape from my chest. I stood up and took pigeon steps to the door.

'Who is it?'

No reply.

'I ain't opening no door until you give me your name.'

I heard a shuffle of feet.

'Open up the door, you low-ranking piece of . . .'

Marcie. I checked the clock. Ten minutes to midnight. I opened the door quickly as I said, 'What the hell are you doing . . . ?'

My words stopped when I saw Jerry in her arms. Wrapped up like he was going on a trip.

'What's going on?'

She thrust him into my arms and dropped a canvas bag on the floor.

'I'm off to Canada. Can't take him with me because he don't like the cold.'

Then she turned around and rushed down the stairs. I tugged my son to me as I followed and yelled, 'Marcie?'

But she was gone. A few seconds later I heard a car scream down the road. I cuddled my boy with my big hands. The same hands that had . . . I let my bloodstained thought go and walked back inside my room.

So I got up, like the rest of black London, on August bank holiday Monday, one friend dead, my son with a neighbour, and set off with Sean to the carnival.

When we got to Notting Hill all you could see was the black uniform of police. Looked liked an invasion. I've never seen so many Babylon at the carnival before. Knowing what had happened last night their presence made me real uneasy. But I tried to put last night behind me. Tried to forget. We set up in what people later started name-checking as Sound System City, which was near the All Saints Road. Anyone coming for that carefree Caribbean jump-up was in the wrong place. This was strictly militant music to replenish wounded rebel souls. The music was the right mix to make a man forget his troubles – mint cool and mellow. North, south, east, west, only one killer tune everyone was mashing up the streets – 'Police And Thieves'. The crowd near our sound system were in a trance. Heads bowed. Rocking and rattling. Eyelids half lowered. Legs a flexible pair of rhythm sticks. Man, that solid groove was just licking me back. I was swaying, blessing the crowd with my verbal vibrations. During our third 'Police And Thieves' exclusive, that's when I noticed the blonde hair pushing through the crowd. I was surprised because not many white people came this far. Maybe they thought it was too black, the music too raw. You got a few of the white lads but not the women. My heart began to beat, because you know I did not need to see the face to know who it was.

What the sweet black rah-rah was the girl doing here?

Anne reached the front of the crowd. I nodded my head furiously, telling her she should meet me at the side. The boys watched me go, not pleased one bit. But I knew they could handle it. Put on a dub cut that was bass heavy.

She met me by the side of one of the speakers. Her face was wet with tears like a panda.

'What the . . .' I admit I swore right in her face because vexation had me in overload. '. . . are you doing here? You're meant to meet with Shakespeare.'

'I was scared. Shakespeare said I should meet you here.'

'You didn't bring it here, did you?' That crazy boom-boom beat from last night was back in my voice.

I was looking around as I said it. I knew that no one would realise what I meant, but you never know. She nodded. I thought she was going to cry again. I grabbed up her arm.

'Where is it?'

'I parked up near the canal towards Kensal Rise.'

My fingers dug into her arm.

'Listen to me. I've got to finish playing this set. When I finish we go and get rid of it. Just stick close by.'

I left her and went back to the sound. I tried to jump into the music, but it kept pushing me back, like I was dirty.

And that's when it happened. All of a sudden a mad ass ripple ran through the crowd. I raised my head. Do you know what I saw?

I just see a line of Babylon appear like a black tidal wave on the horizon. The crowd stopped moving. The music kept playing. The B-line was hard. The Babylon advanced on the crowd, holding their wooden truncheons. Many of them weren't wearing their badges or any other form of ID. The crowd stood their ground, muttering with anger and years of frustration and resentment. Another B-line began to bubble at ground level. Know what it was? The hard chant of 'enough is enough'. The day of reckoning between the young community and Babylon had arrived. Don't know where it came from, but I saw this brick go singing in the air straight towards the police line. That was it, everything just kicked off big time The Babylon jumped back. Then more masonry started flying. I realised that it was coming from a demolition site near by. Then bottles. Then anything the crowd could get their hands on. The Old Bill charged. But a hail of missiles came straight for them. I looked down to find Anne at the same time some people started running and screaming. I couldn't see the girl. Jesus, if I didn't find her someone might find the body. I jumped down from the sound.

'Look after Sean,' I shouted to Desmond.

As soon as I hit the crowd all I could feel was this incredible fury that was stronger than the August heat. I pushed through the pitch battle screaming Anne's name. I ducked as missiles kept flying. I looked around, trying to find her. Kept screaming her name like some maniac. Then I heard my name from somewhere behind me. I turned and there she was, crouched down, holding her head in her hands like a lost baby. I rushed over and grabbed her up.

'Got to get out of here now.'

As we swung around I saw a police car driving towards the crowd. A group of men ran up to it and pelted whatever was in their hands at its windows. The glass smashed. The vehicle reversed with the men still chasing. All this time 'Police And Thieves' was still playing from our unmanned sound system.

'Just keep your head down,' I told Anne.

I grabbed her hand and we ran. Having grown up in this area I knew it well. I slammed my head up and saw a policeman hitting a woman with his truncheon. Man, that wasn't right. I almost stopped, remembered the body and kept moving. The sound of a police chopper circled overhead. We kept running with the rest of the stampeding crowd. We moved to the pavement. A woman, standing in the front garden of a large house, was yelling at her children – two boys, two girls, all under twelve – to hide behind the wall. We ran past them.

'Oi, what you doing with that white woman?' a voice shouted out.

I looked up to see a Babylon running towards me with his truncheon drawn. As he reached us a brick hit him in the face. He fell on his knees, clutching his face as blood poured from it. We kept moving. Must have been a good five minutes before we found ourselves on one of the neighbouring housing estates. We bent over, breathing heavily. A man stood next to us and said, 'It's like Northern Ireland over there, man! The youth are fighting it out with the Babylon. Stones! Bricks! It's all flying around. It's revolution!'

I pulled my head up first. I dragged her away from the man to a lonely spot near the stairwell.

'I've got an idea,' I told her. 'A spar of mine lives on the third floor. Don't move.' I said the last two words slowly to penetrate her head, because the girl still looked like she was in shock. I took the stairs, two, sometimes three, at a time to my spar Mikey D, who lived in a two-bed maisonette. Three minutes later, no questions asked – I think they thought I was going to join the street party – I left with a blue can of paraffin wrapped in a plastic bag. She was still waiting for me downstairs.

'OK, you ready to show me where you left the car?'

We began a mad run towards the canal, with the streets

wailing and the humid air being anchored down by the helicopter's rotor blades in the sky. We passed people scurrying away in all directions. Fifteen minutes later we found the car. I knew that no one would be near by because most people were running scared, trying to get off the streets. We approached the back of the car.

'Take this.' I gave her the bag with the can.

I cupped one hand over my nose and mouth and used the other to open the boot. Underneath the carpet the August heat had already started to make the body smell. I ain't never smelled a dead man before. My belly moved and I started to gag. Dry heaves puffed my cheeks out. I closed my eyes. I got control again. My eyes opened at the same time I heard the helicopter in the distance. I knew we had to act fast.

I couldn't get the damn body in the driver's seat where I wanted it.

'You're going to have to help me,' I called to the girl.

She was standing a good distance away, her hand shielding her mouth. I expected her to protest, but she didn't. She put the can down and stood next to me.

'We need to get him in the front seat. Help me pull down the back seat.'

We leaned over the body and pulled the back seat down. I climbed in the back and grabbed his feet. She held his shoulders. We lifted him and slid him into the front. As his feet touched the ground Anne threw up all over his body. She jumped out of the car, heaving on the ground. I ignored her. Ran to the paraffin can. Came back and scattered paraffin all over his body. From head to toe.

'Start running now,' I yelled at her.

As she followed my command I took out my lighter. Hesitated for one second. Thought about all the good times me and Houdini had. I pressed the lighter and threw it on top of the body. I ran. And ran. I looked back, don't know why, to see the flames jumping in the shape of a body. As I reached Anne the flames hit the petrol tank and the car exploded. The force knocked us to the ground. I looked up to see the boot had been blown off and what was left of the car was rocking from side to side.

As we crouched on the ground I turned to her and grabbed her shoulders.

'OK, this is how it's going to go. You go back to your yard and ring the Babylon and report your car stolen. You tell them you came out of the front door and there were some black men loitering near your vehicle and one of them produced a knife and said, 'Give me your keys, whitey bitch.' They'll like that. Then they got in your car and drove off in it. You didn't see where they went but you thought they turned west. Tell them you think they were going to sell drugs in Notting Hill – they'll like that too.'

She nodded her head. Then I told her, 'And use your posh voice, OK?'

That was it, brother, she ran one way and I ran the other. Back to the carnival, if you could still call it that. As I ran back into the All Saints Road, two policemen just appeared. 'Oi, where the fucking hell are you going, you animal?'

Before I could even answer both of them rushed me and started beating me about the head. I moved my hands swiftly to protect myself, but it was too late. The truncheons cracked over the side of my head and I blacked out. I have never been so pleased to be hit in my life because I didn't have to think about Houdini. I woke up in the Mangrove Restaurant, where people had taken me when they found me lying in the street. It was hard to get out of Notting Hill but I managed to make my way home later that night. I didn't even think about going to the Republic. Sean was waiting for me, all excited because his boys had finally managed to get a gig at the Roxy. He had my little Jerry in his arms. I told Sean to put our faithful 50p in the meter, then I took a long bath. Scrubbed myself silly. Then I was ready to take my little boy in my arms. Every time I sniffed his baby powder, know what I smelt? Dead people and paraffin.

The next day, the newspapers were too busy gloating about the riot to take any notice of the dead black guy in the burnt-out car, but the day after that they reported it. One paper even had an editorial that said something like, 'This newspaper takes no pleasure in the death of a man who burned to death while ferrying petrol bombs to the riots in Notting Hill – but will anyone shed any tears for this black terrorist who abused Britain's hospitality?'

Made it sound like Houdini was from somewhere overseas instead of him being born in Bow, East London. But that was good for us because people in the community were outraged about what had been written about someone who worked hard on behalf of them. That's how the myth got born that the police killed him. The riot was an opportunity, everyone said, to settle old scores. I never went back to the Republic. Desmond and Maximus collected our equipment and we set up somewhere else. I heard that Shakespeare disappeared that night and Anne, well, no one missed a white girl they had never seen. Never saw Shakespeare and Anne again. Oh, I saw them all right, but they weren't Anne and Shakespeare any more, they had become Mr And Ms Respectable. Once the different organisations in the Republic started getting council grants they moved away and set up in other premises. Then the Republic was empty . . .

# TRACK 18: WHO'S THAT GIRL?

'. . . So here I am, dead, cremated the same way as Houdini. After hearing this tale, Jerry, I hope you still love me. His death was an accident. Just one of those tings. I don't know what you're going to make of having that house. Just remember it started out good. I got money from a friend to help fix the house up, but I never once stepped inside it ever again. I know you've waited to hear who Anne and Shakespeare are, but I can't tell you the names. If you haven't buried me in my best jacket and you find it you'll understand why.'

The King coughed. His voice dipped low as he said his final words.

'Son, let me tell you a secret. It is whispered that on August bank holiday the Devil and his six disciples, wearing smiles flashing like molten lightning, travel across the world. Underground. From west to east. From Trinidad to England. Balancing drums on their left hips and bamboo sticks in their right claws. When they reach Notting Hill they beat their drums throughout the multicoloured memories of the day and the black-and-white fusion of the night, making the streets of West London ripple and roll to their badass, hellfire groove.

'Watch the ground beneath your feet, son, because the human experience comes back to one thing – rhythm.

'The sun goes up, the sun goes down.

'The days get longer, the days get shorter.

'People live, people die.

'Simple.'

The tape ran for five more seconds. Then clicked off.

The room that had once been the Sweet and Dandy café was as silent as the sun slipping over the house. They stared at each other across the table. The earlier shock that LT had felt was replaced by numbness.

'All those years,' he finally said. 'Everyone thought the police had killed Houdini and all the time it was his friends. His comrades. My dad.'

She stretched her hands across the table. Put them around the Dictaphone and said, 'But it sounded like an accident.'

'We'll never know because the dead bloke ain't talking.'

He ran his fingers threw his 'fro.

'OK, what should we do?' she asked.

He took one of those gut breaths. Shut his eyes as if he were praying. Then opened them as he exhaled.

'I don't know what we're going to do but I tell you what I'm going to do, withdraw from the Writer in Residence of Ladbroke Grove competition.'

Her hands jumped away from the Dictaphone as fast as the words she uttered. 'You can't do that.'

'How can I take part in a competition that my dad helped set up, only not just sitting on a committee, but by killing someone?'

'So you going to watch your life piss down the drain because of stuff that had nothing to do with you? If you don't get on that stage it will be longer than fifteen years before you see me again.'

A faint smile pushed up the lower half of his face.

'Does that mean you're planning to stick around?' he asked softly.

Their eyes caught. Vulnerable brown touching inviting blue. They both leaned over the table at the same time. Their mouths met in a long kiss. They rushed it because they knew they didn't have time to take it easy. He was the first to pull his lips back.

He whispered, 'When this is all over, maybe I can fix you that hot drink I know you've been longing for. But for now let's talk about what we're going to do about what the King said.'

When they eased back into their chairs, she said, 'OK, let's deal with what we've got so far. We know that Houdini died in the basement of this house. We know that Shakespeare and the King were involved in his death and that Anne was there. We know that Sean Sparkle was part of the group, but he wasn't there the night it happened. So let's move him out of the picture. Shakespeare I know is Beresford Clarke . . .

'I know you don't want to hear this,' she continued, tilting her chin to the left. 'But I was in Birmingham this morning where someone confirmed he arrived there in September 1976, immediately after Houdini's death . . .'

'But he told me he got there in 1973.' His voice was small. Strained. Disbelieving.

'I know you don't want to believe me so I'm hoping to have some proof to show you after the competition tomorrow. Let's push Beresford to the side for the moment and concentrate on Anne. What we know about her is she's about the same age the King would be now, was obviously heavily involved in some radical groups, like the student movement, and had or has a mummy and daddy with a lot of jingle-jangle in their pockets. You sure she doesn't ring a bell?'

He decided that tonight was one for truths. He looked her square in the eye.

'There's only one person I can think whose shape and form slides in nicely.'

'Who?' Excitement pushed her to lean on the table.

'You won't want to hear.'

She waited.

'Your mum.'

Her neck straightened.

'Come on . . .'

'Just listen to me. She was around at the time, you agree?'

She nodded.

'From what you've told me she was deeply involved in the scene.'

'But Irinia said she wasn't part of the East London network.'

'But you did say that her and your father hung out as hippies in Notting Hill.'

'My mother wouldn't lie to me.'

He pushed a harsh laugh into the room.

'The one thing we know about this whole bloody business is that all these self-righteous, let's-get-down-and-save-the-world groupies, not one of them sounds like they've been telling the truth.'

'Not Mummy.' Her tone was stubborn and lost.

'Just like I said not my dad.'

She leaned back in the chair. Let both hands dive through her hair.

'OK. I still think you're wrong, but I'll go and see her and see what she's got to say . . .'

Before she could finish LT's mobile pulsed in his pocket. He pulled it out.

'It's Window. I've got to take this to find out if he's still my manager.'

Three minutes later, LT faced Bernie with a relieved smile on his face.

'Yes. I am back. He wants me to pop over to the club. Why don't you check on your mother while I'm doing that?'

'OK. If Irinia tells me anything I'll give you a bell later. Maybe we can meet tomorrow before the competition.'

'I won't be around. It's just a tradition that I hide myself away to get ready for the competition. I turn my mobile off and soak myself in music. The only way I'm going to make that third record breaking win is to be fully focused.'

'Do you think that's wise, knowing the situation?'

'We'll be all right until after the carnival. It's not like they, whoever they are, can do anything at the Notting Hill carnival, is it?'

*   *   *

Beresford stood with the woman who had once called herself Anne on the roof terrace of his house.

'You can't do it,' she told him harshly.

'I've got no alternative now. The girl's been asking questions about me in Birmingham. He'll know it's me soon enough, if he doesn't already.'

The river wind fluttered across her black headscarf.

'But you can't just kill him like you did his father.'

He looked her full in the eye and laughed. As quick as the laughter came, he cut if off. 'I have a little confession to make, sweet one. I never killed the King.'

'But you told me . . .'

'I never told you anything of the kind. You just assumed I had. The coroner's office was correct when they said he died of natural causes. Don't get me wrong, I did set out to kill him. But when he saw me he collapsed. Apparently the drug he'd been taking for his illness had a high risk of heart failure attached to it. I got out of the car and checked his pulse. He was already dead. I dragged his body and hid it under some rubbish bags, so it would take longer to discover him in order to give my people the time they needed to try and find the jacket. But when they didn't find it I had to find ways of getting closer to the boy to find it myself. So helping the boy on his fool's errand enquiring into the King's death gave me the opportunity I needed.'

'But why didn't you tell me this?'

He looked her hard in the face. She gasped and cried, 'You've been manipulating me all this time.'

'Let's be honest, if I had told you I didn't do it, that little brain of yours might have started thinking. Thinking about running to the police about Houdini's death and how it was an accident. How you were so young. How this big black man seduced you with his ghetto politics and made you to do it. No, Anne, I couldn't take that chance. The best way to keep you in this game was to make you think you were implicated in the King's death.'

'All this to make sure you got your knighthood.'

'Come on, you've spent too many years in a job that's meant

to be about helping the community, but we all know it's really a training ground for learning how to fuck people up. So don't start playing the defenceless little virgin now.'

'You disgust me,' she spat at him.

She twisted away from him, turned her back, ready to leave. Then she stopped and said, 'I'm still asking you to leave those kids alone, especially Berlina Ray, because she's completely innocent in all of this.'

'Too late. My man is primed and ready to go at the carnival. And as I'm a judge at the competition I'll be there to make sure it happens.'

'Irinia, open the door,' Bernie called out as she knocked again at her mother's house.

No response. After leaving the Liberation Republic she'd come straight here. She slumped and pressed the still-tender and bruised side of her face against the cold wood. Shit. She should have brought her keys. She still didn't want to believe what Jerry had said.

'Can I help you?' a voice asked behind her.

Bernie pushed herself upright and turned around, facing the street. A small woman, in a floral patterned dress and a face full of disapproval twisted her strained lips at her.

'I'm looking for my mother, who lives here.'

The woman hitched up her finely plucked eyebrow and ran her gaze over Bernie. Satisfied that she saw some family resemblance she said, 'She's gone away for the day. To her sister's.'

'Did she say when she'll be back?'

'Tomorrow, in the morning. In the meantime can I please ask you to moderate your tone?'

The woman spun on her heels as if she'd squashed something undesirable in the road and left. As Bernie quickened her steps back to the car, her mobile went off. Hoping that it was LT, she clicked it on without looking at the caller display.

'Jerry?'

'Berlina, please listen . . .'

Her feet faltered and she staggered.

'Will you just leave me alone?' she rushed in a shrill tone. 'None of this is my fault. You agreed fifteen years ago to leave me alone, so please do that. And don't you even think about coming anywhere near Jerry.'

She punched off, shattered, breathing hard as she took to the road.

LT gazed up at the building that some claimed was an architectural masterpiece and others scoffed was downright ugly – Notting Hill's Trellick Tower. He held his bag in one hand and the keys to one of the flats in the block in the other. He'd made his peace with Window, who had given him the keys to his friend Barry's flat. Barry had told Window that he was happy for LT to use it to chill before tomorrow's competition. It also gave them an opportunity to meet, for the first time, so they could discuss his possible role in the music@yourfingertips network. LT wasn't sure what he was going to do about his musical future, but he was grateful to Barry for the loan of his place.

His eyes skated up to the floor where Barry's flat was, knowing it would give him a panoramic view of the spot where the King and Anne had burned Houdini's body. Shit, he didn't want to think about that. He dragged the air, sharp and deep, into his chest. He pulled his mobile out of his pocket. Switched it off. He moved towards the Trellick Tower entrance, willing himself to think only about winning the competition tomorrow.

Bernie walked, exhausted, in the breathless night, away from her ride, parked a street away from her home. It had taken her two hours of fighting through London's gruelling traffic to make it back to Hackney. As she turned, a hand grabbed her arm. Her heartbeat dropped as the receding bruise on her face throbbed. She went completely still. A heavy shadow and the tang of lemon shampoo moved around her.

'Just coming up to see you, lady boss,' a voice with a layer of laughter said.

Her heartbeat slipped back into its natural rhythm as she turned to find Schoolboy facing her.

'Any luck?' she asked.

'Luck's not always been my middle name, but it decided to join my joyride today. I managed to get out just as he arrived with some woman.'

'Woman?' She stared at him with complete hope in her eyes.

He nodded.

'What did she look like?'

'Couldn't really tell. Had a headscarf on like she didn't want the world to see her any more. Most probably some brass flute he picked up for a night of pleasure. You know these political men, always humming one tune in public and wailing another in the bedroom.'

He crouched down. Hitched up his tracksuit bottoms. Dug his hand into his sock. Straightened up.

'These what you were after?'

She took the objects in his hand. The King's Dictaphone tape and the digital Dictaphone that her mother had given her the previous year, for her birthday, with her initials, BR, engraved on it. She thrust the objects back at him as she said, 'Hold on to them. I've got to warn him.'

She pulled out her mobile and pressed LT's number. She began to shift her feet, quickly and nervously. 'Come on,' she ground out when the call wouldn't connect. Then it connected, to his voicemail. She punched the phone off.

'Damn, he's not answering. We'll have to go around to his place . . .'

'No point,' Schoolboy said. 'He won't be there. Usually the night before the competition he hangs out somewhere he doesn't reveal to anyone. Usually some girl's yard . . .' He stopped when he saw Bernie raise her eyebrow.

'Although,' he shuffled on, 'I'm sure he's not going to crib with no easy piece this year, you know what I mean? Here, let me try my man Window, he'll know.'

He gave her back the Dictaphone and tape and searched for

his mobile to call his brother-in-law. One minute later he pulled the phone from his face and said, 'Not answering. Don't worry about LT, Window's probably got him stashed somewhere safe. Check him tomorrow.'

As he turned and became another shadow in the night she wondered whether the woman he'd seen at Beresford's was their ghost, Anne. She prayed really hard that this ghost had not come back to life as her mother, Irinia.

# WHO'S THAT GIRL?
## ('76 Club Remix)

The next morning, bank holiday Monday, for the first time in years Bernie used her set of keys to gain access to her mother's home. She had decided to use the keys only when her knock had brought no one to the door. The cool air danced over her as she stepped into the passage. The house felt empty. She called Irinia's name. No answer. She popped the keys back into her pocket and walked into the lounge. That was where she knew Irinia kept all her important papers. In the writing bureau under the window. During her years spent documenting other people's lives she had found that most people were very careless with paperwork.

She hesitated when she reached the early Victorian mahogany bureau that stood as high as her waist. Its flat-fronted writing surface was down with piles of paper on it. She wanted to believe that her mother had nothing to do with all this.

She shifted the papers to the side, revealing three pigeon-holes flanked by a drawer on one side and a miniature cupboard on the other. If Irinia had anything to hide it would be in the cupboard. Well, not exactly the cupboard, but in the secret drawer it contained. Her parents thought she didn't know about it. She found out about it the day her mother had produced photographs of her father with another woman. The photographs were hidden in the drawer. A young Bernie had been standing, unobserved by her parents, watching at the door as they argued.

She opened the cupboard. It was empty. She reached inside and pulled a tiny wooden lever at the back. A drawer slid out from the side of the cupboard. She pushed her hand inside. Felt something hard. Metal. Small. She used two fingers to bring it out. She held it up and looked at it. The blood flooded her face as she gazed at it in shock. She'd come looking for one thing and found something else. Something she didn't want to see. Hadn't seen in fifteen years.

'Berlina?'

She spun around to find her mother standing in the doorway, wearing her gardening gloves.

'What are you doing, darling?' Irinia moved inside as she asked her daughter the question.

'What are you doing with this?' Bernie waved the key furiously at her mother.

As her daughter's face heated up, Irinia's got paler.

'It was hard for me to let go.'

Bernie shouted, 'Is this how all that business got started? How he found out?'

Irinia nodded and started speaking.

'I wrote your name, his name, on a piece of paper and put it in the case, hoping one day he would find it. They left the case with me last week when you never turned up. Obviously he can't use it any more, so he wanted you to look after it.'

Bernie put one hand over her mouth and pressed the key into her collarbone. Irinia shuffled over to her chaise longue and crouched down. She picked up the case and brought it back to Bernie. Bernie looked at it. Wouldn't touch it. She squeezed her eyes, willing the tears that were somewhere inside to go away. She opened her eyes. Shoved the key in her pocket. Ignored the case in her mother's hand and got back on with the job she had come here to do.

'Irinia, just answer one simple question. For once in your life tell me the truth. Are you Anne?' she confronted her mother.

'Anne?'

'Yes, Anne from the Liberation Republic.'

'Like I said the last time you were here, I've never heard of such a place. Really, Berlina, do you think I'd used a crappy name like Anne when I was a young radical?'

Irinia sighed, then carried on talking.

'Do you want the truth? The truth is that your father and I played at being revolutionaries. We spent most of the time popping pills, inhaling pot and screwing other people. Do you know how many demonstrations we really went on? One. Some godforsaken day of marching on a police station in Hackney. Made us look cool to be getting down with our black brothers. We were just escaping, darling. Escaping until reality pulled us in again. And do you know what reality was? Our parents' money. When those trust funds came knocking at our door we packed our duffel bags and were gone. We took our camera the day of the march. You know, to show our friends as evidence that we were fully committed to the movement. Here, let me show you.'

Irinia moved past Bernie and went to the bureau. She put the case on the floor. She bent down and opened the bottom drawer. Ruffled inside for a while and said, 'Here it is.'

She straightened up, clutching a photograph in her hand. She held it out to Bernie. Bernie took it. Peered at a black-and-white snap of her parents standing with a group of people under a students' movement banner that read 'Free Rufus Now'. She realised that it was the demonstration that the Black Fist must have organised in 1976 to help the imprisoned Rufus Williams.

'Irinia, this was in 1976, wasn't it?' she desperately asked her mother.

Irinia came and stood next to her.

'I think so. If I remember correctly, a black teenager had been arrested and mistreated by the police. That's me and that's your father.'

Irinia pointed to the photograph as she spoke. Bernie followed her mother's finger. As Irinia took her finger away, Bernie's eye was drawn to another face in the background. She whipped the photo close to her face.

'Can't be,' she said, breathing heavily.

She looked at her mother and asked, 'Do you know who this is in the picture?'

Her mother looked at where her finger pointed.

'Of course I do. Doesn't everyone? She was a real rabble-rouser back then. Really fancied herself as the female Che Guevara. But like I said, our parents' money pulled us all back.'

'I should have made the connections ages ago about who Anne is.' Bernie shook her head. She looked up at Irinia and said, holding the photograph out to her, 'Can you do me a favour? Put this in your secret drawer.'

Her mother took the photograph at the same time as Bernie began to power-walk to the door.

'But Berlina, we still need to talk about . . .'

Her mother stopped talking when Bernie turned back around. Bernie didn't think. Just went over to the bureau and picked up the case. A violin case. Then she rushed out of the house holding the case that contained the violin that had once belonged to her before she gave it away fifteen years earlier.

LT stood by his rucksack in the sitting room of the flat in the Trellick Tower and decided there were two things he already liked about Barry. That the man he still had yet to meet had a turntable, unlike most of the CD-owning population, and his amazing record collection. Barry was obviously a Bob Marley freak as he had every album the singer had produced. Barry's adoration of the Jamaican Wailer ran to ownership of almost every cover version other artists had made of 'Redemption Song'. From versions cut by Lauryn Hill to Sweet Honey In The Rock, from Joe Strummer to the Chieftains. Funny that he should find himself in the home of a man who bugged out on the one song he would never put on. Too many memories of Hoxton, and now too many images of Emmett Till.

He bent over his bag. Shuffled inside, next to the urn containing the King's ashes, and pulled out a record he'd taken down from the ceiling in his bedroom before he came to Barry's home the previous day. One of the King's dying gifts to him – Junior

Murvin's *Police And Thieves*. It had become a tradition that every year before he got ready for the competition he would choose a rhythm to kick him into the right mood. The previous year had been the hectic chitter-chatter of the Streets. The year before that a little piece of early-morning lovin' courtesy of Usher. This year he knew that it had to be something that reminded him of the good times with the King. Only one tune would do, '76's killer tune – 'Police And Thieves'.

As he moved to put the record on Barry's music system, he thought back to how strange it had been that he hadn't been able to find his own copy of *Police And Thieves* on his record shelf. He always kept it in his '70s roots reggae section. But it hadn't been there. His finger and thumb had rubbed against his chin in puzzlement. Kept rubbing until he remembered that Beresford had been holding it the day that Jane Blake ran out on them in the flat. He'd gone through the whole collection but still couldn't find it. In the end he'd had no alternative but to pull the King's copy, his father's favourite record cover, from his ceiling.

But maybe that was how it was meant to be. For him to be holding something that the King loved, to give him the strength to put on his best performance in a few hours. He reached the music system. Tipped the record cover, so that the sleeve slid out. He slanted the sleeve down, waiting for the vinyl to appear. When it came out, it wasn't a piece of vinyl which landed in his hand. It was a dub plate, much thicker than vinyl because it was made of acetate. It must be one of the King's own toasting versions of 'Police And Thieves', he decided. One of his sound system's exclusives. He put the dub plate on the turntable. Pressed the play button. The arm moved. The needle dropped. The dub plate began to turn. Started to play. He posed his body, ready to dance. Only he never moved because it wasn't the sound of music that came on, but crackling voices. Five voices. Four he'd heard before. Four voices, including the King's, which shocked him. They had the essence of youth about them, but their lifelong texture and resonance were the same. He kicked his gaze to the album cover he held in his hand. Shit, he was a musician and should have realised.

Realised that what he held in his hand was not only called an album cover but a record jacket. The King's best album cover. The King's best jacket.

LT swayed, as he pinned his hand over his mouth, watching the dub plate revolve again and again, spinning out what he knew was a recording of Houdini's death in the basement of the Liberation Republic in 1976.

Berlina Ray showed her journalist's pass to the security guard who stood in the ornate entrance hall of the House of Commons. He nodded his head and let her through. She walked quickly towards the members' rooms. Over the years her work had allowed her to get to know this building very well. She turned into a corridor with statues and grand paintings on the wall. A few minutes later she came to the door she was after. She crossed her fingers, hoping that, despite it being a bank holiday, the person she was after was a workaholic. She knocked and waited. A young man with floppy brown hair and squinting eyes opened it.

'This is a restricted area,' he said, guarding the entrance of the door with his slim body.

'Just say that Anne Hathaway would like to speak to her.'

He looked down his nose at her as if she were a security threat.

'Take my word for it. She will want to see me.'

The man went away. Came back a minute later and said, 'Follow me.'

Bernie followed him into a medium-sized room darkened by wood panelling and recently shampooed green carpet. The woman behind the desk had her head down, writing. She pulled it up.

'Thank you, Thomas,' the woman said, dismissing him.

After he had left the woman's gaze settled on Bernie, coolly assessing what she saw.

'Berlina Ray, isn't it?'

'That's right, Minister of Culture.'

# TRACK 28: TRUTH JIVE

'So how may I help you?' Clarissa Hathaway asked as she eased back in her chair.

Bernie sat down in the leather chair she was not offered. She squinted at the minister, trying to detect the young radical she had once been – the chestnut hair, the stern grey eyes, the artificially tanned face. Bernie realised she was dealing with a completely different woman now.

'Anne was a nice touch,' Bernie started. 'Clarissa Hathaway. Anne Hathaway. Anne Hathaway, the wife of Shakespeare. Anne and Shakespeare.'

The minister leaned forward and placed her hands on the desk. She clasped them together. She spoke in her professionally softened voice.

'Ms Ray, unless you have something you wish to say I advise you to leave before I call security.'

Bernie eased back into the seat, ignoring the minister's threat.

'I just couldn't figure how every time we got closer to the truth a spanner was thrown in the works of Lord Tribulation's musical career. You must have been thanking God every night for that arson attack. Such an ideal opportunity to start screwing around with the King's son's life. I understand now why the King left Joe's Café in such a state. Sure, it was partly seeing his son had disturbed him, but the biggest shock was the face of the person getting ready to destroy his son–you, Minister. Anne, his comrade from the good old days. So you kept it going. Your continuous denouncement of him in the media. The timing of the press turning up outside the funeral. The appearance of Mothers Against Murder Music when he was just about to sign the most important record deal of his career. You pulled MAMM's strings behind the scenes. On their website it says they have a major financial sponsor, and I just bet that is you. Of course, you couldn't have done all this on your own. While you played yin someone had to play yang.'

The minister said nothing. Remained calm, as if she were facing an opponent across the chamber of the House of Commons.

'The other puppet master was Shakespeare, or Beresford Clarke, Order of the British Empire. I took a train trip to Birmingham, and you know what I found? You know what a source told me? Beresford got there in September 1976, not in '73, as he claimed. Then I started thinking about the little tussle with my Dictaphone that put me in hospital. I used my contacts to get into Beresford's home. My contact kept it clean, kept it neat, so Beresford would never know anyone had ever been in his home. Do you know what my contact found?'

She took her Dictaphone and the King's tape from the side of her bag and placed them on the table. The minister's expression didn't change as she looked at the items on the table and said, 'Confessing to a crime could get you arrested, Ms Ray.'

'I don't think you'd have me arrested, Minister. What would you do if the press got their hands on the King's tapes?'

The minister's face lost its sunlamp sheen.

'You should leave.'

Bernie just smiled, tight and taut.

'The King had to go because Beresford couldn't afford to jeopardise his position in society. He'd rather be blind than watch that knighthood slip away. A knighthood, I suspect, you were recommending him for. But you underestimated the lengths to which he would go to keep his secret. Even murder.'

A vein in the minister's throat throbbed.

'I have no knowledge of what you're talking about.'

'Your plan was simple. Your job was to keep the King's son

occupied with trying to save his career while Beresford wormed his way into his life. So you both played him. Good cop, bad cop. Keep pulling, distracting him, and eventually one of you will find what you're looking for. But you didn't find it. We have the tapes and . . .' Bernie paused before she told her lie. 'And the King's best jacket.'

The minister flinched at the mention of the jacket.

Abruptly Clarissa Hathaway stood up, her bob shifting as she walked to the water cooler. She filled a cup. Turned back to Bernie and said, 'I take it you're not taping me.'

'I've got all the tapes I need.'

The minister sat back down with her water. Took a long drink.

'My sources tell me that there may have been an Anne in a black radical group in 1976,' she began. Bernie realised that the minister didn't believe she wasn't being taped. 'This Anne may very well have got involved in things she should never have got involved in. I understand that she was living quietly and peacefully, helping the community, when she got dragged back into a past she didn't want to go back into. She had no alternative. The death of one of her radical black brothers in 1976 was an accident. An accident that came back to haunt her. As for the death of a musician called King Stir It Up, well, I understand that he did indeed die of natural causes, as the coroner's office concluded.'

She took another drink. Lighter this time.

'My sources tell me that Anne is prepared to disappear in exchange for a piece of information.'

Bernie leaned forward and said, 'Depends what the information is.'

Clarissa Hathaway crushed the cup in her hands and threw it in the bin.

'I believe that Anne used to love going to the Notting Hill carnival in her heyday. Now, today is the last day of carnival and Anne heard that a certain Shakespeare was going to take care of a problem he's had for a long time once and for all.'

'What do you mean?' Bernie shot to the edge of her seat.

'Instead of sitting here, Ms Ray, talking about my sources, you may need to get to the Ladbroke Grove Writer in Residence competition, which I believe kicks off in . . .' The minister checked her watch. She turned her face back to Bernie. For the first time Bernie saw the young woman she had once been reflected in her eyes. 'About half an hour. Anne seemed to think that Shakespeare's problem might be taking part.'

Bernie shot to her feet. Grabbed the Dictaphone, tape and bag. She made for the door. Opened it. Then she turned back to the minister and said, 'You might want to tell your sources to whisper in Anne's ear that the best thing for her future well-being would be to stop helping the community before the next election. It wouldn't do for the King's tapes to resurface just before the election. What an embarrassment that would be for the government.'

She turned back to the door and left.

Berlina Ray sprinted with her head down towards her car. Her ruck-sack slapped her back as the wind chewed into her face. As soon as she left the minister she'd tried to call LT. No joy, only his voice-mail. Her only alternative was to get to the carnival as quickly as possible. She flicked her head up as she got closer to the car. That was when she saw him. A man standing by the right side of the Mini. Dressed in black trousers and white shirt. Half devil? Half angel? Which one he was she did not know. But she knew she maybe shouldn't have trusted Clarissa Hathaway. Her sprint eased into a soft run. She noticed something in the man's hand. She stopped. Her teeth clenched the inside of her drying lip. She thrust her hand into her jeans pocket. Wrapped it around her rape alarm. She began moving again. This time in even steps. As she got closer she heard the man whistling Boyz To Men's 'The End Of The Road'. He heard her footsteps. Turned to her. Her chest adjusted back to a normal breathing pattern. A traffic warden holding a notepad and pen in one hand with his cap tucked under his arm.

'Excuse me, miss, is this your vehicle?' he asked in a soft Nigerian accent.

'Yes,' she replied with a beautiful smile.

The warden stepped back, looking at her suspiciously. People smiling at him could only mean bad news.

'Well, I have to give you a ticket . . .'

Bernie didn't answer him. Instead she calmly opened her car door. Got into the driver's seat.

'Miss, you can't . . .'

She sat, back straight. She didn't check her rear-view mirror.

'Miss, I will report you to . . .' the warden said, his voice sticking in his nose.

He moved to stand in front of the car.

She jammed the key into the ignition. Twisted it.

'You can't . . .'

The growl of the engine drowned out his voice. She pushed the pedal to the metal. The warden jumped sideways out of the car's path. It shot the wrong way down the one-way street. She checked the time on the music system: 14:40. Twenty minutes before the competition started. But she still had time because the reigning champion always went last.

She kept her foot down hard.

The Devil and his six disciples were back pounding the streets of Notting Hill and the ground beneath LT's feet. He slammed the phone down, just as an emergency operator connected to the line. Jesus, he didn't know what to do about what he'd heard on the dub plate. Now he understood why they had cleared out the King's place. They needed everything just in case the dub plate hadn't been in the King's record collection. Understood why they tried to burgle his place – to see whether it was in his record collection. That was why May's records were thrown all over the floor when she was attacked in her home. He knew that Beresford had taken his Junior Murvin *Police And Thieves* album, believing it was the King's best record jacket with the dub plate.

Now he knew that Bernie had been right about Beresford. And fuck, when he heard the Minister of Culture's voice, that had flipped him out. Yeah, it was her all right. If there was one thing he knew about it was voices. Her voice might be lower now, but it still possessed that distinctive roll to it. And Sean Sparkle, the boy the King had nurtured, involved in all this shit as well.

Beresford? Clarissa Hathaway? Sean Sparkle? Which one had

called the King to his death? He looked at the phone again. Jackknifed a sharp breath inside his body. It burned his chest. He looked at the clock on the wall. The competition was ten minutes away. If he called the police he would have to wait for them and he'd never make it to the competition by the time he was called to the stage. Would never win the Writer in Residence of Ladbroke Grove crown for the third year running. Would miss his chance, yet again. He moved to the window. Stared at the spontaneous people combustion getting larger on the streets below. Stacked people at ground level, standing on waist-high walls, hanging from trees, on top of rooftops. Stacked colours sparkling, on clothes, hats, scarves, flags, costumes. Stacked flavours from rice and peas to beer, from sweet water drunk fresh from green-skinned coconuts to the fire of curried goat. Stacked sounds from sound systems to mobile floats, from the blast of foghorns and whistles to bugged-out laughter.

The King wouldn't want him to miss this opportunity. But after the competition, that was when he would get Bernie to go with him to the police and give them the dub plate.

He breath beat back to easy having made his decision. He moved to the bathroom to get ready. He used Auntie May's 'keeps demonic spirits away' soap to cleanse his body as he took a shower. As he stepped out of the shower cubicle he heard the front door bang. Heard two voices, one of which was Window. He couldn't place the other voice. Must be Barry. As he wrapped a towel around himself, his manager called, 'Hey, champ, where you at? Come and meet another Hackney whizz-kid.'

'Yeah, I'll be right there,' he replied.

He stopped at the threshold of the room as he considered telling Window about the dub plate. He'd have to tell him about Beresford. He didn't want his manager upset before the competition. He manufactured a smile on his face and went into the hall. He found Window standing with a man of average height, in his mid-thirties, with gentle grey eyes, a smooth white skin and close-cropped brown hair.

'This is Barry,' Window introduced him.

He shook Barry's hand.

'I've been wanting to meet you for a long time, LT,' Barry said, smiling, showing small, even teeth.

'You've got a great music collection, Barry. A hardcore Marley fan.'

Window groaned and said in a mock-despairing voice, 'What did you have to say that for? He's only going to start singing his theme tune, that bloody 'Redemption Song'.'

On cue, Barry opened his mouth and started singing. Stunned, LT listened as the voice filled the room. The voice was older than it had been in 1984. But it had the same texture. The same angel's purity. The same depth. Cramps twisted in his legs. He leaned back on the wall, pushed back to being eight years old. Back to Hoxton. Back, by a teenager his National Front cohorts had called Barry, singing 'Redemption Song' as he prayed for his life inside a skip. When Barry hit the third line of the chorus LT joined in. Abruptly, Barry stopped, his face going as pale as the 'Keep Britain White' sign LT and the King had run past all those years ago.

The man in the baseball cap parked the white van near the Harrow Road at 3 p.m. That, he knew, was as near as he would be able to get. The street was lined with people heading for the same place as him. Except they would reach the carnival before him as he was not going there quite yet. He turned and checked the bag next to him. Holdall. Medium sized. Black. No side compartments, just one zip on the top. He leaned over. Unzipped it. Pushed the canvas material back. Inside were his black clothes. On top of them lay two unsheathed combat knives. Both were the same size – fifteen inches long – but they were different in style and temperament. One was glinting stainless steel, light to the touch with a blade smoothed on both sides. The other had a blackened blade to minimise detection, a saw-tooth edge on one side, and a polycarbonate handle.

He got out of the van with the bag and moved at a brisk pace. He took a short cut he'd found to the Trellick Tower. As he got closer the music began to ripple beneath his booted feet. On the last leg of his journey he couldn't avoid the thick lines of people. Mostly young. Funked out on music, narcs and God knew what else. He kept his head clear as he pushed through. He reached the entrance to the block. Pressed the number he needed on the intercom. His sometimes girlfriend, Linda, answered. She let him in. He pushed inside. She wouldn't ask any questions as he changed into his black clothes and decided which knife to use.

'You all right?' Window asked LT as he watched him put on the King's vintage denim jacket in Barry's bedroom. 'Why didn't you tell me you knew Barry?'

After Barry had realised who LT was, he'd picked up his keys and rushed out of his home. Window had demanded to know what was going on. When LT had told him about Hoxton in 1984, Window had grown silent. LT had headed for the bedroom to get ready, while his manager had stomped to the kitchen.

'Know him?' LT reared back as the words left him. 'You don't know the stress that whole incident brought into my life.'

'We've all got our histories, some more extreme than others. Met Barry when we were young in borstal back in Birmingham. Didn't like each other at first. No way was I going to like some Sieg-Heiling jackboots boy. Then we had to share a room. Circled each other for a long time until we found out we loved music. Barry has worked hard to be where he is now. His past is exactly that, a past, a place he started, had no control over. If you want the best for your future, Barry's your man. By the way, word just came through that May's going to be fine.'

As Window left the room, LT let out a long sigh, relieved that at least something was going well today. He thought about Barry and what Window said. It wasn't easy to slip your hand into the palm of someone who'd been both demon and saviour at the same time. He inhaled deeply. He looked at the white cotton du-rag on the bed. He knew that the headline he'd chosen was provocative, courting trouble. But what was the point of being the son of King Stir It Up and christened Lord Tribulation if he wasn't going to make waves?

'I always rated your voice the first time I ever heard it that night in Hoxton.'

LT stopped as he heard Barry. He wasn't sure what he heard in the voice – hurt? Regret? Guilt? Whatever it was, he said nothing. Instead he continued to look at his du-rag. He heard Barry walk into the room.

'You sure that's the headline you want to wear on your du-rag?' Barry asked quietly as he stopped next to him.

LT curtly nodded his head. Barry picked the du-rag up. Placed it on LT's head. Flattened it. As he moved his fingers to the back to tie it, LT opened his mouth and began softly to sing the chorus to 'Redemption Song'. He didn't know why he did it. Maybe it was because he knew that today ghosts were going to be laid to rest one way or another. Maybe because Barry's fingers were so gentle and soothing on his head.

On the second line of the song Barry joined it. They carried on their duet until Barry fanned the back of the du-rag across the coolness of LT's neck. He stepped back. LT tilted his head farther back in the fine August light jetting through the window, so that the headline was easier to read.

'Murder Music.'

Bernie's wheels had been stationary for ten minutes. The traffic was gridlocked.

'Come on,' she let out furiously.

She looked at the radio clock: 15:15.

She picked up her phone. Punched redial. Voicemail. Again. Every red light she hit she'd tried to contact LT. She threw the mobile back on the passenger seat. The traffic moved. A few inches. Frustration bit into her. She knew she had a decision to make. One that was not going to be popular with the motorists behind her. She closed all the windows. Picked up her phone. Grabbed her bag. Cut the engine. Jumped out. She pointed the fob key at the car. Pressed. The car locked with a clunking sound. She walked to the boot. Opened it. Took out the violin case. Then she turned away from the car.

'Where the fucking hell are you going, lady?' the motorist behind her yelled as she ran towards the nearest Underground station.

'You ready for this?' Window asked LT as they stood inside Barry's front door.

Barry looked at them, an encouraging smile on his face. LT nodded at both men.

'Window, make sure no one gets this,' LT said as he passed his bag to Window.

Window took it. Opened the door. LT took a deep breath. Moved forward into what he knew was going to be one of the longest afternoons of his life.

Bernie rushed to the nearest exit in Notting Hill Underground station. People were milling and chilling all around her. She spun around, not sure which was the quickest way. She pulled her bag from her back. Dug inside. Found her carnival map. All Saints Road was the other side of the carnival. She swallowed, dizzy with dehydration. Her teeth bit into her lip as she slung her bag over one shoulder and her violin case over the other and set off through the pulse of happy revellers around her.

The man who had entered the Trellick Tower wearing a baseball cap left his girlfriend's flat at the same time as a huge cheer rose from ground level. He set off with the saw-tooth knife in his back trouser pocket.

As LT walked towards the crowd he didn't need to contemplate his entrance. He'd already decided. He wasn't going around the back like the other performers. He was going, Moses-style, straight through the crowd. Using the classic street walk called smooth 'n' sexy. Head held high, shoulders back, legs moving in short, even steps, one foot in front of the other. Never rush it. Always take it easy.

As a policeman moved two barriers and the multicoloured crowd parted.

He took it easy.

As the crowd gasped when they read his du-rag – 'Murder Music'.

He took it easy.

As cameras flashed all over him.

He took it easy.

He reached the steel barriers that drew a line between the audience and the stage. Red, gold and green lights circled the mobile stage from the lighting hanging inside the aluminium roof. Three large black speakers were stacked on the ground, on either side, like bodyguards. LT smiled as he remembered that the King called them houses of joy. The promoters had arranged for a full screen behind the acts to show real-time film of the performers for those who couldn't see properly. Across the screen in large red, gold and green graffiti-style writing was the tag line: 'THE WORD REVOLUTION WILL NOT BE TELEVISED. IT WILL BE LIVE.'

Instead of his own performance being transmitted, LT had arranged for something quite different to appear on the screen.

M.C. Insanity waited by her decks on the right. The four judges sat at a table on the left side of the stage. He gulped as he looked up at Sean Sparkle and Beresford Clarke. He wondered which one had killed the King. Or maybe it had been the Minister of Culture. The crowd cheered as the people's MC, DJ Lady Hectic, strode up to the mic.

'OK, people of the metropolis, this is the one you've been waiting for. Will he? Won't he? You know who I'm talking about. Will the current boy wonder be able to put his troubles behind him and make it three in a row? Will he impress the judges? I give you the man that's setting this town on fire – Lord Tribulation.'

No one clapped. No one spoke. No one moved. He jumped on to the stage. Nodded to Lady Hectic. Took the mic from her hand. Turned to the crowd. He wiggled his toes in his trainers. Felt the stage. Smooth and fluid. Able to handle his weight and his heavy music at the same time. The stage was high enough for him to connect with the crowd, low enough for him to groove with the bass line. His eyes swept the kaleidoscope of people in front of him. A man dressed all in black at the front of the stage watched him with anticipation. Yeah, the crowd were ready. He nodded to M.C. Insanity. She did her thing at the decks. Vivaldi's Winter Concerto with that bonfire R 'n' B beat sizzled over the crowd. LT's voice boomed out as he started rapping the lyrics to 'Gasoline Ghetto'. That was the signal for the crowd to move into their hellfire groove. A montage of images and dates flashed on the screen behind LT to the beat of the music.

1955: a black-and-white photograph of Emmett Till smiling, wearing a hat, with the pose of a boy getting ready to become a man.

1963: Malcolm X in militant mode regaling a crowd in Harlem.

1965: civil rights demonstrators marching from Selma to Montgomery being beaten with billy clubs and teargassed by the police.

Flames and smoke as Watts burned during a civil disturbance.

1976: a teenager carrying a dying child through the Soweto uprising.

Bob Marley smiling as he strolled along a London street.

1981: the silent image of the burnt-out ruin of a house on New Cross Road.

The music died away. LT held the mic close to his lips. He stopped rapping. He moved to the edge of the stage.

Silence. Only the noise of sound systems in neighbouring streets and the shouting and squealing of revellers following them could be heard. The crowd watched him, transfixed.

Bernie fought her way through the crowd that stood outside the barriers, trying to get a glimpse of the Writer in Residence of Ladbroke Grove slam. She reached a barrier. A tall, imposing policeman blocked her way.

'I've got to get through.'

He didn't even answer, just shook his head.

'I'm part of the performance.'

He lifted both eyebrows, but stood his ground. She knew that if she tried to climb over she would be pulled back. Maybe even arrested. She twisted her lips as she frantically thought of what to do next. The excitement of the crowd behind her pressed the violin case on her back. Her violin. Except it didn't really belong to her any more. Everyone went still as the music stopped. She quickly pulled her rucksack from her back. Took off the violin case. Opened it and pulled out her violin. She held it under one arm and the bow under the other. She pulled the violin case and the bag awkwardly on to her back. She took a deep breath. She knew this was going to be hard, but she had to do it. No other way would she get in. She tucked the violin on the left side of her chin, pulled the bow up. She counted one, two, three. Touched the bow to the strings and began to play Vivaldi's Winter Concerto. The policeman smiled, moved back the barrier and let her through.

*　*　*

LT's mic hand slipped down as he heard the violin. Beautiful, precise, elegant. He strained over the heads of the twisting crowd, looking for the player. The crowd began to shift, making a path for whoever it was. He stretched on tiptoe, catching the sun flashing on blonde hair. He didn't need to see who it was. Bernie. A large grin spread across his face. He eased back down, pushed his mic hand up as she made her way to the stage. Someone was already pushing back a barrier when she got there. She walked up the steps, still playing. She got on to the stage, moved passed M.C. Insanity towards him. She stopped on his right. Her hand stopped moving. He ran his eyes over her. Her jaw was moving, as if she had something to say. But she kept quiet.

He took up his wide-leg stance. Nodded to M.C. Insanity.

'Babylon is a bitch,' he roared.

M.C. Insanity flicked her fingers. The beat kicked in. Bernie picked up her violin moves. A new segue of images flashed on to the screen.

1976: photographs and film of youths clashing with the police at the Notting Hill carnival.

The B-line dropped. The crowd went wild. LT danced towards Bernie as he rapped high and hard.

'I need to . . .' she started to say as she played.

But he couldn't hear her because the crowd were pumping high and up. He danced away from her, back to the centre of the stage. He finished rapping as the screen filled with the image of the black athletes from the 1968 Olympics doing their iconic Black Power salutes. LT bowed his head and thrust his clenched fist in the air. The light reflected his homage across the screen.

The judges threw down their pens and began to clap. There was no formal announcement – there didn't need to be – as the crowd began to climb over the metal barriers on to the stage. They pushed Bernie out of the way as they mobbed and congratulated him. She tried to push through but they propelled her back. She drew in her breath when she saw a man dressed all in black with his hand moving in his pocket standing next to LT. Bernie punched through the crowd until she reached the edge of the stage. She jumped down, her eyes frantically searching. She saw a policeman, in his black uniform and helmet, getting ready to mount the stage. She ran over to him. Grabbed his arm and yelled, 'You've got to help me, someone is going to hurt him.'

The policeman nodded and pushed her hand away. As he leaped on to the stage and turned his back she saw a black handle sticking out of his back trouser pocket.

Bernie had seen handles like that before from her days reporting around the world. Sometimes she'd seen them sticking out of bodies. She didn't even think. She rushed back on the stage towards the judges' table and ran up to Sean Sparkle, who was on his feet.

'They're going to kill him,' she cried up at him.

'What?'

'Don't question me. Someone dressed as a policeman. Just help him.'

Bernie looked at the other judges, still clapping. Two of them. With Sean that made three. She realised that one was missing. Beresford Clarke. She spun around. Couldn't see him. She turned one more time. Then she found him. Standing next to LT.

'He's got Jerry,' she yelled at Sean, pointing to where they stood.

He followed her finger and found LT and Beresford just as the older man put his hand on LT's shoulder. Then he spotted the 'policeman' approaching LT from the other side of the small crowd surrounding his mentor's son. Bernie and Sean rushed through the crowd.

Through the euphoria and noise a hand gripped LT's shoulder. He swung around, his smile blazing with his success. The smile drained away when he saw the imposing figure in front of him. Beresford Clarke. LT didn't even think. Reflex made him step back. But the buoyancy of the crowd pushed him forward again. Beresford's hand shot out. Grabbed LT's hand. Held him in the tightest handshake.

'Let go of my hand,' LT growled.

He tried to pull his hand out of the older man's. But Beresford held him in a vice.

'Congratulations, son.'

LT grimaced as the pressure on his hand increased.

'I said let go,' he grunted.

The hand tightened.

'Can't do that. Just as I can't let you disturb the very ordered life I've built for myself.'

Suddenly Beresford's other arm snaked out, hooked around LT's waist and snapped him forward. LT slammed into Beresford's body. He became smothered in the heat and odour of bay rum from the body, locking him in place. LT tried to heave back but the iron will of Beresford's bunched muscles and experience held him, so it seemed they were in an embrace.

'I found the jacket. I played what was inside,' LT ground out, hoping the shock of his words would distract the older man, making him loosen his grip.

But the grip squeezed him closer. Beresford pushed his mouth close to his ear. The words he whispered bruised the side of LT's face.

'The problem with the King was he was a one-man show. Did what he wanted when he wanted. He should have got rid of that tape recording of all that nasty business instead of making it into a dub plate. Instead of leaving it in his record cover.'

LT strained, desperate to break the hold.

'What are you going to do?'

Beresford's arm became taut, a chain around his waist. The older man whispered in his beautiful, bedtime-story voice, 'At least everyone will remember you as the rapper who won the Writer in Residence of Ladbroke Grove three times.'

Desperately he looked down into Beresford's face. Saw his eyes. Unmovable, black, granite. LT had seen him with those eyes at the press conference, determined to win the day. Now LT knew that Beresford was getting ready to finish another job. He saw Beresford look over his shoulder. Beresford smiled. Nodded. LT's back arched forward. He didn't know what was behind him, but he knew Beresford did. Whatever it was he knew that Beresford was ready to drop his deadly bass line.

Sean rushed through the crowd with Bernie following. As they muscled through, their eyes darted between the 'policeman' and Beresford.

'Get out of the way,' Sean yelled.

Realising who he was, some people moved. But most didn't. Bernie saw Beresford look over LT's shoulder. His eyes connected with the man dressed as a policeman. He nodded.

'Shit, we need to hurry,' she yelled at Sean's back.

Sean used both hands and elbows to shove people. Bernie saw the 'policeman' shift closer to LT's back. She saw one of his arms move. She knew he was pulling his knife.

'Oh my God,' she whispered.

Sean began to run faster, using his body to barrel people aside. Bernie saw the man's arm move back around. She knew he had his knife.

'We're not going to make it,' she cried.

*If you relax, your opponent will too and that's when you strike.* As LT wriggled he remembered Bernie's words when she had him pinned against the wall in his father's flat. He counted. Classic four on the floor.

One.

Two.

Three.

Four.

LT relaxed his body. Beresford loosened his grip slightly. That was when LT struck. He quickly tensed. The older man shook with surprise. LT leaned in and hooked his arm around Beresford's waist. Spun him a full one-eighty degrees. He let go. Beresford staggered back. His footing gave way as he crashed on top of the man behind him. LT breathed with relief when he saw that the man was a policeman. Beresford's weight made the policeman tumble to the ground. LT heard a sharp cry as Beresford arched up. Then he collapsed back down. The crowd scattered back. The man underneath Beresford pushed at him frantically. Beresford slumped off, slipping on to his front. That was when LT saw the knife sticking out of Beresford's back. Someone in the crowd screamed.

Four hours. That was how long LT and Bernie had been sitting in the hypnotic brightness of Sean Sparkle's lounge. That was how long LT had been answering the two murder squad detectives' questions. Now he watched Sean's retreating figure as he showed the satisfied policemen to the front door.

As soon as the scream echoed through the crowd, pandemonium had broken out. The assailant ran off. The police scrambled on to the stage. By the time an ambulance arrived Beresford had already been pronounced dead. The police wanted to question LT at the local station, but Sean Sparkle persuaded them to do it at his home. Once LT realised that Beresford had been the person the King had met in Hoxton and that Sean hadn't been involved in the King's death, he had decided not to reveal anything about 1976 to the police. Also, there was still the final puzzle that the King's dub plate had revealed, which only Sean could resolve for him. So when the police's questions came, he took it easy, didn't rush it as he told them untruths.

An unprovoked attack.

Beresford Clarke had been congratulating him.

No, he had never seen the man dressed in a police uniform before.

Absolutely no idea why anyone would want to attack Mr Clarke.

Sean came back into the room. Went over to pull a drink from the cabinet in the corner.

As Sean turned around the front door intercom sounded.

'If you don't mind, Mr Sparkle, I'll get it,' LT said, already rising.

He knew who it was and what they had. When he opened the door his manager was standing there with his bag. Before he passed it to him, Window said, 'I'm sorry. This is the first time my eyes have let nostalgia cloud what they should have seen.'

'None of us saw it. Except Bernie. Beresford was a master at playing all of us.'

After Window had left, LT moved back into the main room. Didn't sit down. Instead he said to Bernie, 'Why don't you go and have a long look at Mr Sparkle's gold disc collection in his studio downstairs?'

Surprised, she tilted her head to the left to check him over.

'But . . .' she began.

Her words trailed off when she saw the stubborn set of his mouth and realised he wasn't going to ask her twice. She got up and left.

'What's going on?' Sean asked as he moved across to LT.

LT didn't answer him. Instead, he placed the bag on the floor. Hunched down. Unzipped it. His hand clutched the item sitting on top of the King's urn. He pulled it out. He straightened up, holding the King's best record jacket. Sean took two steps back when he saw it.

'Where's your turntable?'

Sean pointed to a cabinet on the wall. LT moved across. Opened it. He tipped the record jacket so that the dub plate eased out. He put it on the turntable. Pressed 'play'. The arm moved. The needle fell. The sound of crackling voices filled the room.

'*Houdini, how could you do this to us?*'

It was Beresford's distinctive voice, but stretched with outrage.

'*Man, you might have been able to sleep at night, but I couldn't.*'

Ragged breathing and the sounds of rough soles scraping across a hard surface replaced the voices.

'*You pig squealer,*' *shouted a woman's voice.*

A clank sounded as the scuffling became more intense. Grunts filled the air.

'*Take your hands off me, man.*'

'Houdini, calm down. Let's talk about this.'

The King's voice.

'Calm down? I-man can't sleep at night knowing what we've done. I helped evict my own people. When the NF attacked that man it might as well have been my hands giving him the licks. Those explosives and guns are going to turn up in the hands of the NF. This whole mess is turning me crazy.'

'Let's sit down, man, and we'll work this out.'

The King's voice again. Calm. Reassuring. Suddenly, there was banging and erratic breathing.

'Let go of my arm.'

'No way, man.'

The King's voice was forceful. Then the sounds of a full-range scuffle ripped the air.

'Houdini, let go of me.'

The King's voice was loaded with distress.

'Houdini, let him go.'

Beresford's voice was instant and loud.

'I can't breathe.'

The King's voice, as if someone was crushing his windpipe.

More bangs and thumps filled the air. Then something crashed, hard, followed by a low scream and then a moan. The dub plate filled with heavy breathing. A half-breath in, a half-breath out. As if someone was catching their last breath.

'Oh my God, Sean, what have you done?'

The dub plate continued to revolve in silence.

LT turned to Sean, whose face was now as white as the clothes he wore.

'You were the King's boy, weren't you?'

Sean answered with a short, shaking nod.

'Then don't disrespect me by giving me any bullshit lines now I'm looking into your eyes.'

'All right.'

'Why did the King lie on the tape and say you weren't there?'

The other man gave LT a quick glance, his expression guarded. But he started speaking.

'Simple. To protect me. The day he took that fifty p from my hand was the day he became the shadow at my back. Sort of like one-way traffic, him always looking out for me. And that was the problem, we never thought about what would happen the day I had to look out for him.'

He stopped speaking. His mouth opened. Caught the air. Took in a big breath. He moved his body so that he stared in LT's direction. But his gaze went over his head, as if he were watching something. From the shifting light in Sean's eyes, LT knew he was remembering.

'It was me making the tape for a dub plate, not the King,' Sean finally said, his voice quiet, almost lonely. 'So I was in one room and they were in the other. I knew there was some serious shit going on because they were all arguing. Just wouldn't stop. Just as I got the tape up and running they burst into the room.'

Sean's breath hitched high in the room, as if he were back under the low-level ceiling of a basement.

'Houdini and Shakespeare were really slogging it out. The King being the King, he couldn't just watch them try and kill each other, so he stepped in to pull them apart. But Houdini just wrapped his hands around the King's throat. Started squeezing. Squeezing. All I knew was that the man who had loved and looked out for me was in trouble. I suppose after all those years of having the living daylights beaten out of me by my dad, the rage just came out. I don't even remember moving. I suppose I pushed him, hit him, I don't fucking know. The next second, Houdini was falling backwards. I lunged for him.' LT watched Sean's hand flick sideways. 'But I couldn't reach him in time.' His hand fell flat at his side. 'He hit his head against one of our houses of joy. He started breathing really erratically for, I don't know, thirty seconds. Then he stopped.'

Sean twisted his head away. Jerked his hand through his hair.

'What I don't understand,' LT began, 'is if he wanted to protect you, why keep it all these years?'

'You know why he kept it?' The older man flicked his head back towards LT. 'To protect himself. From me. He told the others he got rid of it, but he made sure I knew that wasn't true. He was scared. We were all shit scared. Keeping that recording was his way of telling me to keep quiet. Remember back in those days he didn't know how my life was going to turn out. What if I'd become a resentful drunk like my old man? What if one day my tongue got loose and I went to the Old Bill and told them the King was involved in a death? It was his way of making sure I never did that. In some respects I was glad he kept it because it made sure I never became a replica of my dad. Instead I became the man I am today.'

'Why didn't he just keep it as a tape? Why make a dub plate?'

'You know the King. He hated tapes, except his Dictaphone tapes for his lyrics. Said that tapes deteriorated too quickly. They were no place to keep your music. Everything had to be on vinyl or acetate. Mind you . . .' He smiled, as if remembering the fun of those old musical days. 'You can't play those dub plates too often or they go as well.'

'So why try to destroy it now after all these years?'

A harsh expression battered Sean's face as he replied, 'When my old man was dying, he got in contact with me. Praying for forgiveness and all that kind of crap. When people know they're dying they just want to tie up all the loose ends. It was the same with the King. He wanted his best record jacket with that dub plate to be cremated with him. That way he could protect me and himself.'

'But how did Beresford and the Minister of Culture find out he still had it?'

The expression on Sean's face softened as he quietly said, 'Your interview on the telly.'

'I don't get it.'

'The King rang me up to tell me that you were going to be doing an interview.' Sean momentarily stopped when he saw the surprise on LT's face. 'The King was really proud of you, and you may not have known it, but he made it his business to know what you were doing all the time. Anyway, I tuned it to watch your interview. And that's when I started feeling sick because you talked about the dub plate . . .'

'I don't think . . .'

'Remember when the interviewer asked you how you got your defining Ice Shack musical sound?' LT nodded. 'A half-breath in, a half-breath out . . .'

Sean trailed off.

'Oh my God, that was the sound of Houdini dying, wasn't it?' LT shot out. 'All this time my fans have been dancing to a sound that was based on the last breaths of a dying man. No wonder the King collapsed when we were watching the interview together in the hospital. I thought it was the dope he was smoking. But it wasn't, it was what I said about the record on the interview.'

'Beresford and Clarissa Hathaway must have seen the interview and realised after all these years that he had kept it.'

'I don't get it. Why would they have thought that he was going to expose them? If he did that, wouldn't he have been exposing himself as well?' LT said.

'They knew he was already dying and I suppose they thought, what would he have to lose by telling the tale? If there's one thing I know about, it's powerful people. They become paranoid. Think that every last bit of shit they did in the past is going to come helter-skelter back at them. Beresford, Clarke OBE, Clarissa Hathaway, Minister of Culture, were donkey's years away from Shakespeare and Anne. No way were they taking the chance on finding out whether some old-time musician was going to rat on them.'

'Why didn't you warn me?'

Sean sighed deeply. 'Remember, I live in the States now, so I only realised what was going on when you asked me about the King's best jacket when you came to see me. That really fucked me up. You don't know how many times I picked the blower up to call, but each time I got scared. I was never as strong as your dad. And I suppose I never thought that Beresford would go this far – you know, try and kill you.'

Sean looked at him, the sparkle in his eyes too bright. His mouth opened a few times, but no words came out, as if he were afraid to ask the next question. The decision was taken out of his hands by a voice at the door.

'What are you going to do with the dub plate?'

They swung around to find Bernie standing in the doorway as the rumble of her question bounced in the room.

The King's former boy and LT's old girlfriend watched him as he tried to make his decision. His eyes caught Bernie's. Overwhelmed brown meeting frank blue. He shifted his profile towards Sean. Their eyes caught. Resigned brown meeting forlorn blue. LT made his decision. He turned around. Leaned over the turntable. Pulled the dub plate up. Raised his knee and broke the record into two over it. He stepped towards Sean. Held out the pieces and whispered, 'I've heard better versions of "Police And Thieves".'

Sean's shoulders fell flat as he took the broken dub plate.

LT picked up the bag. Put out his hand to Sean Sparkle and said, 'It was good meeting you, Mr Sparkle.'

The older man ignored his hand and took him into a hard embrace. He let LT go. Looked at him with those sparkling blue eyes and said, 'Now the King's gone you let me take care of you. Record contract. Anything you want, just let me know. Come over to LA soon.'

LT nodded. He moved towards the door with Bernie. As he reached the threshold he turned slowly back and asked, 'When your dad contacted you, begging for forgiveness, what did you do?'

'Told him to piss off. Whatever hole he was dying in I knew he was still the same evil bastard he'd always been. But the King, he was a good man.'

LT nodded again as he watched the sparkle flare back into Sean's eyes. He turned back towards the door with Bernie and his bag and left.

'What are we doing here? The carnival's more or less over,' Bernie asked quietly, her voice anxious as LT cut the engine of his car.

They both stared at Ladbroke Grove, bathed in the thick night. He didn't answer her. Instead he turned to the back seat, where his bag was. He grabbed it and got out of the car. He was glad she asked no more questions as she followed him. They began walking, past a few stragglers still unable to let the long-dead carnival go, and street sweepers. He stopped outside a record shop. Bent down and placed the bag on the ground. He unzipped it and tenderly felt inside. He cupped the urn in his hand. He straightened as he raised the King for his final goodbye. He heard 'Oh' slip from Bernie's lips. He turned to her and smiled. A full smile. She understood what he was going to do. She reached over and pulled off the lid.

LT took a deep breath and said, 'There will always only be one king who can stir it up.'

He let the ashes fall into the oncoming wind.

As the ashes floated away he found Bernie's hand and slipped his hand into hers. Their eyes caught. Shattered brown meeting . . . she quickly looked away. She sucked in some air. Kept her face averted as her small, quiet voice fell into the wind.

'We need to talk. I need to . . .'

Her words stumbled when he let go of her hand and cupped her chin. He pulled her head towards him and said, 'My brain hasn't got any more space, so whatever it is, let's save it for another day. It's just me and you now, so let's go and find that hot drink I know you're after.'

His arm wound around her waist and he moved her gently towards the car.

# TRACK 24: DROP THE BISCUIT
## (Featuring Bernie)

'This is where the studio is going to be,' LT told Bernie as they stood in the basement of what had once been the Liberation Republic.

It was almost four months since the events at the carnival and four days away from the start of the new year. They had been some of the fullest five months of LT's life. Beresford's killer had been apprehended a day after the carnival. He claimed he'd been sent by Beresford Clarke to kill Lord Tribulation. The police didn't buy his explanation. Neither did the newspapers, which universally reported Beresford's death as a tragic incident that had robbed the community of one of its most memorable leaders. The Handsworth Road had held a grand send-off for one of its own. LT had not attended. Five days after the funeral Clarissa Hathaway had resigned as an MP owing to 'family obligations'.

LT had spent most of that time trying to get grants and funds to start his own music programme for young people, which he named the Emmett Till School of Music. Everyone had been pleased that he was using 16 Rhodes Square as a way of putting something positive back into the community. Especially after that terrible business at number 12. Most of the residents of the square had been won over when he'd suggested that the first two music students should be the boys hurt in the fire, who were both back at home but still recovering. The media approved of this and now treated him as a favourite son. That made him chuckle. And as for MAMM, they simply disappeared.

After he had won the competition, Paradise Records, plus a few others, had breezed back to his door. He turned every one of them down. For what? The chance of becoming partners with a former child racist who sang with him while he was laid out in a dirty skip. He'd been impressed with Barry's operation. Artists didn't make mega-bucks, but enough to constitute a steady and secure wage. When he'd insisted on a partnership, Barry had smiled, taken his hand and embraced him. That had felt good. Right. He'd even been over to LA so Sean Sparkle could give him a greater insight into the business.

Bernie wound her arms around his neck, which brought his mind back to the basement. She leaned over and kissed him. On the pulse on his neck, where he loved it. The violin key that she now wore once again around her neck, just as she had when they were young, left its imprint on his T-shirt. She whispered low in his ear, 'Why don't you show me what you're going to do with the rooms upstairs.'

She jumped back and giggled as he tickled her. They both ran from the room, holding hands. They reached a bedroom on the second floor. He pushed her against the wall with hands as soft as the breeze sneaking through the half-open window. Looked into her blue eyes. He almost liked the shine there now. He knew she hadn't dabbled in any C since Beresford's thugs had attacked her. But there was still a part of her eye that remained dull. He decided he would ask her soon what he could do to help get that shine to spread all over. She still hadn't played her violin since the carnival. He decided to leave that one alone. When she was ready she would do it.

Their lips fused. He shifted his lips to her ear and whispered, 'What do violinists use for birth control?'

Instead of answering him she began to giggle. He licked her skin and gave her the punchline.

'Their personalities.'

Her giggles mutated into a high laugh. She grasped his hand. As she led him to the bed the black fist knocker banged against the front door. They leaned against each other and groaned.

'I'll get rid of them,' he promised as he bounced from the room.

He took the steps two at a time. Reached the door. Opened it. A tall white man, maybe fifty, maybe older, LT couldn't tell, stood there sweating, with red eyes, as if he had been crying. His thick, black wool coat sagged on his body as if he had lost weight recently.

'I'm here to see Berlina Ray.' The man's precise, well-modulated voice was soft, but demanding.

LT knew he'd heard that voice somewhere. He never forgot a voice.

'She expecting you?'

'She'll see me.' His tone was weary.

LT remembered where he'd heard the voice. On Bernie's answering machine the night she was attacked.

'Come in. I'll get her for you.'

The man stepped into the hall. LT called out Bernie's name. He knew that the conversation might be private, but he got the feeling from the man's clenched fists that Bernie might need some help.

Bernie came skipping down the stairs.

She stopped rigid on the second-to-last step.

'I'm not prepared to see you,' she called out.

She turned her back, gripped the banister and took a step up. The man rushed forward at the same time. LT grabbed the back of his coat.

'Easy, mate,' he said.

The man ignored him and called out to Bernie, 'He still wants to see you. He can't stop talking about you.'

Bernie's shoulders began to shake. LT knew she was crying. He let go of the man and rushed up the stairs to her. He curled his arm around her. Held her tight.

'He still doesn't know, does he?' the man threw up the stairs.

LT felt Bernie go rigid. She shook him off. Turned to face the man. Wound her arms tight around her middle.

'Why have you done this in front of him?'

'Because he wants to see him as well.'

LT stared at the man. Then at Bernie.

'Is this something I should know about?' he asked both of them.

'That's not for me to say,' the man began. 'He wants you to visit him on New Year's Eve. If you decide to visit him, you'll need this.'

He placed a white envelope on the first step.

'Yesterday he got five years,' the man said weakly.

He turned around. Left the house. LT turned to Bernie, a scowl ruffling his features.

'Bernie, what's going on?'

She eased down to the step as if her back was finally ready to break. LT sat down beside her. Suddenly she gripped his hand. Tight. She kept her head down as she talked. The wet of her tears soaked into his palm.

'Shit, this is so hard. The reason I don't play my violin is because I gave it away. It belongs to someone else. Well, it did, until I got it back recently. Remember all that business fifteen years ago? The reason I left. I got rid of the baby, but not the way you think.'

The pressure of her hand increased.

'I gave him up for adoption. I was just too young. So my mum organised it. There was this couple she knew – he was white, she was black – who couldn't have any kids. So we decided that the best thing to do was for them to bring the baby up as their own. From the beginning I said I didn't want any contact after that. But the one thing I did do was to give him my violin . . .'

'So that's why you never played again until the carnival?'

Her head remained low.

'Just couldn't do it. I tried. But it never felt right. Mummy, being the woman that she is, just couldn't quite let it go. What is it they say about the bond between grandparents and their grandchildren? I didn't find this out until after we met again. My mother decided to hide our details in the material of the violin case, hoping one day he would find it . . .'

'Now he's found it he wants to see you? See us?'

Her hand squeezed his.

'If only life were that simple. He found it and came looking for me, just before you and I met again. But I wouldn't see him. I didn't want a face haunting me, day and night. I suppose he was hurt so he decided to find you.'

'But he hasn't come to me.' He looked at her, puzzled.

She gulped a strained breath.

'On the night before your concert at the Minus One he tried to see you, at another concert. But you weren't signing autographs. So he found what he thought was your fan mail address in a magazine article you'd done. Only the address was wrong. Number twelve Rhodes Square . . .'

LT leaped up. Stood over her and whispered, 'No way, Bernie. Don't tell me what I think you're going to say.'

He saw the youth's – no, his son's – face as he had looked at him on the stage at the Minus One club. His brown eyes and Bernie's long, elegant neck.

His body trembled. Then sagged against the banister. He felt her touch on his back. He heaved her off.

'Don't touch me. Just don't touch me. That's where I've heard that man's voice before, on your answerphone the night you were attacked. All those funny calls you got, like the time we went to find answers about where the King had died, this was what it was about, wasn't it?' He knew he was yelling, but he couldn't and wouldn't stop.

Her words pierced him as she rubbed her hand over the violin key around her neck.

'His father wouldn't leave me alone, or my mother. She kept trying to get me to meet them, but I couldn't. She said I should tell you, and I tried to tell you after we scattered your father's ashes . . .'

He cut her off as if he hadn't heard her speaking.

'All this time what they said about me and that arson attack was true. Except it was never the music, it was me. That kid set the fire with one of my "He's The Daddy" du-rags when all the time that's exactly what I was, his dad.'

'No . . .'

He straightened up.

'You need to go.'

She put her hand out to touch him. He moved back, dazed. She ran downstairs to get her bag. When she came back he was standing in the same position. She turned her back, chest heaving, and left.

He wasn't sure how long he stood there. But it felt like fifteen years. Finally he moved down the stairs towards the envelope the man had left on the step. He picked it up. Opened it. It was a visiting order to see Curtis Lawson at Marshfield Youth Offenders Institution. The numbness in his legs pulled him down to the stairs. He gripped the visiting order as he thought about losing a father and gaining a son.

On New Year's Eve, LT locked his four-wheel-drive outside Marshfield Youth Offenders Institution. He was glad it didn't look too much like a real prison. But still, the thought of the boy inside it made him feel bad. He took out the visiting order in his pocket and started towards the main entrance. After he had taken a few steps he heard a familiar voice call his name. He closed his eyes. He hadn't seen or heard from her in two days.

He turned to look at Bernie. She stood next to her faithful Mini, dressed in a way he hadn't seen before. Long skirt, a pair of heels and make-up. At least she wanted to look her best for the boy. Curtis. He made himself say it in his mind. He couldn't manage the son bit yet. Wasn't sure he ever would or that Curtis would want him to.

'Can I come with you?' she asked.

Her clothes might look fine but her face looked gaunt. He nodded. She played with her butterfly clip then walked towards him. They didn't speak as they reached the front gate. He pressed the intercom. As his arm came down, he took her hand in his.

# TRACK 25: BONUS TRACK

When Curtis was released on parole his birth parents told him a secret.

'It is whispered that on August bank holiday, the Devil and his disciples, wearing smiles flashing like molten lightning, travel across the world. Underground. From west to east. From Trinidad to England. Balancing drums on their left hips and bamboo sticks in their right claws. When they reach Notting Hill they beat their drums throughout the multicoloured memories of the day and the black-and-white fusion of the night, making the streets of west London ripple and roll to their badass, hellfire groove.

'Watch the ground beneath your feet, son, because the human experience comes back to one thing – rhythm.

'The sun goes up, the sun goes down.

'The days get longer, the days get shorter.

'We all fall down, we all have to get up.

'Simple.'

## Coming Soon

# GEEZER GIRLS

4 Women
  1 Last job
    But will it be the last thing they ever do?

**10 years ago ...**
Fifteen-year-old Jade Flynn and three other girls were forced to become the sole occupants of the fourth floor of St. Nicholas care home for children. Forced to take part in 'special community projects' – drugs dealing, money laundering, gun running. Forced to work for a man they nicknamed The Geezer.

That is until a shocking event made them rebel. Made them steal some merchandise that didn't belong to them.

So they ran.
    Disappeared.
            Ceased to exist.


**10 years later ...**
Jade Flynn is now living a respectable life as Jackie Jarvis and is
getting married. She invites her three friends to be her maids of
honour. But someone else turns up as well – The Geezer. He gives
them two choices – he can either kill them or they can do one final
job for him and then return to their respectable lives. So they agree
to become his Geezer Girls one last time.

But can they trust him?
Would you?


*This time if they cease to exist
        they won't be coming back.*


Dreda Say Mitchell
**GEEZER GIRLS**
*OUT NOVEMBER 2008*

# KILLER TUNE
## SELECTED SONG LIST

BLOOD AND FIRE – Niney

FIGHT THE POWER – Public Enemy

GET IT ON – T-Rex

HANDSWORTH REVOLUTION – Steele Pulse

IF IT'S MAGIC – Stevie Wonder

JOHNNY TOO BAD – The Slickers

KLU KLUX KLAN – Steele Pulse

LIVING FOR THE CITY – Stevie Wonder

MANY RIVERS TO CROSS – Jimmy Cliff

PASTIME PARADISE – Stevie Wonder

PEOPLE GET READY – The Impressions

POLICE AND THIEVES – Junior Murvin

PRESSURE DROP – Toots and the Maytals

REDEMPTION SONG – Bob Marley

SUZANNE BEWARE OF THE DEVIL – Dandy Livingston

THIS WILL BE, (AN EVERLASTING LOVE) – Natalie Cole

TOUCH THE SKY – Kanye West

WHAT'S GOING ON – Marvin Gaye

VIVALDI'S WINTER CONCERTO ~ Vivaldi